D0210790

PROPERTY OF:
RANCHO MIRAGE PUBLIC LIBRARY
71-100 HIGHWAY 111
RANCHO MIRAGE, CA 92270
(760) 341-READ 7323

ALSO BY AMY SOHN

Fiction
Run Catch Kiss
My Old Man

Nonfiction
Sex and the City: Kiss and Tell

Prospect
Park West

A Novel

AMY SOHN

Simon & Schuster
New York London Toronto Sydney

Simon & Schuster
1230 Avenue of the Americas
New York, NY 10020

This book is a work of fiction. Names, characters, places, and incidents are products of the author's imagination or are used fictitiously. Any resemblance to actual events or locales or persons, living or dead, is entirely coincidental. Although several well-known people appear in this book, the references to them, their dialogue, their conduct, and their interactions with other characters are wholly the author's creation.

Copyright © 2009 by Amy Sohn

All rights reserved, including the right to reproduce this book or portions thereof in any form whatsoever. For information address Simon & Schuster Subsidiary Rights Department, 1230 Avenue of the Americas, New York, NY 10020.

First Simon & Schuster hardcover edition September 2009

SIMON & SCHUSTER and colophon are registered trademarks of Simon & Schuster, Inc.

For information about special discounts for bulk purchases,
please contact Simon & Schuster Special Sales at 1-866-506-1949
or business@simonandschuster.com.

The Simon & Schuster Speakers Bureau can bring authors to your live event.
For more information or to book an event contact the Simon & Schuster Speakers Bureau
at 1-866-248-3049 or visit our website at www.simonspeakers.com.

Designed by Jill Putorti

Manufactured in the United States of America

10 9 8 7 6 5 4 3 2 1

Library of Congress Cataloging-in-Publication Data

Sohn, Amy.
    Prospect Park West : a novel / Amy Sohn.
       p.   cm.
    1. Social classes—New York (State)—New York—Fiction.   2. Brooklyn (New York, N.Y.)—Fiction.   I. Title.
    PS3569.O435P76   2009
    813'.54—dc22   2009002264

 ISBN 978-1-4165-7763-8
 ISBN 978-1-4165-7766-9 (eBook)

I made you to find me.

—*Anne Sexton*

Prospect Park West

Tiny Love

REBECCA ROSE felt about Park Slope the same way she felt about her one-and-a-half-year-old daughter, Abbie: basic unconditional love mixed with frequent spurts of uncontrollable rage. On this particular Monday afternoon, the rage was winning. It was two-thirty and Abbie was napping. Rebecca had already cleared the lunch dishes, folded the clean laundry that had been sitting in the dryer for a week, and spent an hour reworking an article she was writing for *Cosmopolitan* called "Beauty Secrets You Don't Want Your Man to Know About." Her final order of business was to sit on the living room couch, pop in a DVD of Roman Polanski's *The Tenant,* and masturbate to the scene of Polanski molesting Isabelle Adjani in a darkened Parisian movie theater.

As she lay back against the cushion and fast-forwarded to the scene, she was startled to see a man outside her window. He was not a muscular and Chippendales-esque Peeping Tom seeking to witness her afternoon transgression but a Pakistani facade worker named Rakhman who liked to sing praises to Allah while applying scratch coat. He was working his way down the building. The lower shutters were closed, but Rebecca had forgotten to close the upper shutters, which meant that Rakhman could see right in.

Rebecca and her husband Theo's four-unit brownstone coop building was populated entirely by yuppie couples with kids, including Apartment Four: a gay black guy who lived with his teenage son and his boyfriend. Since Rebecca and Theo had bought their apartment two years before, the coop board had authorized interior painting, new carpeting, boiler replacement, and facade renovation. All the renovating was good for Rebecca's property value but bad for her profligacy, because it meant a constant parade of workers out the window. This was one of the unfortunate consequences of being bourgeois: Your life was in such a constant state of improvement that it became nearly impossible to live.

The neighborhood itself was testament to this. On Rebecca's block alone, Carroll Street between Eighth Avenue and Prospect Park West, half a dozen buildings had undergone facade renovations in the past year. Rebecca could not even push Abbie down Seventh Avenue to Connecticut Muffin to grab a French roast without bracing for the roar of jackhammers. Down on Fourth Avenue, a gritty strip of tire repair shops, gas stations, and glass cutters, new modernist buildings featuring million-dollar lofts were going up each day.

The Rakhman sighting made Rebecca too uncomfortable to pleasure herself in the living room, even with all the shutters closed. If she wanted to come before Abbie woke up, she would have to do it on her bed, an area that these days was better suited to the excretion of baby poo than any more appealing bodily fluids. As Rakhman trilled loudly in Arabic about his black-eyed virgins (a term that made Rebecca picture women who'd been socked in the face), she made a quick escape down the hallway to her bedroom, tiptoeing in so as not to wake Abbie in the baby room next door.

For a moment Rebecca considered using Rakhman as masturbatory fodder; in his early thirties, he wasn't bad-looking, with a lean fit body and shiny brown skin. Still, although she had married a gentile, she could not imagine making love to an Arab. Too scary, too *Munich*.

She shut the bedroom door, closed the curtains, and turned on the air conditioner. It was only the first week of July but a hundred and three outside, thanks to global warming. She lay under the crimson high-thread-count Calvin Klein bedspread, leaned over the side of the bed, and pulled out a Chanel shoe box. In the living room, with the added stimulation of the DVD, she used nothing more than her right index finger and a small dab of lube, but in the sexless and toy-cluttered bedroom, she was going to need special assistance.

Inside the box, along with an assortment of other toys, was Rebecca's pale pink Mini Pearl egg vibrator. She had bought it at the sex shop Toys in Babeland on the Lower East Side, before there was a Babeland in Park Slope, right next to Pintchik hardware.

The "egg" was smaller than a real egg, closer to the size of a jumbo wine cork, and it was attached to the battery compartment by a slender white cord. During her twenties, Rebecca had used it with many of her paramours, on them and on herself. "Paramour" was a title the men probably didn't deserve. Most of her relationships premarriage lasted only a few months or half a dozen dates, whichever came first, just long enough for the thrill of new sex to fade or for her to find a guy who interested her more. Unlike some of her friends, who found one-night stands dehumanizing, Rebecca enjoyed them. She would pick up the men—comedians, drummers, actors, or screenwriters—at bars on the Lower East Side or in the East Village, usually with a girlfriend as a wingman, thrilling in the chase.

Though the sex itself was rarely spectacular, Rebecca loved the lead-up: the banter, the glances, the hand-holding, the cab ride, and the very first kiss, which she felt was pure no matter how drunk both of them were. She didn't see one-night stands as tawdry or cheap. She felt they were perfect, in that she could write the biography of herself that she wanted to (confident, witty, sarcastic, sought after), then say good-bye before the guy knew her well enough to see how much of it was fiction.

Rebecca was not unattractive, but even as a teen, she'd been aware that her body was a bigger selling point than her face. She had curly Andie MacDowell–style hair and deep brown eyes, but a pinched, angry expression no matter what mood she was in. Once, at a party at Barnard, she had overheard two women whispering about her, and one of them had remarked that she was a "butterface—a great body, but her *face.*"

Rebecca had been humiliated but after a few minutes realized that the girl had verbalized something Rebecca had known all along. Her face had never hurt her in the eyes of men, who cared much more about her body. They almost acknowledged as much, saying things like "Your breasts are the perfect size" and "You're so fucking hot," which was different from "You're so beautiful." Because she knew her selling point was her figure, she took great pride in her body and felt at ease in bed in a way she didn't always feel out of it.

In her bedroom Rebecca regarded the Mini Pearl as an old friend, remembering the days when she and Theo had used it together, to spice up the sex or to get a laugh. Before Abbie, they had made love a few times a week. When her married friends complained that they were having less sex married than when they were single, she would chuckle sympathetically but secretly pity them, certain it would never happen to her. *You must not like sex,* she would think. Or, *Didn't you know your husband wasn't into it before you married him?* Even late in her pregnancy, her drive hadn't tapered off, and she had been surprised to find that Theo's hadn't, either. They had even joked about the therapy the baby was certain to have once it uncovered the memory of the penis knocking at its skull.

But then Abbie came, a hurricane, and everything changed. At Rebecca's six-week postpartum appointment, the midwife, a mustachioed mother named Leeza, examined her and told her, "You can have sex whenever you want." She asked what Rebecca was planning to do for birth control, and Rebecca, who had not had to use contraception in over a year, shrugged and said, "Condoms, I guess."

That night she brought home a bottle of chilled East End chardonnay, put Abbie to bed, and handed Theo a pack of lambskins. The pain during sex surprised her, since Abbie had been delivered by cesarean, by the attending OB, after two hours of fruitless pushing. But Rebecca was not discouraged. She reasoned that the sex would take time and more chardonnay to improve.

A few weeks later, after no overtures from Theo, she touched him tenderly in bed. He moved her hand away and turned to her with an expression she hadn't seen before: terror. "We don't have to rush this," he said, and that was that. In the ensuing months, though he kissed or massaged her occasionally, he had not once initiated sex.

It had been sixteen months since they had made love, a period so staggeringly, embarrassingly long that Rebecca didn't like to think about it. As the drought continued, she grew too hurt to try to make a move herself, and the two of them had become cool to each other, like hostile roommates.

She had thought about separation, but the possibility made her uncomfortable and anxious. Though she considered herself a feminist whose needs were as important as those of her husband, she was also a product of a nuclear Jewish family, and she saw divorce as a shame, a *shanda*. She knew this was an outdated way of thinking but could not shake it.

If she had been prepared for Theo's rejection, she often told herself, she might have been able to cope with it. But of the many worries Rebecca had had about becoming a mother, prolonged involuntary celibacy had not been one of them. For a man to reject his own wife, an attractive wife with intact anatomy, no less—that was galling. Didn't he know what he had in her? Did he honestly think he could shut her out, for this many months, without repercussion?

Other new moms she met complained about their husbands' boyish libidos, fretting guiltily about their *own* lack of interest: "Gary wanted to do it before my episiotomy stitches had even healed" or "After my postpartum checkup, I lied and told Dave the doctor said six more weeks." Not once had Rebecca heard a mother infer, even obliquely, that she was hard up. There was no chapter in *What to Expect When You're Expecting* entitled "Daddy's Drive: Dead or Just Dormant?"

Some of the mothers who complained about being chased were fat or unkempt, and Rebecca would listen to their laments, in shock that men would find them desirable. Five-seven and naturally slim, she had shed all her baby weight soon after having Abbie. Once large B's, her breasts had bloomed into small C's, and she had no stretch marks on her belly, unlike the Baby and Me swim mothers she saw in the Eastern Athletic locker room, with long purple scars winding down their abdomens. Even her cesarean scar was below the hairline.

She had always enjoyed sex more than Theo did, but he had never turned her down. And she liked it that way, liked initiating with the certainty that she could make him hard after only a few seconds.

She and Theo had met at a mutual friend's birthday party in December 2003. She had just turned thirty-one, and though she wasn't anxious about marriage the way some of her peers were, she felt that she had slept with every smart artistic cutie south of Fourteenth Street and was beginning to wonder how she was going to meet anyone new.

She'd been standing at the cocktail table in her girlfriend's apartment —littered with tonic, liquor, and sodas—when Theo came up next to her and joked that no one had opened the Mountain Dew yet. His riff didn't seem to come naturally to him, and she'd been aware that he was flirting, trying to be clever because he had noticed her. There was something charming about this to Rebecca after her long run of one-night stands and so-called boyfriends. Theo wanted to court her, and she couldn't remember the last time any man had courted her.

They got very serious very quickly, with him moving into her Fifth Avenue apartment in the Slope the April after they'd met. Theo was an architect and had a maturity and self-sufficiency that the hipster guys lacked. The opposite of the coddled Jewish boys who brought laundry when they went home to their parents, Theo was a solitary, independent WASP who had been raised by a single mother and learned to take care of himself early on. On their first official date after the birthday party, he invited her over to his Lower East Side apartment and made four individual pizzas, his own tuna tartare, and a strawberry rhubarb pie with a lattice crust.

Dark-haired and trim, he resembled Clark Kent. Unlike the drummers and stand-up comedians, Theo had a real job, though he was scrimping by as a junior associate when they met. He was worldly and well traveled, having lived in Madrid and worked for Rafael Moneo after graduate school at Harvard. His cramped one-bedroom was filled with original modernist furniture pieces, like a Carlo Mollino side table and a few mismatched Eames chairs that he had bought at el Rastro flea market. Rebecca, who had grown up in a suburban Philadelphia stone cottage whose decor had not changed since the early seventies, admired Theo's aesthetic sense and, more important, the fact that he had cultivated it on his own.

After he proposed to her at Lever House, his favorite building, and slipped his grandmother's engagement ring on her finger, she felt only joyous anticipation about what was to come. She'd had her wild years and was ready to become part of a twosome. She loved all the couply things she got to do with Theo. They went to museums and gallery shows, read Malamud aloud to each other in bed, and visited ethnic restaurants in Queens. She felt confident that even after they had children, their mutual need for each other—his to take care of someone and hers to be adored—would be the glue that held them together. Theo would be a good father. He was clearly the better cook, but he also knew how to use a hammer and mop a floor. Naturally, he would know what to do with a baby. She could do the breastfeeding and leave the rest to him. But she never anticipated that he might care about the baby so much, he would stop caring about his wife.

Now, after all these months of rejection, she vacillated between worrying that he found her ugly to raging that he found his own behavior acceptable. Knowing how important sex had been to her before motherhood, had he somehow rationalized that she no longer cared? Or had he envisioned this happening at the dinner party three years before, when he told her she could cheat?

It was at Lisa and Kevin Solmsen's apartment in Carroll Gardens that Theo gave her cunt blanche. She and Theo had been married a year and were, she thought, truly happy, besotted for different reasons, but in a haze of mutual new love. She was a senior editor at *Elle,* and he was at Black & Marden architects in Tribeca. The other guests were mainly publishing people and artists, married couples, some with babies. Everyone was chewing overcooked duck and getting drunk on Chilean merlot, and somehow the Clinton marriage came up, which naturally led to a discussion of the definition of adultery.

Rebecca was enjoying the repartee when Theo, usually shy, put down his glass and said, "I wouldn't care if Rebecca cheated on me with another man—as long as she didn't fall in love. I mean, as long as there are no feelings involved, I don't care if she gets her pussy eaten by a businessman in St. Louis."

The other couples fell into stunned silence. Rebecca arched an eyebrow, stood up, and said, "Excuse me while I go book a flight," and everyone roared in laughter.

Despite her glib reaction, she had been shocked. Why was he saying this in public? If a man loved a woman, wouldn't the thought of her with another man send him into a fit of wild rage? What kind of man (who wasn't a cripple) felt it was all right for his wife to stray? She could not tell whether he had said it out of braggadocio ("This is a bluff; my wife would never cheat because she loves me too much") or honesty, and eventually decided on the former, chalking up his pronouncement to the red wine and late hour.

But lately, she had been thinking a lot about St. Louis, the metaphorical city. It was as though Theo had known that someday he wouldn't be able to meet her demands and, in the guise of tipsy dinner-party chatter, preemptively offered her an out.

In order to have an affair, she had to find someone to do it with, and in Park Slob that seemed impossible, so neutered were the men. Rebecca wasn't even attracted to most Park Slope fathers, but she pursued them because they were the only men she interacted with on a regular basis, since she was self-employed and worked at home. In hopes of arousing interest on the playgrounds, Rebecca dressed for sex. While other mothers wore cargo shorts, P.S. 321 T-shirts, and sneakers, Rebecca chose Marc Jacobs minis, Splendid scoopnecks with high-end push-up bras for maximum cleavage, and four-hundred-dollar Miu Miu fuck-mes. Just the week before, when Sonam, her part-time Tibetan babysitter, was with Abbie, Rebecca had trekked into Nolita to buy herself a gold lamé romper at a boutique.

But even her romper drew no interest. Standing next to a sideburned dad at the Lincoln-Berkeley playground swings, she would arch her back and wait for him to ogle. He would allow himself to be engaged in conversation but then drop the phrase "my wife" in the first few sentences, as though she didn't already know he was henpecked by the fact that he lived in Park Slope, an urban Stepford teeming with young white families. Earlier that summer a cute blond dad in an Obama T-shirt had struck up a flirtation, but after a few minutes he mentioned something about his partner, Rick.

Children of miserable seventies divorces, these nesting, monogamous thirtysomethings had 1950s morals—New Victorians, a newspaper article had labeled them. If there was sex going on in their households, it was impossible to see from the way the parents related to each other. The parents of two were the most depressing, the bodies gone to pot, the looks of resignation and regret. They traded children, barely acknowledging each other, their faces lighting up only when a baby clapped or smiled. They were like factory workers on the same assembly line, watching the clock and thinking, *Only eighteen years to go.*

Rebecca wished she'd come of age in the era of 'ludes, key parties, and women's lib, when sex was everywhere and cheating was a given. At least then if your marriage was sexless, you had an out. That new TV show *Swingtown* was trying to tap into seventies nostalgia, but Rebecca had grown bored after a few episodes, feeling it was too PG to be hot.

Whenever Rebecca thought about her lover, she imagined him as a gray-haired man in his forties who carried his money in a clip and smoked without apology. Maybe because she had seen the movie *Sex, Lies, and Videotape* when she was coming of age sexually, she always pictured Peter Gallagher.

But until she found Peter Gallagher, she had to resort to pleasuring herself every afternoon during Abbie's nap to iconic seventies films: the paraplegic Jon Voight going down on Jane Fonda in *Coming Home* (the hottest portrayal of impotence in American cinema), Donald Sutherland and Fonda in *Klute*, George Segal raping Susan Anspach in *Blume in Love*. In these movies she had found the archetype she was seeking, a man who took without asking.

In the bedroom she wriggled out of her jeans and sheer cornflower-blue Cosabella boyshorts, placed the Mini Pearl against her, and flipped the switch on the battery pack. Nothing happened.

She turned the switch off and on again. Still nothing.

The batteries were dead.

Then she remembered Abbie's mobile.

It was a black-and-white Tiny Love Symphony-in-Motion that her parents had brought Abbie as a newborn gift on their first visit. On the mobile you could select Mozart, Bach, or Beethoven, and when Rebecca's father mounted it to the crib, she had joked, "How come there isn't any Mahler?"

Every day for Abbie's nap, Rebecca would deposit her in the crib and turn on the mobile, and it would lull Abbie to sleep. If Abbie stirred, Rebecca would flip on the mobile. Hypnotized by Beethoven's Fifth, Abbie would go back out.

Abbie was most likely in REM sleep now, so Rebecca was pretty sure she could sneak in and grab the batteries without waking her. She crept to the mobile, pried out the batteries, turned, and padded out.

She shut her bedroom door tightly. Batteries in place, underwire bra unlatched and hiked up, left hand on right nipple, right hand on egg, panties and jeans in a fireman pile on the floor, she got to work. She was Isabelle Adjani, and she had beckoned Polanski to the film because she was oddly attracted to him despite his ratlike appearance. Inside the dark dampness of the B-movie theater, she found herself so drawn to him, perhaps sensing his future pedophilia, that she put her hand on his crotch. He got hard immediately, looked both ways, and slung his arm around her, dropping his hand to her breast and squeezing it. Instead of being repelled, slutty IsaBecca reached for him and kissed him sloppily on the mouth, not caring about the dirty old men all around.

Rebecca ratcheted up the vibrator to level two. She squeezed her nipple harder, imagining the soft unsullied director's hand of Roman Polanski. As her muscles tightened and she began to sweat, certain she would come within seconds, she heard the clear, near cry of her baby girl.

Rebecca went into denial. This wasn't a full-out waking but a slight stirring, a shifting of position, and Abbie would soothe herself back to sleep in a moment or two.

A louder and more urgent cry. Rebecca flicked the vibe to level three, thinking of Roman Polanski. She put the pillow over her head, giving up on the nipple stim. But through the foam she could still hear her daughter wailing. It sounded like a poopy cry.

Goddamn it. She threw off the pillow and went into the bedroom. As soon as she walked in, she could smell it. She picked Abbie up and carried her to the changing table silently. The less you shook things up, the better the chance of her falling back asleep. Rebecca changed Abbie swiftly, depositing the used diaper in the bin. "Shhhh," she said, and put the baby back in the crib. "Go back to sleep. Shhhhhh."

Abbie stared up at her indignantly and screamed at the top of her lungs. The mobile hung above her face, mute. Rebecca had to make a Sophie's choice: her own orgasm or her daughter's sleep. Tiny love or Tiny Love.

She knew what Marc Weissbluth, MD, author of *Healthy Sleep Hab-*

its, Happy Child, would say: Babies with inconsistent or too-short naps were more likely to develop attention deficit disorder, learning disabilities, and adult insomnia.

Still, it was with great reluctance and considerable irritability at the many ways motherhood had ruined her life that Rebecca trudged back into her bedroom, removed the double A's from the vibrator, and replaced them in Abbie's mobile. Abbie fell back asleep within minutes, but Rebecca could not gather the energy to conjure *The Tenant* once again. She lay on her bed, arms folded across her chest, glaring at the useless pink phallus beside her. A few minutes later, her intercom buzzed.

The Gold Coast

KAREN BRYAN Shapiro didn't think of herself as neurotic so much as attuned to the demands of urban motherhood. She didn't think it was unusual that she kept a small bottle of unscented Purell antibacterial gel in her handbag and used it several times a day on the hands of her son, Darby, whose name had been chosen years, thank you very much, before actor Patrick Dempsey picked it for *his* baby boy.

She didn't think it unusual that she made Darby wear preventive One Step Up kneepads at the Third Street playground so he wouldn't skin his knees while running, even though the asphalt was covered with black rubber mats that made the skinning of knees nearly impossible, or that there was a three-foot-wide bathmat on the floor of her tub so Darby wouldn't slip and fall during bathtime, or that she had applied to seven, count 'em, *seven* Brooklyn preschools when Darby was fifteen months old, including Grace Church, Brooklyn Heights Montessori, and the Early Childhood Center of Garfield Temple, to be sure he got into one. (He'd gotten into the temple, but only because she had spent nearly $1,800 to join the congregation. Darby's classmates were a combination of Jewish children of members and *goyish* kids whose mothers referred to it euphemistically as the Garfield School.)

Karen didn't even think it was particularly odd that Darby, who was four, still insisted she put him in a pull-up diaper when he had to make a number two, after which he would remove the diaper, wipe himself, and change back into his underpants. Karen believed that no matter how humiliating it was for her to have to diaper her four-year-old on the playgrounds, the humiliation was nothing compared to the guilt she would feel if she created a lifelong intestinal disorder in a child who'd been pressured too hard to train and withheld his movements in protest.

Though she did not believe in pushing her son to do things he wasn't ready for, she did believe in pushing the world to make things better for her son. This was a dog-eat-dog world, and Karen felt that if you didn't do everything you could to give your child an edge, he was destined for a life of mediocrity.

Because of this, Karen did not think it unusual that she was ringing the buzzer of a total stranger at a quarter to three on a weekday afternoon because she had heard there was an apartment coming up for sale in the building. Karen had learned about the apartment from a Garfield School father who'd heard about it from his wife's doula's dog runner. The father, Neal Harris, said the owners were selling it, in an open house on their own, that Sunday, and though they would put up an ad in the *New York Times* online real estate listings Thursday, Karen wanted to get a sneak preview.

According to Neal, it was a smallish, nine-hundred-fifty-square-foot three-bedroom with decorative fireplaces and an open kitchen, but its primary appeal was that it was located in the P.S. 321 school zone. Karen and her husband, Matty, had been looking at apartments for the past two years, attending open houses with Darby nearly every weekend in the hope of finding a decent place. But they had already been outbid on several apartments they had loved, and even with the correction in the housing market that had started during the spring, Karen was beginning to fear that they'd never bid high enough to win anything.

They lived in a rental on Fourteenth Street between Sixth and Seventh avenues, which meant their apartment was in the P.S. 107 zone. And although 107 was getting better due to a highly successful fundraising reading series featuring Paul Auster and Jhumpa Lahiri, 321 still had the better test scores.

Karen had read in *New York* magazine that apartments in the 321 zone cost an average of $100,000 more than similarly sized apartments in 107, but felt that was a small price to pay if it meant your kid went to a school that was 62 percent white instead of only 43. Sure, 321 only went up to fifth grade, and the local middle school, M.S. 51 on Fifth Avenue, was like a boot camp for wilders, but there were plans for a charter middle school in the district that would surely be up and running by the time Darby was twelve.

The Carroll Street apartment's asking price was $675,000 and Karen felt that if she and Matty offered $700,000 up front, before the open house, the sellers might not feel the need to hold it at all. It would be a stretch to afford the monthly payments, but if the apartment seemed expensive now, in a few years they would feel they'd gotten it for a song. Besides, if she could just talk to the owners, they would see that she was Good People, nice and board-approval-worthy, with a well-behaved child, no pets, good credit, and a household income of $286,000 a year.

The apartment was not only on a name street, which meant the northernmost, priciest area of Park Slope, but a park block. Better, it was in short walking distance of the Prospect Park Food Coop, where Karen was already a member. It took over twenty minutes to get to the Coop from the South Slope, which made it a considerable pain to shop, not to mention to do her and Matty's monthly work shifts. (All adult household members had to perform shifts, but because Matty worked so hard, she did both. She worked on the child care team so she could bring Darby along; the Coop's many pro-family policies were one of the reasons Karen had joined.) The North Slope was also closer to the central branch of the Brooklyn Public Library and the Montauk Club, where Karen already schlepped twice a week for her Weight Watchers meetings, and she was convinced the move would be an investment in not only her health but her well-being.

Karen was thirty-two but looked several years older due to the twenty pounds she had not been able to shed postpartum. Five feet four, she had clear, pale black-Irish skin like her mother's, and her dark hair was short, in a "mom cut" she had gotten when Darby was a baby and wouldn't stop playing with it. She tried to make an effort with her appearance—carrying a Brooklyn Industries bowling bag as her purse and wearing foundation every day—but after four years of stay-at-home motherhood, she had learned to dress functionally, for the playgrounds, in loose tops, jeans, and black-and-white MBT walking shoes she had bought at a Pilates place on Union Street.

MBT stood for Masai Barefoot Technology, and the shoes, with huge sloping soles, forced you to roll your foot as you walked, in mimicry of the long-striding Masai people of eastern Africa, who had no cellulite. Karen had seen only marginal improvement in her own cellulite in the six months she'd been wearing the shoes but had not yet lost hope.

There was a gruff female voice on the intercom: "Who is it?"

"Um, I'm here about the open house," Karen answered, trying to sound as casual and unpsychotic as she could.

"What open house?" the voice replied angrily.

"Um, the one on Sunday?" Karen had started uptalking soon after Darby was born, having learned it from other neighborhood stay-at-homes who had learned it in boarding school. "It's a three-bedroom? For sale? By owner?"

"That's Number Two," the woman said shortly. "This is Number Three." A baby wailed loudly in the background. "What's wrong with you?" Karen wasn't sure if she was addressing the baby or her.

Not sure if she was still on "listen," Karen said, "I actually tried Apartment Two already? But there wasn't any answer? And I was just wondering if you'd mind showing me your apartment instead, so I could get an idea of the layout. I promise I'm not an ax murderer." She giggled anxiously. "I'm here with my son. Darby."

Karen didn't hear anything for a while, and when she buzzed Three again, there was no response. A second later, she heard a noise from above, where a scary Arab man was working on the exterior. A head popped out of a window. The woman looked mad.

"Oh, hi there!" Karen said hopefully. "See? There he is. Darby." She pointed to her Maclaren stroller, which was parked at the bottom of the stairs. Though most of Darby's peers no longer used strollers, Karen always used one because the walk from the South Slope to the North was so long and she couldn't deal with him dragging his feet when she had to get somewhere. "I'm Karen. Karen Bryan." Karen always excised her married name when she felt it would help.

"Well, Karen Bryan, I'm glad I got a good look at you," said the woman.

"Why's that?" Karen asked nervously.

"So when you come to the open house, I can point you out to Tina and Steve and tell them not to accept your bid because I will personally ensure that this board never approves you." The window slammed shut. From the scaffold, the Arab stared at Karen blankly.

She retreated down the stairs, shaking with humiliation. She would not tell Matty about this turn of events. He was tough, like all lawyers, and she knew he'd give it to her if she told him she'd already botched things.

Karen and Matty had met at Bates during her sophomore year; he went to Bowdoin and had come to visit a friend. At lunch they chatted, and after that they stayed in touch. She enjoyed his company and thought he was funny but didn't consider him husband material until a few years after she had graduated, when she was working as a social worker at an elementary school in the Bronx and living with three roommates in Curry Hill.

Matty, who had graduated from Cardozo, was in mergers and acquisitions at the white-shoe firm Simpson & Holloway, and called frequently to take her out to dinner. She enjoyed his company but never thought of him romantically. He was tall but awkward, with bushy eyebrows and an irritating habit of picking at his cuticles. She would dine with him, chatting amicably, and then say goodbye in front of her apartment building, and he went along with it as though he wasn't interested in her either.

One night, as they were sitting at a Pakistani joint not far from her apartment, she looked across the table at him while he was telling a funny story about a coworker and she realized that Matty Shapiro was in love with her.

It had been hard for her to accept that any guy could be in love with her; she was used to being the supportive second fiddle to girls more beautiful than she was. When she and her Bates girlfriends went out, guys didn't hit on her. Karen stayed at the bar and listened as the other girls got progressively drunker and asked advice about the lunkheads whose appeal, beyond the physical, was never clear to Karen. Her own premarital sexual history amounted to an ill-fated one-night stand at Brooklyn Tech High School and a few party hookups at Bates—all with Indian or Asian guys who didn't speak to her afterward.

Though it had been hard at first to imagine having sex with Matty, she knew at that fateful dinner that he adored her and would never cheat or leave. More important, she knew that soon he'd be making enough to support a family on one income. She'd only had her MSW for two years but Karen found her work at the school depressing: the absent or dead fathers; the addict mothers, the violence, and even the children's language, which would have made a hooker blush. One boy, an eight-year-old who looked fourteen, was nicknamed The Wiper by the other children for his tendency to blow his nose into his hand and wipe it on classmates when they weren't looking.

She was tired of the commute on the 6 train, tired of living in a two-bedroom with three roommates. If she married Matty Shapiro, then someday they could get a brownstone in Park Slope. They could send their children to private school and summer camp and make sure they got into good colleges so they could lead happy and productive lives.

A year after that Pakistani dinner, she and Matty were married, and a year after that, they moved from his place in East Midtown to the South Slope and she got pregnant with Darby. But their apartment was cramped and Darby was getting bigger, and Karen felt that it was time for them to go from renters to owners.

Karen released the brakes on Darby's stroller. She had been planning to shop at the Prospect Park Food Coop after she saw the apartment— she had volunteered to buy chips and dip for an organizing meeting of The Audacity of Park Slope, a local group that was trying to get Barack Obama elected president—but she decided the shopping could wait. She wanted to do something purely selfish. She pivoted the Maclaren toward Prospect Park West.

Prospect Park West was the ritziest and most regal street in the neighborhood, known in the 1880s as the Gold Coast, a fact that Karen knew from attending the open houses of its most expensive properties, or the most expensive properties not to require a prequal for entry.

Although many of the buildings were hideous postwars, sprinkled throughout the twenty-block street were breathtaking Victorian mansions with wraparound center staircases and original detail.

Every time she walked on the Gold Coast, Karen would peer into the buildings and imagine herself living inside, wondering what it was like to sleep in a room that overlooked Prospect Park. There were people who believed that money didn't buy you happiness, but Karen thought those people were morons.

Consumption was inconspicuous in Park Slope in a way it wasn't on the Upper East Side. The women with rich husbands never called them hedge fund managers or investment bankers. They just said, "He's in finance." If you were rich in Park Slope, you tried to hide it. But there were giveaways, and these giveaways got under Karen's skin: the mothers who mentioned that their kids went to Saint Ann's; the two-thousand-dollar Mulberry handbags that some women took to the playground; the Southampton beach stickers on the Subaru Foresters parked on the streets.

When she got to the intersection of Prospect Park West and Carroll, she crossed to the park side, walked two blocks south to Garfield Place, and sat on a green bench facing a strip of mansions. The air was thick and sticky, and passersby wore looks of glazed weariness, eager to get into the comfort of air-conditioned apartments. Babies lolled in strollers, red-faced, while West Indian nannies patted them with hankies. A black kid in a do-rag passed by, and Karen gripped her purse tightly. You had to be careful near the park.

The week before, she had read in the *Brooklyn Paper* about a rape by the ball fields. The victim was in a car with her boyfriend at one-thirty in the morning on Prospect Park Southwest when the rapist came up to the window. The boyfriend came out to confront him, the two got separated, and the attacker caught up with the woman and raped her. There had been a police sketch in the paper—he was medium-skinned, six feet three, lanky, mid-twenties—Karen had been on the lookout for the guy ever since.

Karen parked Darby's stroller beside her. "But I don't wanna do Mommy Time!" he said.

"Just for a little while," she said. "Then we're going to go shopping at the Coop, and you can go upstairs to child care and play with the toys."

"This is boring!"

"Have some Pirate's Booty," she said, handing him a bag. Mommy Time was one of the few occasions on which she fed Darby to placate him; generally, she didn't believe in distracting children with food.

He ingested a few pieces, still pouting. She placed her bowling bag beside her on the bench and removed a pair of Ray-Ban knockoffs, a green iPod shuffle, and a half-eaten package of Paul Newman–brand chocolate-flavor Newman-O's. She put on the sunglasses, placed the iPod buds in her ears, and pressed play, thrilling at the opening chords of Sade's *Stronger Than Pride,* an album she first heard when she was fourteen at a basement party in Fort Greene where everybody was making out with somebody except her.

Then she planted her MBT shoes on the sidewalk, removed a Newman-O from the bag, and bit into it, delighting in its crisp sweetness and lack of trans-fatty acids. She chewed and swallowed quickly, then took out another, lulled by the dulcet tones of Sade and blinking across traffic at the regal white double-wide mansion of two-time Oscar-winning actress Melora Leigh.

Melora had won her first Oscar (Best Supporting Actress) in 1977 at age nine, for playing the role of Al Pacino's daughter in *The Main Line,* a dark but brilliant Paul Schrader film about a Philadelphia heroin junkie. Before that Melora had enjoyed an ordinary childhood in the West Village, the only child of a schoolteacher mother and a photographer father. And then one day—as Karen knew from countless interviews in which Melora recounted the story—the casting director Mary Jo Slater had spotted her in line at Joe's Pizza and brought her in to audition for the Pacino.

It turned out Melora had "it," and she quickly became one of the best-known child stars of the late seventies, along with Cynthia Nixon and Kristy McNichol. She worked steadily, appearing in after-school specials, serious features, several Broadway plays, and a famous commercial for Duncan Hines cookies.

But by the late eighties, she began to have trouble convincing audiences to buy her in adult roles. She went to Columbia for a year but dropped out. She starred in a string of bad romantic comedies and a few short-lived TV series, unable to find her niche. In 2002, when the thirty-four-year-old Melora was only a blip on the radar screen of the nation, she won the lead role in Paul Thomas Anderson's biopic *Poses*, which was based loosely on the life story of the 1950s experimental film director Maya Deren.

Thanks to coaching by the acting guru Harold Guskin (who Melora had credited in many interviews), Melora gave one of those brave, heart-wrenching performances you see only once in a blue moon. The movie took off, going on to earn $100 million at the box office. Loving a comeback story, the Academy had awarded her a second Oscar.

Melora's husband of three years was the lesser-known but incredibly good-looking red-haired Australian actor Stuart Ashby, who had been cast against type in *Poses* as Melora's first husband, a Czech Jew named Sasha. Karen and everyone who'd even once skimmed an *Us Weekly* knew the story of how they had met and fallen in love on-set. Melora had been single when she met him, having recently adopted a Vietnamese baby named Orion on her own, but Stuart had been practically married to his six-feet-tall Aussie actress girlfriend, Natalie Sullivan, who was known for her critically acclaimed period roles and porn-star figure.

The attraction to Melora was too much for him to bear, however, and he swiftly eighty-sixed Natalie to be with Melora. Soon they were appearing at film premieres and ducking out of Per Se, refusing to talk to the press, while Paul Thomas Anderson told interviewers, "I don't claim any credit. All I can say is that Melora and Stuart are special people." They made their first public appearance at the 2004 MTV Video Music Awards, and after he moved into her Spring Street loft several months later, Stuart legally adopted Orion. They had his last name changed from Leigh to Leigh-Ashby, and the couple was married in a low-key ceremony at Angel Orensanz Foundation for the Arts on Norfolk Street.

Melora was slender and wan and, according to the Internet Movie Database, five feet ten, which Karen knew was accurate from her several run-ins with her in the neighborhood. Melora had long, perpetually shiny Carolyn Bessette–style blond hair. Like other Park Slope celebrities (Steve Buscemi, John Turturro, and the *Law & Order: Criminal Intent* star Kathryn Erbe), Melora made no attempt to disguise herself when she walked through the neighborhood. Karen understood: There was no need to slum it when you lived in Brooklyn. You put on a meta-phorical baseball cap and dark shades the moment you set up shop across the East River. Once in a while *Us Weekly* would run shots of Emily Mortimer and Alessandro Nivola in Cobble Hill, or Adrian Gre-nier in Clinton Hill, but the photo credit was always the same, Phil Parnell, as though only one photographer was industrious enough to cross water.

Melora's career had been in a slump ever since she had moved to Brooklyn. Though some blamed her choice in roles, Karen felt she was merely refocusing. Since *Poses,* she had starred in a horror film called *Creeping* that tanked at the box office; a Lionsgate drama about Jane Austen's real-life relationship with her sisters that got solid reviews but went basically unseen; a romantic weepie, *You Just Call Out My Name;* a sci-fi thriller based on the *Usurpia* comic book series in which she played a mutant crime-fighter named Princess Xaviera; and a well-reviewed Neil LaBute play. Though some critics had already written Melora's professional obituary, Karen was convinced that it was only a matter of time before she found another script that was as strong a showcase as *Poses.* Once that happened, she would make a second comeback.

Karen had spotted Melora a handful of times in the neighbor-hood since Melora had purchased the six-bedroom 362 Prospect Park West, at the corner of Garfield Place, in March 2006. (Karen knew from PropertyShark.com not only how much Melora had paid—$4.7 million—but also that she had bought it in the name Main Line Trust, even though she and Stuart had been married at the time of purchase.) Karen had seen her window-shopping on the Slope's hip Fifth Avenue; emerging from a car in front of the mansion, with Bergdorf bags and what seemed to be a cold sore on her lip; and trying on a top at the Seventh Avenue clothing boutique Loom, murmuring into her cell phone, "Don't be depressed."

But Karen's absolute favorite Melora Leigh sighting, which she had recounted to playground mothers many times and posted on Gawker

Stalker under the handle "bklynmama," had occurred at the Park Slope Yoga Center a year and a half before. It was a Saturday morning, and Karen had decided it was time to do something about her pear-shaped body, so she had announced to Matty, "You're taking Darby. I'm going to get some exercise." Daunted by the prospect of any activity that might force her to break a sweat, she had decided to take a Basic Vinyasa class.

On her way out the door, she had stopped to check her e-mail and gotten caught up reading a thread from the local message board, Park Slope Parents, about whether it was okay for children to walk up the playground slides. As a result, she got to class ten minutes late and had to wait outside the door until after the opening chant. The only free spot was in the far back corner. As she unfurled her rental mat, she was startled by the sight of Melora Leigh sitting next to her in a lotus.

Melora was wearing a pair of maroon split-seam yoga pants and a tight dance-style white tank top with no bra. (She had always been small-breasted, and Karen loved that, unlike most of Hollywood's leading ladies, she had opted not to get a boob job.) Up close she was even more beautiful than in the closing shot of *Poses,* where she overdosed on sleeping pills in her bathroom. Her skin was translucent, her hair swept into a high bun with a few loose strands by her temples, and Karen thought her body looked even longer than her purported five feet ten inches.

Karen, who had assumed a Basic class would be easy, was surprised to find herself sweating like a horse as she sneaked peeks at Melora during Warrior Ones and tried to discern whether she'd gotten thigh lipo. Forty minutes into the class, as the yogis were maneuvering themselves into Cobra, Melora farted. Audibly.

The other women near her turned to stare, assuming it was Karen. Irritated by the accusation, Karen took on a look of denial, and then Melora said softly, "Excuse me. Those Cobras really get me," and the women laughed and then gazed at her worshipfully. Melora was not only beautiful, talented, and rich, she could admit she had dealt it when somebody smelt it.

Karen thought of this run-in now, as she passed a zero-trans-fat Newman-O fart herself. She came to this bench a few hours a week, praying she would catch a glimpse of Melora in an upstairs window blow-drying her hair or adjusting the level of what Karen was certain was central air.

Underneath the Sade, Karen could hear an urgent whine. Exasperated, she ripped out the earbuds. "What is it?"

"I'm done," Darby said, handing over the empty Pirate's Booty bag, as if she were a human garbage can. "I want to go home."

"Just a little longer."

"But you always say that, and it's always a lot longer."

"Darby, that's one."

"But, Mom!"

"That's two." She had learned this trick from a book called *1-2-3 Magic* and found it worked surprisingly well. You established a punishment suitable to the age (for Darby, it was no dessert), and when the child began to act up, you counted. If he was still acting out by the time you got to three, he got punished.

Darby said nothing more, and Karen reinserted the earbuds, gazing up at the third-floor window. She was beginning to think this whole exercise was futile. It was summertime. Rich people didn't stay in the city in the summer. The Hampton Jitney had even started a Brooklyn route along Prospect Park West. Karen had seen it pass by a few times and envied all the rich people behind the tinted windows who she imagined reading the *New York Observer* and sipping iced skim lattes.

Melora, Stuart, Orion, and their entire staff were probably stationed at their cottage in Bridgehampton, going to Robert Wilson parties in Watermill and having Jessica Seinfeld over for margaritas. The only people who stayed in the city during a heat wave were those who had to. Karen and Matty had taken a week off in April during the Garfield School's Passover break, to visit his parents in Miami, and were taking his second vacation week between Christmas and New Year's. But now she regretted not saving a week for the summer.

A light went on in the window. There was a gauzy curtain, but through it Karen made out the outline of a tall woman swinging a little boy around in a circle, airplane-style. They were here! Though all she could see was the silhouette, she knew from the long, flowing hair that it was Melora. The bodies were jubilant and relaxed and gave off a joy that Karen herself could not remember ever feeling, even as a small child growing up with her sister in Midwood, Brooklyn, in a shingled two-story with a driveway and a yard.

This was what it meant to be rich. All the big stuff was taken care of, so you could enjoy the little stuff, like playing with your children. Instead of thinking all the time about how to make things better, you could be present in the moment—something Karen had been striving to do ever since she read *Everyday Blessings: The Inner Work of Mindful Parenting,* by Jon and Myla Kabat-Zinn.

Karen wanted to race across the street and pound on the door until Melora let her in and spun her around, too. A moment later, the figures retreated, but long after they had, Karen stared at the curtain, still seeing the outline of mother and son.

Orientation

WHILE ORION was in the third-floor playroom with the nanny, Annika, Melora was on her way to orientation at the Prospect Park Food Coop. She had decided to join at the suggestion of her publicist, Lynn. Since her move to the Slope, she had passed the sprawling Seventh Avenue building many times, with its quaint 1970s-style sign and legions of organic-food-eating, Michael Pollan–reading members, and it had amused her in a distant way, a quirky neighborhood institution that she hoped never to enter.

But in April she got the new Green issue of *Vanity Fair* in the mail, with Madonna on the cover, splayed up against a plaster globe, and realized that she was going to have to get on board with the whole environmental thing. She'd always been politically engaged: In the nineties Tim and Susan got her involved with the Innocence Project; long before it was the trendy thing to do, she bought a Prius for her house in Silver Lake; and it was not without consciousness of the PR value that she later committed the most extreme and headline-making act of recycling—adoption.

But even with a live-in nanny, mothering Orion had been trying enough that Melora had no plans to get all Angelina and take on a brood of twelve, which meant she would have to find another way to be visibly progressive. A few weeks before, she had met with Lynn to discuss the upcoming premiere of *The Dueling Donnellys,* a Gary Winick romantic comedy about an overprotective sister who puts her brother's (Vince

Vaughn) fiancée (Kate Hudson) through a brutal set of tests. She and Lynn were talking about her red-carpet interviews, and Melora had said, "I feel like doing something for the environment would help my Q rating."

"Why don't you get involved in that food coop in your neighborhood?" Lynn had replied offhandedly. "My sister-in-law belongs. Loves it. Says the produce is better than Fairway." Four feet eleven, Jewish, and sixty, Lynn had been in PR since the seventies and always thought outside the box.

"*Food coop?*" Melora had said. "Ugh. Isn't there a work shift?"

"Yeah, like three hours a month. Can you think of any other celebrity who does a mandatory monthly work shift? These days it's all about being at one with the hoi polloi. Isn't that why you fired Lisanne?" A few weeks before, after Stuart convinced her that they needed to streamline their lives, Melora had fired her personal assistant, Lisanne, an incredibly competent twenty-six-year-old Brown semiotics grad.

"You've got a built-in publicity platform," Lynn went on. "The place has nine thousand members, any of whom could call in a Page Six to tell them what a saint you are for doing your own work time. And it could be a very useful bit to drop when you sit down at Gemma with Adam Epstein."

The independent film director Adam Epstein had come on the Hollywood map in 2004, after writing and directing *The Undescended,* a dark and brooding coming-of-age tale set on the Upper West Side, which went on to be nominated for three Oscars. A New York–bred private school kid who was often mentioned in the same breath as Darren Aronofsky and Noah Baumbach, Adam had made two other films: *Eva and Andie* (2006), an indie *Beaches* starring Sandra Bullock opposite Epstein's wife, Jessica Chafee; and *Mumbai Express,* a George Clooney thriller (2007). Since spending all that time in India, Adam Epstein had become a committed humanitarian and die-hard environmentalist. He'd recently directed two pro bono spots for the Natural Resources Defense Council, shot in black-and-white like Truffaut movies, and now every time he gave an interview, he talked about global warming.

Melora was up for the title role in his new film, *Yellow Rosie,* about a Valium-popping, borderline psychotic wife of a Texas oilman, played by

Viggo Mortensen. It was scheduled to begin production in August in Bulgaria, standing in for Texas. Adam had cast Nicole Kidman but Kidman had just bowed out, claiming she was suffering from exhaustion. Adam had contacted Melora's CAA agent, Vanessa Andreadakis, saying he wanted to cast Melora instead. He told Vanessa he was a huge fan of Melora's work, and Vanessa had already finalized the salary ($1 million plus back end) with the producer, Scott Rudin. It was a done deal, except for the contract, which would be issued after the meeting. Adam said it wasn't an audition so much as a mutual opportunity to make sure he and Melora were in sync creatively.

Melora was terrible in meetings, shy and withdrawn, and often got feedback that she came off as entitled. She would have preferred to do a screen test. If you were shy and a nobody, people pitied you, but if you were shy and famous, they despised you. She'd been surrounded by adults at an early age before she ever learned how to be around her peers, and as a result, she was uncomfortable with other people. She had worked hard with her shrink on behavioral techniques for dealing with her social anxiety, but she was nervous about the meeting anyway and felt it couldn't hurt if she and Adam had a safe topic of discussion.

Lynn said that if the conversation lulled, she could always shift the subject to the Coop, sustainability, and the many benefits of shopping local. So Melora decided to join and have Lynn leak it to the press in a release she was sending out about Melora's Sierra Club fall fund-raiser hostessing gig.

The Coop's third-floor meeting room was fluorescent-lit and dingy and filled with a nauseatingly unattractive mishmash of hipster couples, Hasidic wives, and butch dykes, all sitting in hard-backed black metal chairs. It reminded Melora of an A.A. meeting. (She'd been a friend of Bill W. in 1993 and 1994, until she decided she was drinking only to get over her breakup with Fisher Stevens.)

The orientation leader, a large-boned blonde in a saggy waffle tee, was saying something about 40 percent savings off retail prices when Melora came in. Everyone turned to the door. She had tried to low-key it to appear down-to-earth—she was wearing cutoff Levi's and a Wildlife Conservation Society T-shirt—but she had neglected to low-key her purse, a $1,495 black patent-leather Yves Saint Laurent Majorelle handbag.

In the back Stuart raised his hand to beckon her over. Sitting next to him was their lesbian chef, Shivan, a French Culinary Institute grad they had poached from Robin Williams.

As Melora settled into her seat, she was alarmed to spot Maggie Gyllenhaal in the front row, bouncing her daughter, Ramona, on her lap. Gyllenhaal and her boyfriend, Peter Sarsgaard, had bought a brownstone on Sterling Place six months after Melora closed on the mansion, and they had gotten way more press for their purchase than Melora had—in part because Gyllenhaal was pregnant at the time, and in part because her profile had soared after she said the U.S. was responsible for 9/11. Melora couldn't stand the fact that this slummer, who had paid only $1.75 mil for *her* North Slope town house, was joining the Coop, too.

But there was another reason she was unhappy to see Maggie Gyllenhaal. Stuart had written his first screenplay, set in Brooklyn, and wanted Gyllenhaal to play the female lead, a Prospect Heights cop. Melora wanted to play the role herself, but Stuart had been insisting that Melora wasn't "weathered" enough, even though she was nearly a decade older than Gyllenhaal.

"What's *she* doing here?" Melora murmured to Stuart.

"I ran into Peter at Third Street playground and told him we were joining," he answered in his Aussie twang.

"You did not," she hissed.

These days he didn't seem to understand her needs at all. She hadn't said specifically that she was joining for the publicity, but she had expected him to understand that it was an ancillary benefit. In PR, the whole game was to get there first.

The orientation leader, wearing a name tag that said "Nicki," kept having trouble with the overhead projector and making jokes about the "mommy brain" she had developed since giving birth to her second baby fourteen months after the first. Her face was attractive enough, but she had a defeated look that made Melora wonder why these women couldn't wait a couple years between children. This was a neighborhood in which secular women aspired to a Hasidic lifestyle.

After the painfully long two-and-a-half-hour orientation, Nicki led them next door to the membership office, where Melora had to sign up for a work team and pose for an ID card photo. The photographer was a hijabbed woman who didn't even do a double take when she saw her. Perhaps Melora had overestimated the PR value of Coop members; between Al Qaeda and the Weather Underground, a good portion of them would have no idea who she was.

Melora decided she would do the Shopping team, which meant she could work one of the barcode scanning machines and be spotted by the maximum number of people. Her goal was to do one shift, hope it elicited a few mentions, and then make Shivan do all the rest. She expected Stuart to pick Shopping, too, but he said, "I want to do Food Handling. More meditative. I'll bag raisins or something."

Nicki took the group downstairs for a tour, announcing that they could buy anything they wanted with their provisional ID cards. The produce aisle was jammed with shoppers, stressed and hot from the humidity outside. A guy with a BabyBjörn grabbed two kinds of peaches from different bins and put them in the same bag, and an old woman in a wheelchair shouted, "Those aren't the same price!"

"I know they aren't!" he bellowed back. Everyone seemed to have too much time on their hands, and Melora had spent her life trying to become someone with too little.

Stuart raced up to her with a big green stalk in his hand. "It's aloe!" he said. "Great to have around if Orion gets a scrape on his knee or whatever." He spotted a bin of baby bok choy and grabbed a bunch. "I'm going to have Shivan make stir-fry tonight. Dr. Bob said baby bok choy keeps the pitta dosha in check."

In the spring, he had gone off to the Raj, an Ayurvedic spa in Iowa, and come back with this talk of doshas and moderating his fire. He had already eliminated coffee and processed sugars and had become incredibly preachy about the whole thing. As he plopped the baby bok choy into his basket with a self-satisfied grin, she had a sudden urge to mash the bunch into his face.

Lately, they hadn't been connecting well, and as much as she blamed the Raj, a part of her felt the real culprit was Zoloft. Melora had been on the pills since Orion had gone, seemingly overnight, from an angelic little baby to a screaming, whining, hyperactive, snot-nosed toddler.

When Melora had adopted Orion, she had wanted desperately to have a child, although she had no desire to birth one naturally. The tabloids had her visiting sperm banks, but they got it wrong: She was terrified by the thought of having her body transformed by pregnancy, and doubly so by the thought of squeezing a living being out of her most precious part. But she did want to be a mother, to have someone love her unconditionally and forever. Over the years she'd had a string of dysfunctional relationships—Fisher, Robert Downey, Jr., Sean Penn, John Cusack, and just before Stuart, Ryan Gosling—and she wanted someone in her life who would never leave.

She met Orion visiting Ho Chi Minh City on UNICEF work (she'd been a spokesperson since she was fourteen) and fell in love at first sight. The first year of motherhood had been a delight, in part because of the round-the-clock baby nurses, and in part because Orion was such a mellow baby. But at two and a half, he became so difficult that she began to question the wisdom of adopting him at all. After one horrific fight when he woke up in the middle of the night and insisted she feed him chocolate ice cream, she grabbed him tightly by the arms and screamed, "You little motherfucker!" The next morning she booked an emergency appointment with her psychiatrist, an owlish Upper East Side Buddhist named Michael Levine.

"I want medication," Melora said.

"What kind of medicine were you thinking about?" he asked, as though he were prescribing Robitussin or Maalox instead of brain-chemistry-altering drugs.

"Something to take the edge off. I can't go calling my kid a motherfucker. Give me something that makes him easier to love."

"We all want our children to be easier to love," he said. He had a teenage daughter and sometimes complained about her in sessions, which alarmed Melora because it seemed so inappropriate.

"What should I start with?" she said. "Zoloft?"

He leaned back in his Aeron chair and sat in a lotus position. "Probably. Women like it, and the side effects are minimal."

She filled the prescription that day. Two years later, she was still on it, having upped gradually from twenty-five to a hundred fifty milligrams a day. She wanted to be the best at everything she tried, including motherhood, and felt that if the pills took the edge off and made her a more normal mom, it was silly not to take them. Besides, it was only for the wonder years. Once Orion was six or seven, she'd wean off.

Because of the pills, she had never again called Orion a mother-fucker, but she had also become unable to orgasm. After discovering the side effect, she had switched temporarily to Wellbutrin and then Effexor, but Wellbutrin gave her headaches and Effexor made her put on weight, so eventually, she returned to Zoloft.

Ever since then, in bed with Stuart, she had been faking it. She was pretty sure he didn't suspect—she was an expert at faking, having done it for years with Sean Penn—but the deception made her anxious, and the anxiety made her needy. Because she was keeping a secret from him, she feared that he would find out and see her as less of a woman.

These days she didn't trust Stuart, didn't feel safe around him. Either she snapped at him for small slights or asked him constantly if he loved her. Ever since he starred in Doug Liman's hit *Rolfers,* a science-fiction fantasy about interdimensional time travel, he'd been in hot demand for action films. He was gone a lot, shooting in Baton Rouge or Bulgaria, and his absences made her feel vulnerable and alone.

As she watched Stuart caress, and then shake and sniff a honeydew melon, she was not sure what was wrong with her that she could not muster that level of enthusiasm for anything. This was another down-side of Zoloft. It took the edge off, but the highs were lower, too. Even shopping excited her less than it used to. In the early days of her marriage, she'd go to Madison Avenue and buy bags full of Sonia Rykiel and Chloé, delighting in her finds. Now she shopped and was already bored with the purchases by the time they were delivered.

Stuart was always telling her how grateful she should be to have money, a career, and a family who loved her. It was the humble Aussie side of him—he felt lucky about his own career because he'd grown up a punk-rock surfer in South Sydney—but she didn't relate.

Despite his fame, he was genuine. This made Melora jealous. He could make himself at home in almost any situation, while she tended to skulk in the corner of the room. People stuck to Stuart but wanted to get away from her, and this embarrassed her. You couldn't be a power couple if only one of you had any power.

Many nights they socialized separately, because she found it so unbearable to have to talk to people she didn't know. When they did go out together, they often fought, and then he would accuse her of ruining his night. If they were really unlucky, a paparazzo would snap a photo and the next day the tabloids would say they were on the rocks.

When they met on *Poses,* Melora had been focused and ambitious. For the three months of shooting in the West Village and Astoria, she, Stuart, and the crew guys would play poker and tell dirty jokes; that was how the two of them began flirting in the first place.

But these days she never laughed. She resisted sex and even his frequent offers to go down on her, because it depressed her so much to have to fake it. The only sexual act she enjoyed with him was anal-bead play; in submission, she found the thrill that sex had otherwise lost.

They were in the express checkout line now, having said goodbye to Shivan, who wanted to keep shopping. Suddenly, Maggie Gyllenhaal strode toward them, pushing Ramona in a Maclaren. "Stuart!" she said, hugging him. "Thank you so much for turning us on to this place." Stuart and Maggie had worked together on a Sundance indie about nurses in an inner-city ER and stayed in touch. Had the two of them done it on *Sirens?* Was this Maggie's way of rubbing it in Melora's face?

"You know Melora?" Stuart said to Maggie.

The women nodded. "We met at the Costume Institute Ball last year," said Melora.

"That's right," said Maggie. "So nice to see you again." And then she widened her eyes, bowed her head in what Melora could not tell was genuine or manufactured deference, and said, "I don't think I told you that night how much I love your work."

There was something backhanded about the compliment, as if Maggie was aware that she had replaced Melora as one of Young Hollywood's ones to watch and was making a comment about how obsolete Melora had become. Melora wanted to slap this skinny hipster who was famous only because she'd flashed her tits in *Secretary,* and tell her not to be so entitled because in a few years she'd be considered over the hill, too.

"When are you going to send me your screenplay?" Maggie said. So Stuart had already told her about the role.

He glanced at Melora. "Um, as soon as I do the next pass."

"I can't wait to see it. Have you read it?" she asked Melora.

"Oh, you'll love it," Melora said.

"So what do you think of this place?" Stuart asked Maggie brightly.

"Fantastic," said Maggie. "I'm making a black cod Veracruzano for Peter tonight, and I got all the ingredients here except for the fish. If you guys haven't picked your shifts yet, do Shopping, Wednesdays at one, Week A. Then we can all hang out!"

With that, she traipsed down the aisle. Melora's throat got tight, and as she sucked in a breath, it felt like she was at the top of a mountain. A lifelong claustrophobic and not a fake one like Paris Hilton, Melora had trouble even sitting inside a movie set trailer for longer than fifteen minutes. Now she had to deal with these crowds, these miserable crowds. She was nauseated, and she didn't know how much was Maggie Gyllenhaal and how much was the weird smell of body odor and nutmeg.

"Next!" shouted the checkout worker, a cute Asian girl in a tank top that displayed her pencil-eraser nipples. Stuart eyed her. This was all Melora needed. Stuart loved Asian chicks, ogling them openly on the sidewalk and at parties.

"Well, g'day, Stu Ashby," said the girl in an Australian accent. She wasn't only Asian but *Australian* Asian. *Great. Now we'll be here forever.*

He and the woman went on, doing the whole Aussie geography thing. Grimacing, Melora turned away, accidentally bumping a harried-looking dad who was pushing an orange Bugaboo. She wanted to get the hell out of this place and away from all these losers.

The room felt close and overpoweringly warm, even through the wind-power-controlled AC. She wanted to be angry with Stuart, but it was her own fault. Because of her own desire to get some publicity about her environmentalism, she had provided Stuart with access to cute twentysomething fucksluts with visible hip bones. And Maggie Gyllenhaal.

It was as she was thinking the term "twentysomething fuckslut" that she noticed a black man in front of her. He was moving swiftly, and he smelled of urine and had a faint beard. Clearly he was homeless. How had a homeless guy come to be a member of a food coop?

Though he carried no groceries, he was making his way to the exit, where he jostled a tall white guy who was fumbling with his iPhone.

Melora watched as the homeless man plucked the wallet out of the guy's jeans pocket. He didn't even do it stealthily. The act was overt and slow, so slow she was convinced iPhone would notice right away. But iPhone went on fiddling as the homeless guy slipped out past the exit worker, a Susan Sontag type who eyed him suspiciously but said nothing.

Melora could not believe how clumsy the man had been. He had done it right out in the open, and yet she seemed to be the only one who had noticed.

She flashed back to the time she was fourteen and pilfered a Mars bar from a candy store on Amsterdam, on a dare by Trini Alvarado, her classmate at Professional Children's School. She remembered the thrill she had felt touching it and hiding it in her pocket, then seeing if she could make it out of the store without being caught. The storekeeper was oblivious, and Melora had made her exit easily, then raced down the sidewalk, exuberant, the wind catching her hair, Trini running after her and howling. They sat on the steps of Lincoln Center and split the candy. She had never tasted anything that good. After that she shoplifted on and off for months, until one day a shopkeeper caught her, threatened to call the cops, and scared her so badly she never did it again.

Melora followed Stuart toward the exit. There was a long line of people next to them on the cashier line, to pay in cash, and, as she moved, she saw Bugaboo Dad leaning into the stroller to comfort his baby. An overstuffed, open Skip Hop diaper bag was strung across the gargantuan handle, containing sippy cups, an Elmo doll, and a man's wallet.

Before she was fully aware what she was doing, Melora leaned forward with a cough, plucked the wallet from the diaper bag, and deposited it swiftly into her Majorelle.

She glanced around quickly. Stuart was running the aloe leaf across his face, and the other shoppers were so stressed about the long lines that none took any notice of her. Her breath came more easily, and her heartbeat slowed. She felt calm and safe, as though watching a scary movie, tucked away safely in the darkened theater.

When Bugaboo Dad arrived at the cashier station, he reached into the bag and then patted his pockets, confused. He tried the bag again, removing everything in it before shaking his head, more in confusion than in fear, and telling the cashier, "I think someone took my wallet."

There was a sudden urgent shuffling near him as other shoppers checked their pockets and totes to make sure their wallets were still there. The iPhone guy cried out, "Mine's missing, too!" Melora stole a quick glance at Sontag, waiting for her to say something about the homeless man. Instead, she glanced guiltily out the door.

"What's going on?" Stuart murmured.

"I don't know," Melora said, and then, using the skills that had garnered her two Academy Awards, skills she had been honing since she was a child, took on an expression of alarmed concern.

There was a loud shout and Bugaboo Dad was on the floor on top of a tall, broad-shouldered Rasta as two Jewish-looking middle-aged men tried to pull him off.

"What the hell you doin', man?" the Rasta shouted to the dad. "You blood clot!" Bugaboo Baby was screaming now, and several other babies in nearby strollers piped up in sympathy, like dogs howling at the moon.

"Leave me alone!" shouted Bugaboo Dad. "This guy stole my wallet," he said to Sontag. "I know he did! And *his,* too!" He pointed at iPhone, whose face was wracked with panic.

"You betta be careful whatchoo say around here!" shouted the Rasta.

"Someone should search him," Bugaboo Dad said, more weakly now.

"That's not right," said Sontag. "You can't go searching someone without evidence." Then she went into a speech about personal liberty.

Melora felt like she wasn't on Zoloft at all. She felt invigorated and cleansed, the way Stuart had described himself feeling after he returned from the Ayurvedic spa. She felt that if she looked in a mirror, the whites of her eyes would be clear.

She squeezed Stuart's hand and he squeezed back. For the first time since she had set foot in the Prospect Park Food Coop, she was glad that she'd joined. And to think it was all because of a homeless thief. This kind of thing never would have happened at the Gourmet Garage in SoHo. There were no homeless in SoHo.

The Teat Lounge

LIZZIE O'DONNELL noticed a commotion through the Coop door as she passed. A white woman was arguing with a black man about something. Altercations like these made Lizzie relieved she wasn't a member, even though she and her husband, Jay, could have benefited from the savings.

She had considered joining when she was pregnant with her son, Mance, due to the generous parental leave policy (one year off for each baby), but had decided not to after realizing what a pain it would be to schlep groceries all the way to her Park Place walk-up. Her mother-in-law, Mona, had been a member for thirty years, back when her husband was still alive, but Lizzie had signed up for FreshDirect. Although some of the deliverymen made her nervous with their shifty eyes and what appeared to be prison tattoos, she felt that overall it was worth it not to have to carry groceries up three flights of stairs herself.

Despite the name of their street, Lizzie and Jay actually lived quite far from Prospect Park, on the northern side of Flatbush Avenue, in Prospect Heights. Prospect Heights had been almost all black since the sixties but in the nineties began to gentrify. Vanderbilt Avenue, the area's commercial street, now boasted chic restaurants, women's clothing boutiques, and a high-end bakery. Still, the property values in Prospect Heights were below those in the Slope, so far below that Jay and Lizzie jokingly referred to the neighborhood as TooPoSlo, Too Poor for the Slope.

Jay, who was black, had grown up on St. Marks Avenue, a few blocks away, and loved Prospect Heights. Mona still lived there. Jay liked having her so close and was always telling Lizzie that she should let her babysit for Mance, but after a year and a half, Lizzie had not let her do it once. It wasn't that she didn't trust Mona, who had done a great job raising Jay and his sister, Sabrina, alone; she didn't feel comfortable with her. Because of that, she was reluctant to hand over her son.

When Mona came to visit, Lizzie always felt she was judging her—for still breastfeeding after a year and a half, for waiting so long to introduce solid foods, for letting him sleep in their bed sometimes. Jay always said that it was who she was—formal, a retired schoolteacher—but Lizzie felt that Mona didn't like her because she was white.

Lizzie and Jay's brick walk-up was between Vanderbilt and Underhill, in the footprint of the developer Bruce Ratner's proposed Nets arena, which meant that it might be knocked down in order to build the arena. Lizzie and Jay, a funk musician, had looked into buying in Kensington but opted to stick it out in Prospect Heights because their landlord charged them only $1,350 for their seven-hundred-square-foot one-plus-den.

It was a little after six o'clock, and Lizzie was meeting her friend Rebecca and Rebecca's daughter, Abbie, at the Tea Lounge, a huge café on Union Street, around the corner from the Coop. As she walked in, she stopped to peruse the fliers on the enormous bulletin board by the door. There was a flier for an Obama fund-raising group—The Audacity of Park Slope—and Lizzie was smiling at the name when next to it she saw a police sketch depicting a broad-faced black man with squinty, deep-set eyes. At the top it said, WANTED FOR SEXUAL ASSAULT. He was listed as mid-twenties, six-three, medium-skinned, and was last seen wearing a black hoodie. Lizzie hated how, in wanted posters, the men always looked so black, with exaggerated African features. It was as though in remembering the crimes, the white people who gave the descriptions exaggerated the blackness in fear.

She moved toward the back of the room and got in line to buy a coffee. The Tea Lounge was a five-thousand-square-foot room filled with vintage furniture. It was populated by self-employed hipsters, grad students, nursing mothers, and an assortment of nannies of different races, all of whom barely tolerated one another. Every Wednesday morning Lizzie took Mance to the Tea Lounge for a baby sing-along led by Roy, a goateed Jeff Tweedy look-alike whom the mothers had nicknamed Hot Roy.

As Lizzie waited for Rebecca, she spotted half a dozen moms and their babies gathered around a nearby table. A heavyset, raspy-voiced woman was regaling the other mothers. Her son was strapped to her chest in an Ergo carrier, facing her, and he kept trying unsuccessfully to crane his neck to see behind him. "By the time they brought the epidural," the woman said, "I was so happy I kissed the anesthesiologist on the lips!" The women shuddered in hysteria. Lizzie could always pick out the Funny Mom in a group of new mothers: She was the loudest and usually one of the least attractive, and she didn't actually have to be witty, according to any sort of objective standard. She just had to crack mild, baby-centric, infuriatingly palatable jokes in a sarcastic but never bleak tone and all at once she was Will Ferrell.

Lizzie frequently felt different from other mothers, partly because her baby was black and partly because she was young. Most Park Slope stay-at-home-mothers (SAHMs) were at least a decade older than the thirty-year-old Lizzie, and because many of them had struggled to have children, they were neurotic and overattentive in a way that spooked her.

Lizzie, five-eight and naturally slender, dressed in vintage clothing and, with her short black bangs, was often told she resembled Bettie Page. Though hardly a fashion plate, she felt appearance mattered and had become especially attentive to it after reading a book called *The Post-Pregnancy Handbook,* which said a mother could improve her mood simply by trying to look good. Ever since then she had been careful to put on lipstick and mascara each day and had invested several hundred dollars in sexy, supportive German nursing bras from Boing Boing, a maternity store on Sixth Avenue.

Lizzie didn't consider herself depressed, but a year and a half into motherhood, she was finding it less satisfying than she had hoped. It was completely isolating, and yet you were never alone. The exhaustion, the constant work of it! She never played guitar or answered e-mails anymore, or even lay on the couch spacing out. Even when Mance was asleep, she was always straightening.

It didn't help that Mance was a challenging baby, moody and difficult, who hadn't gotten any easier with time. Dressing him each morning was like the climactic fight scene between Alan Arkin and Audrey Hepburn in *Wait Until Dark,* leaving her exhausted before the day had even begun. She wondered if she would have felt less alienated from him if he had been white, but when she had thoughts like that, she tried to push them out of her head, too guilty to give them credence.

When she first found out she was expecting, she had been elated. Lizzie's parents had split up when she was seven, and though she felt her mother had done a good job under the circumstances, she'd been so preoccupied with supporting the children that she hadn't been the most attentive mother to Lizzie or her sister, Katie. Lizzie wanted to do a better job.

And even though she knew her baby would face extra challenges, being biracial, she'd been excited. It made her giddy to imagine the looks on people's faces as she pushed her black child down the street. She wanted to shake up all these settled Slopers.

The first few months of her pregnancy she had been certain she was having a daughter. People told her she was carrying a girl because she put on weight in her butt and carried low, and since a girl was what she wanted, Lizzie believed them. Lizzie loved the idea of raising a bold, beautiful, biracial girl, with curly hair she would put in little pigtails. She wanted to feel like she was similar to her child, in gender if not in race.

But at the twenty-week ultrasound (which she had attended alone because Jay was traveling with his band) when the technician exclaimed, "You're having a boy!" Lizzie burst into tears.

When she called Jay to tell him, she made sure she sounded calm, but she was secretly dismayed by his response: "I always knew I would be a father to a son."

What the hell is that supposed to mean? she had wondered. Was he saying there was something superior about boys? Was he saying only weak men had girls?

For the next few months she had tried to wrap her mind around the idea of having a boy, but she couldn't see him, the way she could see her daughter, even when the sonographer gave her and Jay printouts to take home. Back then, in the spring of 2006, Barack Obama was a senator and had not yet declared his candidacy for president and Lizzie had only a faint idea of who he was. Lizzie hadn't known any biracial men except for a gay guy in her class at Hampshire with waist-long dreadlocks, so she had no model for her unborn child.

The birth itself had been triumphant: fast and natural, only six hours of labor at the Brooklyn Birthing Center, aided by aromatherapy and counterpressure massage. Mance was so light-colored when he came out that he didn't seem to be a different race at all, but when he latched on for the first time, she stared down at him like he was a stranger, which he was. A boy at her breast. It was like making out with someone you'd just met at a bar. It felt sexual, and the hungry way he drank caught her off guard at first.

They had named him after Mance Lipscomb, an old Texan blues singer who had been rediscovered in the sixties, but so far the only person who had known the reference was Hot Roy from sing-along. Mance Lipscomb was the son of an ex-slave, and Mance was short for "emancipation." Lizzie liked to point this out to people who inquired about the derivation, to make them think about slavery while they absorbed the meaning of a white mother and a black son.

After her maternity leave ended, Lizzie planned to go back to her job as an associate publicist at Knopf, but after three months, with Mance still breastfeeding on demand, she realized she wasn't ready. She only earned thirty-two thousand a year anyway, and a full-time nanny would have cost at least twenty-five, which meant that after taxes it would be a wash.

Mance had been a colicky infant, and though he vexed her, she felt his mood would only be worse in the company of a nanny. Besides, she reasoned, the early months were the worst; everyone said that. But all this time later, she still felt as overwhelmed as she had at the beginning. She wasn't sure whether to go back to work or have another baby and regarded each possibility with a different kind of dread.

It would have helped if she could have talked to Jay about any of these feelings, but these days he was rarely around. They had met at Pete's Candy Store in Williamsburg. He was the opening act for a friend's band, and when she walked in, he was onstage, playing slide guitar and singing a bluesy song containing the line "You feel like a promise, you look like rain," and she found herself imagining he'd written it for her. Jay had dark black skin and closely shaved hair, and he was wearing a guayabera shirt and dark, slim-fitting jeans. She found herself drawn to his powerful, deep voice, which contrasted with his slender frame.

After the show, someone introduced them, and when they shook hands, Jay's eyes seemed to linger on her. Jay was exotic, even though she knew it wasn't PC to see him that way, and yet he turned out to be just similar enough that she felt a connection with him.

Despite the racial difference, they had a lot in common. She had gone to Hampshire, he to Oberlin, both on scholarship. They both had single mothers and had grown up without a lot of money. They were creative but realistic, both trying to find ways to turn their talents into stable jobs.

That night, they talked about his music style, which he said he had altered after trying to get a career going writing R & B singles. He did okay at it, but it didn't satisfy him, and then one day a friend played him a Muddy Waters album and it was like someone had turned a switch. There was a song called "Two Trains," and when he heard it, he realized he wanted to sing like that. Now his music was a mix of blues, funk, and folk.

She was so taken with his idealism and ropy forearms that she got drunk on whiskey and wound up sleeping with him at his apartment on Park Place that night. A year later, they were married in a small ceremony at her childhood home in Woodstock.

These days it was hard to remember that first perfect night. Since he was never home, for all intents and purposes Lizzie was a single mother. He traveled with his band, One Thin Dime, playing midsize venues in white college towns, and had a cult following of frat kids who would smoke pot during the gigs and dance like they were doing Irish jigs. The concerts were well attended and the record sales strong, but all the money went back into session fees, rehearsal spaces, and album production. So even though the band had good name recognition, it always felt like she and Jay were scraping by. She and Mance were on a cata-strophic health insurance plan, but Jay wasn't on it, claiming he didn't need it. Lizzie worried all the time that something terrible would hap-pen to him and they would go bankrupt, like the families on those frightening public service announcements they were always showing on CNN.

When Jay was home, he would sit at the computer in his tiny office off the living room, working on his mailing list, calling venues, or prac-ticing. He had told her that when he was in his office, he was not to be bothered unless it was an emergency. So she would sit a few feet outside his door, comforting the wailing baby as Jay refused to come out. When she told him it wasn't fair, he said he didn't think it was fair that he had to earn all the money.

Rebecca came into the Tea Lounge, pushing Abbie in her stroller, and raised a hand to Lizzie. "How disgusting is this weather?" Rebecca said, kissing Lizzie wetly on the cheek.

"Oh, it's horrible," Lizzie said. "I hate being stuck in the city for the summer."

Rebecca was always physical, which was one of the things Lizzie liked about her. She seemed so at ease, and she was sarcastic and funny. They had met on the Third Street playground in June. Lizzie had been guiding Mance over the shaky bridge when she spotted Rebecca, wear-ing a form-fitting Petit Bateau tee, helping her daughter slide down a pole. When Rebecca caught Lizzie staring, she said, "I shouldn't be helping her. When you have a girl, you only have to do one thing. *Keep her off the pole.*"

Lizzie had laughed, and then Rebecca had admitted it was a Chris Rock line. They chatted for a few minutes, introducing themselves and the children, who turned out to be only weeks apart.

A few days later, Lizzie ran into Rebecca again. This time they ex-changed numbers, and now they got together once or twice a week.

"God, they're old," said Rebecca, pointing to the mothers arranged in a circle around a coffee table. "Nothing is more frightening than the sight of a granny mom nursing at the Teat Lounge." Lizzie giggled. Re-becca always called the Tea Lounge the Teat Lounge, but Lizzie laughed every time anyway. "I mean, I get that they're old, but I don't get why they refuse to make an effort with their looks."

"They've spent their lives making an effort," Lizzie said, "and now they have the kid so they don't have to."

"It's not like this in Tribeca," Rebecca said. "I once took Abbie to the Washington Market playground, and I saw a hot woman pushing her kid on the swings. She turned out to be Christy Turlington. I felt so bad for the normal mothers in Tribeca. They must have such low self-esteem."

"In Park Slope *we're* Christy Turlington," Lizzie said. One of the reasons she liked to be with Rebecca was that they cut a fine swath. Lizzie dressed like Parker Posey in *Party Girl,* crazy vintage schoolgirl chic, while Rebecca dressed like an art gallery assistant moonlighting as a prostitute. Their outfits, juxtaposed against the two strikingly attractive children in front of them, drew looks from other mothers. Lizzie enjoyed piquing the boring Park Slobbers and knew Rebecca did, too.

"I swear to God, I've seen one MILF since I've lived here," Rebecca said.

"Melora Leigh?" Lizzie asked.

"Besides Melora Leigh. She's tall and slim, and she has long, really light blond hair that she braids on her head, and she always dresses in, like, seventies vintage. She looks like Heidi. And she's married to this tan guy, Jewish I think, with curly Adonis hair and a surfer body."

"I think I've seen them!" Lizzie said. "Two boys?"

"Yep. They go to Third Street a lot. I have no idea why they choose to live here. They look like exiles from Santa Monica or something. I call them the Hotties."

The women paid for their coffees and sat on a couch in the corner. Rebecca eyed the new mothers, who were laughing loudly about something. "Did I ever tell you about the Boing Boing new mothers' group I went to?" Lizzie shook her head. "Abbie was two weeks old, and I found out they were meeting by the picnic tables in the park. I had gotten all dressed up so I'd look cute, and I had pushed her all the way up the hill. I said, 'I'm Rebecca and this is Abbie,' and I swear to God, this one mother stared right at me and did not say a word."

"Noooo!"

"She didn't even introduce herself."

"You should have left."

"I did after about twenty minutes. It was too depressing, all that bullshit about how many ounces of milk a baby needs and whether it can sleep on its stomach. It was like *Consumer Reports: The Play*."

Lizzie lifted Mance out of his stroller and put him to her breast, careful to drape him with her shirt. She often got stares when she breast-fed him, maybe because the sight of a black baby nursing from a white mother was so startling in Park Slope. "How come you're breastfeeding so long?" Rebecca asked.

"I'm enjoying it, and they say as long as the mother and child are enjoying it . . ."

Rebecca gave Lizzie a skeptical look. Lizzie didn't like that Rebecca was so snide. In a lot of countries women nursed until the children were three or four years old. Lizzie had noticed a strange double-standard in the neighborhood: If you were a strict mother, you were allowed to pass judgment on other mothers, because you were an underdog, outnum-bered. But if you were more attachment-oriented, you weren't allowed to. You couldn't look down on mothers who chose not to nurse or sleep-trained their children, because then you were a stereotype: a hippie, earth-loving Park Slope mom.

"How long did you do it?" Lizzie asked.

"Only six months. Then she got a cold and lost interest, so I cut her off. I'll tell you one thing I miss about breastfeeding. Breastfed babies don't get constipated. Abbie got so blocked up after I weaned that I had to give her an infant suppository. Whoever invented those should get a Nobel." Lizzie giggled. "So did Jay get back from his tour yet?"

They often complained about their absent husbands. "He comes back Saturday night," Lizzie said. "I feel like he's been gone for months." She noticed Rebecca's shorts, which were black crinkled taffeta. "Those are really cute."

"Marc Jacobs," Rebecca said. "I got them at this boutique on Atlantic Avenue. They cost two hundred dollars. I can't afford that, but I'd had a long day with Abbie, so we got on the bus and went over. When Theo saw the credit card bill, he freaked out, but I said, 'You take care of a baby three days a week, and you can go buy yourself some two-hundred-dollar shorts.' "

"Good for you," Lizzie said. If Jay were as successful as Theo, Lizzie would probably spoil herself, too. You had to reward yourself when you were with a baby all day. That was why there was always a line of mothers out the door of Häagen-Dazs with babies too young to eat ice cream.

Lizzie found Rebecca so refreshing that when they were together, she was often nervous that she'd say something stupid and screw it all up. She wanted to have her over for dinner and show her off to Jay, so he could see she knew someone cool, even if that someone was a mom.

Abbie got fussy and Rebecca asked if Lizzie wanted to come back to her apartment so she could feed her. Lizzie nodded, taken aback. They had never been to each other's apartments. That was common in the Slope—you could know a mother for months without being invited over; instead, you met on playgrounds, relieved you didn't have to straighten your apartment. If Rebecca was inviting her over, it meant they were real friends.

Rebecca's building was clearly a coop—Lizzie could tell from the well-maintained interior and the homogenous mailbox labels. The living room featured vintage modern pieces, all expertly arranged. It was monochromatic and artful, and on the wall were a few abstract paintings, one with neon-looking stripes. Compared to other Park Slope living rooms Lizzie had seen, it was practically a showroom; most other families with young children had shabby hand-me-down chintz couches and ugly childproofing blockades around the perimeters.

They sat at the dining room table, and Rebecca offered to feed both babies. She made mac and cheese and broccoli. Lizzie held Mance on her lap and fed him while Rebecca fed Abbie in her booster seat. Lizzie was pleased to see that Mance ate more than usual, and she felt it was because he was doing it with another child. The children were adorable next to each other, Abbie with her wide eyes and blond hair, Mance brown-skinned with his mini-Afro.

"I'm getting hungry myself," Rebecca said. "Do you want to have dinner here?" Lizzie glanced at her watch. It was close to seven. She couldn't believe it. That morning, when she was nursing Mance, bleary eyed and barely awake, she'd felt like dinnertime was a million hours away, and now it was almost here. This was why you needed other mothers as friends, to make the day pass more quickly.

"Oh, I wouldn't want to put you out."

"It's fine," Rebecca said. "Theo's not getting home till ten anyway, and I don't like to eat alone. I'll make us something simple." She went into the kitchen and put some water on. She emerged with a bottle of white wine and two glasses.

"I don't know," Lizzie said. "I usually nurse him before bed and—"

"Perfect. Drinking before nursing is a surefire way to get a baby to sleep through the night." Rebecca filled both glasses. Lizzie knew she shouldn't drink, but she felt twitchy and excited at the possibility of doing something she wasn't supposed to. Jay got to have all the fun these days—on tour or out with friends. Why couldn't she do something forbidden?

They clinked. "To the first normal mom I've met in the neighborhood," Rebecca said.

"Ditto," Lizzie said. She took a small sip.

"You gotta wean him," Rebecca said.

"Why?"

"For your own good. It's voluntary enslavement. In France a woman's considered a hippie if she nurses beyond three months. There's a stigma against it. They want their bodies back and their independence."

This sounded hostile, but Lizzie chose not to respond. She didn't want to get into a debate on the politics of nursing. As she sipped, the alcohol warmed her lungs. All she'd had for lunch was a yogurt, so the wine was going right to her head. Her cheeks flushed, and she got the mildly buzzed feeling that even if nothing was all right, everything would be all right.

"God, this is good," she said. "What is it?"

"Terre di Tufi. It's mostly Vernaccia, but there's some chardonnay, too. Are you a wine person?"

"Not really. I've always wanted to take a wine class, but I've never had the time."

"I didn't get into wine till I had Abbie. Childbirth turns women into alcoholics."

The children were finished eating, and Rebecca plopped them on the floor in front of a Baby Einstein video, which they watched, transfixed. Lizzie didn't let Mance watch videos, but she could see the appeal: It stunned them into a coma.

Mance seemed to have gotten more easygoing since he started spending time with Abbie. They were too young to interact, but Lizzie felt he was aware he had a friend and liked being around someone his own age instead of stuck with his mother all the time. In Park Slope all the SAHMs seemed to feel that constant mother-child contact was best for the child, but Lizzie thought kids needed to be around their peers.

The women moved to the couch. Lizzie sipped her wine, imagining Jay setting up for his gig in Charlotte. She wondered whether *he* had started drinking for the night. His favorite drink was Wild Turkey, because he had read that Mance Lipscomb used to drink it. Had he had one glass already, comped by the bar, or two? When he drank, did he think about the fact that he was a dad? Did he worry about drinking too much? Maybe the difference between a mother and a father was that a mother could never bracket parenthood, but a father could.

Rebecca was refilling Lizzie's glass generously. It had never occurred to Lizzie that if you combined a pleasurable activity, drinking, with a burdensome one, mothering, it made it fun.

As Lizzie drank, she found herself opening up. She told Rebecca about her constant state of exhaustion. She told her how angry she was at Jay for being selfish when he was home and traveling more than he needed to, and how frustrating it was to be alone with Mance all the time. She told her about Mona, who always seemed to be judging her.

"What does she judge you for?" Rebecca asked.

"You know, for attachment parenting. She was really strict with Jay, probably because she's a widow and she had to be. I get that. My mom was tough, too, after my dad left, but Mona has no sense of humor. She made fun of me for buying a nursing pillow when he was born, even though I was just trying to help my back."

"Did you try telling her to mind her own business?"

"I can't do that. She's my mother-in-law."

"So?"

"Jay's really loyal to her. He wants us all to be one happy family."

"Except he doesn't want to have to be there."

"Exactly."

"How come you were in such a rush to have Mance, anyway? Did you say you're twenty-nine?"

"Thirty."

"You look younger. You could have postponed purgatory."

Lizzie knew she had an opportunity to tell Rebecca the story of how she'd met Jay, and decided to take it. She wasn't afraid. "I never believed in the biological clock," Lizzie said carefully, "but when I was twenty-seven, I got hit by this uncontrollable desire to have a baby."

"I never had that. For me it was more 'What the hell, I'm going to do it sometime, so might as well do it now.' "

"For me it was a bigger deal." Lizzie took a deep breath. "When I met Jay, I was living with a woman."

Rebecca raised her eyebrows with the kind of interest that Lizzie had rarely seen on any new mothers' faces, because most of what mothers talked about was so boring and inane. She knew Rebecca was interested because Rebecca was aware of this, too—the rarity of two mothers talking about something provocative—but Lizzie wanted to tell her.

During her sophomore year at Hampshire College, she had fallen in love with a woman in her Gender and Genre class who had very strong feelings about the male gaze in *Vertigo*. Her name was Sarah Boschen, and she was a beautiful and high-profile lesbian activist on campus. Despite the fact that Lizzie was a child of hippies, she had never been with a woman, and she found Sarah eye-opening and brilliant. Sarah was a year older, and after she graduated, she got an administrative job with the LGBT Alliance on campus so they could keep living together. When Lizzie graduated, they moved to a one-bedroom in Bushwick, Sarah working at the Lesbian Herstory Archives in Park Slope, Lizzie landing a job as assistant publicist at Knopf.

"So what happened? You had lesbian bed death and realized you missed cock?" Rebecca asked.

"That wasn't the problem. We had all these gay friends in the Slope having kids, and one night after we went to a baby shower Sarah said it bothered her that all these dykes were getting knocked up because she'd never wanted children. I realized that I did. We had a big argument about it. Sarah said that lesbian moms were tools of the patriarchal hegemony. I said it was an issue of personal choice. We started fighting a lot, and then one night I went to Pete's Candy Store to hear a band, and it turned out Jay was the opening act."

"And?"

"I moved out a couple days later."

The wine was swirling around in Lizzie's head, and she felt light-headed and free. Rebecca's eyes traveled down Lizzie's body, and she said, "I would not have pegged you as a dyke."

"You mean a hasbian," Lizzie said.

"Hasbian!" Rebecca said, giggling.

"You never heard that? There's wasbian, and then there's Hechebian, for Anne Heche, which is a really opportunistic lesbian. Sarah kept saying it wouldn't have been as bad if I was leaving for another woman, but the last I heard, she was living with a guy, too."

"Figures. The most militant ones are always the straightest."

"I was never militant."

"You mean you never got a buzz cut and put on forty pounds?"

"Neither did Sarah. She had long hair, too. She just didn't want to have babies. Have you ever been with a woman?"

"There was one party at Barnard where this chick attacked me. We made out for a little, and I was cool with it, but she never spoke to me again. Even though she was the one who kissed me."

"Did you like it?"

"No, mainly it felt weird. I never thought about it much, after. I think if I were bi at Barnard, I could have experimented. A woman can experiment with no repercussions, but a man can't. 'Build a thousand bridges and you're a bridge builder, suck one cock and you're gay.' "

Lizzie couldn't remember the last time she'd heard a woman say the word "cock." She couldn't believe she was having this incredible night and that it was all because of Mance. Now that she knew how hard it was to raise a child, there were times when she missed Sarah and wondered if she had made a mistake. But sitting here drinking wine with a woman she knew only through motherhood, she felt fortunate. She had met someone who was smart and funny and badass, and it had happened because of her son.

"So does Jay care that you used to be gay?" Rebecca asked.

"At the beginning he did. His mother is kind of religious. But he went to Oberlin, and half the campus was gay."

"I bet he worries he can't measure up. Right? How could any man be better at sex than a woman?"

"Oh, I don't think he worries. He's very confident in his masculinity."

"Do you guys do it a lot?" Rebecca's face was open. If Lizzie hadn't been buzzed, she might have gotten shy, but she felt like Rebecca was daring her to be as bold as she was.

"How often is a lot?" Lizzie asked.

"Well, how often do you do it?"

"I guess four times a week or so. When he's here that long."

"*Four times a week?*" Rebecca's eyes widened. "Are you sure you're bisexual?"

Lizzie found herself in the odd position of being embarrassed by what she thought was a healthy sex life. "I'm not bi. Anymore."

Why did everyone have to put a name on everything? If she had to label her sexuality in the way everyone did at Hampshire, she would say she was a straight-identified-former-lesbian-who-still-sometimes-wondered-about-women. She was interested in women's bodies and faces, and even now, as a card-carrying member of the breeder bourgeois, she observed women with a level of interest that she'd never had in men. She had expected motherhood to make her forget about women, as though procreating with a man would turn her straight forever, but it hadn't. Breastfeeding aroused her, one of the reasons she was unwilling to stop. She felt as though she were on display all the time, with her breasts out in front of strangers, and it excited her a little to catch a cute single girl staring at her breast and then looking away. She had an entire private sexuality that had nothing to do with Jay and even though the sex with him was good, it felt distant from the scenarios she imagined while they were doing it, which usually involved some combination of women, men, and wolves.

"You think four times a week is a lot?" she asked Rebecca. "I thought it was average. How often do you do it?"

There was a clap of thunder outside, and Mance let out a frightened cry. It had clouded up while they were sitting there but Lizzie hadn't noticed. She scooped him up from in front of the television and bounced him up and down, but he cried more. He startled so easily. Still standing, Lizzie put him to her breast, but this didn't placate him as it usually did. She was struck with a wave of guilt. She had been so busy drinking she had been ignoring Mance, and now he needed her.

"I totally forgot about the pasta," Rebecca said, rushing toward the kitchen.

"Don't worry about it," Lizzie said. "We should be getting home anyway."

"Really?" Rebecca said, eyeing the window. "It looks pretty bad out there."

"I'll be fine."

"Well, at least let me lend you an umbrella," Rebecca said, retrieving one from the closet. When she handed it to Lizzie at the door, she said, "I had a lot of fun with you."

"Me, too," Lizzie said.

"We should get drunk every night."

Lizzie fumbled with the lock, cradling Mance in her arms. Rebecca hugged her tightly and rubbed her back. Her hands were firm and strong. It reminded Lizzie of the time a teacher at Park Slope Yoga Center gave her a massage during Shivasana, except that had only happened once, and ever since she had wondered what was wrong with her that yoga teachers never chose her for massage. "Get home safe, okay?" Lizzie nodded. Rebecca kissed Mance on the cheek and then leaned in and kissed Lizzie on the lips. It started out ambiguously—wet but closed-mouthed—but neither of them pulled away, and soon it turned into a French.

Lizzie felt her whole body thrill. Rebecca was a good kisser, confident, and her mouth was sweet from the wine.

Motherhood was sensual, but the relationship was so parasitic. Lizzie often felt that her body, her hands, her arms, her breasts were all for Mance, put there to gratify his needs. Rebecca's touch was for her.

But she was frightened by the feeling of being wanted in this way by someone she liked and respected. Lizzie pulled away and rushed out the door.

Outside, the rain was coming down in sheets. Lizzie got the umbrella open, but it was hard to push the stroller with one hand, and she walked crookedly, soaking her left side. The streets were deserted and the sky dark. She didn't like being alone on the street, even early at night, even in Park Slope. She headed down Carroll past Eighth Avenue, toward Seventh because there would be more traffic, more stores, and she felt she'd be safer there. She turned right toward Flatbush Avenue and crossed at Park Place toward home.

As she walked, she thought about the kiss. She felt like Rebecca had done it manipulatively, as some sort of test or dare, because she knew Lizzie had once been with women and wanted to see if she had the power to attract her.

As she crossed to the far side of Vanderbilt, she saw a tall black man leaning against an iron gate, midway between Lizzie and her place. He seemed young and was wearing a dark hooded sweatshirt. He turned toward her.

Her pulse raced. Walking with Mance in Prospect Heights, she passed a lot of black men, even a lot of black men in hooded sweatshirts. But now the wanted poster at the Tea Lounge came flashing before her. Normally, when she passed a black guy on an empty street, instead of instinctively crossing the street, she tried to gauge the threat level from a distance. Did he look like he was out for trouble, or was he on his way somewhere? Did he have a knapsack? How did he wear his pants? As the mother of a black son, she felt it was important that she not stigmatize black men. She imagined Mance grown up, walking down a street and having white women cross the other way.

This guy made Lizzie uncomfortable. He was standing outside in the middle of a thunderstorm with no umbrella, which didn't make sense. His skin seemed medium, like the poster said, and though she couldn't make out his features, there was that hoodie. Lizzie kept thinking of the horrible police sketch.

The guy was staring straight at her. She stood still, debating the possibility of rushing past him to her door, then decided it was better to be cautious. There was a rapist on the loose. She couldn't mess around.

She spun around and hightailed it back to Vanderbilt, where she turned the corner and darted into the bodega she went to all the time to buy milk and juice. There was a big sign on the door that said ARENA with a slash through it. She thought about calling Mona and asking if she could come over for a visit, but she had never been alone with her when Jay wasn't there. And if Lizzie got upset and confessed about the man on her block, then Mona would think she was a racist, a paranoid white woman incapable of raising a strong black son.

Lizzie wanted to call Rebecca but was too ashamed. She didn't want to admit that she felt unsafe in her own neighborhood. It would only emphasize the money differences between them.

The bodega's proprietor, José, saw the frightened look on Lizzie's face and asked what was wrong. "A guy on my block," she said. "There's a guy."

José dispatched his heavyset middle-aged brother-in-law Norberto in search of him, and Norberto came back saying no one was there. Norberto offered to walk Lizzie to her door. She said she wanted to wait a few minutes more, and José offered her a cup of tea, but she declined. As grateful as she was for the assistance, she was also ashamed to have told him. Now every time she came in to buy something, he would re-member this.

She thought about Jay, away at his gig in Charlotte, and was furious at him for not being there, for being the reason she was alone with Mance all the time. Who did he think he was, abandoning her week after week, with Mance still so young and dependent? It was as though his music bought him some sort of special liberty other fathers weren't allowed. Rebecca's husband, Theo, worked long hours, but by the look of their apartment, he had to be making good money. Jay netted only $60,000 a year after paying his band, barely enough to support the fam-ily, and still wouldn't consider getting a real job on the side.

As she headed out with Norberto, she scanned the block nervously, convinced the man was hiding somewhere. But he had evaporated.

"You see him?" Norberto said.

"No, he's gone."

Norberto waited for her to get in the front door. As soon as she did, she shut it, locking the top lock, too, and leaned against it, head in her hands. Out of the corner of her eye she saw Mance, still in the stroller, behind the rain shield, and for a moment he looked foreign, like someone else's kid.

Failure to Progress

"BYE, SWEETIE," Rebecca was saying to Abbie, walking backward toward the gate of the Third Street playground. It was a scorching July Thursday, three days after Rebecca's thwarted masturbation, and she was looking forward to getting a break from her daughter. Rebecca's babysitter, Sonam, diminutive and deferential, with a forehead of life-long suffering, took care of Abbie Tuesdays and Thursdays while Rebecca worked on freelance article assignments, window-shopped, or did her Prospect Park Food Coop shift, like today. Abbie adored Sonam but was going through a phase of separation anxiety, and today she was screaming in agony, "Mommy!" with tears streaming down her pink cheeks.

The sanctimommies had turned to stare, casting Rebecca looks of bald accusation. Rebecca figured they were being nasty because of her wardrobe, the gold lamé romper, as out of place on a Park Slope playground as a pair of Jimmy Choo stilettos. "Jesus Christ," Rebecca wanted to tell them. "They all cry like this when their mothers leave. It's manipulative. It doesn't mean anything."

"Mama's coming back soon," said Sonam.

"I'd be crying, too, if my mama were leaving me," said Cathleen Meth, a frazzled, curly-haired redheaded SHAM (Rebecca preferred to call stay-at-home mothers SHAMs) whom Rebecca had met in a prenatal class at Park Slope Yoga.

Cathleen, who was five-one and heavy and wore a baggy T-shirt with mom jeans every single day regardless of weather, was helping her very blond son, Jones, navigate the low climbing structure for tots. Next to her was Jane Simonson, a tall, pert mother of three whom Rebecca had met a few times before. Jane was nursing her youngest, Emily, in a sling while keeping an eye on August, two, who was going down the little slide on his stomach.

Cathleen and Jane made an odd combination—Cathleen messy and door-mattish, and Jane Pilates-fit and neat. To Rebecca the draw was clear: Cathleen felt Jane imbued her with status, and Jane was happy to have a follower, however dowdy. Motherhood was high school for unemployed people.

"I'm going to my Coop shift," Rebecca told Cathleen, as though this reason for leaving were morally superior to, say, earning money.

"Why don't you work Child Care," said Cathleen, "so you can bring Abbie? That's what I do. Jones loves it up there." Rebecca wanted to tell her that any woman who would choose to spend more time with her child than she had to was insane or masochistic. But as usual, she bit her tongue.

Rebecca could never imagine doing the child-care thing twenty-four-seven. Every time she looked at the SHAMs' faces, she felt vindicated in her choice to work. They were the ones who were supposed to be most gratified by motherhood—because they had quit their jobs to devote themselves to it—but they always looked stressed out and miserable. As they tended to their children, they wore expressions of joyless focus, as if they were doing open-heart surgery or defusing bombs. The working moms, who would come racing onto the playground at five-thirty or six, were the only ones who seemed to enjoy their kids—maybe because they got a break.

Sonam led Abbie to the sand box, a dirty, wet, bacteria-laden mud pit that mothers referred to as the "sand" box, making disdainful air quotes with their fingers. "I wouldn't put her in there," Cathleen said, more to Rebecca than to Sonam. "Stray cats go in there at night."

"August got ringworm from the sand," said Jane.

Who were these people? Rebecca had never felt alienated from other women until she became a mother. At *Elle* there were definitely some fembots, but even they were smart, or ambitious, or so stylish she couldn't help but admire the way they put themselves together. Her girlfriends outside of work had been in the literary scene, slutty bipolar smokers who were into indie rock and Proust. They carried Labyrinth tote bags, rode the F train, and spoke in voices dripping with irony and heartbreak.

But Rebecca had not met anyone like that in Park Slope. The SHAMs were wives of bankers and hedge fund guys. They threw baby showers, wore diamond rings, and went by their husbands' last names. And the working moms were rarely around.

Occasionally, Rebecca would meet a mother who seemed different—smart, or self-employed, or sardonic—but inevitably, the woman would prove to be insane. A cheerful kindergarten teacher, Jeannie, invited Rebecca and Abbie to her Garfield Place apartment one Sunday afternoon, and she and Rebecca chatted amicably until Jeannie's daughter, Ella, pooped in her diaper. When Jeannie tried to change Ella, the girl threw a fit, kicking and screaming on the table. Jeannie dropped her back on the floor, shrugged, and said, "Sometimes she doesn't like to be changed." For the next half hour Ella walked around happily in her own shit until the stench grew so unbearable that Rebecca made an excuse and left.

There was a poetry teacher mom, Joanna, whom Rebecca had met at the Teat Lounge when Abbie was a baby. Joanna was pretty and pulled together and had a large buoyant boy, Colin. They got to talking, and soon Joanna had told Rebecca all sorts of exciting things: she was a medicated manic-depressive who was on Paxil, had stopped taking it during pregnancy but had gone back on in the thirty-seventh week after having a breakdown; she wasn't going to have another child because she couldn't handle being off the meds; she had stolen her husband from his first wife. Rebecca found her negativity and drama-ridden experience so refreshing that she told Joanna to read *A Life's Work,* a dark British book on motherhood that Rebecca had devoured.

A week went by, and then another, without Joanna calling, and finally, Rebecca tried her. "I can't believe you recommended that book to me," Joanna said.

"I thought you'd appreciate the honesty."

"That woman hates her child. I don't hate Colin."

"I didn't say you did."

"It's like she believes she's the first person in the world to become a mother."

This got under Rebecca's skin. "You know, people always say that when women write books—'She thinks she's the first one in the world to . . .' whatever it is—but they never say it about men. It's like women don't have a right to describe universal experiences, even though men have been doing it for thousands of years: war, heartbreak, suicide. And I happen to think Rachel Cusk says some things that no other woman was brave enough to say before."

Rebecca knew by the long pause that followed that she had gone too far in the Barnard department. She had double-majored in English and Women's Studies, and sometimes she could get militant.

"I just feel like we're really different, you and me," Joanna said. "We don't have the same ideas about things at all." Rebecca had assumed that because Joanna taught poetry, she would be interested in books and ideas, but she realized Joanna only wanted someone to talk to over coffee. After that they never spoke again, exchanging uncomfortable glances when they passed, pushing strollers, on Seventh Avenue.

It was impossible to make friends with Park Slope mothers. If they weren't asexual fatties, they were earth mamas who breastfed till seven. As soon as you opened up to one, you got sucked into her psychosis.

So far Rebecca's only official mom friend was Lizzie O'Donnell. Lizzie was sweet and a good listener, and unlike other SHAMs, she was cute. Who would have guessed that she used to be a rug muncher? It intrigued Rebecca, mainly because it distinguished Lizzie from the other mothers. Though most Park Slope mothers dressed like lesbians, it hadn't occurred to Rebecca that some of them might actually *be* lesbians.

Rebecca hoped she hadn't ruined everything by kissing Lizzie. She'd been tipsy, she remembered that, and Lizzie had told her she used to be with women, which was obviously a come-on, so Rebecca had decided to have a little fun. She hadn't thought much about it before she did it.

She'd enjoyed it. It had been so long since she and Theo even kissed. When they did touch, passing each other in the hallway, they practically flinched.

But Lizzie had been so strange about it—pulling away and running out the door—that Rebecca was certain she had been offended, which seemed a bit of an overreaction. There was something too serious about her; her eyes were so intense. Rebecca wouldn't have been surprised to find that someone had a restraining order against her.

She hadn't called Lizzie later that night, not sure if she was supposed to apologize or pretend it hadn't happened. She hoped Lizzie would call her. It would be just Rebecca's luck to lose the one semi-decent friend she'd made—all because she got blitzed and sucked a little face. She really needed to get fucked one of these days or she was going to do something *really* stupid.

Rebecca waved to Abbie, trying to ignore her plaintive wails, and slipped out of the gate at the southern end of the playground. She pulled it shut behind her, but it swayed open a little. A woman with a newborn strapped to her chest gave Rebecca the evil eye and hurried over to latch the gate even though the baby was preambulatory.

Rebecca ambled down the path toward Prospect Park West, feeling her spirits lift higher the farther she got. Her shoulders felt lighter and her arms hung lightly at her sides, because she wasn't struggling to push a stroller with a twenty-five-pound baby in it.

When she was single, she hated being alone, found it embarrassing and pathetic. It was depressing to sit in her walk-up on Fifth Avenue, but to go out with a girlfriend to a bar and see if you could get laid, that was exciting. Most weeknights during her twenties, that was what she had done—and on her down nights, she stayed home feeling antsy and lonely.

But these days she saw solitude as promising. When Theo was home, she would search for excuses to run errands, bolting out to return a video, or taking out the garbage for the pleasure of getting a few minutes of silence.

She walked north on Prospect Park West to Second Street and then down the slope toward Seventh Avenue and the Coop. When she was halfway to Eighth, a gate opened and a man came out. He ogled her in the romper and then blanched in embarrassment as he recognized her. "Rebecca."

It was David Keller. David, a successful comedian, had been her boyfriend for a year and a half, starting in December 2001. In the time since they had broken up, during which she had met and married Theo, given birth to Abbie, and gone freelance, David had become internationally famous, a fact that caused her no small amount of pain.

He was six-two and Jewish, with a large beak nose that didn't look beak to women because most of them were too short to get a full-on view. As a result, he seemed more attractive than he actually was. He had dark shiny brown hair that he wore in a 1940s cut under stingy brims he bought from the Austrian company Mühlbauer.

They had met at a Christmas party on Pitt Street. She was at *Elle* and he was waiting tables while doing alternative comedy downtown. They spent the party bantering on the frigid fire escape, and then he kissed her under the moonlight and she was smitten. This was soon after September 11, when Christmas parties were tentative and no one knew if it was all right to celebrate anything. It turned out David lived on Fifth Avenue, too, so they split a cab back and drank at O'Connor's, then went back to her place and made out.

One night at a loft party thrown by a male journalist friend of Rebecca's, David told the story of the time he threw up on Salman Rushdie at a Chinese restaurant. There were a lot of journalists and authors at the party, and by the time he finished the story, he had a crowd of half a dozen collapsing in laughter.

On their way home, Rebecca suggested he perform at an open mike on Allen Street, where she knew the MC. He reprised the Rushdie Vomit story, bringing down the hundred-seat house. It wasn't long before he was doing regular gigs at downtown performance spaces and bars. His act was a cross between stand-up and storytelling and usually involved some sort of gross humiliation. After each show, a crowd of cute twentysomething girls would approach to tell him how cool he was, their eyes wide with admiration. His Woody Allen–esque self-effacement, combined with the fact that he was much more attractive than Woody Allen, made him an object of lust.

Rebecca found his tales of heartbreak, road trips, and germaphobia amusing enough—but after hearing them over and over again, she grew bored. She was aware that some of her resentment came from jealousy, but that did nothing to quell it. She had an unpublished novel that she thought was pretty good, *Willow Grove*—a comedic coming-of-age based on her high school experiences in suburban Philly—but by the time she met David, it had already been rejected by nine publishers. And now it was in a box under the bed.

A few months after David started performing, a top book editor came to one of his shows. The guy told David to write down some of his stories, and he did. He got an agent and went out with a submission, and there was a ferocious bidding war among six houses for his memoir. He finally sold *Are You My Mommy?* for $250,000, and then Jack Black's production company purchased the rights for another $300,000.

David bought a spacious loft on Union Street with the money but didn't ask Rebecca to move in, saying he didn't want to rush things. When they went out in the neighborhood, he would get recognized by adoring fans, and he chatted them up at length as she waited. Then he would take her back to his apartment and fuck her with extra enthusiasm.

When he got a $1 million development deal for a half-hour dramedy pilot on CBS about his life, they celebrated with a romantic dinner at their favorite restaurant, al di là. Over ice cream in espresso he broke up with her, saying they were "growing in different directions."

After the pilot deal, David flipped the Union Street loft for $900,000 and bought a double-wide, double-deep brownstone on First Street. It was a huge deal, written up on Brownstoner and Gothamist. Asking price was $3.6 million, and according to the Corcoran listing, it was sixty-five hundred square feet, with stained-glass windows and a conservatory. The garden was so deep that it stretched all the way to Second Street.

In her wanderings with Abbie, Rebecca frequently passed the yard in the back and ogled his professionally landscaped garden. A few times she'd seen him sitting at his patio table entertaining friends, an odd hodgepodge of people like Mos Def, David Cross, Darren Aronofsky, Rachel Weisz, and Liv Tyler. She would hurry past, not wanting to seem like a stalker.

She had run into David on the street half a dozen times since Abbie had been born, and though she always made small talk, she hated the idea that this bachelor was living it up in a $3.6 million brownstone alone, without even needing the space. It depressed her. She was aware that by many women's standards, she, too, would be considered a success—handsome husband, cute baby, flexible freelance career, two-bedroom coop in a great school district—but these signifiers felt empty to Rebecca. In Abbie's birth records, the doctor had written that her cesarean was due to "failure to progress," and around David she always felt a failure to progress.

"Hi, David," she said.

"How's it going?" David asked. "Where's Abbie?"

"With her sitter," Rebecca said.

"Do you have pictures?" he said. She showed him a few on her phone. "She's so big and beautiful! Wow!"

He seemed genuine in his interest, so genuine that she was surprised she didn't feel more gracious. Abbie was beautiful, with long blond hair and enormous doelike brown eyes. Rebecca would see other women on the playground, fretting over their monkey-faced boys. Why wasn't she prouder of her gorgeous girl? Was it because Theo lavished so much praise on Abbie that Rebecca was jealous? Or was it that he lavished so much praise she never got a chance to really notice Abbie for herself, see how beautiful she was? Rebecca frequently felt that if she could only hand her motherhood to a woman who would appreciate it, everyone would be happier.

"So how's everything going?" David asked.

She told him she was freelancing, and that Abbie was really cute these days, and that Theo was working on a new condo project in the West Village. She was conscious of trying to make her life sound rich and fulfilling, if not exciting.

Without her asking what he was doing, he said, "I just found out that Al Maysles is going to shoot a documentary about me."

"I thought he was dead," she said.

Rebecca saw some motion in the yard, and then the gate opened and a tall brunette was standing next to him. It took a moment for Rebecca to register the face, but when she did, she felt like she had swallowed a ball of dough.

"Rebecca, this is Cassie," David said redundantly.

Cassie Trainor was a knockout, raven-haired, six-foot-tall twenty-five-year-old wunderkind Alaskan singer-songwriter whose first album, *Stick Your Finger Down My Throat,* had gone platinum. Since then she'd had a mediocre-selling second album, *Addictive Personality,* followed by another platinum album, *Codey.* She had recently won attention for starring in a racy Marc Jacobs ad photographed by Juergen Teller in which she squatted in a see-through bra and panties, hyperventilating into a paper bag.

Rebecca had read on Gawker that David and Cassie had been spotted together at a Broadway opening but had found the news so disturbing that she wrote it off as a fabrication. Now there was no contesting the truth. Her ex-boyfriend was dating an internationally famous pop star, and Rebecca was a Park Slope mother who couldn't get her husband to fuck her.

"Hey," Rebecca said, extending a hand.

"Rebecca has the most beautiful little girl," said David. "Abbie. She was named for Abbie Hoffman."

"What a great name," Cassie said in a pipsqueak voice.

"Show Cassie the pictures."

"She's so cute!" said Cassie as she looked at the phone. She seemed genuinely bowled over, baby-lustful.

"Thanks," Rebecca said, wondering who was on top during sex—if Cassie was submissive, as Rebecca had been, or more dominant, spinning around on David's face while hurling anti-Semitic epithets. The best thing about Rebecca's relationship with David had been the sex; it was the only time his narcissism was appealing.

"I gotta get going," Rebecca said, taking the phone back. "I'm late for my Coop shift."

"You're a member?" Cassie said. "We're thinking of joining." So they lived together. It got worse and worse. "How's the produce?"

"It never ripens."

"Hey, Rebecca," David called as Rebecca headed off. "Cassie's doing a show at Southpaw next Wednesday night. She's being interviewed by Philip Gourevitch, a fund-raiser for the *Paris Review.* I'll put you on plus one. You should come."

"You definitely should," said Cassie.

Rebecca smiled and nodded, but there was no way she would go.

The problem with the world was that people like Philip Gourevitch interviewed people like Cassie Trainor.

"Motherhood agrees with you!" David shouted as she made her way down the street, feeling ridiculous in her romper. She wasn't sure which infuriated her more: that David had become a starfucker or that he'd become a star.

The food handling room in the Coop basement was quiet, as usual. The only sound was the tinny din of WNYC coming from a small transistor radio. The room was bright and silent—you couldn't hear any of the hubbub on the shopping floor above. Rebecca greeted her team leader, Terry, a bearish bearded gay guy, and Helen and Carla, two menopausal librarians on her shift.

"Look what the wind blew in," said Terry. "Did you come from Studio 54?"

"It's hot out," she said. "Leave me alone."

The regular crew of misfits was there, all wearing bandannas and aprons, as specified by the health code. Rebecca noticed a tall man with his back turned, perusing a sign about hand washing. As he turned to face the group, Rebecca blushed.

He was as good-looking in real life as in the movies. She had first noticed him in that Soderbergh thriller where he played best friend to Matt Damon's CIA agent. She'd wondered what he'd been doing in a supporting role when he was so much sexier than Matt. Then he'd starred in *Poses* with his future wife. After that there had been a string of action movies, including a brainy thriller costarring Clive Owen called *End of the Day,* for which he'd received an Oscar nomination.

She knew he lived on Prospect Park West with Melora Leigh and, like all Slope residents, knew the mansion, but had never seen him until now. The last place on earth Rebecca had expected to run into Stuart Ashby was the Prospect Park Food Coop—the bowels, no less. Why did anyone who lived in a mansion need to shop at a food coop?

She had seen Melora on the Third Street playground once, reading a script while a blond nanny pushed Orion on the swings. Rebecca didn't understand why any mother would go out with her child and her nanny at the same time but figured that for a celebrity, it was the best of both worlds: She got to be seen with her kid without actually having to take care of him.

Stuart eyed Rebecca's romper with surprised appreciation, then let his eyes hover, as though he didn't care if she saw that he was checking her out. "We have someone new on our team," said Terry. "Stuart." He said his name in a mock-breezy tone. "I was hoping you could train him, Rebecca." She could count on a gay guy to be an enabler.

Stuart smiled sheepishly. "I'm a very fast learner." Helen nudged Carla, who also blushed.

"Rebecca's going to show you how to bag nuts," said Terry.

"That would make us nut bags, then, eh?" said Stuart. Helen giggled loudly, but no one else did.

"You keep making bad puns, we're going to kick you off the shift," said Rebecca.

"That's all right. I'm shiftless by nature."

There was something old-fashioned about him. It was as though his good looks gave him insurance against coming off as a dork, even though his jokes were horrible.

"I have a few announcements before we start," Terry said. "The Minority Issues Task Force is looking for new members. They're holding a meeting this Tuesday if any of you want to go. I don't know if you read the *Coop Courier,* but lately, there have been a number of complaints of racial bias at the Coop. There was an incident involving two pickpock-etings the other day, and apparently, an African-American member was accused of stealing." It was so typical. People were always getting up in arms at the Coop about one thing or another. " 'The goal of the Minority Issues Task Force committee is to eliminate bias in the Coop and advocate on behalf of those who feel they have experienced discrimination while shopping or working.' "

"I'm discriminated against every time I have to wait half an hour to buy my food," Rebecca said.

"Maybe you should join, then," said Terry.

"*You* should go," Rebecca told Stuart. "You're in an oppressed group."

"Which one is that?"

"Celebrities. You can't get any of your needs met here. No personal assistants, no bottled water, no *Variety* magazine."

"Yes, but they do have an excellent supply of neti pots," he said. He seemed to be flirting, but it had been so long since anyone had flirted with her that she felt as though she had lost her play-dar.

Terry and the other team members went to other parts of the basement to work on other projects. Rebecca put on a yellow bandanna and showed Stuart the bin of mixed nuts. The downy red hair on the back of his hands made her imagine the tint of his pubic hair. There was a vulgarity to redheads. They were overt, sexual, in a way brown-haired guys weren't. You met a redhead and you thought about cock.

"You start with the tamari roasted, and I'll do mixed nuts," she said.

"Could you say 'mixed nuts' again?" This was not what she expected from a married celebrity. Weren't they supposed to be withholding and cold, so as not to give off any whiff of availability? Either his marriage was in trouble, like the tabloids said, or he was messing with her head.

"So you put these on"—she handed him a pair of cellophane gloves—"and then you scoop out one handful with the scooper and bag it in these." She pointed to a stack of clear plastic bags. "Each handful should be about a third of a pound. You weigh them the first few times to get the hang of it. Tie each bag in a knot, like this, after twisting the plastic. And then when we're done, we'll put the labels on."

"Yes, ma'am," he said.

She stood perpendicular to him at the butcher-block table, the scale between them. Stuart speared the scooper into his bin. "Excellent technique," she said.

"Are you going to rag on me for the next two hours?"

"Two hours thirty-seven minutes."

She couldn't believe she was alone in a room with the undivided attention of a celebrity. He couldn't be flirting. He probably acted this way with everyone. Famous people wanted everyone to like them, even nobodies.

"That bag's a little big," she said, eyeing the scale. "Almost a pound. Clearly you have a distorted sense of size."

"Maybe I just really like nuts."

"I like nuts, too. Especially salty ones. Kind of sweaty-salty, you know? Like right after the gym but before the shower."

He stopped midplunge and shook his head. "Who are you?" he said.

"Rebecca Rose."

"Are you sure you live in this neighborhood, Rebecca Rose?"

Maybe she'd gone too far. This was what happened when you didn't get laid for a year and a half. You turned into a guttermouth. But what was the point of pretending to be normal when she was alone in a small room with an Oscar-nominated actor? In Park Slope you didn't know the next time anything exciting would happen.

Rebecca had a sudden instinct to take a cell phone picture of herself with Stuart Ashby and send it to David Keller, with the table and nut barrels cropped out, of course. What did it matter if David Keller was living with Cassie Trainor when she was two feet away from Stuart Ashby?

Rebecca set a bag of mixed nuts on the table between them. It was cold in the room, and she was glad to be wearing almost nothing, aware that her nipples were hard. "So is it true you're not on the deed?" she asked.

"How'd you know about my deed?" he said with a frown.

"This is brownstone Brooklyn. We take real estate very seriously here. I hear she bought it with her trust. Was that part of your prenup or something?"

"What are you—a bloody journo?"

"Yep. Freelance writer for women's magazines. It's mostly lifestyle, but I do a few blow jobs for the extra money. *Allure* and *Women's Health*." She wanted him to bend her at the waist like a Barbie, rip the romper off her body. "You know what's weird about celebrity interviews?"

"What's that?"

"About a third of the way in, the celeb always spills some anecdote about her sad childhood. You know, the father who abandoned her or the mother who died when she was young. Then she says some stupid platitude like 'People have always left me.' And you can tell it's something her shrink said. She tries to pass it off as original, but most celebrities are so vapid they're incapable of reflecting on themselves beyond parroting some observation by a Beverly Hills shrink to the stars."

"Burbank. The shrinks to the stars are mostly in Burbank."

"Whatever."

"For your information, my parents have been married forty-five years."

"That's right, that's right. And you were discovered in a Jocelyn Moorhouse movie, right?"

"You're killing me here. That's Russell."

She knew it was and had said it to toy with him. "I love *Proof*. He was, like, twenty-five when he did it. About the blind guy. I saw it at the Walter Reade in a festival of Australian cinema."

"Did they show *Dead Calm*?"

"Oh my God," Rebecca said, feeling warm. "The greatest thriller ever made."

Stuart twisted a bag and set it down. "That was before Noyce went Hollywood and did all the Tom Clancys. *Dead Calm* is a primer for thriller makers, although it would have been better if it were eighteen minutes shorter. I love the way he uses the camera in that, mounting it at the top of the mast."

"Yeah, although after you see *Knife in the Water*, you realize what a debt he owed to Polanski."

"Roman Polanski's one of my favorite filmmakers," he said. He was staring at her with a look she hadn't seen from any man in quite some time: aroused interest. He seemed to be attracted to her for having things in common with him. She hadn't talked this way with Theo in so long. They barely had the energy to watch movies, and when they did, late at night, afterward they would get up and take turns in the bathroom, too tired to talk about what they had seen. When you were falling in love, you couldn't stop talking to each other, but in only a few years, you ran out of things to say.

"I was watching *The Tenant* the other day," Rebecca said. "If you want to know the truth, I kind of have a thing for the young Polanski."

"But he looks like a gerbil."

"I've never been into conventionally attractive men."

Stuart's head jerked back as if she'd offended him. Maybe he had taken it to mean that she didn't think he was attractive, which wasn't the case at all—or maybe he thought she saw him as conventionally attractive and hence wasn't interested. She wanted to correct herself, to scream out that he was hot, that he could have her right there in the room if he wanted.

"It's funny you mentioned *The Tenant*," he said, "because I'm actually writing something that's inspired by it."

"A screenplay?"

He nodded. Why didn't he say "screenplay" in the first place? "It takes place in the neighborhood," he said.

"What's it called? *Slippery Slope*?"

"No, but that's good. *Atlantic Yards*. It's sort of a thriller about gentrification and terrorism."

"What's thrilling about gentrification?"

"Well," he said, "ultimately, it's more about the clash between different types of people. There's a terror cell run out of a muffin shop, and a corrupt borough president funneling money to the terrorists, and then there's this weathered Seventy-eighth Precinct cop who catches on to the scheme and winds up saving the day. She's a woman. And I'm trying to figure out a way to work in that rape on the ball fields."

Rebecca was impressed—it sounded messy and full of itself, but with *Crash* having won Best Picture he might be onto something. Stuart said he was going to direct it himself, and star, and that he already had financing of $5 million from a Cuban sugar heir he'd met at the Beatrice Inn. He was shooting it in the spring on location in Brooklyn if everything came together.

"I think it's pretty good," he said. "I've been writing at the library, and I feel like the atmosphere is really helping."

"You write at the library?" It struck Rebecca as very Hollywood to write in a public library, to act like one of the masses.

"Yeah, at Grand Army Plaza. On the second floor. There's a lot of homeless, but I try to let the smells make their way between the lines." He smiled, like it was a joke. Everything he said came off as an imitation of celebrity. She couldn't tell if he did it intentionally. Either he was smart enough to know how stupid most actors were or he was as stupid as the rest of them. "Anyway, I'm really interested in doing something about post–September eleventh apocalyptic paranoia, you know? Every time I pass those Lebanese shops on Atlantic Avenue, I wonder what's going on inside them, and then I feel guilty for wondering. I guess what I'm trying to do is take a snapshot of the collective malaise of modern New Yorkers. In the guise of an action-packed thriller."

"I like it. It sounds very *Panic at Needle Park*," she said.

"How do you know so much about movies?"

"I'm a junkie. I almost applied to Columbia grad school for film but decided I probably wouldn't get in. I've been catching up on seventies cinema during my daughter's nap time." She hadn't been sure whether to mention Abbie but figured it was stupid to lie. She was a thirty-five-year-old female Food Coop member wearing a wedding ring. There was a 95 percent chance she was a mother.

"What's your daughter's name?"

"Abbie. With an 'ie' and not a 'y.' We named her after Abbie Hoffman. He was—"

"I know who Abbie Hoffman was."

"Really? That's impressive, because most celebrities have no sense of history."

"I saw a documentary about the Chicago Eight at Sundance." She couldn't remember the last time she and Theo had bantered like this. She missed the banter as much as she missed the sex. "So how old is she?"

"One and a half. Thankfully, she's over the alien blob phase. Angelina Jolie got all that flak for calling Shiloh a blob, but it's true. They can't do anything at the beginning."

"Oh, I didn't mind the alien blob phase," Stuart said. "I love babies. They embody the spirit of the Buddha."

Rebecca burst out laughing, not sure if he was kidding. "Are you a Buddhist?"

"In the past I've meditated every day, but now it's more something I try to incorporate into my life."

"So you're like an alcoholic who doesn't go to meetings."

"That's a good line. I think I'm going to use that."

"I find the whole Richard Gere thing ridiculous," Rebecca said. "Like kabbalah. Buddhism is another bandwagon for people with no inner life."

"You think I have no inner life?"

"Well, you probably have more than the average Hollywood star because you're Australian and your ancestors were criminals."

He was frowning. She had wanted to taunt him, but she hadn't intended to come off as a raging bitch. Before she had a child, she would have been able to tell the difference, but now it was impossible. When you spent this much time alone, you lost your social barometer. Motherhood gave you automatic Asperger's.

Rebecca's breath was short, and she felt clammy even though the room was cold. She'd had her chance and she'd blown it. Stuart would switch his shift and she'd never see him again. He'd be out of her life as fast as he came into it. She would miss him terribly if she never saw him again, never got to talk like this, even if this was all that happened. She wanted to know that the next time she showed up, she would see the red hair on those hands. But there wouldn't be a next time now.

"Did you ever hear the story of the two Zen monks?" he asked.

"Uh-oh," she said. "*Charlie Rose* moment. Cue the zoom."

"I told a different koan on *Charlie*. These two monks are walking along a path back of beyond, and they come across a caravan carrying a wealthy woman and her suitcases. She's not very nice to them. The monks and the caravan come to this muddy river, and the attendants discover they can't cross with the woman and her possessions. The older monk volunteers to carry her across on his back so the attendants can carry her things.

"But when they get across, the woman doesn't say thank you. She's rude to him, and she pushes him away to get back in her caravan. The two monks keep going, and after a while, the younger monk says, 'I cannot believe that old woman! You were so nice to carry her across the river on your back, and she didn't even say thank you! She was so rude!' The master turns to his student and says, 'I put her down two miles ago. Why are you still carrying her?' "

Stuart blinked at Rebecca, and she saw warmth in his limpid eyes. "What are you carrying?" he asked.

He held her gaze, easy and steady. It was as though he knew her without knowing her, saw through the bluster. All these months she had been trying to find some way to transcend the hurt, to make sense of Theo's neglect so she could forgive him for it, but she hadn't been able to. She had married him because he could take care of her, and now he no longer did. Her husband had become an enigma, and she didn't know whether to leave him or accept that this was the way it would always be.

She stared back at Stuart and wanted to cry, but she was afraid that if she started, she wouldn't stop and she'd fall into a heap on the cold floor and Stuart would have to summon medical help. She wanted him to hold her in his arms and kiss the top of her head. This was why she had kissed Lizzie, she realized: It had been so long since she'd been touched by a grown-up. Touch was like water or food; you needed it or you'd shrivel into nothing.

"I'm carrying nuts," she said, her voice cracking. "A lot of mixed nuts."

He set another bag down on the counter, and as she reached for it, their hands brushed. It was like an electric shock. They didn't move, the sides of their hands touching, each of them looking straight ahead but not at the other. The touch was so intense that she got wet. When you wanted someone, even the smallest contact was a turn-on.

She remembered feeling this way at that party where she'd met Theo at the cocktail table. He'd asked her questions and touched her lightly on the arm with each one, a rhythmic reminder of his enthusiasm, and she'd enjoyed his attention so much that each tap was like a shock.

She could feel Stuart's pulse in his hand, and she thought about his very expensive blood. This was a man so warm-blooded, so vital, that people paid money to watch him breathe.

There was a squawk, and over the intercom a shopper asked where she could find a case of Vintage seltzer water. Stuart took away his hand and plunged the scoop into the barrel.

Open House

THE CARROLL Street open house on Sunday was the usual pushy affair, with potential buyers slitting their eyes at each other as they passed in the narrow hallway. According to the information sheet they had been handed at the door, the apartment had not one but two fireplaces, one in the living room and one in the master bedroom. Karen had always wanted to throw a dinner party with a fire, and she could see herself doing it here, even though the sheet said the fireplaces were decorative, which meant the fire would be gas.

Six days after ringing that awful woman's bell, Karen's excitement for Apartment Two had not waned. Everything about it was perfect. She could picture her name on one of those NRDC return address labels: "Karen Bryan Shapiro, 899 Carroll Street, Apartment Two." Apartment Two sounded regal and high-class. Now her address labels read "8R," the R for rear apartment, the R that blared MIDDLE CLASS, because it meant everyone knew you lived in a rental with multiple tenants per floor.

Apartment Two (and she had already decided she would spell out the Two) meant a coop, a small building, a purchase. It meant you'd made it. Sure, it was one step down from the most coveted address, an address like Melora Leigh's that came with no apartment number at all, but this was only a first step. In a few years, after Matty had made partner, they could trade up to a single-family, even if it had to be in Gowanus.

As long as they didn't wind up buying in Midwood, she would be happy. Her parents still lived in the house Karen had grown up in, and though they made noises about giving it to her someday, she couldn't stand the idea of living in the same area she'd started out in. That meant you'd gotten nowhere in life.

If Karen lived in this apartment, she could sit on the bench across from Melora's mansion as often as she pleased. Living in the North Slope, she'd be bound to run into Melora. Maybe they would even become neighborhood friends, the kind where you didn't know the person's name but would smile each time you passed.

She had to get this place. She just had to. It was summer, slow real estate season, and there were twelve names on the sign-in sheet, small compared to the frenzied open houses of the spring.

Karen hoped the mean woman in Apartment Three wouldn't ruin everything for her. She hadn't meant to be so aggressive, ringing another buzzer. She was only trying to get an edge. If they were lucky enough to get the apartment, Karen hoped the woman wouldn't sway the board against her. Who even knew if she would remember her name? Practically every other mother in Park Slope was a Karen.

Holding Darby's hand, she followed Matty down the hallway to the second bedroom, passing the bathroom, where a woman was flushing the toilet. What a real estate neophyte. Only idiots flushed toilets at open houses.

The second bedroom had a bunk bed on the left, against the exposed brick wall. The opposite wall was crammed corner to corner with toys, dressers, and two desks, each with hand-painted names: Kylie and Jonah. Judging from their belongings, the kids seemed to be school-aged, and Karen could not fathom how they had stayed so cooped up for so long.

Matty was looking out the window at the garden below. "The garden's not shared," he said, pointing to the information sheet. "It's exclusive to Apartment One."

"I know," she said, "but the roof is shared. Maybe we could throw parties up there."

"It's a ladder. You can't get food up a ladder."

"I want to go to the playground!" yelled Darby.

The master was big for Park Slope, probably three hundred square feet, with a decent-sized closet and floor-to-ceiling built-ins. The tiles on the fireplace needed some work, but the mantel, original, was in good condition. She could imagine the photos of Darby, her parents, and her grandparents arrayed in silver Restoration Hardware frames. The closet was ugly, with white particleboard shelves, but maybe Karen could get California Closets to deepen it and turn it into a walk-in.

"It's big, isn't it?" she asked Matty. "And there's a view of trees."

"And Apartment One's garden."

"Oh, come on, the only way you get an exclusive garden is if you buy a ground-floor, and everyone knows they come with noise issues."

He moved down the hallway back toward the living room. The third bedroom was walled off from the living room, and it was done in pale yellow, a crib abutting the far wall. *Three* children! No wonder they were moving to Northampton.

The sellers, Steve and Tina, were standing anxiously at the kitchen counter, where they had displayed a bowl of green apples, clearly a tip they had learned from a Realtor friend. In her years of attending open houses, Karen had seen a lot of chocolate chip cookies and Granny Smiths, put there to make prospective buyers think about bounty.

Steve was broad-shouldered with white teeth, and Tina was a pretty blonde with no makeup. They were Karen's age but clearly had more money. More important, they were smart enough to have bought in spring 2004, just before the housing market peaked. Karen had looked it up on ACRIS, the Automated City Register Information System. They'd paid $475,000. And only four years later, they were asking $675,000.

But the price was a steal—a three-bedroom on a park block for under $700,000. That was a steal for a *two*-bedroom. Three-bedrooms were scarce in the neighborhood, and the few on the market were in bigger, prewar apartment buildings.

Karen could see her family here. The more she thought about it, the more certain she was: If they lived in this apartment, she would be able to have a second child.

Because Karen and Matty had made Darby on the first try, she'd never anticipated that she would have trouble conceiving a sibling for him. She and Matty had decided to try again when Darby was two and a half. Karen had read in *Your Three-Year-Old: Friend or Enemy* that by three, most children had developed a good self-concept, and she felt that three and a half would be the ideal age to introduce a sibling.

But as the months went on with negative tests, she began to worry. Karen hated that her younger sister, Colleen, a pediatrician in Scarsdale married to an investment banker, already had three sons, Patrick, Logan, and Kieran, while Karen had only one. She hated that Colleen was lapping her in the baby race. There was an order to things—the older daughter married first and procreated first. It wasn't supposed to happen this way.

People in the neighborhood, other parents, were starting to ask if she was going to have another, and she would nod confidently, pained by the truth. People who'd never struggled with fertility were so casual about babies. It didn't occur to them that the stakes might be high for other people.

When Karen and Matty had been trying for a year with no luck, she went to see her OB, Dr. Lucibella, at NYU Medical Center, because she had read that infertility was defined as a year of trying with no conception. It turned out Dr. Lucibella specialized in infertility issues, and she ran some tests and put Karen on Clomid to stimulate ovulation. But the pills made her nauseated and moody, and after three cycles, she opted to stop and turn to natural methods.

While surfing on an infertility website, she had learned about a book called *Taking Charge of Your Fertility,* by Toni Weschler, which taught you to use waking basal temperature and other fertility signs to maximize your chances of getting pregnant. Karen had started charting her cycles, but so far she hadn't had any luck.

Though the ultrasound Dr. Lucibella had ordered found Karen's uterus to be in good shape, she didn't believe the results. She was convinced her womb had been damaged after what happened at the junior-senior dance at Brooklyn Tech when she was sixteen. Karen had been standing alone against a wall when a heavyset Haitian trumpeter in her chemistry class named Jean Pierre-Louis came up next to her. "You wanna go somewhere?" he said abruptly, and Karen, stunned and curious, shrugged and said yes. They sneaked out to a chemistry classroom to make out on the floor. Things got intense quickly, and then she felt something inside her, and she started to say something, but when she looked at his face, she realized he had already finished.

"I'm sorry," he said.

"It's okay," she said.

The next month she missed her period. When Karen told her mother, Eileen, a small, brisk woman who was impossible to rattle, she made an appointment for her with her own ob-gyn at Lenox Hill. The recovery from the procedure had been horrible—Karen felt woozy and sore for days. When she was lying in bed that night, her father came in to clear her soup plate and said, "Everyone makes mistakes." Karen had burst into tears, ashamed of her own stupidity.

As the months passed, it got better. Because she knew that having a baby at sixteen was not a smart thing to do, she never really felt guilty, and eventually, the memory grew fainter until she was almost able to pretend it had never happened. When she filled out forms about prior pregnancies, she put "one," and when gynecologists asked about it, she told them the story and they never asked more questions.

In fact, she hadn't thought about Jean Pierre-Louis in years, until Dr. Lucibella mentioned secondary infertility and Karen decided something terrible had happened to her womb during the procedure all those years before. When Karen thought about it, it made sense. You couldn't go removing a fetus and expect there to be no repercussions. Darby had been a miracle baby, a gift from God, a lucky shot. Somehow he had wanted to be born so badly that he had implanted in her despite the inhospitable environment. But in life you got only one lucky break.

Karen wanted to be a mother of two. And she didn't want to adopt. You didn't know what you got with those kids—the messed-up parents, the bad genes. There was an adopted boy at the Garfield School who was a product of a rape in Mexico, his mother had told her, and although Karen lauded the adoptive mother, she knew she would be terrified to do the same. (Melora Leigh's situation couldn't really compare. When you were that rich, it didn't matter how troubled your children might be, because you could spend hundreds of thousands of dollars on their future mental health. Even a child of a rapist would turn out all right if he had celebrity parents.)

But in the living room of 899 Carroll Street, Karen felt confident that she wouldn't have to consider adoption because she was going to get pregnant. Her fertility troubles all boiled down to stress. Karen and Matty's apartment was too small, so her eggs sensed that they would be coming into a world that had no room for them, and hence they never fertilized. It was clear and very simple. If they moved into 899 Carroll Street, Karen would be able to conceive.

"I think we should offer seven hundred right now," she told Matty.

"Seven hundred? Are you out of your mind? It's a buyer's market! All the papers are saying the market is starting to deflate. I think they're asking too much."

How could he be such an aggressive lawyer and such a wimp when it came to Brooklyn real estate? He was the breadwinner, but she often felt like she ran the show.

"In this neighborhood it's always a seller's market!" she said.

Karen saw a little girl coming through the door and recognized her as Tilly Harris, a classmate of Darby's from the Garfield School. Tilly's father, Neal, had been the one who told Karen about the open house. Tilly's mother, Arielle, and Neal came in, Neal carrying Tilly's baby brother in his arms. Neal was one of the few stay-at-home dads Karen knew, and because he didn't work, she didn't understand how they could afford that orange Bugaboo in which he was always pushing the baby. Arielle was a graphic designer, and Karen figured her business had to be extremely successful for the money to stretch far enough for a Bugaboo.

"Thanks for telling us about this place," Karen said to Neal as they came over to say hi.

"You like it?" Neal asked, looking around as though impressed.

So as not to get him too excited, Karen answered only, "It's all right."

"So do you guys own?" Arielle asked.

"Rent."

"Us, too. But with the baby, our apartment has been way too cramped. We decided that with the values dropping it was a good time to buy." Karen introduced them to Matty. She was always introducing

Matty because he was too busy to come to the Tot Shabbats, even though he was the Jewish one, not she.

"Do they share a room?" Karen asked Arielle.

"No, Tilly has her own room, but this week they've both been in our bed because the AC in their rooms broke."

"And in this weather! That's awful."

"Tell me about it. Between the AC going on the fritz, our car being in the shop, and Neal getting pickpocketed, it's been the summer from hell."

"You were pickpocketed?" Matty asked.

"Yeah. In the Food Coop. Can you believe it?" Neal told them the terrible story of how it had happened. "I still think it was that Rasta, but they never searched him, and now I have no way of proving it."

Karen was horrified. The next time she went to the Coop she would have to watch her bowling bag extra closely.

After Neal and Arielle went to check out the bedrooms, she went over to Tina and said quietly, "We'd like to make an offer. We love your place and can really see ourselves here." Matty was shooting daggers at her from across the room.

"That's great," said Tina coolly.

Karen ushered her toward the bay window so the others wouldn't hear. "Seven hundred," she said.

Tina didn't even flinch. She nodded, took out a BlackBerry, and typed something in. "I think I told you we've decided to do this as an open auction," Tina said, "because we think it's fairer for everyone." That was a lie. The purpose of open bidding was to scare everyone into going higher than they would in a best-and-final. "We're asking everyone to get their bids in by six o'clock tomorrow, and then you'll have a chance to go above. Depending how things play out, we may or may not do a third round. I'm sorry, your name is—"

"We're on the sign-in sheet. Bryan. I'm Karen Bryan," she said, proffering her hand. She had to drop the Shapiro. She was dealing with a Tina Savant, the kind of woman who would never be in the predicament of choosing to drop the Shapiro.

Sometimes Karen felt that life came down to getting there first. The winners seemed to be the ones who had married, procreated, and bought property early, confident in their future earning potential. She and Matty had done two out of the three—she was married at twenty-six and pregnant with Darby at twenty-eight, which was practically Jamie Lynn–young in this day and age—but they had missed the boat on the real estate thing. At that time Matty was still paying off his college and law school loans, and she'd saved almost nothing from social work, so it hadn't occurred to them to buy property. Now she wished they'd had more foresight. If only they'd bought before the boom, scrimped somehow to make it happen, then she would be a Tina Savant and not a Karen Shapiro.

"That's my husband, Matt," Karen added. She waved to him in the corner, where he was looking anemic. "And our son, Darby."

"Darby," said Tina. "Isn't that the name of Patrick Dempsey's boy?"

"Yes," Karen said quickly. "But we thought of it first."

Respond, Don't React

MELORA REMOVED the wallet from the bedside table drawer and flipped it over in her hands. The thrill of stealing had been so intense it had carried her through the past six days. It was as though by touching the wallet she anointed herself with a magical salve that made her relaxed and happy at the same time.

When she had gotten home from the Coop the Monday before, she had sat on the edge of her bed and gone through the wallet. It was a strange feeling to hold someone else's closest possessions in your own hands. For a woman you needed the whole handbag to get the soul, but for a man you needed only the wallet. It was a black Coach, and on his driver's license, Neal Harris's address was listed as Garfield Place, only a block from Melora. He looked young in his photo, more handsome than the frazzled dad Melora had seen in the Coop. There was three hundred in cash, but she didn't spend it and didn't plan to. As she had examined the Visa, Blue Cross Blue Shield, and Park Slope Yoga cards, she had felt a twinge of guilt, but she wasn't going to return the wallet. She had been sure of that. Remorse wasn't the same as stupidity. Instead she had tucked the wallet in the drawer, underneath a copy of *Eat, Pray, Love* given to her by Michelle Williams but as yet unread.

Since that fateful Monday evening, Melora examined the wallet whenever she was anxious or unsettled, and the contact calmed her immediately. Today Stuart, Annika, and Orion had gone to the Prospect Park Zoo, and she was lonely. She missed her husband, though not her son.

She wondered if her melancholy had been caused by going off Zoloft. The morning after she took the wallet she had stopped the medication. Though she knew Dr. Levine probably wouldn't approve, she had felt ready, and didn't see the point of waiting till her next appointment to do it.

The night before had been Melora's first without Ativan, which she usually needed to drift off. Though she had lain awake for several hours next to Stuart, eventually, she did sleep and realized she probably never needed them anyway.

She heard the front door opening and a shout from Orion downstairs. She slammed the drawer shut. Stuart came into the bedroom, sweaty and exuberant. He plopped down on the bed next to her.

"Did you guys have fun?" she asked.

"He loved it. They had this ruler where you could measure how far you jumped, and he went as far as a wallaby."

She took in Stuart's physique. They had made love that morning, and though she didn't come, she got closer than she had since she'd gone on the Zoloft, so when she faked, she convinced herself it was only a partial fake and not a total.

Now she wanted him again, was hungry for him. This was a strange new benefit of the drug weaning: Her desire had soared. She leaned over and kissed him gently. He kissed back. She lifted his shirt and made her way down his torso. She couldn't remember the last time she'd given him head.

She unzipped his shorts and took his cock into her hand. She crouched over him and enveloped it in her mouth, moaning with pleasure. It had been so long since she had been a wife to him. She wanted to please him, to make him happy. She had spent so many months making things difficult, and now she wanted to make them easy. He got only semi-hard, and after a minute he sat up in bed.

"What is it?" she asked.

"I really wanted to work on my screenplay. Can we do this later?"

He zipped his fly. She sat next to him against the headboard, thigh to thigh. Melora hated not getting what she wanted.

But instead of letting the anger take over, she decided to slow her reaction time, something she'd been working on with Dr. Levine. "It's not about cutting off the feelings," he always said. "It's about slowing down your experience of them so you don't act out." They used to say the same thing in A.A.: "Respond, don't react." She had been trying to internalize these platitudes for years, but this was the first time she really understood them. You got in trouble when you rushed things, and what the Zoloft did was prevent you from rushing. Now, without the drug, she would have to learn to do it herself.

She allowed herself to feel the sting of Stuart's rejection and then tried to imagine what he was feeling. He had to be depleted from taking care of his son all afternoon, even though Annika had been with them. Of course he wanted time to himself. It didn't mean he didn't love her; they just had different needs.

She was surprised by her compassion, and yet it felt familiar, like an old coat that still fit. Sometime long ago she had known how to put someone else first.

"Of course we can," she said.

"I'll be back by dinner," he said, standing up. He went toward the bedroom door. She didn't understand why he wrote at the library when he had a beautiful room of his own in the mansion. This was the whole reason they'd been staying in the city instead of going to their place in Bridgehampton—Stuart said Bridgehampton was too distracting for him, because of all the social obligations, a logic that Melora found unconvincing, since lately he'd been out every other night in the city.

When she'd read the screenplay the fall before, she'd thought it was stupid—a movie set in *Brooklyn*? What was the point? There were too many plot twists, and she felt the role of Lucy was underwritten. He had shown the first draft to Paul Thomas Anderson, with hopes of getting him signed on as a producer, but Paul said it didn't speak to him, and Stuart had been discouraged. Secretly, Melora had been relieved, hoping this meant that Stuart would put it to bed.

But then in the spring he rewrote it, and when she read it, the twists seemed to make more sense. He showed that draft to the Cuban sugar heir and got the five million, and now she was worried that he was going to get it made. That was part of the reason she had been so anxious lately. Stuart's idol was George Clooney, because Clooney had been nominated for a screenwriting Oscar and was considered a legitimate

producer. Melora didn't want Stuart to become the next George Clooney because then he would want Clooney-level pussy.

"I didn't know you were sending Maggie Gyllenhaal *Atlantic Yards*,"
she said.

"Oh, Lor," he said, turning and letting out a big sigh. "When are you
going to let this go? The character is too gritty for you."

"I can do gritty. I've been doing gritty since I was nine."

"But I want something understated. I don't want the lead to call attention to the performance, all Nicole Kidman in *The Hours*. I want
Lucy to blend into the scenery."

"Maggie Gyllenhaal grew up in Los Angeles! No one's going to believe her as a Bensonhurst cop."

"Why don't you direct the movie yourself, then?"

Melora softened her tone. She had become combative when what
she really felt was pained. "I don't think you want to direct me," she
said.

"I'd love to direct you. You're a director's dream."

"So then why don't you draw up a contract?"

"I just don't think you're right for this."

"Come on. I saw the way you looked at Maggie in the Coop. Admit
it. She's on your Hump Island."

"There's only one woman on my Hump Island," he said, coming
over to the bed. He put his arms around her and planted a big exaggerated kiss on her lips. "And that's Emily Mortimer."

After he left, Melora sat on the bed for a minute, trying to decide
what to do. Normally she would have flipped on the bedroom TV—
but if she was going to watch TV during the day, she might as well
be on Zoloft. She thought about drinking some wine, but it was early.
What did normal people do on weekend afternoons? She heard a yelp
of delight from upstairs. Of course. Sometimes she forgot she was a
mother.

In the playroom she found Orion and Annika building a weird
Gothic world with his Playmobil. Annika noticed Melora in the doorway right away, but it took a minute for Orion to turn.

"How was the zoo?" she asked him.

"We saw a baboon. His butt was red."

"That was the female," said Annika.

"Did you go on the carousel after?"

"I'm too old for the carousel. Carousels are for babies."

He was growing up before her eyes. He had done so well in the Berkeley Carroll threes program, even though she'd been nervous about the long school day. In the fall he'd be in pre-K, a little boy.

She wanted to believe that she'd given him a normal childhood. Hers had been abnormal, and she often wished she could do it all over again. Before she started acting, she and her parents would go to a country house in Amenia every summer. She would swim in a pond with her mother, float on her back, and stare up at the clouds. They would go on hikes and build fires at night. Now, when she closed her eyes, she could barely picture that time before her parents split up, before she became an actress.

They had divorced soon after Melora got famous, after arguing constantly over whether she should get out of the business (Bob thought yes, Marcy thought no). Marcy became her manager, eventually quitting her teaching job to handle Melora's career full-time. She went to all the auditions with Melora, flew to L.A. with her for screen tests, and converted the pantry of their brownstone into an office. Melora hated being so closely wed to her mother—she enjoyed the acting, but she didn't enjoy her mother's investment in her success. When Melora was twelve, Bob left Marcy for the mother of one of Melora's classmates and they moved to Santa Fe, where they had two children together.

After that, he saw Melora only once a year, though he sent photos of his daughters. Melora always believed that her professional success had been the catalyst for her parents' divorce. At the beginning Melora, like Bob, blamed Marcy for being overinvested in her career. But it was too hard to hate the parent you were stuck with, so eventually Bob became the enemy. Even if he didn't want to be married to her mother, Melora felt it was wrong for him to abandon his daughter.

She often fantasized about how things would have turned out differently if Mary Jo Slater had never spotted her at Joe's Pizza. Melora loved her early memories of the cocoon of their house on Charles Street, of the intimacy that came from being an only child. But these days she had to struggle to picture Bob and Marcy in the same frame. The later memories—getting her period on a Mickey Rourke film at fourteen, going to the 1982 Oscars with Michael Jackson as her date—those stood out, but not the early ones. She could hardly remember being four.

She stared at Orion, thinking about how slender and soulful he'd been when she brought him home from the orphanage. The joy of having this person who would never leave was so thrilling that it got her through the exhaustion of those early months, though the baby nurses helped, too.

These days she and Orion hardly ever saw each other, although she was home much of the time. Annika or Stuart took him to his playdates and birthday parties because Melora didn't like socializing with other parents. But there were other times when he was around, up in the playroom with Annika, no one else there, and Melora would hide in the bedroom, not wanting to see him.

The intensity of motherhood was often too much to bear. Sometimes she thought about sending him to boarding school when he was older so she could have Stuart all to herself, but she worried this would scar Orion for life. You didn't adopt a child to ship him away.

She attributed her ambivalence to the Zoloft, even though she had taken the Zoloft because of her ambivalence. The drugs she'd gone on to become a better mother hadn't made her easygoing. Instead, they'd made her afraid of her son. What kind of mother was afraid of her own child?

Melora had an idea. Annika was probably exhausted and in need of a break, and Stuart was off at the library, so he couldn't intervene.

"You want to go to Häagen-Dazs and get a cone?" she asked Orion. "Just you and me?" Häagen-Dazs was only four blocks away, but she had never taken him.

Orion looked up at her as though waiting for her to say she was kidding, and then he raced out the door and down the stairs. "You want me to come with you?" Annika asked softly, as if Melora, and not Orion, were the child.

"I'll be fine," she said. On the way downstairs she stopped in the bedroom and opened the bedside table drawer. She hesitated for a second and then shut it before bounding down to join her son.

Soft Swinging

LIZZIE WAS sleeping soundly when Jay came in. She glanced at the clock. Eleven-forty. He had returned from his tour the night before, but instead of spending time with her and Mance, he had dashed out the door at nine for a friend's gig at some club on the Lower East Side.

Jay always made too much noise when he came in, as if he didn't care that he might wake her up or that when Mance was sleeping—the crib was in their room—she needed all the rest she could get. She heard him go into the kitchen and open the refrigerator. When he came into the bedroom, he flipped on the lamp, opened a biography of Levon Helm, and swigged from a bottle of some Belgian microbrew. He liked to drink obscure beers, American and European, and was always shopping at Bierkraft on Fifth Avenue, getting into long conversations with the staffers. When Lizzie made fun of him he would say, "What's the matter? Black people can't drink microbrews?" and though she would laugh, she saw something hostile in his eyes.

"What are you doing?" she whispered angrily.

"Reading."

"It's midnight. I was in REM sleep."

"I'm wired. I need to read for a little."

"Then go in the living room. You're going to wake up Mance."

He threw a shirt over the light to dim it, but it didn't make a difference. She wanted to kick him out of the bed and make him sleep on the floor. She could put up with the absences, even the spaced-out way he played with Mance, but not this. This was cruel. He was acting like he was a rock star and she was a groupie. Didn't he have any idea how hard things were? Didn't he have any compassion for what she was trying to do for his own son?

"Please put the book away," she said.

"In a few minutes." He took a swig of the beer.

Maybe she was being too hard on him. This was his way of unwinding. He was overworked. The touring was exhausting. He was trying to do so much—boost his career while supporting a family—that he was depleted, and his exhaustion made it hard for him to see what a jerk he was.

She needed to unwind, too. The last few nights she'd taken to drinking Terre di Tufi with dinner, alone, after she'd given Mance his final nurse of the night. She had expected Jay to ask her about the bottle in the kitchen when he got back, but so far he hadn't. He hardly noticed anything anymore.

The night she and Jay met, they took a cab from Williamsburg to this very apartment, and after they made love, they lay awake in Jay's bed and talked. They came at each other in reverse. They talked the way you talked before you had sex, not after, when the getting to know each other was part of the seduction. It was as though they had both known, that night, that they would be spending their lives together, didn't see the point in postponing the sex, and now that they'd made love, they would get to the business of finding out each other's secrets.

As they lay there holding hands, they told stories. They couldn't stop talking—about his music, her job, their families, and their childhoods. They tried to trace their earliest memories, and in the ease of being with him, she remembered things she hadn't known she remembered: a time she fell, ice skating, at a birthday party; a miscarriage her mother had had when Lizzie was a toddler.

She told him about the day she met Sarah and how she had fallen in love with her because of the way she moved her lips when she said "the male gaze." He told her how he used to have snowball fights in front of his parents' brownstone when he was a kid and how it felt getting nailed in the cheek. She told him about the woman who sat next to her at her publishing job and the strained, tense phone conversations she would have with her boyfriends, and how Lizzie finally began to listen to music on her headphones so she wouldn't get the bad relationship karma. Jay said, "You mean you didn't want to 'catch the fight,' " and Lizzie laughed because she knew he was smart.

He was bright and observant, and she loved his music even based on the few songs she had heard that night. She felt selfishly that now his voice would belong to her. When you fell in love with an artist, you got the art for free.

Now, in bed with him reading next to her, she could not muster understanding for this brooding, egomaniacal man. She would have to tell him things needed to change.

She flopped over onto her side and covered her face with her pillow, hoping he would put the book away. As she was beginning to hate him, she heard the book clunk on the tabletop. He pulled her toward him and turned her over. She could taste the ale on his mouth.

He made love to her in his predictable way: a minute of tweaking her breasts with another minute sucking them; three minutes of cunnilingus; a hover-over blow job followed immediately by ten minutes of thrusting (she came quickly, even though she was angry with him; she was often startled to note that her emotional state had nothing to do with her ability to reach orgasm); withdrawal; and a puddle on her stomach. While he was inside her, she imagined Rebecca Rose's husband making love to Rebecca while she breastfed Abbie.

Jay mopped the semen off her belly with a white towel he had stolen from Crunch gym on Flatbush. He said the club overcharged for membership and he had to even things out by stealing towels; she had explained that maybe the reason they charged so much for membership was because they kept having to buy more towels.

"You smell good," he said softly, nuzzling her neck.

"It's so hard for me when you're not here," she said.

"I know."

"And then when you are here . . . and you come back so late . . . Don't you want to be with us?"

"Of course I do. But I need time to myself, too. It can't just be about work when I'm away and being a daddy when I'm here. I need something in between."

"I need time to myself, too," she said.

"I keep telling you, you should have my mom come babysit. She'd love it. You could go get a manicure or something. She doesn't know why you don't ask for help. You should give yourself a break."

He was right. They had free babysitting right here in their own neighborhood, and yet she never took advantage. But she wanted Jay to offer to babysit, too, not every night he was home but once in a while, so she could go out. She had the idea that it might be fun to go to dinner with Rebecca one night, even though they hadn't spoken in six days and she wasn't sure she would ever see her again.

The morning after they got drunk together, Lizzie, not wanting to put herself out, had waited for a call. But none came. By Mance's nap on Wednesday, Lizzie had decided to send Rebecca a thank-you note for the playdate. It was the gracious thing to do and would require that Rebecca call her back. She didn't know Rebecca's address, so she took Mance to the building (hoping she would run into Rebecca nearby) and then copied down the number: 899 Carroll.

On handsome stationery she had gotten as a gift from her mother, she wrote, "Just wanted to say thanks so much for having us over. Mance adores Abbie! And the wine was great. Can't wait to see you again.—Lizzie."

After she wrote "Can't wait to see you again," she tore up the stationery, thought for a second, and wrote it all over again, ending with "See you soon," which sounded much more noncommittal.

But when she stuck it in a mailbox on Flatbush later that day, she immediately regretted sending it. Rebecca was going to think she was crazy. Nobody sent notes anymore and Rebecca had to know it. She would see it as overformal and desperate. No woman wanted a friend who was desperate.

Lizzie's shame at sending it had only increased as the days passed. It was Sunday, which meant she'd definitely gotten it, and Lizzie still hadn't heard anything.

She got out of bed to go to the bathroom. When she came back a few minutes later, Jay was asleep, the come rag in a heap on the floor. She checked on Mance, who was stirring slightly in his crib but asleep, and went to the living room window. She scanned the street. Empty.

Lizzie went into the kitchen, poured herself a glass of wine, and brought it to her desk, a tiny secretary in the living room. She opened her computer and went to the Park Slope Parents site. She often surfed on Park Slope Parents when she wanted reassurance that she was not the unhappiest mother in the world.

On this night only one post caught her eye. It began "OT: Something fun?" Since PSP subject headers tended to be more along the lines of "Toddler sleep woes" or "Traveling to Sicily with newborn," Lizzie was curious. She read on:

> We are a local couple with two children who go to school with some of your very own children. We are educated, responsible parents and we are into soft swinging. Many of you know us and some of you have even passed us on the street or in front of your child's school or in one of the playgrounds. We thought this would be the ideal forum to meet like-minded, bright, imperfectly attractive, professional people. We are posting with an anonymous e-mail address in the hopes you will contact us there. Single moms encouraged also.

The return address was slopeparents@gmail.com.

Lizzie scrolled down to read the responses: "My parents were swingers in the '70s and as a result I have been in psychotherapy my entire adult life." "This is not the forum for such inquiries. Why don't you post this on an AOL chat room instead of polluting our parenting board with your sick desires?" And the predictable "I'm definitely interested in swinging but usually it's at the playground with my son Jasper."

She covered her mouth to keep from laughing, afraid she would wake up Mance. Then she took her phone out of her bag. It was twelve-thirty in the morning. She couldn't call. But during one of their get-togethers a few weeks before, Rebecca had mentioned that she was a night owl. Lizzie figured she might be up. *You awake?* she texted.

A minute later, she got the reply: *Yeah.*

Can I call?

Sure.

"I'm sorry to bother you so late," Lizzie said when she got Rebecca.

"It's okay. Abbie's up, and we're trying to decide whether to go into her room. I got your note. That was sweet. Totally unnecessary. What's up?"

"I saw this hilarious post on Park Slope Parents. This couple said they're interested in soft swinging."

"On Park Slope Parents?" said Rebecca. "Impossible. The only time anyone in the neighborhood has sex is to get knocked up."

"What's soft swinging?"

"No sex. Everything but."

"How do you know?"

"I did a story on the new monogamy for *Mademoiselle*."

"But what's the point of doing it if there's no sex?" Lizzie asked.

"Come on, you used to be a lesbian. Are you saying a woman can't experience pleasure unless she's getting fucked?"

"Well, yeah. When I was a lesbian, I always got fucked. Isn't the whole point of swinging that you get to have sex with someone else?"

"This is Park Slope. People are wimps. Whoever posted it probably thinks fucking is infidelity. Like President Clinton."

"You should see the responses," Lizzie told her. "People got really offended."

"It doesn't make any sense," said Rebecca. "Swinging in Park Slope. That's like walking into an ice cream store and asking for a glass of water." Lizzie could hear Abbie crying in the background, and then a man's voice, clipped and angry. "I should go," Rebecca said.

Lizzie took a deep breath. "Do you want to do something this week? With the kids?"

"Sure. I'll call you."

It sounded noncommittal, but Lizzie tried not to put too much stock in that. It was practically the middle of the night, after all. Rebecca didn't have the luxury of a lengthy conversation.

Lizzie clicked the "Respond to post" link. Her Gmail handle was

TooPoMama, and it didn't show her real name when she sent e-mails. She thought for a second and then wrote, "Hi there. My name is Victoria and I'm a single mom responding to your post. I'd like to park my slope in your living room." She kept writing and before long she could hear Jay snoring from the bedroom.

Graduated Extinction

"DO NOT go in there!" Rebecca snapped at Theo. It was almost a quarter to one in the morning. Abbie had woken up screaming, and then Lizzie had called, and by the time Rebecca hung up, Theo was threatening to go into Abbie's room.

Abbie had been doing this on and off the past few weeks, waking up in the middle of the night and then being inconsolable. The mobile, which worked like a charm for naps, was useless at night. The only thing that stopped Abbie's wailing was if Rebecca or Theo stroked her back for up to an hour or took her into their bed—a solution Rebecca despised, because she felt it set a bad precedent.

To try to deal with the problem methodically, Rebecca had bought three sleep books: Weissbluth's, Richard Ferber's *Solve Your Child's Sleep Problems,* and for Theo's benefit, Elizabeth Pantley's *The No-Cry Sleep Solution.* She wanted to try a Ferber technique called graduated extinction, where the parents ignored the child's cries for longer and longer intervals, but so far the longest Theo had gone without picking Abbie up was five minutes.

"Listen to her!" he said, upright in bed next to her. "How can you let her wail like this?"

"She's not wailing. She's gotten out of one sleep cycle, and she's about to start another. Each time we go in there, we're going to stimulate her more."

"Where did you read this—in one of your stupid books?"

"Maybe."

"You read too much," he said. "You always have such an agenda." He pounded the night table for emphasis. "*Ow!*" He rubbed his elbow, agonized. Since Abbie's birth, Theo had suffered a seemingly endless series of physical calamities, which caused him to cry out and then clutch and rub the offending part in agony. First there had been a broken toe due to a bad stub, then a calf muscle that tore as he was playing pickup basketball, and now a bad bout of elbow bursitis whose cause was unknown. Because of her resentment toward him, Rebecca was unable to summon any sympathy for his ailments. She had never considered herself wildly empathetic, but early in their courtship she babied him when he needed it. Now, when Theo yelped in pain, she felt nothing and stared at him blankly, refusing to offer even "Oh, honey, are you all right?"

Her stoicism led to frequent harangues from Theo about her emotional coldness, which resulted in rejoinders from Rebecca about what a baby he was, which usually resulted in her sleeping on the couch. Over time her couch exile had lost some of its emotional punch; Theo no longer begged her to return. It was hard to sexually extort someone when you weren't having sex.

"I just want her to sleep through the night," she said, "so you and I can sleep through the night." She felt that if they could not teach their baby to go to sleep on her own, they were going to wreck her for life. What was going to happen when Abbie got to college? No wonder so many twentysomethings were on antidepressants. "Ferber says that all kids are capable of doing it by six months, and Abbie's a year and a half."

"Ferber? Isn't he the one who said you should let your baby cry until she vomits?" There had been an article about Ferber in the *New Yorker* years before, and every fragile child of divorce who read it had vowed never to let his child cry it out, even though Ferber later admitted sometimes taking his children into his bed.

Theo was a fragile child of divorce, although he wouldn't have called himself that, and Rebecca had always suspected he'd been drawn to her because her own family was so stable and *heimish*. Raised in Westport, he was the son of an investment banker and homemaker who had split up when he was only six. His father moved to New York after the divorce, and Theo and his mother had moved around a lot afterward—eight cities in ten years. Though his mother was living in San Francisco, now happily remarried to a psychiatrist she had been set up with on a blind date, Theo had never forgotten what came before. Early in his relationship with Rebecca, he had told her of his parents' screaming fights when he was a boy, the time he walked in on his mother sobbing in the bathroom after his father hurled a plate at her, and the terrible snowy night they told him they were separating. He had told her of bad sitters, cheap day camps with violent counselors, and his mother's many dubious suitors.

Rebecca's own parents, public school teachers, had recently celebrated their fortieth anniversary, and particularly since she'd had Abbie, she regarded their marriage as idyllically structured. She and her older brother, Todd, were punished if they mouthed off, the family ate dinner together every night, and—as far as she recalled—she and Todd always slept in their own beds. Her parents weren't mean or strict but were lovingly firm. When she had asked her mother recently about her own infant sleep patterns, she had said that to get Rebecca to sleep through the night she would send her father in with water—a suggestion from the pediatrician. In those days parents asked their pediatricians for advice; now, if you did that, you were a child abuser. When she told Theo the story, he had been horrified, saying that was why Rebecca had so many problems with men before she met him.

With Abbie, Rebecca was trying to repeat her own childhood, while Theo was doing everything he could not to repeat his own. Because she felt so defensive about her childhood, she found herself glorifying its simplicity. Her parents had managed to dine out, throw parties, be there for their friends, and raise two children—all on far more modest incomes than she and Theo had. Her parents seemed to believe children should be the backdrop to a good life, not the end-all and be-all of one.

Theo, on the other hand, viewed Abbie as his reason for being, a sentiment that Rebecca experienced as a double blow given his devotion to her before Abbie was born. Now that she had brought Abbie to him, it seemed he no longer needed a wife. She had been the passage-way, the vessel (though her surgical delivery made her feel like she had failed even at that), and now she was redundant.

"I would never let her cry until she vomited," Rebecca told Theo, pulling the covers up to her chest. She slept in expensive lingerie every night, but lately the effort seemed hollow, a caricature of a sexy wife.

"How long would you let her cry, then?" Theo asked, scowling.

"I don't know, half an hour?" He looked at her, in shock. "But Weiss-bluth says on the second night it goes down to like two minutes!" she added.

"Shh. Stop yelling. You're scaring me."

Was she really scary? Wasn't a mother allowed some degree of in-sanity in the middle of the night? As a teenager she had been allowed to rage. In Jewish families everyone screamed and then forgave, but if you yelled at a WASP, it was an unpardonable sin.

Theo was getting out of bed. "What are you going to do?" she shouted helplessly.

"I'm giving her some milk."

"She doesn't need milk. The pediatrician said we shouldn't be feed-ing her at night because it only encourages her to wake up."

"Yeah, well, Dr. Silver isn't here right now," he snapped from Abbie's room. She could hear him lifting Abbie from the crib. "It's okay," he said, his tone syrupy. "Daddy's here." No matter how Rebecca tried to spin Theo's protectiveness—it meant he loved Abbie, it was because of his difficult childhood, it would fade with time—she seemed unable to experience it with any attitude other than jealous rage.

"Please don't feed her," she called desperately. But he was already carrying Abbie down the hallway.

She knew she could follow him and keep yelling at him, but she didn't want to yell in front of Abbie. This was the problem with having a bad marriage and a young child: When you were merely trying to hold your ground, you had to worry that the fighting would screw up your kid.

In the living room she could hear him putting on the TV. She got out of bed and stood in the hallway. Abbie was in his lap, drinking a bottle of milk. Theo was staring at a commercial for Coors Light. A bunch of office workers were dancing around to the tune of "Love Train" as snow fell from the ceiling like confetti.

"This commercial always reminds me of September eleventh," he said. So he knew she was there. "They're all sweaty, and then the paper's flying in the air like after the towers fell. I can't believe they show this in New York. They should know people are sensitive to this kind of thing."

One winter Sunday earlier that year, she and Theo had taken Abbie to the Third Street playground together, and Rebecca had realized she had forgotten Abbie's blanket, the one he liked to cover her with when they put her in the swing. Theo told her to go home and get it. Rebecca said it wasn't really that cold, which it wasn't, and Theo snapped, "Be a mother for once!" She shouted back that he was an "overprotective freak," and he said, "There's a reason!" She waited for him to allude to his parents' divorce, but instead he said it was because he'd witnessed the second plane hitting the World Trade Center from the roof of his office in Tribeca. "If September eleventh hadn't happened," he said, "I would be a different kind of father." She listened, stunned, not sure how to respond. If she challenged him, she would look unsympathetic, and if she bought in to it, then she'd never get her way as a mother. In what world could maternal instinct trump post-traumatic stress disorder? It seemed Al Qaeda was to blame for the downfall of her marriage.

Rebecca retreated to the bedroom and opened her computer, thinking that since she was awake anyway, she might as well do an edit on the story she was writing for *Marie Claire* about real women who solved their chronic debt problems. The stories she was assigned read like *Oprah* teasers, and she had written so many of them that she often felt déjà vu while composing them. The freelance life had turned out to be less fulfilling than she had hoped; while the assignments came regularly and she was making about $60,000 a year, she felt empty writing them. She hated providing "service" with no voice and fretted that she was a shill for the cosmetics companies whose ads kept the magazines in circulation.

After a quick pass on the story, she closed the document and went to the Park Slope Parents site. She chuckled at the responses to the swinging post, then opened her mail program. There was a message from David with the details on Cassie Trainor's gig.

She decided she would go. Maybe she could ask Theo to sit. He was always saying she should go out more—not that *they* should go out more but that *she* should. Half the time when she got a sitter to come so they could go to dinner, Theo had her cancel, claiming he was too tired. This insulted her as much as the sexual rejection because it made her feel he didn't want to be with her apart from Abbie. She wasn't particularly interested in Cassie Trainor's music, but it had been so long since she had been invited to anything. And even if the interview was bad, she would get a few hours alone, without Abbie or Theo, to drink wine and maybe even bum a cigarette.

Theo had turned off the TV and was carrying Abbie into her room. Rebecca could hear him soothing her, but despite the bottle of milk, the crying only got more intense.

Theo came in with the crying baby and set her on the bed. "She's not sleeping with us," Rebecca said.

"It's the only way to get her to go out."

He laid Abbie between them, and she instinctively flopped on her belly and began to drift off. Lying beside Abbie, Theo put his hand on Rebecca's shoulder. Now he was being nice—now that their baby was between them.

She flinched. She hated that the only way he could muster any affection was in the triangle of family. Normal guys saw their wives as women, not just mothers.

"I can't sleep with her in the bed," she told him.

"Then sleep on the couch."

"But it's *my* bed."

"But *you're a mother now.*"

She grabbed her pillow and blanket and raced to the couch. Even if she didn't sleep at all, she wasn't going back, wasn't going to give him the satisfaction of having Abbie between them.

But after a few minutes trying to get comfortable, she began to feel something worse than rage: indignation. Now he had gotten just what he wanted. He had his daughter snuggled up next to him and not his wife. Why did Rebecca always cave to him? It was as bad as his caving to Abbie. It seemed that her only two options were to give in to Theo's way of doing things or to divorce him, and she didn't like either one.

Though her childhood had been relatively stable, her father had a bad temper. When she was a teen, they often butted heads. Sometimes when she was talking on the phone to a girlfriend at night, he would decide she'd been on too long and pull the cord out of the wall, right in the middle of Rebecca's conversation. Her cheeks would burn with humiliation, yes, but also a sense of injustice. She hated the fact that as long as she was dependent, living under the roof of this mostly good but slightly crazy man, there was nothing she could do about his behavior.

She thought about her father now, as she lay on the couch trying to get comfortable. It was one thing to feel a sense of injustice as a teenager when your options were limited but another to feel it as a wife, a wife in the twenty-first century. It was so pathetically retro to feel unhappy in her marriage when she could get a divorce. It seemed shallow to leave a man for not making love, but it was in fact grounds for divorce. Jewish law said so, and so did the state of New York. Constructive abandonment, they called it.

But every time she imagined it, she stopped at the vision of telling her parents. Since she could never tell them the truth about what had gone wrong, they wouldn't understand. They would see her as a failure, if not as a wife then as a mother. Only a bad mother opted to be single.

Surely the repercussions of divorce would be worse than the repercussions of a sexless marriage. What would divorce do to Abbie? How would Rebecca date again? She couldn't imagine herself going to the playgrounds as a divorced mom. So far the only single moms she'd met were lesbians who'd had their babies alone, and they all looked pretty miserable. It didn't make single motherhood look like a raging party.

What if she divorced Theo and still couldn't find anyone else to make love to her because men didn't want to be with the mother of a toddler? Then she would be hard up and alone, and broke, probably, since he would be so furious that he would ensure she got a bad settlement. She didn't want Abbie to grow up a child of divorce and turn her into the same fragile adult that Theo was. She wanted her to be grounded and strong.

And so she told herself, for the hundredth time in the past year, that what was going on between her and Theo was only temporary. She had to think long haul. Abbie wasn't ten; she wasn't even two. Children were a notorious libido killer, so it wasn't as though Rebecca and Theo were the first couple to experience this. It was too early to start worrying.

Burying her face in the cushion of the sofa, she thought about Stuart Ashby, standing so close to her in the food handling room. For the three days since they had met she had thought about him all the time. When she was out with Abbie, she kept thinking she saw him. At the Coop she did a double take at every tall, fair guy. She was so desperate to see him that she had grown illogical; as the days with no contact passed, Stuart's doppelgängers began to look less and less like him. One day she had been certain she saw him at Neergaard pharmacy, looking at deodorants, but it turned out to be Cathleen Meth, saying, "Jones, don't touch that!"

She thought about him so often that when she was caught up working on the debt article and half an hour went by without her reconstructing a memory of the food handling room, she would realize it and be surprised that so much time had gone by with no thoughts of Stuart. When she woke up each morning, she would lie in bed a few minutes remembering him, and at night, when she had trouble falling asleep, she replayed every moment of their time together, and the memory buoyed her until she drifted off.

Thinking about him had become a project. It was as though she were a playwright concocting a new play. She looked forward to Abbie's naps the way a mistress looks forward to an assignation, because they meant she had a long stretch of time to lie on her bed and think about how she and Stuart might be together. She would create different scenarios and then delight in being able to play them out any way she wanted. They would run into each other on the street, and he would take her back to the mansion and fuck her in the Japanese garden. He would get her number somehow and summon her to a suite at the Carlyle or Lowell. She would walk out of her apartment to find him on her stoop. He would invite her to an office in Manhattan where he worked sometimes, roll down the shades, and have her on the desk in something out of *Mad Men*.

In these scenarios she could commit adultery without any of its real-world complications, like convincing Stuart to do it and keeping it secret from Theo. Stuart wanted her, and they would find a way to be with each other like the couple in *Punch-Drunk Love*.

Rebecca knew that whatever the real-world next step was, there was purity in this first phase: the wanting without the action. The most unadulterated part of adultery was thinking about how to do it. In this way she felt as though she were having an affair with herself. She was more attracted to herself when she looked in the mirror, and she put extra effort into her wardrobe, especially the lingerie. She even noticed that her body felt healthier, and her energy was higher than usual. After meeting Stuart, she had felt alive, and it was frightening to feel alive when you had felt dead for so long.

Restless, she went into the kitchen and grabbed her pot stash from the freezer; though Theo didn't know it, she had an affable white hippie dealer, a Wisconsin grad named Renee, who came by every few months to replenish. Rebecca rolled a joint and smoked it out the window before going back to the sofa.

Though stoned, she was even more restless, so she went to her second insomnia cure. As she touched herself, she tried to fit Stuart into her standby fantasies—Stuart Ashby as Roman Polanski, Stuart Ashby as a doctor who discovers that the only way the starving Rebecca can survive is to feed her a steady diet of his semen in a secret examining room for the rest of her life—but none of the fantasies seemed to work. After a while she stopped touching herself. She kept remembering his hand against hers, and when she raised her wrist to her face, she could smell him still there.

Lee Nielsen had finished uploading the new content to the author website he was designing, and now he was straightening the apartment. The place was always so messy with Marcello's toys everywhere, and sometimes Kath let the clutter build up. He didn't blame her—it was hard being a full-time mom to a two-year-old. It was nine-thirty on a Wednesday morning, and Kath had taken Marcello out to the play space, Kidville, for Little Maestros music class.

He loaded a few stray breakfast dishes into the dishwasher and sponged down the countertops. The garbage was full, so he decided to take it out. In their old building, the Ansonia Clock Factory in the South Slope, there had been a trash compactor down the hall. Lee and Kath had sold their loft a few months before, anticipating a fall in housing values. The profit, $328,000, was in a high-yield CD, and now they were renting a two-bedroom in a brownstone on Polhemus Place, a one-block street in the North Slope. They hadn't decided if they were going to buy again or even stay in the neighborhood. Kath had some friends who had moved to Ithaca, who touted it as "Park Slope outside of the city." Apparently, it was progressive and scenic, and since Lee was self-employed, there was no reason they had to stay in the city.

Lee put a twist tie on the garbage and went down the stairs. As he rounded the landing, a mouse scurried out in front of him. He jumped, startled and then embarrassed that a tiny mouse had caused his pulse to race. He had seen one in their apartment a few weeks before, but he'd been hoping it was a one-time thing. Now he would have to tell the landlord, an obese Italian woman who didn't seem to take their complaints very seriously. She'd probably ask them to spring for the exterminator themselves.

Outside, he shoved the garbage in a bin. It was a bright sunny day, early enough that it hadn't gotten too humid yet. As he turned toward the building, he saw a black man approaching, heavyset with a lazy eye, and thought for a second that it was the actor Forest Whitaker. But then the man stopped in front of Lee, flashed a shiny gun, and said, "Give it to me."

It was daylight. On a weekday. On one of the most beautiful blocks of Park Slope. Things like this just didn't happen.

Lee looked around for help, but the street was empty, one of the problems with living on a short block. And there was that gun. Sure, it probably wasn't even loaded, but if Lee ran, he might get shot. Shaking, Lee reached into his back pocket. He had seen the man's face clearly—and as he took out the wallet, he tried to memorize the features so he could give a good report to the police.

Lee passed over his wallet. The guy removed the cash, about two hundred dollars, fingered it, and handed back four singles but kept the wallet. Then he slid the gun out of sight and ambled slowly down the street. Lee stood there watching him go, and when the man turned the corner, he took out his cell phone to dial the police.

Pigeons

KAREN WAS eyeing Darby on the big-kid monkey bars at Harmony playground when she got the call. "So I'm calling everyone about the bids," Tina Savant said. "As of last night we're at seven-eighteen."

Karen's heart sank. She had really believed they would be near the top with seven hundred. She could feel the apartment slipping away.

So she said, "Seven thirty-five." It was clean and beautiful, a statement. Over fifty thousand above asking. She knew it was wrong to go up without consulting Matty, but she was certain he would tell her to bow out.

Tina was quiet. If Karen hadn't had an impact with the initial bid, she knew she was having one now. It was a strange feeling to know you'd gone so high you'd surprised the seller, frightening but also exhilarating.

And even if $735,000 felt like a lot, in a few years it would seem like nothing. In a few years a large coffee at Connecticut Muffin would cost seven dollars, and a *New York Times* would cost twelve.

"That's a very strong offer," Tina said.

"Is it the highest?"

"I haven't reached every—"

"But is it the highest so far?"

Tina paused and said, "Yes." Then she added, "But of course everyone will get a chance to go up. I'll give you a call tomorrow, by the end of the day, to let you know where we are."

Karen was so excited she could hardly walk. The apartment was within reach. Two years of near misses had taught her how to play the game.

Darby was off the bars and running to the sandbox. Public school had gotten out three weeks before, and the playground was crowded and frenetic. Karen had thought about putting Darby in the Garfield School's day camp for the summer, but she worried that he would miss her too much. Summer was the time they got to bond, like when he was a baby, the two of them alone for twelve hours a day. Soon he'd be in kindergarten full-time, and then she would miss him, so she decided it was better to be with him while she could.

The sprinklers were on, and children were running around in them, scantily clad. Today Darby wasn't interested in the sprinklers. Karen was relieved. She couldn't stand the sight of these boys and girls in their wet superhero and Dora underwear. Playgrounds in the summer were a pedophile's paradise. She had read an article in the *New York Times* about a pedophile in Los Angeles who trolled playgrounds and fairs for little girls and blogged about it; he could not be barred because he had never actually done anything to a child. It had disgusted her so much, she had to throw away the newspaper as soon as she'd read it.

On the playgrounds she was always keeping her eyes peeled for lone men. Darby had long, feminine lashes, exactly the look pedophiles went for, and with cell phone cameras so easy to come by, you had to be careful or your kid might wind up on the Internet as part of a child-pornography ring.

The other week at Harmony playground, a little girl got snatched, and minutes later, the place was crawling with cops. Karen later read on Park Slope Parents that it was a custody dispute, which consoled her only a little.

As she followed Darby to the sandbox, she thought about how much better she liked Harmony than Third Street. Her friend Jane's son, August, had gotten ringworm from the Third Street sandbox, and ever since then Karen hadn't let Darby play in it.

Darby was already making trouble, engaged in a tug-of-war with another child over a Super Soaker. Darby was screaming, "I want it!" and the boy was shouting, "It's mine!"

"What have I told you about taking other people's things?" Karen shouted. The other boy's back was to her, but his model-good-looking blond nanny was facing Karen. Karen could tell she was a nanny because of three things: She was in her twenties, she had nice breasts, and she didn't look tired.

As the nanny's charge turned and Karen saw his face, a tingle went down her spine. Every woman in America had seen photos of this boy, with his spiky hair and caramel skin, and every woman in America knew his name, which had soared in popularity during the past few years in response to his celebrity.

Karen grabbed the toy out of Darby's hand and placed it in the nanny's hand. "I'm so sorry," she said. "He shouldn't have taken that without asking."

"That's okay," the woman said in a slight accent.

"I'm Karen," she said, proffering her hand. "Bryan."

"Annika. Åkersson. And this is Orion." The announcement was as redundant as if Jack Nicholson had shown up at a Lakers game with JACK written in red ink on his forehead.

"Orion," Karen said. "What a beautiful name." Annika's eyelashes fluttered a bit, as though she knew that Karen knew that Orion was famous and didn't appreciate the deception. Karen would have to cool it.

"Say hi to Orion, Darby," she said.

But Darby was skulking away, having spotted a lone plastic dump truck that no one was using. Karen yanked him back. "Maybe you two can work things out," she said. She turned to Annika. "He thinks the world revolves around him."

"They all do at this age," Annika said. "What is he, four?"

"Yep."

"Where does he go to school?"

"Well, now he's off for the summer, but he's over at the Garfield School."

Annika frowned, confused. "Where?"

"On Garfield Place?"

"You mean the synagogue?" She said "synagogue" in a thick Scandinavian accent, making the word even more foreign than it sounded in

English. Karen nodded. "What are those things on his knees?" Annika asked.

"I have him wear kneepads so he doesn't hurt himself."

Annika squinted at Karen as if Americans were crazy. Karen took a parachute toy from her bowling bag. "Darbs, why don't you show Orion how this works?" she said. The boys ran off to the center of the playground as the two women followed, walking slowly in the heat.

"So where are you from?" Karen asked.

"Sweden. A suburb of Stockholm called Täby."

"So how did you get the job working for Melora?" Annika seemed to soften, as though Karen's acknowledgment of Melora's fame made it clear she wasn't trying to pull a fast one.

"I was working for Julianne Moore's neighbors in the West Village. They moved to Connecticut and I wanted to stay in the city, so Julianne recommended me to Melora."

"So you live with them—with Melora and Stuart?"

"Yeah."

Karen tried to imagine what Annika's room looked like, if she had an entire floor and her own kitchen. Karen made small talk with Annika, who told her that she had come to the United States to train at Gleason's boxing gym in DUMBO after seeing *Million-Dollar Baby* and becoming inspired by Hilary Swank's character.

"That's wonderful," Karen said.

"But I don't go there anymore," Annika said. "I started dating my trainer, and we broke up. He's a world champion from the Dominican Republic. He kept saying he was going to leave his wife, but then she got pregnant and he changed his mind. Now I go to Kingsway in the city. But I liked Gleason's better."

Women always revealed such personal things on the playground. No one was going anywhere, so you sat there and spilled your guts and then looked at your watch and hurried off in opposite directions.

"That's such a shame," Karen said, "that you have to suffer because he broke it off."

"It's my own fault. I shouldn't have gotten involved with a married guy in the first place," Annika said, "but Martin and I were in love. I never loved anyone like him. Orion, give him a chance with it! He told me he was unhappy. I really believed he was going to leave his wife. I was so surprised when he told me she was pregnant again. Their fourth."

Her voice cracked and she started to cry. Karen offered her a tissue, keeping a careful eye on the boys, who had abandoned the parachute and were going down the big slide. It was hard to focus on the children and Annika at the same time, but she wasn't going to take her eye off her son. "You poor thing," she said, patting Annika's shoulder while steering her closer to the slide.

That was when Karen noticed a group of black children coming in from the park. There were about six of them, boys and girls, and though they were all under ten, they were raucous. One of the boys was fat and tall—a nine-year-old in the body of a teenager. They reminded her of the students she had worked with up in the Bronx, bigger than their years, and loud, desperate for attention even if it was negative attention.

They proceeded to chase one another up and down the slides, yelling too loudly. Karen shook her head. "No one watches these kids," she said.

This was another thing Karen hated about the playgrounds in the summer. When school was out, the black kids came. And they weren't neighborhood kids, either. Every year in late June, like clockwork, they overtook the sprinklers of the white playgrounds—running and screaming. The week before, Karen had seen a black boy careen into a two-year-old girl in the Third Street sprinklers, so hard that she skinned both knees and hands. Rich people never had to contend with the rough kids because they were gone from mid-June, when private school got out, till the week after Labor Day.

Orion and Darby had wandered near a group of toddlers who had set out a bunch of sunscreen bottles on the shelf of a climbing structure. They were running a mock store, with other children acting as customers. Nearby, the big black boy was chasing a pigeon with a stick.

As one of the white girls pretended to sell a friend a bottle of Coppertone, the black boy let out a loud whoop. Suddenly, he was beating the pigeon with a stick as the children watched, mouths agape. "*Stop that!*" Karen cried, racing over. "*What are you doing?*" But by the time she grabbed the stick from his hand, the pigeon had stopped moving. It was still, blood coming out of its chest, eyes open.

Darby raced into his mother's arms as Orion clung to Annika. The nearby mothers and nannies ran over to swoop up the sobbing children. One mother dialed 911. A Russian nanny threw a newspaper over the bird.

Karen strode over to the boy, who had moved away from the pigeon but was sneering with a few of the black girls. "What is wrong with you? Why would you do that?"

"I didn't mean to kill him," he said, head down. "I was only playin'."

"It's against the law to harm an animal," said Karen. "You could go to jail for that. We've already called the police."

The boy seemed chastened. Karen sat on a bench next to Annika, wondering where the cops were. They never came when you needed them. "I can't believe it," Karen said. "They're animals, those children. This is why we need Obama to be our next president: so he can set a model. They have no role models."

Annika nodded distantly, as though not wanting to engage in political debate. "Mommy, why'd he kill the bird?" Darby said.

"Some people do terrible things to animals because they don't understand how precious they are."

Orion murmured, "Lotta blood."

"It was an awful thing that boy did," Karen said, "and I don't want either of you to do anything like that to an animal. Ever. You should have respect for all living creatures."

"She's right," Annika said. "Those boys were very bad."

A cop van had arrived on the pathway, and an officer, young and Puerto Rican, got out. Karen looked around for the black boy, but he and the others had left. She went to the officer and told him what had happened, but he didn't seem to take it very seriously.

Darby was pale and shaken up. "I want to go home, Mommy," he said.

Though concerned for her son and distressed by the pigeon incident, she was also disappointed. She had just begun to make headway with Annika, and now they would have to leave. "It's been a rough morning for him," she told Annika. "Say goodbye to Orion, Darb. Maybe you two can play together again."

"Can he come over?" Orion asked.

"Sure," Karen said. "Maybe sometime. If it's okay with—"

"I mean now," Orion said. Annika looked hesitant.

"Maybe another time," Karen said in the authoritative mother tone that always turned Darby oppositional.

"I want to go over now," Darby said, seeming to forget about the pigeon.

"I'm not sure if it's okay with Annika."

"You can come," Annika said finally. "It's all right."

"Are you sure his mother wouldn't—"

"It's okay." The Swede nodded as though trying to convince herself.

Karen wasn't sure it was really okay but said gingerly, "Well, it *would* be nice to get out of the heat."

"The house is really comfy," said Annika. "Melora and Stuart have central air."

When they got to the mansion, Karen folded Darby's stroller and held his hand as they alighted the steps. As they stepped into the entryway, Karen gasped. The mansion was even more incredible than she had imagined. There was a beautiful oak staircase right in front of the door that seemed to ascend into the heavens. To the left was a spacious, high-ceilinged living room decorated with a glass table on an abstract black base, a cowhide chaise, and a brown couch with no armrests. Not a toy or child's item was in sight. Even though she knew an interior decorator had probably furnished the place, she had the feeling Melora had really strong opinions about what she wanted where.

Annika turned to the burglar alarm pad and Karen peeked over her shoulder. Annika moved her fingers so quickly Karen wasn't sure what the combination was—6727, or maybe 67227. She'd have to try the numbers later on her phone, to see what they spelled out.

Annika hung her keys on an elaborately carved key rack to the right of the door, attached to a mirror where Karen could imagine Melora looking at her reflection every day. "Do you want something to drink?" Annika asked.

"Sure, any kind of diet soda would be wonderful."

"Melora doesn't allow sodas in the house," Annika said. "How about some lemonade?" Karen nodded, and Annika disappeared down a flight of stairs.

Darby was taking Orion by the hand and leading him up the stairs. Their son—at a playdate with Orion Leigh-Ashby! If Colleen could see her now, it wouldn't matter that she had three sons and Karen had only one. She would think Karen was living the high life in brownstone Brooklyn.

Karen made her way around the living room, inspecting the abstract art on the walls—blobs and smears, that kind of thing. There was a painting of an angry woman that looked like it had been drawn by a child. Karen thought it said de Kooning in the corner. Were they that rich? There was a working fireplace with a stunning original mantel, and Karen pictured Melora reading on the chaise in the winter, curled up under a blanket, never cold, always comfortable.

To the rear of the living room was a dining room with a stunning chandelier, built-in cabinets, and a floor-to-ceiling wine rack. Eight high-backed white leather chairs were arranged around a long table. Karen imagined the fabulous dinner parties. De Niro had probably eaten here, and Willem Dafoe, and all the young hipster Brooklyn celebs. They probably drank five-hundred-dollar bottles of wine and then smoked cigars and laughed until it was light out.

Annika came in with two lemonades and handed one to Karen. It was perfect, sweet and tangy. "This is delicious," Karen said.

"Would you like a tour?"

"Sure."

Annika led her down a small set of stairs behind the front staircase to the lower level, which contained a professional chef's kitchen with all Sub-Zero appliances and a huge butcher-block island. "So they must have a cook," Karen said.

"Yeah, she's out shopping. They joined the Coop, so she's been going there a lot."

Karen was shocked. "Melora joined, too?"

"Yeah." Karen wondered why a celebrity would join the Food Coop, but everyone was into organic these days, and the Coop had the best vegetables in the neighborhood. Karen had stood in line behind Maggie Gyllenhaal the other day, so maybe it wasn't implausible.

Adjoining the kitchen was a breakfast nook with bay windows overlooking the immaculately decorated private garden. A den showcased a state-of-the-art stereo system with a humongous flat-screen television built into the wall.

On the third floor was the playroom, facing Prospect Park West. Behind it Annika pointed out the door to the master bedroom but didn't open it, instead breezing past it down the hallway. The fourth floor contained a bathroom; a small Zen prayer garden with a waterfall; Annika's bedroom, whose walls were decorated with posters of black boxers; and Stuart and Melora's studies.

Matty did his work in bed mostly, and sometimes on the kitchen table. He would kill for a study of his own and these people had two.

"What an incredible home," Karen said, looking out Annika's dormer window onto Garfield Place. "I didn't know real people lived like this."

"They're not real," said Annika with a grin. The women headed down the stairs. "Let's go sit in the garden. We can finish our lemonade."

Karen hesitated and said, "Um, I have to use the bathroom. I'll meet you down there."

Annika gestured to the bathroom off the hallway. Karen went in, then waited a minute for Annika to go downstairs and slipped down to the third floor and into the master bedroom. Her hands were sweaty, and she wiped them on her shorts.

In the real estate listings it would have been called a "master bedroom suite" because it came with its own dressing room and an adjoining bathroom. Karen stood in the dressing room, which adjoined the walk-in closet, and tried to imagine how her life would be different if she got dressed there every day. It probably changed your whole outlook to have that kind of privacy. Your husband would never see your Spanx or your dirty underwear. You could freshen up before he saw you in the morning and emerge not only immaculately dressed but perfectly made up, with a pulled-together visage, flushed cheeks, and pink glossy lips, so that you always looked like you'd just had an orgasm.

The bedroom decor featured mirrors with elaborate frames, hanging on dark cork walls. A crepe lamp in a Kleenex shape dangled over the bed, which was covered with a high-thread-count black duvet and so many throw pillows it felt like a hotel room.

Karen sat on the bed. It was firm, not too bouncy, probably one of those $25,000 Swedish horsehair numbers that they were always advertising in the *New York Times*. She turned onto her back and stared at the ceiling, imagining Stuart Ashby making love to her on this bed.

Before she and Matty started trying to conceive, they had sex once a week, on date night, after dinner at Applewood. Karen didn't come during sex, but once in a while Matty would go down on her until she did. She actually preferred it when he didn't go the extra mile; it was so exhausting, and who had the time? She preferred brief missionary because it made him happy and because she had read in *Great Sex for Moms: Ten Steps to Nurturing Passion While Raising Kids* that mercy sex was better than none at all. But now that she and Matty did it only on the four days a month when she was fertile, so he could store up his sperm in between, she enjoyed the fact that once her peak day had passed, she didn't have to do it again for another month.

Karen rolled onto her belly, lifted the comforter off the pillows, and inhaled. She could smell a sweet perfume, musky but subtle, and recognized it immediately: Soften, by Melora Leigh. It had come out a few years before and sold astronomical numbers at Bendel and Saks. Karen owned it and wore it every date night but felt it was too extreme for the playground.

She opened the bedside table drawer and examined the following items: a pill vial reading "Lorazepam—no more than 8 mg. daily," prescribed by a Dr. Michael Levine; a nail file; a tube of Sonya Dakar Youth! age-defying lotion; a pair of Tweezerman tweezers; a white tub of La Mer moisturizing cream; a plastic chain of white beads of varying widths, with the widest next to a circular loop; a copy of *Eat, Pray, Love,* a book that Karen had read in her book group; and a thick man's wallet.

Curious as to what a man's wallet was doing in Melora Leigh's bedside table, Karen opened it. She was startled by the sight of Neal Harris's face smiling at her from his driver's license, the very same Neal Harris she had run into at the Carroll Street open house and whose daughter, Tilly, went to the Garfield School with Darby.

She fingered the wallet, wondering how it had come to be in Melora's bedroom. It was so incongruous. There was no reason the wallet of a plebeian should have been in the bedside table drawer of an aristocrat.

And then everything clicked.

She remembered the story Neal had told about the pickpocketing at the Coop. Annika had said Melora was a member. That alone didn't mean she had taken it. It could have been Orion, on a shopping trip with his mother or the cook. Or maybe Stuart had stolen it and then socked the wallet away under the book because he was certain Melora would never read *Eat, Pray, Love.*

But Karen had a suspicion, a suspicion so strong and unmistakable it was almost like her first labor contraction with Darby, that it was neither of these. Of course Melora had done it. It went along with what Melora had said about her childhood in all those interviews, how she was forced to grow up too fast. Karen knew a little about social anxiety disorder from reading *Nurturing the Shy Child: Practical Help for Raising Confident and Socially Skilled Kids and Teens* after Darby had gone through a painfully shy phase around two and she was at odds about what to do. The book said that sometimes children who overachieved at a young age missed out on the opportunity to develop peer relationships and had trouble in social situations as adults. That was probably what had happened to Melora.

She felt pity for Melora for having done what she had, but at the same time she felt a sense of possibility. In the two years Melora had been in the neighborhood, Karen had not exchanged a word with her, but now she was certain she would.

Hearing footsteps, Karen leaped off the bed, adjusted the comforter, slipped the wallet into her shorts pocket, and dashed out into the hallway to the stairs as though just coming down. Around the bend, Annika gave her a funny look. "Are you coming?" she said.

"Yep." Annika frowned suspiciously and eyed the bedroom door,

but Karen had shut it all the way and it stayed closed, not betraying her.

In the garden they had lemonade and butter cookies. As Karen nib-
bled, she put her hand in her pocket and stroked the wallet. She had
been feeling so out of place in this magnificent house, but now she felt
at home. She closed her eyes and imagined she was Melora sitting in
the backyard of her own house. From the chaise Karen couldn't hear the
traffic on Prospect Park West, just a tiny breeze rustling through the
branches of the Japanese maple.

The Coop Courier

THE NEXT morning at nine o'clock Melora was running down Prospect Park West toward the Third Street entrance to the park. Usually, she didn't awaken till well after ten, but this morning she had risen at eight-forty without an alarm, seen the sun streaming through her windows, and decided to give the loop a try, though it had been months since she'd last gone running.

When she stumbled downstairs into the kitchen for a coffee, Shivan was the only one there. She told Melora that Stuart was at the library and Annika was out with Orion. Melora had been irritated that she'd been feeling like such an early riser when everyone else had left the house long ago, but she decided that progress came in baby steps.

As she ran down Prospect Park West, she was struck by affection for a neighborhood where she had never felt completely at home. She passed yuppies on their way to the Grand Army Plaza subway stop and nannies pushing babies. The air was cool, given the humidity of the days before, and she breathed in through her nose, enjoying the summer scent of blossoms and oak.

In her Stella McCartney for Adidas tracksuit and a WGA East baseball cap she'd gotten on the picket line, she thought she almost blended in with all the ordinary Park Slopers. She wasn't a movie star; she was another neighborhood mother on a morning jog.

She ran the loop easily and in good time. Usually, she had to stop at Drummer's Grove to rest and then walk most of the way up East Drive to the Soldiers' and Sailors' Memorial Arch, but not on this morning. She was a new person, a new Melora. It was as though she didn't even know the old Melora, the one who took 150 milligrams of Zoloft a day, needed Ativan to sleep, and felt nothing when her son was brought in to kiss her good night. That Melora was going through the motions, but the new Melora was Really Living.

From the drive she could see Long Meadow to her left, a few dog walkers and soccer players. Her breath shortened. *You're almost there.* She passed the war remembrance rock, which signified the final, most challenging stretch. She could see the Memorial Arch over the trees, the statue of a woman in a horse-drawn chariot. Stuart had explained the history to her one day at the greenmarket; he'd learned it from a PBS documentary about Brooklyn. In the middle was Columbia, holding a sepulchre in the air. On each side were two winged figures—Victory, Stuart said—leading horses and blowing a trumpet to announce Columbia's arrival. He said Columbia represented the United States, an allegory for the Civil War.

As Melora ran up the hill, she stared up at Columbia, imagining the goddess rooting her on, encouraging her to clean up her act, and she was so focused on the statue that she didn't notice the two black teenage boys lurking by the trees to her left. One was wearing a do-rag, and even though they were young, they were scary.

She reached into her jacket for her cell phone. "Yo, Princess Xaviera!" the shorter boy shouted. "Where yo saber?"

She breathed a sigh of relief. "Oh, I left it at home," she said lightly, then quickened her pace. They didn't follow. She heard them laughing behind her. What were they saying? Were they mocking her body or age, staring at her ass? They should have seen it when she was on Effexor.

When she got out of the park, she stopped at a stone bench and stretched, relieved to be out in the open with people passing by. Prospect Park was so strange. One moment you were isolated and vulnerable, the next you were in a busy public plaza surrounded by dozens of people.

As she lowered her head to her thigh to stretch her hamstring, she decided that instead of going home immediately, she would take a detour to the health food store on Seventh Avenue, Back to the Land, and pick up a fruit smoothie. The Food Coop didn't have a juicing station, and even if it had, she had no plans to set foot in there again. She hadn't been back since she had taken the wallet the week before. She had gone about her business in the neighborhood, careful not to walk past the Coop, afraid that if she did, she would want to steal again.

She would take her smoothie home and drink it while reading the papers in the breakfast nook, maybe have Shivan fix her some salmon, too, or an egg-white omelet. Melora had the *Times* and the *Post* delivered every day, but usually, she didn't make it through very much of the *Times,* unless it was a Thursday, in which case she read all of the Styles section.

Maybe today after she read the papers, she would go to one of the boutiques on Fifth Avenue, to buy a new top. She wanted something new to wear for Stuart, something revealing and obviously expensive. After she shopped, she would get a mani-pedi and reread *Yellow Rosie.* She was meeting with Adam Epstein the next day for lunch, and she was excited to tell him her ideas about Rosie and how the entire character had crystallized for her when she saw her, in a dream, in a single-process bouffant. If it went well, she could even mention *Yellow Rosie* on the red carpet for *The Dueling Donnellys* the next night.

After Adam Epstein, she was supposed to see Dr. Levine, and she wasn't looking forward to it. At their last appointment, a few days after the wallet incident, she had felt obligated to tell him but hadn't, certain that it would lead to bad things. He would think she had a problem and would want to talk to her about why she had done it, and then she'd have to tell him about the times she'd shoplifted as a teen. He might want to put her on a different antidepressant, or worse, an anticompulsive like Topamax, which she'd been on for a brief stretch of hair pulling in 1998 and hated due to the bloating and hallucinations.

Or he might insist she up her sessions to two times a week, only furthering her dependency on him. She'd been feeling so energized this week that she'd had the idea to drop from every week to every other, and she wanted Dr. Levine to be on board. She hadn't always been so dependent; there had been a time when she could handle her own problems. When she was twelve and on the set of a Movie of the Week with Lindsay Crouse, a fat costume assistant was in her eye-line for a crucial one-shot, and Melora had asked the director to make the woman move. She wanted to be that girl again, that bold brave girl. The best thing to do was cancel.

As she walked down President Street toward Seventh Avenue, she took out her cell phone and dialed his number. "Hi, Michael," she said into his voice mail. "I'm going to have to cancel our appointment tomorrow. Something came up. But I'll see you next Thursday at four."

She hung up, wondering if he would buy the part about something coming up. He hadn't been her shrink five years for nothing.

Inside Back to the Land, she went to the juice counter and ordered a strawberry papaya smoothie. As the kid was fixing it, her phone rang. Dr. Levine. She was a little nervous at first but decided it was ridiculous not to answer. It was only a scheduling thing; she didn't have to avoid his call. She lowered her voice and stepped back from the counter to take the call. "Hi, Melora," he said brightly. "I got your message. Is everything all right?"

"Yeah, why?"

"You said something came up. I wanted to be sure everything was okay."

"Oh yeah, it's just . . . a meeting. For the Adam Epstein movie. I can't reschedule."

"Break a leg with that. It sounds like it was written for you."

"I feel like it was, too. I feel . . . strangely . . . optimistic." She couldn't help herself. She was too buzzed, too high. "We'll talk about it when I come in, but I just . . . I don't know, I was thinking of maybe coming in less often. I've been feeling really good about things, and I thought I could try going a bit longer. Between sessions."

"That's probably something we should discuss in person."

"Of course, of course."

"But I think it's great you're feeling so good. That's a very strong indicator. So I'll see you next Thursday, then."

When she hung up, she felt lighter. On the way out of the store with her smoothie, she noticed a shelf littered with pamphlets and newspapers. A headline blared, COOP DETERMINED TO FINGER PICKPOCKETS. It was the *Coop Courier.*

Melora grabbed it and went outside.

> This week, Coop member Neal Harris, 34, reported
> that his wallet was stolen from a stroller bag while he
> was in the cashier line. In addition, Coop General Ad-
> ministrator Vivian Shaplansky said there has been a
> rash of thefts of inventory, with dozens of food items
> ranging from Stonyfield Yogurt cups to Murray's
> Chicken Thighs disappearing from the shelves without
> showing up in the computers as paid for.
>
> "I would hate to think that any Coop member
> would steal either from another member or from the
> Coop itself," said Shaplansky. "I am guessing this is the
> work of non-members who managed to get past the
> entrance workers. Hopefully people will be more vigi-
> lant about guarding their bags and we will not have to
> take extreme security measures."
>
> "The fact that something like this would happen
> at a place where we're supposed to be a community,
> that enrages me," said Harris, a stay-at-home father of
> two. "This is not Key Food. It's really sad to see this
> happen at the Coop. My wife and I are thinking of
> moving to Montclair."
>
> The Coop installed a dozen video cameras on the
> shopping floor in 2004 after a similar rash of thefts.
> Shaplansky said the Coop has begun a thorough re-
> view of the tape, along with the NYPD, in hopes of
> finding the perpetrator or perpetrators. "Because we
> know the time and location of the thefts," said Shap-
> lansky, "we expect to find the culprit soon."

Melora jerked her head up. A wave of vertigo passed over her, and
she sat quickly on the bench in front of the store. *Fuck fuck fuck.* That
was it. It would have been one thing if she were anonymous, one of
those generic Park Slope mothers with crow's-feet and scoliosis, but she
was famous. Any idiot who'd been to the movies could finger her. Her

career would be ruined before she got her second comeback. She didn't want to be the next Winona Ryder. Winona had done nothing since the shoplifting; that Sundance comedy about the Ten Commandments didn't count.

And to think all Melora had wanted was one tiny little Page Six or *Us Weekly* item about joining the Coop. Even if she got off with community service and a fine, there was no way Adam Epstein would cast her. He'd decide she was too high-risk. The production companies were fanatical about insurance bonding, and if he couldn't get bonding, he couldn't book her. That was why Woody Allen didn't hire Ryder and Downey for *Melinda and Melinda*. Not that a role in *Melinda and Melinda* would have helped anybody's career.

She thought about the *Dueling Donnellys* premiere the next night. She was supposed to do a red carpet. How could she do that, smile through her teeth, knowing she was headed for the slammer?

Nobody liked to work with messed-up women. They expected women to be on the ball at all times, while men could carry guns or get blow jobs from black whores and nobody cared.

Her carotid throbbing insanely, sweat pouring down her neck, she dialed Dr. Levine. Voice mail. When she was trying to avoid him, he answered, and when she was trying to reach him, it went to voice mail. Some kind of sick joke.

"Michael?" she said hollowly. "I was wondering if you had any openings later this week. Can you call me as soon as you get this? It's Melora."

How could she have been feeling so strong a moment ago and so weak now? Why hadn't she waited till the fall to join the Coop and gone off with Orion and Annika to Bridgehampton for the summer? You always got into trouble when you stayed in the city past June.

How long would it take to review all the security tapes? Had they started already, before the article in the newspaper went to press? The Coop people knew when the pickpocketing had occurred, because Bugaboo Dad had complained about it. It couldn't take too long to look at the video, at most a few days. They'd make her serve time. Even if Adam wanted to cast her, he couldn't. You couldn't work from jail.

Just two blocks till home, she told herself, rising to her feet unsteadily.

She headed south on Seventh Avenue, abandoning the smoothie. The scent of the gingko trees nauseated her.   .

She had to get some perspective. Maybe it would all blow over. Maybe she was getting worked up over nothing. The thing to do was stay calm. She would have to get through the Epstein lunch. But how could she do that with all this to worry about? How was she even going to get a full night's sleep tonight? She would definitely take a couple Ativans before bed.

In fact, she would take a milligram or two as soon as she got home. Maybe she would swallow them with wine, since Ativan took ninety minutes to work. Stuart had ordered half a dozen cases of sauvignon blanc from Reverie Vineyard and Winery in Diamond Mountain for a dinner party in April. Dafoe and Robbins had polished off a case at the party, and since then Melora had finished a bottle every couple of days, sneaking it during the day and then having more at dinner with Stuart. Now there was only half a case left.

She could taste it, crisp and buttery, in her mouth. *Reverie.* If she could just have a glass of sauvignon blanc when she got home, then she wouldn't worry about the stupid video camera thing.

Don't sweat the small stuff. Let go and let God. Home, then wine. Home, then wine. And everything will be okay.

Mom Job

ON HER way to meet Rebecca in Prospect Park Wednesday morning, Lizzie stopped at her mother-in-law's. Mona had called to say she had something for Mance, and Lizzie, feeling guilty for never visiting, said she'd come by and pick it up.

Mona, tall and austere with perfectly coiffed hair, ushered her into the living room, which was decorated with antique furniture and doilies and looked like it hadn't changed since 1969, when she and her husband had bought the brownstone. There were framed photographs on every surface of Mance, Jay, Jay's sister, Sabrina, Mona's late husband, François, and dozens and dozens of black relatives. Black people at parties, and dinners, and church, smiling and happy. It was like walking into a stranger's home, except this was where her husband had grown up.

"Look at him!" Mona exclaimed, reaching for the baby. He began to cry.

Lizzie took him back and said, "He's been in a bad mood because of the heat."

The TV was on. CNN. A commentator was talking about the *New Yorker* cartoon depicting Barack and Michelle as Black Power radical extremists. He was saying something about how "clearly the cover was meant to poke fun at the Republicans vilifying the Obama family and not the Obamas themselves."

Mona made a hissing noise and shook her head. "That might be true," she said, "but it doesn't mean people won't get the wrong idea."

"Nobody who reads the *New Yorker* is the kind of person who would get the wrong idea," Lizzie said.

"What's that supposed to mean?"

"Just that people who read the *New Yorker* are smart enough to understand satire." Mona was glaring at her as though Lizzie had said something racist herself. Around Mona nothing she said came out right. "So what did you want to give me?" Lizzie asked.

"It's so hot. Don't you want to stay for some iced tea?"

"No, no, I'm on my way to meet a friend." Mona frowned. Lizzie felt she had been too abrupt but didn't know what to say to correct it.

"I bought him this at that store on Vanderbilt," Mona said, and fetched an orange floppy sun hat with a six-inch rim and earflaps.

It was hideous. It looked like something you'd see in a pediatric cancer ward. Even in another color, Lizzie wouldn't put it on him. "Isn't it adorable?" Mona said.

"Oh, I love it," Lizzie said, and placed it on his head. He cried and she took it off. "Thanks so much. We should get going soon." She made a move for the door.

"Black skin burns, too," Mona said, as though Lizzie were rejecting it out of racial cluelessness. Lizzie hated that Mona was so patronizing. Mance was Lizzie's own son. She knew how to care for his skin and hair. Jay had shown her.

"I know."

Lizzie waited till she was out of view of the brownstone to stuff the hat into the diaper bag. She felt like Mona didn't understand her. When Mance was older Mona could take care of him, but not now. It was too soon.

Rebecca had asked Lizzie to meet her at the Third Street entrance, and when Lizzie got there, she was tired. Third Street was a long walk from Lizzie's apartment, but it hadn't occurred to her to ask Rebecca to come to the Underhill playground, right around the corner from her. When you lived in Prospect Heights, you were expected to cater to the needs of the Slopers, not the other way around.

As Lizzie approached the entrance to the park, she didn't see Rebecca so she stopped the stroller and looked up at the two stone panthers abutting the path. "Look at that!" she said to Mance. "Do you know the difference between them? It's the ears, sweetie. One has its ears pricked up, and the other's ears are slicked back." She'd heard another mother pointing this out to her daughter once.

It was hard to know what he understood, though that was true with all babies of this age. One minute they were right with you, and the next they were zoned out, as clueless as newborns. Though she sometimes felt self-conscious, she made an effort to talk to Mance all the time in a light, pleasing singsong that child development experts called motherese. This was the way you were supposed to teach them language, by narrating for them when they were too young to talk and by questioning them when they were old enough to understand you better.

Lizzie spotted Rebecca coming toward her, pushing Abbie. She feared that she had cereal stuck in her teeth and ran her tongue over them quickly. Rebecca was smiling broadly as she came down the street. "Hi there," she said.

Lizzie reached into her bag and pulled out a wrapped bottle of Italian wine that she had bought at a liquor store on Vanderbilt.

"What's this?" Rebecca said, looking more taken aback than flattered.

"I was in this store in my neighborhood and told the guy you liked Terre di Tufi, and he recommended this. It's from Sardinia."

"You didn't have to do that."

"I don't mind. You fed Mance dinner."

Rebecca unwrapped it and regarded it for a minute before stowing it in her stroller bag. "You look great," she said. Was she hitting on her or merely being friendly, one mom to another?

Lizzie had put a lot of thought into her wardrobe: She was wearing a Loomstate T-shirt she'd splurged on at a Fifth Avenue boutique the day before. "Ugh. I look disgusting." She clutched the side of her waist. "I'm so fat. I used to have good boobs, but now I feel like a deflated Dolly Parton. After I wean him, I think I'm going to get a mom job."

"What's a mom job?"

"Tummy tuck, breast lift, and lipo. It's thirty grand, but I figure if I start saving now, I can do it in time for my fiftieth birthday." She was kidding, she would never do it, but knocking her own body was a way of seeing what Rebecca thought of it.

"You definitely don't need a mom job," Rebecca said, laughing. "You're a MILF." They pushed their strollers down the pathway into the park.

"I am not a MILF," Lizzie said. "I am the furthest thing from a MILF. I am a mother nobody likes to fuck." She tried to picture the letters in her head. "A M-NLF."

"Come on! You said you guys do it four times a week!"

"Well, yeah," Lizzie said. "I guess some men have less energy for sex once they become dads, but Jay is not in that category. A guy has to spend time with the child for the child to exhaust him."

Jay was gone again, off on some gigs in New England. He had left the morning before, awakening at five, and though Mance had slept through the packing, Lizzie hadn't. Jay had put his duffel on the bed and stomped around the room while he filled it, and after he left, she couldn't fall back asleep. Instead, she lay in bed tossing and turning until Mance woke up at seven. When she came out to the coffeepot, it had been on so long it had burned.

"What about Theo?" Lizzie asked Rebecca.

"What do you mean?"

"Did he have less energy for sex when he became a dad?"

"You could say that." Rebecca's face looked hardened and ugly.

"I've heard that can happen sometimes," Lizzie said.

They were on the roadway in the park. Rebecca stopped the stroller and looked at Lizzie. "How long do you think someone's allowed to not fuck you before . . . before you know there's a problem?"

"I don't know," Lizzie said, not sure what the right answer was. "A couple of months?" Rebecca didn't say anything. "Like six months?" Rebecca made a "keep going" gesture with her hand. "How long has it been? A year?" The gesture. "A year and a half?"

Rebecca was silent. Lizzie didn't know what to say. So this was the reason for the kiss. Rebecca was hard up. It had nothing to do with Lizzie. If Lizzie hadn't gotten laid in a year and a half, she'd be thinking other mothers were hot, too. It was like men in jail turning gay.

"Maybe he has erectile dysfunction," Lizzie said. "You should tell him to try Viagra."

"He doesn't like to talk about it."

"Have you guys seen anyone about it?"

"He thinks couples therapy is the gateway to divorce," Rebecca said.

"Well, no sex isn't that good for a marriage, either." Rebecca nodded. "Have you tried to talk to him at all?" Lizzie asked.

"He always clams up. Or he says it's because I'm mean to him. I don't know if he's right. You know what? I shouldn't have said anything about it. It's embarrassing."

"Why?"

"It's not normal. A man's supposed to want to do it. I mean, men spend their lives getting sexually rejected. But women spend their lives turning men away."

"That's kind of a stereotype."

"But it's true!"

Rebecca looked so miserable, pushing Abbie. Lizzie wanted to tell her something reassuring but didn't know how to or what to say. She wanted to tell Rebecca that any guy who wouldn't fuck her was crazy. She wanted to tell her that if she were with her, she'd never let that happen.

Lizzie couldn't believe Rebecca's husband had stopped making love to her. It was hard to imagine that someone could change that much on a dime. Maybe their sex life had been mediocre before Abbie and now she wanted someone to pin it on. Lizzie felt sorry for her friend but also wondered if there was more to the story.

Inside the park, they stopped to find a place to sit down. Lizzie pulled out a picnic blanket and spread it under a tree. They sat the kids down next to each other, and Lizzie took out some bubbles for them, helping them wave the wand even though they weren't old enough to know how to blow.

"I wrote those swingers back," Lizzie said.

Rebecca turned to her. "*What?*"

Lizzie giggled, remembering. "I pretended to be a single mom named Victoria. Some guy wrote back. Andy. Says his wife is Alexandra. Probably not their real names. They have two sons. He wants me to grab a drink with them tomorrow night at the Gate, to see if the chemistry's right." She had e-mailed back and forth with Andy the past few nights and had enjoyed creating a woman she thought he would like, blond and busty.

"Are you going to go?" Rebecca asked.

"*We're* going to go." Lizzie kept her voice light and easy, although she was desperate for Rebecca to come. If Rebecca came, Lizzie might stand a chance with her. It would be too hard to seduce her one on one; Lizzie needed the subterfuge of the couple.

"You think I'm pathetic because of what I told you," Rebecca said. "You think I'm desperate."

"No, I don't. We're not going to do anything anyway. I just want to see what they look like."

"They're probably fat," Rebecca said. "Did he say how old they are?"

"Late thirties. It'll be fun. I told him I was blond. I'll say you're a redhead. That way we can spy on them without them knowing it's us."

"It sounds kind of stupid."

"Come on. Haven't you ever wanted to do something to see how it might turn out?" Lizzie was getting more excited the more she thought about it. Her whole life belonged to Jay and Mance now. She wanted to have a secret from them.

"Did you tell this Andy that you're a hasbian?" Rebecca asked.

"Victoria is not a hasbian. She and her husband are separated, and her son is named Cyrus. She's a paralegal and she lives in Windsor Terrace."

"Did you give him your dimensions?"

"Yeah, but I augmented a little. I think Victoria has a mom job."

Rebecca giggled and removed a joint from her shirt pocket. She stuck it in her mouth and rummaged for a lighter in her purse. Rebecca was richer than Lizzie but so low-class. Lizzie didn't know if she acted this way—the wine, the pot—to get a rise out of Lizzie or because she really had some sort of substance problem.

"What are you doing?" Lizzie asked.

"What does it look like?"

"You'd better be careful," Lizzie said. "The cops are all over the park."

"Please. You think they're going to look twice at us? I can't believe you haven't already figured this out: Nobody notices mothers." Rebecca lit up, took a drag, and offered it.

Lizzie shook her head and said, "I have no tolerance."

"Suit yourself."

"I got drunk last week at your apartment," Lizzie said. Rebecca blew the smoke away from the kids. "I don't know if it's childbirth or getting older. I was so out of it when I left your house." She told Rebecca about the man on her block. She wanted Rebecca to know she saw her as a friend, to know she had wanted to call her.

When she finished the story, Rebecca said, "You should have called me," and choked a little on the joint.

"I figured you would think I was being ridiculous," Lizzie said. "I was buzzed from the wine. It probably wasn't even the guy from the poster."

"But that doesn't mean he wasn't dangerous. I heard there was a shootout at the Underhill playground in January. Isn't that right down the block from you?"

Feeling defensive about her neighborhood, Lizzie said, "It wasn't on the playground. It was on the street outside the playground. A drive-by. No one was hurt. Besides, Park Slope is just as dangerous. A guy posted on Park Slope Parents this morning that he was mugged at gunpoint in front of his apartment on Polhemus Place."

"That's awful!"

"Then all these people posted to say that he shouldn't have named the street because he was lowering their property values. Can you believe that? People are so naive. They think Park Slope's safe because there're all these celebrities, but it's still Brooklyn. I don't think any of the celebrities live here, anyway. I've never even seen Melora Leigh, even though she has that mansion on Prospect Park West."

"I met her husband the other day," Rebecca said, stubbing out the joint on her shoe.

"Really?" Lizzie asked. "Where did you meet him?"

"He was on my Coop shift," Rebecca said. "I got to train him. Alone. For almost three hours." Her face was flushed and she sounded like a schoolgirl. It was odd—a side of her that Lizzie hadn't seen before.

"What did you talk about?" Lizzie asked.

"Movies, mostly. He actually knows a lot about them."

"Why would Stuart Ashby join the Prospect Park Food Coop?"

"It's the new PC celebrity bandwagon," Rebecca said, and shrugged.
"Apparently Maggie Gyllenhaal's a member, and some guy from *Oz.*"

"So what was he like?" Lizzie asked. She didn't like the excitement in Rebecca's eyes. She knew Rebecca was probably excited because she wasn't getting any at home, but still it bothered Lizzie. It was so uncreative to be infatuated with a celebrity.

"Cool. Funny. Very down-to-earth."

"Do you have a crush on him or something?"

"No, why?"

"You should see yourself. You look kind of insane."

"No, I don't."

Rebecca was starting to annoy her. All she wanted to talk about was Stuart Ashby. It had been a long time since Lizzie had to indulge one of these idiotic conversations with a woman, straight or gay. Only a moron fell for a second-rate movie star. Why couldn't Rebecca see that there was someone wonderful, if not famous, sitting right opposite her?

Abbie started to wander over to a fallen log, and Mance followed. Lizzie didn't like them being so far away. "You think they're all right?" she asked Rebecca.

"*Dr. Spock* says a child who's never been bandaged has not been parented well." Rebecca flopped down on the blanket and looked up at the trees. Lizzie lay down next to her but kept peeking at the kids.

They were quiet for a while, staring up at the sky, and then Rebecca said, "Do you ever feel like things didn't turn out the way you expected them to?"

"Uh-huh," Lizzie answered.

"And that it's too late to do anything about it? And that if only you'd been able to see into the future, you would have made different choices?"

"Yeah, all the time," Lizzie said. "Sometimes I wonder why we had to have a baby."

Rebecca turned to her and frowned. "Come on, now. No, you don't. I do, but you don't."

"There are times when Mance has been such a pill all day that I can almost understand how women could hurt their babies. Not that I would. I just wish sometimes that I could shut him off, like a faucet. But I never can because Jay's never around to help. And then I start thinking that it's never going to end, even when Mance is grown up. I'll always be worrying about him no matter how old he is or where he is, even if he's in a different city. And I wonder why I did this to myself."

"Nobody thinks about all of that when they have kids," Rebecca said. "They only think about the good stuff. It's the only way the species can continue."

Their shoulders were touching. Lizzie felt like Rebecca understood her. It was so hard to say any of this to the stay-at-home mothers because they all seemed so gratified by having had kids. You were a traitor if you were a stay-at-home who admitted you didn't like it.

Lizzie felt the expansiveness that came from being honest. She liked Rebecca, if only for giving her a chance to say what she felt. She wanted to lie here next to her for hours, talking about everything.

Lizzie watched Rebecca's chest rising and falling with her breath. She wanted to keep talking but didn't know the next thing to say. "I like to be with you," she said, something she said to Mance all the time because she thought it was important that he hear it. Rebecca looked at her like she was a dolt, and Lizzie felt ridiculous. You couldn't talk to an adult the way you talked to your kid.

Rebecca was frowning at the children. Lizzie turned to see what had happened. Abbie was standing on the log, about to topple over. It was small and low, and even if she had fallen, she would have been fine, but Rebecca raced over as though Abbie were imperiled, murmuring, "Now, that's a little too far."

Reverie

IN THE kitchen Melora grabbed a bottle of Reverie from the refrigerator. She took out a twenty-ounce balloon glass and the bottle and hurried upstairs to the master bedroom. She sat on the edge of her bed, poured half the bottle into the glass, and tossed it back. She had to get a grip. If she could get a grip for twenty-four hours, until the Epstein lunch, then she would ace it and nothing else would matter. Adam wouldn't care about something as ridiculous as a shoplifting charge. He was indie, for God's sake. Maybe he'd consider a shoplifting charge good publicity; despite the critical praise for *Eva and Andie,* it had only done $4 million domestic, and Vantage would want better numbers for *Yellow Rosie.*

But no matter what she told herself, she couldn't shake the dread. She was a goner. That very morning she'd been feeling so alive and healthy, and now it was all going to shit.

She tried Dr. Levine again. Voice mail. "Hi, Michael, um, it's Melora again. I really need to see you. Something terrible has happened. Well, not terrible. I mean Orion's okay and Stu's okay. It's just . . ." She had to impress upon him the dire nature of the situation but resented that she couldn't get him on the line. Wasn't this supposed to be one of the benefits of fame—that you had everyone you needed on call? When this blew over, she was going to have to rethink whether he was committed enough to be her shrink. "I'm starting to feel really scared about something, and I need to talk to you so we can make sure that it's okay. So call me. Please. As soon as possible."

How could she have been stupid enough to go off of Zoloft without consulting her psychiatrist? Stuart had told her about a story he'd read in the *New York Times Magazine*: A middle-aged man went off Effexor against his doctor's advice and had horrible brain zaps, shocks to his head, for months afterward. What if she got a brain zap in the middle of her lunch with Adam Epstein—at Gemma, where everyone would see?

She was going to jail. They were going to find her on the tape, and she'd have no defense. She wouldn't even be able to say she was researching a role, because Winona had already tried that, and it had turned her into a punch line.

Get a grip, get a grip. She swallowed a huge gulp of wine. *Take it easy.* She had a tendency toward obsessive rumination—that was what Dr. Levine called it when you kept playing out negative outcomes in your head. She took two Ativans from her table drawer and let them dissolve under her tongue so they would work more quickly. She'd gotten this tip from her aesthetician, who told her during a treatment that she took one milligram of Ativan a day, every three hours, sublingually.

Calm down. Cool it. Maybe she was jumping the gun. Maybe there wasn't even a camera in the area where she'd been standing. And even if there was, the lighting in the Coop was so fluorescent and distorting that she would probably be unrecognizable.

But there was other evidence besides the tape. The wallet. The wallet! What if Stuart discovered it and was planning to turn her in? She hated the fact that she was worrying about this, but she didn't trust him. Lately they had no rapport, and they weren't a team.

She opened the bedside table drawer and took out the copy of *Eat, Pray, Love,* feeling for the wallet beneath. It was gone! Like a terrier after a rat, she pawed through the items: the pills, the Tweezerman, Youth!, La Mer, and the anal beads. Trying to cover every square inch of the drawer, she pulled it out as far she could, and the drawer tumbled out onto the floor upside down.

She went around to Stuart's side and rifled through his drawer, too, but all he had were a couple of movie scripts, a novel called *Bangkok*

Nights, and *Balance Through Ayurveda.* She bounded to the playroom, opened each of the toy chests, and threw the contents on the floor. She ransacked Orion's bedroom. Nothing. She dialed Annika. "Did you take anything from my room?" She could hear children playing in the background.

"What do you mean?"

"There was something in my bedroom, and it's mithing. Missing."

"It wasn't me, Melora."

"So someone else took it?"

"No. No one's been in your room."

"What about Orion?"

"I don't let him in there when you're not around. Maybe it was the housekeepers. You should ask them." The housekeepers were a Burmese brother-sister pair who also worked for Liev and Naomi; Melora doubted they would do anything that might jeopardize their chance at political asylum.

"If you had someone over here and you're lying about it, I'm going to find out." Melora was certain Annika was hiding something. She'd never liked the Swede—the girl played everything too close to the belt.

"Has Orion had any playdates, any friends over?"

There was a pause and then Annika said, "No. All his friends are away."

Annika was a lousy nanny to the stars because she didn't know how to lie. Melora would check with Shivan later.

She brought the bottle and glass from the master into the adjoining bathroom and drank from the glass as she ran the bath. Maybe the cops were already onto her. They'd staked out her mansion and sent in detectives to retrieve the evidence in the middle of the night. They knew what she'd done, and they were going to arrest her right in the middle of her Epstein, for the extra publicity. With Bloomberg as mayor, the NYPD was just as bad as the LAPD, victimizing celebrities to prove a point.

She poured some L'Occitane Lavender Harvest bath salts into the tub and watched the bubbles form. She could feel the Ativan and the wine working already, creating a halo of calm around her brain. Ativan allowed you to see the awful things that were going to happen without worrying about them. It didn't make you delusional; it made you capable. *Everything's going to be fine.*

She got in the hot bath. She had to be Buddhist and have faith that things would work out, or twelve-step and let go and let God, or listen to Dr. Levine and not waste time worrying when operating with incomplete information. The third was the hardest thing to do, but these benzodiazepines helped. One tiny pill—or had she had two?—produced the same effect as thirty years of practicing meditation. Stuart spent all that time in his Zendo, and she didn't get it. Why would anyone choose the long route when there was a short one?

She sank her head beneath the bubbles, closed her eyes, then came up and finished the glass of wine, setting it beside the tub. The still half-full bottle was on the marble sink vanity, sweating. *More wine!* She had to have more wine! She began to salivate; the bottle seemed to salivate, too.

But in order to get it, she would have to get out of the tub.

The water was so warm, and the last thing she wanted to do was get out when her muscles were starting to relax. She could stay in the bath and try Shivan from the bathroom phone, but she didn't want Shivan to know that she was drinking in the morning. This was one of those times when she really wished she hadn't fired Lisanne.

With reluctance, she climbed out of the tub, put one foot on the Italian marble floor, and reached for the sink. As she did, her wet foot slipped out from under her, and her forehead slammed into the beveled edge of the vanity. "Goddamnit!"

It hurt like hell, but she was distantly aware that she didn't really care. She saw spots before her eyes. When they finally cleared, she looked into the mirror. There was a gash above her right eye, dripping blood down her cheek. It was like looking at someone else's face. She rinsed off the blood, but the cut above her eye was still oozing. She grabbed a few tissues and pressed them against the cut, then removed them to inspect the damage. It was deep, so deep she probably needed stitches.

But she couldn't afford an emergency call to her plastic surgeon, Dr. Resnick, who had done such a wonderful job with her thigh lipo. From her mood he would suspect she'd taken things and insist on calling Dr. Levine, who might want to have her committed. And even if it were someplace safe, like Silver Hill, where she'd enjoyed a very pleasant coke rehab in 1998, she couldn't jeopardize the Adam Epstein lunch. But as she stared at the blood dripping down her face and the hollow, crazed look in her eyes, it occurred to her, in a mild, distant, Ativanian way, that it was possible she already had.

Play Ground

REBECCA TOOK Abbie to the Lincoln-Berkeley playground when she was feeling burnt out on the Third Street playground übermoms. The playground stretched from Lincoln Place to Berkeley Place and was next to P.S. 282, an elementary school with mostly black and Hispanic students. Lincoln-Berkeley drew a more low-key crowd than Third Street, perhaps because of its proximity to Fifth Avenue, which had lower property values than the streets closer to Prospect Park. Despite its limited shade, ugly asphalt, and outdated play structures, it was a favorite of the West Indian and Tibetan nannies and their charges.

It was noon, getting close to lunchtime, and Rebecca was hoping to tire Abbie out before her nap. The sprinklers were on when she got there, but Abbie screamed when Rebecca put her in, so she took her over to the swings. Rebecca noticed Cathleen Meth a few feet away, pushing Jones. Evidently, the übermoms had found out about Lincoln-Berkeley.

"I didn't know you came here," Cathleen said.

"I live really close," Rebecca said.

"I'm staying away from the playground parks for the time being. Did you hear about the pigeon?"

Rebecca shook her head, and Cathleen told her about a black boy who had killed a pigeon on Harmony playground. The story was so grotesque that Rebecca wasn't even sure it was true. "How did you find out?" she asked.

"I read about it on Park Slope Parents." Jones made a face, and Cathleen leaned in and looked at him. Then she made some weird clicking noises and he made them back. A few minutes later she had removed a portable yellow potty from her diaper bag and planted Jones on it with his pants down, clicking her tongue against her teeth. "We're doing EC," she told Rebecca.

"What's that?"

"Elimination communication. He's basically toilet-trained."

"But he's not even two."

"I started at six months. He always had his number two in the morning, so I would take him to the potty and read to him, and he got used to never going in his diaper." Cathleen clicked some more. Surely this woman had something better to do with her time than toilet-train a baby, Rebecca thought, before realizing that in Park Slope that was never the case.

After another minute of what was apparently a lack of action, Cathleen said, "Maybe you don't have to go," whisked up Jones's pants, and carted him away in her arms.

Over Cathleen's shoulder Rebecca saw him scrunch up his face. Then he let out a grunt and Cathleen cried out, "Oh, Jones!" and raced him to the water fountain to clean him.

Rebecca noticed some motion by the nearby Lincoln Place gate and turned to look. She was always looking at the playground gates in hopes that someone exciting would come in. She was almost always disappointed.

This time she wasn't. It was Stuart, holding Orion's hand and telling him what appeared to be an elaborate story. Rebecca could feel sweat dripping down her armpits and wondered how long it would take for it to smell. Still, she felt good about her wardrobe selection—a short denim miniskirt, a sleeveless tight Joe's Jeans shell with a unicorn on it, and wraparound gladiator sandals. Her long hair was in two braids, and she wore a pair of amber Ray-Bans. As Stuart entered the playground, she looked away, heart thudding, but he had already seen her and said,

"It's you." He came to the iron fence dividing the swing area from the playground.

"I bet you thought you wouldn't see me till the next shift," she said.

"No, I had a feeling I would see you before then. It's that kind of neighborhood. Eventually, you run into everyone you know."

"What do you mean?" she said. "You guys don't know anyone around here. You're too famous."

"Sure we do." Orion bolted into the sprinklers, where he sat on one of them, draped his shirt over, and filled it up so it ballooned out.

"Okay, name three friends you've made since you moved here," Rebecca said. "And you're not allowed to count anyone in a service industry."

"Well, there's the guy who owns Blue Apron Foods—"

"Ah-ah," she said, wagging her finger.

"Okay, there's our lovely FedEx guy, Mark—" She shot him a look. "Wait a minute! I've got one. I had a very pleasant chat with a fellow next to me on the StairMaster at Eastern Athletic."

"What's his name?"

"John Henry. So there."

"John Henry's a trainer! I used him for a couple months till it got too expensive."

"I guess you're right. We're dicks."

She wanted him to whisk her off to an alley and pound her against a wall, but there weren't any alleys in Park Slope except Fiske Place and Polhemus Place, and they were just short streets. She wanted to put her mouth on his and taste if his breath was salty or sweet. She wanted to live with him in a house far away where he kept her on a leash and made her go by a different name.

"So what have you been doing to stay cool in this weather?" she asked.

"Not enough."

Orion came over and tugged at his father's shirt. "Come in the water, Daddy!"

"I don't have a change of clothes, sweetie."

"Take off your shirt," Rebecca said. "Give these mothers something to dream about."

Stuart hesitated and then took off his T-shirt and ran in with Orion. Stuart's torso was built but lean. His skin was pale and freckled, and he didn't look like as much of a gym bunny as Rebecca had expected, which she liked. Most Hollywood actors were overpumped. The boy howled with laughter, and he and Stuart ran back and forth a few times, Stuart carrying him and spinning him around.

Rebecca took Abbie out of the swing and over to the baby slide. After a few minutes Stuart came over, sopping wet and panting, and sat on a bench nearby. To Rebecca's disappointment, he put his gray shirt back on. It said CONEY ISLAND STEEPLECHASE and was one of those expensive fake-retro shirts that probably cost eighty dollars at Barneys.

"I was thinking about your screenplay," she said.

He perked up. "Yeah?"

"And I think it has a lot of potential. I mean, the whole idea of post-9/11 paranoia is really interesting. No one's ever made a movie about it. About how that event changed New Yorkers, changed the way they look at each other. In a way *Do the Right Thing* was the best 9/11 film ever made, and that came out before it happened."

"That's one of my main models for the script! A perfect film! Although it would have been better if it were eighteen minutes shorter."

"I think you should let me read it. I mean, I'm not Syd Field or anything, but I feel like I could help you with the mise-en-scène."

"The what?" He looked at her like she was pretentious. It struck Rebecca that she might have blown the whole thing. "I had a chance with a Hollywood star once," she'd tell Abbie someday, "but then I said 'mise-en-scène' and totally cockblocked myself."

"You know, the design aspects. I'm good at that, and I know the neighborhood really well. I'll write some—what do you call it? Coverage. And I could give you some advice on that female character. You know, the cop. Are you going to cast Melora?"

He got an uncomfortable look and said, "Actually, I was thinking of Maggie Gyllenhaal."

"Really? How come you don't want to cast Melora?"

He said, "Melora's booked for the next four years."

There was obviously some drama between them. She had to stop this line of conversation. When you wanted a married man, you couldn't make him think about his wife.

"What the hell," he said after a beat:

"What do you mean?"

"I'll show you my screenplay. It could use a fresh pair of eyes."

"Why don't you bring it over sometime?"

"Give me your number." She told it to him and he typed it into his iPhone.

"The best time is during Abbie's nap," she said. "Or on one of my sitter days, Tuesdays or Thursdays."

Cathleen Meth, a clean Jones in her arms, was approaching with Jane, who as usual had Emily in the sling. "Hi, Rebecca," said Cathleen, blinking at Stuart. The women stood there, waiting to be introduced but Rebecca refused to indulge them. Finally, Cathleen couldn't take it any longer; she leaned in to Stuart and said, "You were so great in *End of the Day*."

"Totally robbed of that Oscar," said Jane.

"You don't want to have too many in one household," he said.

"I've always wanted to know," Cathleen said. "What does Melora do with hers? I mean, where do you keep them?"

"One's a toilet paper dispenser," Stuart said, "and we use the other one on Orion when he gets out of control."

"You use the other one on Orion!" Jane said, tittering.

"So how do you two know each other?" Cathleen asked.

"Summer camp in Vermont," Rebecca said. "He was a dishwasher, I was a camper. Very sordid story." She waited for him to correct her, to be pragmatic, but he seemed to enjoy getting a rise out of them as much as she did.

"Let's just say it's a miracle I was allowed back in the country," he said.

The women looked at them, confused, not sure whether to believe it. Rebecca wanted to get away from them, but she didn't want to leave him alone with them, either. She couldn't bear the thought of sharing him with these harpies.

"Stuart?" she said. "Would you mind helping me out with my stroller?" She angled her head to the Berkeley Place exit, where she had parked the Maclaren.

"What's wrong with it?" asked Cathleen.

"I'm having some trouble with my left wheel."

"You know, there's a store in Brooklyn Heights that—"

Rebecca grabbed Stuart's arm and ushered him toward the gate. He knelt and pretended to look at the wheel, murmuring, "They were scary. Real stickybeaks, eh?"

"Yeah. I don't know how either one got a guy hard enough to make a baby."

"Me, neither. I saw a fat mum on Seventh Avenue bending down to talk to her kid, and there was a leopard-print cotton thong coming out of her ass. It had a Victoria's Secret label. I thought, *No secret there.*"

"Some guys are into BBWs."

"What's that?"

"Big beautiful women. It's a fetish."

"How do you know about all this?"

"I did a story on female body image for *Glamour*. They wanted something positive about large women, so I interviewed these BBW fetishist guys. Most of them are very . . . small." She strapped Abbie into the stroller.

"You going?" he asked.

"It's too hot for her," she said, thinking it was better to keep him wanting more. "Let me know when I can read *Atlantic Yards*."

She walked to the gate and tried to push it open before realizing it pulled. All the gates pulled in, to make it harder for little kids to get out. She winced, feeling like an idiot. She'd only done this about seven hundred times, but the one time she wanted to look cool, she got it wrong. When she looked back at Stuart, he was flashing a big sarcastic thumbs-up.

On Saying Yes

MELORA AWOKE in her bed at four that afternoon to the sound of her ringing phone. For one brief beautiful moment she didn't think about the *Coop Courier,* but then it all came crashing back like a nightmare.

Maybe it's Dr. Levine. I'll go to his office and he'll help me and everything will be all right. But when she grabbed the phone from her bedside table, she saw Cassie Trainor's name.

Melora and Cassie had met at the 2006 Glamour Women of the Year awards at Carnegie Hall and became instant BFFs. They were often photographed attending premiere parties, shopping, and dining at posh restaurants. Because of the fifteen-year age difference between them, the photos always had captions like "Educating Cassie" or "Mama and Cass."

"Are you coming to my Southpaw thing tonight?" came the pipsqueak voice. For the past few weeks Melora had been out of touch with Cassie, not in the mood to go out and not wanting to be around anyone. She remembered that Cassie had e-mailed her about it—something literary—but Melora had deleted it and then forgotten.

"Oh, sweetie, I totally spaced. I have that Adam Epstein lunch tomorrow, so I was going to go to bed early."

Melora considered the possibility of confessing what she had done. Cassie had taken every drug imaginable and was an avowed nymphomaniac, so Melora didn't think she would be overly judgmental. Still, there was nothing Cassie could do to help her, and Melora was so paranoid she thought at this point it was better that nobody know.

"But I was hoping you'd be there," Cassie said.

"What was it for again?" Melora asked, going to her Majorelle and fishing out a pack of American Spirits.

"The *Paris Review* fund-raiser," Cassie said as Melora opened the balcony door. "I'm playing a few songs and then doing a discussion with Philip Gourevitch. I'm so nervous. He's an expert on genocide, and I have to talk to him about process. There's going to be, like, two hundred people there, and I hate public speaking, which is why I want you to come. Are you smoking?"

"You know I quit," Melora said. She held the phone away from her mouth and blew the smoke out onto the street. "So why'd you agree to do it?"

"David's friends with Phil. I guess Philip Gourevitch thought if I did this, it would be good for the magazine. Help them get a younger demo. It's at eight. You'll be home by ten."

"I have to rest, Cass," Melora said. "You'll tell me all about it."

"You never do anything anymore. You used to be a yes person, but now you're a no person. Like in that piece by Dave Eggers."

Melora had met Dave Eggers briefly at a party at Vince Vaughn's house several years before but had never gotten around to reading any of his books. She couldn't remember the last book she'd read. Probably *The Reader,* the spring before, after Kate and Nicole pulled out but before Kate signed on again. "What piece?" she asked.

"On saying yes. He says, 'What matters is saying yes. Saying no is so fucking boring.' I'm putting you on the guest list. Bring Stu."

After she hung up, Melora went into the bathroom, removed the butterfly Band-Aid she had affixed to her gash, and inspected the damage. It had clotted over, but it was ugly, and there was no way she could cover it up with makeup. It would only look worse tomorrow.

She dialed Levine and left another message, then opened the medicine chest and took out the vial of Zoloft. She swallowed a pill. Then another for good measure. It would take a while to work, but the placebo effect could kick in sooner. She took an Ativan from the vial she kept next to the Zoloft and broke it in half. How many had she taken so far? It was so hard to keep track. As long as it was under eight, she'd be all right. That was what it said on the label. The label instructions were like the gas gauge on your car: too conservative to be believed.

What killed Melora was that she had brought the whole situation upon herself, all because of her hunger for some extra press. There were a lot of things you could do when you needed press, but only idiots went and joined smelly, overcrowded socialist food coops.

She was startled by a knock on the bathroom door. She hadn't thought anyone else was home. No one was ever home. "Honey?"

She threw some water on her face, put on a fresh Band-Aid, grabbed a white towel, and wrapped it low, turban-style, around her head. She opened the door.

"You all right?" Stuart said. "When I came in, you were sleeping."

She wanted to trust him, to tell him everything. Maybe he could help her—when she had that breast cancer scare a few years before, he had been very levelheaded, and when *People* magazine put her on the worst-dressed list after the 2007 Oscars, he had been cool about that, too.

But she was terrified. Children loved you unconditionally but not adults. He had seen the change in her over the past few years, and he didn't seem to like it. If she told him what she had done, it would only push him further away. His love had faded into something paternal and distant.

"I went running this morning," she said. "It tired me out."

"You ran? That's great, honey," he said, wrapping his arms around her and kissing her neck.

He could come with her to Cassie's gig. She should say yes. At best, it would be a distraction from all her worries. At worst, it beat lying in bed replaying every sentence of the Coop newspaper article.

"Cassie's doing this interview tonight for a *Paris Review* fund-raiser," she said. "I was thinking we'd go."

"I was going to try to get some writing done tonight," he said.

He was always working on that goddamned screenplay. And now he was sending it to Maggie Gyllenhaal. Melora's greatest fear was that *Atlantic Yards* would get made, elevate him to a new level in his career, and make a real star out of Gyllenhaal. Then they would fall in love during shooting and he'd leave Melora to be with her . . .

She stared at him, trying to tell him that she was about to go under but that he could save her if he would only keep her company. "Please come with me," she said.

"If it means that much to you," he said with a shrug.

Melora and Stuart took a cherry-scented Family car service Lincoln Continental to Southpaw, even though Stuart suggested they walk. Melora, who had explored little in her years in the neighborhood, wasn't sure where on Fifth Avenue Southpaw was located, so Stuart directed the driver. Stuart walked around Park Slope a lot exploring locations for *Atlantic Yards,* a habit Melora found incredibly irritating, since the film wasn't yet a done deal.

The driver was obese and listening to blaring Spanish radio. Stuart and Melora had given up their car and driver, Ringo, at the same time they gave up their assistants, agreeing that it was better for the environment. Melora regretted this now, feeling ill from the freshener.

She cracked the window and breathed in the summer air. She was wearing her hair over her face to hide the Band-Aid. So far he hadn't seemed to notice. She hoped she could hide it from Adam Epstein the next day.

She kept thinking about the missing wallet in the drawer. Whoever had taken it was on to her and wanted to hurt her. Was Stuart *Gaslight-*ing her? Melora had been up for the Ingrid Bergman role in a Callie Khouri remake a few years before, and she had watched the original as research. It had struck a chord with her—the way Boyer tricked Bergman into believing she was crazy, all so he could search the attic for her aunt's jewels. He talked to her in such a patronizing way, and Bergman had so little self-esteem she had no choice but to act like a child.

"I love that skirt on you," Stuart said, and raised it up over her knees, massaging her thigh. She was wearing a blue organza Sonia Rykiel ankle-length skirt and a Marc by Marc Jacobs white-and-polka-dot smock from his 2004 cruise wear collection. "So how are you feeling about the lunch?"

It was the worst question he could have asked her. She was afraid that even with the Ativan, she wouldn't be able to sleep that night and she would show up to the meeting bleary and inarticulate. "You know," she said with a shrug.

"I think you get too worried about these things. Just be yourself and you'll be fine."

But this wasn't true. To be herself was to be withdrawn and sullen, and with everything that had happened, it was going to take enormous might merely to come off as stable.

"You're right," she said. "I'm always too hard on myself."

When they got out on Fifth Avenue, there was a line of skinny white guys and fat Goth girls stretching all the way around the corner. The girls were there because of Cassie's mordant lyrics, and the guys were there because of her well-regarded cameo in the second *Harold and Kumar* movie.

They paid the driver, and Stuart escorted Melora swiftly to the door as some of the hipsters gawked. Inside, Melora gave the check-in girl their names, and she handed them two tickets that said "VIP."

Melora headed straight for the bar and ordered a dry martini. Stuart got a beer. When he wasn't looking, she slipped a half Zoloft into her mouth with another Ativan and swallowed them with the martini.

She downed the drink quickly and then asked for a second. "Your meeting tomorrow," Stuart said. "Maybe you should take it easy." He was acting so protective, but his eyes looked fishy. Why was he so invested in her meeting? He was a huge Adam Epstein fan and had been since *The Undescended*. He knew Epstein's Hollywood stock had gone up lately, with the box office success of *Mumbai Express* and his upcoming Lemony Snicket adaptation with Michael Chabon. Maybe Stuart wanted to slip *Atlantic Yards* to Adam Epstein and was afraid he'd lose the chance if Melora lost the role.

He squeezed her shoulder protectively. It was hard to know what was in her head and what was real. Dr. Levine would tell her to try to separate her problems and not—what was the word he used?—catastrophize. Only when you separated things could you begin to deal with them.

She drank the second martini in four fast gulps. Why oh why had she put that wallet in her drawer? Why hadn't she done what a normal criminal would do and tossed it in a garbage can on the way home?

She thought she heard her phone ringing in her bag and pulled it out to see if it was Dr. Levine, but when she looked, there weren't any new messages. Stuart was eyeing her suspiciously, so she pretended to type a text message.

The lights were dimming, and they went to the tiny VIP section in the back, a raised platform with a dozen chairs. Brooklyn was an awful place to be important. The venues were unsegregated, and none of the restaurants had back rooms.

Penny Arcade, Ryan McGinley, Zac Posen, Michelle Williams, and Spike Jonze were all there with friends, sitting in metal folding chairs. She pictured their faces as they read about her pickpocketing trial in the tabloids, laughing at her misfortune.

Zac, who had designed the Oscar dress she had worn the night she'd won for *Poses,* waved to Melora. She smiled through clenched teeth. As she climbed the steep stairs to get to her seat, her heel caught on the carpeting, and her foot buckled beneath her at an odd angle. It felt like it was exploding. "Are you okay?" Ryan McGinley asked.

"I'm fine, I'm fine."

"Are you sure you're all right, honey?" Stuart asked, helping her up. "It looks like a sprain."

"Of course I'm all right!" she snapped. It was sprained, she could feel it, but what was she going to do—hobble out of Southpaw like a loser before the show even started? If she went to a doctor, he might insist on keeping her overnight or putting it in a cast. She couldn't meet Adam Epstein in a cast.

She limped carefully to her seat, passing her wince off as a grin. "I told you not to order that second martini," Stuart said as they sat.

She wanted to smack him. Who did he think he was, telling her what to drink? She had fallen only because the steps were so steep. It had been a terrible idea coming here. She should have followed her first instinct and stayed in bed.

Cassie and Philip Gourevitch came onstage, and the audience clapped for a long time. Cassie was wearing a heather-blue pocket

T-shirt and black jeans. Her shoulders were bony, and her hair was twisted into a sloppy bun. Philip Gourevitch joined the audience in applauding her, and when the noise finally died down, he thanked her for coming.

"I'm really nervous," Cassie said. "I didn't want to do this. Just don't be mean, okay? I can't stand it when people are mean." She was so childlike and sullen. Melora had spent her career trying hard to please people, and Cassie had spent hers trying not to. Now Cassie was more successful, and Melora wondered if she'd approached it all wrong.

"I won't be mean," said Gourevitch. "I'm going to start with a banal question: Can you describe a typical day?"

"Well, the first thing I think about when I wake up is what colors I'm going to wear."

"You mean what will match?"

"No, it's not about that," she snapped. "It's more about the way different colors emotionally inform things. The palate, I mean? Like this morning it took me four hours to get dressed."

"And is this outfit what you were wearing this morning?"

"Of course. You think I changed for you?"

"I don't know." He did a smirk to the audience, and there was a faint titter.

"I need to make sure that the colors I'm wearing match my mood. So, anyway, I spend a lot of time thinking about what colors to wear, and then I feed my cats."

"What do your cats wear?" Gourevitch asked.

"They don't wear anything," Cassie said, irritated. "They're cats." Philip Gourevitch mugged to the audience. Cassie noticed this and looked down, brooding. Melora had no idea why she had agreed to do this.

And yet Cassie seemed to have the audience's sympathy. No one was mocking her for her words. They were on the edge of their seats.

Melora was jealous. This crazy-beautiful thing worked for Cassie. If Cassie had a meeting with Adam Epstein, she could act as blitzed out as she wanted, and it would only make him want her more. Melora was fifteen years too old to get away with that.

"Do you consider yourself obsessive?"

"I'm very OCD. If you read the *Spin* interview that's out right now, I talk a lot about that. I was on medication for it, but now I'm off it." This made Melora nervous. Cassie hadn't said anything about this the last few times they had talked. "I feel like I have my life back. It's good for my art. I don't think anyone who's medicated can be a real artist. It's kind of a copout. When your instruments are your brain and your heart, you can't pollute them with all that stuff."

Melora's ankle was screaming for attention, and she didn't know how much longer she could stay. She kept thinking about the meeting the next day. Even if she could hide the cut over her eye, how could she hide the limp? She looked like a charity case. She was going to show up looking like she'd been in a car wreck. That was useless for an Adam Epstein picture—a Cronenberg, maybe, but not an Adam Epstein.

Girls' Night

REBECCA HAD worn a red Splendid V-neck and tweed pencil skirt to the Cassie Trainor gig because she wanted to look good but not like she was trying to look good. Underneath her shirt was a Wacoal Halo bra she had bought before she got pregnant and had been delighted to find she could still fill. Theo had agreed to babysit, saying he was looking forward to "girls' night with Abbie," a half-joke that Rebecca found unfunny.

Rebecca almost never went out at night anymore. After she and Theo had gotten married, the party invitations stopped coming—when you were a married woman, no one was interested in you. Only three years before, she had been on Bret Easton Ellis's Christmas-party list; now she had to pull teeth just to get invited to the *Elle* party, which was boring anyway.

She had considered inviting Lizzie along to Southpaw but worried her friend would embarrass her. Lizzie seemed like she never got out. And she had become so intense and needy since that first misguided kiss—with her thank-you note and the bottle of wine—that Rebecca was considering cutting her off.

When Rebecca came in the club, Cassie and Philip were taking the stage. She found a seat halfway back and craned her neck to the VIP section to see if David was there, looking proud of his girlfriend. She didn't spot him, but sitting next to Ryan McGinley and Zac Posen were Stuart Ashby and Melora Leigh.

She turned her head quickly back to the stage, her heart jumping to her throat. Stuart knew Cassie? Or maybe Melora did. It was as though fate was intervening to make sure Rebecca and Stuart saw each other again. Maybe he would stay after the show and she would get to speak to him, joke with him. She would also have to meet Melora Leigh, but that was all right. She'd never seen her up close, and now she could find out if she had acne or bad hair.

After the show, which culminated in Cassie dancing wildly while singing some new dark tunes accompanying herself on guitar, Rebecca went to the bar to buy a drink. David approached, kissed her on the cheek, and said, "So what did you think?"

"Intense. Where were you sitting? I didn't see you in the audience."

"I was too nervous. I was in the wings."

David Keller had been waiting his whole life to say things like "I was in the wings" about his girlfriend, Cassie Trainor. Rebecca tried to imagine what her life would be like if she and David had stayed together. He probably would have left her for someone like Cassie.

Still, if they had married and had a child, she didn't think David would have stopped having sex with her. He wouldn't want to replace a woman with a baby. David scoped every attractive woman he passed on the street, and even when he and Rebecca had fought, it only seemed to make their sex better. Theo, even before their problems, had never been into makeup sex or angry sex. He liked to do it only when they were getting along. Before Abbie, that was most of the time.

Melora was coming over to the bar with Stuart on her arm. She looked angry, and she seemed to be limping. Rebecca wondered if Melora came easily, like the Charlize Theron character in *Celebrity*, and if they did it every night. Their nanny was probably a live-in, so child care never got in the way of sex. They could jet off to Cabo San Lucas whenever they wanted. To narcissists and the rich, separation parenting came instinctively. They could write a book for Gen X moms called *Famous Women Don't Stop Fucking*.

David waved excitedly and beckoned Stuart and Melora over. "How do you know them?" Rebecca asked David.

"Melora and Cassie are very close." Rebecca wondered what David thought of Cassie's histrionics. Did he see her the way Rebecca did—

narcissistic and unstable—or was he so whipped that he could only see her as vulnerable?

When Stuart saw Rebecca, he squinted, surprised, and seemed to flush. It flattered her that she could make him blush. David kissed Melora on the cheek and shook Stuart's hand but didn't introduce Rebecca. She could feel David's discomfort, his nervousness that she was going to shame him in front of these important people, and she wanted to scream at him not to assume she was worthless just because she had a kid.

"What happened to your foot?" David asked Melora.

"Oh, I slipped a little on my way in. It's nothing."

David seemed to determine that he had an obligation to introduce his civilian ex-girlfriend to his celebrity friends and said, "Melora, Stuart, this is Rebecca Rose." Rebecca shook their hands. Stuart held her palm a second longer than was appropriate, but Melora didn't pick up on it.

"Rebecca has the most adorable little girl," David said. "Who's watching her tonight?"

"Her dad." Rebecca was standing face-to-face with a two-time Oscar winner, and he had to humiliate her by bringing up Abbie. It was as though he was trying to distance himself from her, his own high status as a Cassie Trainor–dating bachelor from her low status as a Park Slope mother of a toddler.

"How come when a woman goes out," Rebecca said to David, "everyone asks who's taking care of the kid, but when a man goes out, it's assumed that his wife is?" Melora chuckled. Maybe she wasn't so bad after all.

"Because a woman's role is in the home," said Stuart.

"Shut up, Stuart," Melora said, weaving a little. She was drunk. So this was why he was unhappy: His wife was a lush.

"I think you guys live right near me," Rebecca told Melora.

"Oh yeah?" Stuart said, raising an eyebrow.

"I'm on Carroll between Eighth and the park. I love what you've done with the garden." Melora seemed irritated that Rebecca knew not only that she lived in the Slope but the precise location of her home. Celebrities felt entitled to privacy even when they made a public-relations choice to live among the masses.

"So how old is your daughter?" Stuart asked Rebecca. There was a twinkle in his eye, as though he enjoyed pretending they'd never met.

"One and a half."

"Cute age," he said.

"How old is your son now?" Rebecca asked Melora. "Four?"

"Yes," Melora said curtly.

"I've heard four is terrible," Rebecca said. "Very oppositional."

"A little," said Melora, "but at least he can wipe his own ass. I hated changing all those diapers."

"What are you talking about?" Stuart asked. "You never changed any."

"You're a liar!" she said. "I changed them all the time!"

"No, you didn't, honey. I did. And the nannies."

She shot him a death glance and stormed off. Rebecca and David watched as Stuart followed her. They exchanged words, Melora gesticulating angrily.

How could Stuart stand being with someone so stuck up? Maybe it was a turn-on to him that she was such a bitch, and what he really wanted was a woman who would boss him around. If he did, then Rebecca had nothing to offer. She wanted Stuart to boss her around, order her to mop his floor, take calls from Hollywood while he was inside her mouth.

Rebecca had seen a side of herself in Melora. She had spent the last year and a half of her life bitching at Theo. She bitched at him for everything imaginable except the one thing she was really angry about. She yelled at him if he left the bathroom floor a little wet after washing his hands. She told him his dinners were mediocre or had been prepared better the last time. She mocked him when he farted in bed because it made her feel that he didn't want to be sexy to her. She harangued him for staying too long in the office or bailing on her when she wanted to go to a restaurant. She never asked him about his work, and when he told her about it, she listened with only one ear. Because she was so hurt by his rejection, she felt that he didn't deserve any of the pleasures that came along with having a wife.

Stuart and Melora were still arguing, and she could see Melora heading toward the door, scowling. Stuart tried to follow, but his wife shook him off violently, and then he shouted something ugly back that Rebecca couldn't make out. People were staring. It was a big deal to see a public couple publicly fighting. Rebecca was pretty sure she beat Stuart and Melora in the lousy-marriage department, but at least in her case, nobody had to know.

American Spirit

"IT'S HUMILIATING!" Melora was shouting.

"Well, it's true. You didn't do nappies. It was always me or Fatou." Fatou was the Senegalese nanny they'd had on Spring Street. "You want everyone to think you're a supermom, but that's a lie."

"I changed diapers, and you know I did!" she said, hearing the words slurring in her mouth. She definitely had changed a few. He was always rewriting history. That was half the reason she felt crazy all the time.

"You're drunk."

"I'm not drunk. You don't understand anything about me. You don't know me."

"No one knows you, Melora."

That was it. "You're such a self-satisfied prick!" she cried.

"What?"

"That's a line from your movie! 'No one knows you, Lucy.' That's what the Al Qaeda guy says after they sleep together!"

"Look at you. You can't even walk straight."

"It's nothing, it's not even a twist. I'm fine!"

"Let me take you home so you can rest it."

"You're not taking me anywhere!" A few heads turned to stare. She spun on her six-hundred-dollar Stephane Kélian heel and stumbled out. She wanted him to follow, but the door shut behind her with a thud.

Everything was going to pieces. Her brow was throbbing as she headed onto Fifth Avenue. She needed a cigarette. The Ativan, Zoloft, and martinis had gone to her head.

A group of young hipsters was standing on the sidewalk in front of Southpaw, smoking and deconstructing Cassie's performance, a stringy-haired blond girl attesting that the new songs were her best since "Stick Your Finger Down My Throat." Melora kept her head down and moved to the side of the door, fumbling for her pack of American Spirits.

She put a cigarette to her mouth, rummaged for a light, and realized she'd left the lighter on the balcony at home. A skinny guy in a maroon trucker cap that said ODESSA COMPRESSOR REPAIR was smoking and talking to some friends. Making sure her hair was covering the cut, she assumed the slouching posture of a bored Gen Y–er and asked for a light. The guy looked up and seemed to recognize her but said nothing. These kids were too cool to kiss up.

He removed a Zippo from his pocket, and Melora reached to take it, but he shook it open with a flourish, and the shiny blond mane, which had commanded $3 million in a national Garnier campaign, caught on fire.

She saw the flame before she felt it. "Oh my God!" she screamed. She dove to the ground and rolled on the pavement as Odessa hit her head with something again and again. The motion around her stopped, and she realized the flame was out, although she could smell the singed hair.

"Jesus Christ!" Odessa screamed. "I'm so sorry!"

Stunned, Melora rose to her feet. The hipsters were gaping at her in shock, confused by the conflicting emotions of witnessing something horrifying and witnessing it happening to a celebrity.

He offered her a hand, but she shook him off and stood up herself. Her head felt like it was still on fire. She smelled the September-eleventh-like stink of burnt hair.

She could tell by their stunned looks, their incredulous squints, that it wasn't good. This was *Rescue Me*.

"You fucking asshole!" she said.

"I'm really sorry!" he said. "It was an accident!"

"You're a goddamn moron!" She swiveled toward a window behind her and inhaled sharply at the reflection. To the left of her left temple was a beach barbecue pit the morning after. She ran her hand over it, remembering the last time her hair had been this short: at eleven, when she did a low-budget feature shot on Long Island about the children of the Terezin concentration camp.

This did not bode well for her Adam Epstein meeting. You didn't want to look holocaust unless you were up for a holocaust role. Why had she gotten herself into this mess?

If only she hadn't taken so many Ativans. If only she hadn't taken the wallet. If only she'd taken the wallet but tossed it in a can. If only she hadn't cut her brow. She was beginning to wonder how she'd gotten through the first thirty-nine years of her life intact.

She pulled at the remaining long hair by her ear to see if there was any chance of covering the patch but there wasn't enough. She couldn't pull a combover.

She could feel the Cassie groupies staring at her as she regarded her reflection. Odessa called out, "Do you want us to call 911?" Without answering, Melora turned and limped up Fifth Avenue, not sure where she was headed but certain that she had to get away.

Sophomoric

WHEN STUART came back to David and Rebecca, he looked rattled. "Sorry about that," he said.

"Is everything okay?" David asked.

"She's under a lot of pressure right now. So where's Cassie, anyway? I thought she was going to socialize," Stuart said.

"Downstairs," David said. "I should go be with her, actually."

"Philip Gourevitch was too hard on her," Rebecca said. "I mean, Cassie's just a singer. She's not committing genocide or anything."

"I *know*," David said.

"Although some might consider that second album a form of genocide," she added.

At this Stuart let out a chuckle. "The critics were savages," David said, frowning. "They wanted her to have the sophomore curse."

"Well, the album was nothing if not sophomoric," said Stuart.

Rebecca grinned. They were conspirators. She wanted a conspirator almost as much as she wanted a lover. David looked from one to the other, but she didn't care that they'd pissed him off. It was way more fun mocking Cassie Trainor than showing Cassie Trainor baby pictures on her cell phone. And she had the courage only because Stuart egged her on.

She thought about David's massive success and hot famous girl-friend, and then she thought about *Willow Grove,* the novel stowed in a container under the bed with her winter clothes, and realized she hadn't even looked at it since Abbie was born. She had been stung when she got all those rejections, unable to think about reworking it or even start-ing a new one. She'd heard stories about writers who got a lot of rejec-tions before something took off, but when nine publishers rejected you, all with vague reasons, it meant you weren't a writer.

Instead of feeling bitter and angry, she felt like it all came down to luck. David Keller wasn't more brilliant than she was, just luckier. She'd been off track for a while, busy with Abbie, but in the fall Abbie would start Beansprouts preschool two days a week, and Rebecca was hoping to get back to the novel. All mothers took time off after they had kids to get their priorities in order. The only thing separating her from David Keller was focus.

Dane Cook was standing about ten feet away talking to someone, and he waved at David. Clearly relieved to have an excuse to slip away, David said, "Excuse me," and strode to greet him.

"I didn't expect to see you here," Stuart said to Rebecca. "So how do you know David?"

"We used to go out," she said, working hard on making her mouth seem slack and casual.

"Really? What was that like? He fascinates me."

"It's kind of a long story. It was like a reverse *Star Is Born*."

"Who were you—Barbra Streisand or Kris Kristofferson?"

"James Mason."

"You picked the wrong guy. You need too much attention to be with someone like that."

How did he understand her so well when he hardly knew her? It was a form of seduction for someone to tell you who you were. "The scary thing about dating a narcissist," she said, "is that you start to be-lieve his lies. You're not allowed to think any less of him than he thinks of himself, which means you have to put him on a pedestal all the time. I wasn't any good at that. I make a bad codependent."

"That's okay. I'd rather be a dependent than a codependent."

"Why's that?"

"The dependent gets to drink." She imagined getting drunk with Stuart at O'Connor's or Mooney's, staying up with him into the middle of the night. "So who left who?" he asked.

"Oh, he left me. He got too famous. And he needed someone more introverted. I think that's why he likes Cassie. Even though she's famous, she's an introvert."

"Do you think that in a relationship, there's only room for one extrovert?"

"Absolutely."

"So are you the extrovert now, with your husband?"

"Yeah," she said. "Actually, that's not true. I was."

"What happened?"

"We had a baby. Now Abbie's the extrovert, the center of attention. All babies are. It's impossible to compete with a baby."

"A mother shouldn't compete with her own baby."

"You sound like him now." She could hear bitterness in her tone and didn't like it. But Stuart had provoked her. It was his fault that she'd opened up like this.

"Maybe he's onto something," Stuart said.

"Maybe you should mind your own business."

"He's definitely onto something." His face was hard. She wanted to back up and erase what she had said. The whole point of having an affair was not to be the miserable and unpleasant person you were in your marriage.

"I should go find Melora," he said.

She stood there dumbly and nodded. He was leaving because she had become ugly. That was what Theo said to her when she harangued him for being too beholden to Abbie: that she was an ugly person. He didn't understand that her rage came out of frustration. She wouldn't care that he was so protective of his daughter if he could simultaneously show affection for his wife.

The few times she had tried to talk about their issue, he would say vaguely, "You're a part of the problem, too" or "Maybe if you were a little nicer . . ." They were in a chicken-and-egg situation. He felt he would make love to her if she treated him more kindly, while she felt she would be more kind if only he would make love.

She had read an article about Angelina Jolie and Brad Pitt that said they had visited a crisis counselor who'd had them make lists of everything they didn't like about the other. Apparently Angelina enjoyed the exercise, coming up with lots of complaints, but the only thing on Brad's list was how he wished Angelina were nicer. Maybe that was all men wanted.

As she was beginning to lose hope that Stuart would ever speak to her again, he said, "Catch you later. I'm going to call you about the screenplay."

"Okay," she said. "Whenever you want."

"You can help me with the misogyny."

"You mean the mise-en-scène," she said, but he was already gone.

"Don't you dare talk to me that way!" Chris said to Jason, elbowing in his bedroom door.

"What are you going to do about it?" Jason shouted. His voice cracked on the second syllable of "about," and he was embarrased. Though almost six feet tall, he was only fourteen, and sometimes his voice still cracked.

"You can't go treating this place like a hotel!" Chris said. "It's a school night!"

Jason had been smoking a blunt in the park with this new Tibetan chick at his school, Tsering. She had told him it was the first time she'd smoked, and then they'd kissed. It was good.

"I'll come home when I feel like it," he said to Chris. "What are you gonna do about it?" Chris didn't have an answer. "That's right. You can't do shit. You can't do nothing."

Chris had made Jason back in his thirties before he realized he was gay. After Jason was born his mom took off. Now she was a waitress in Florida. When he had some money, he was gonna go down there and meet her.

Fred, Chris's boyfriend, came in and put his arm protectively around Chris. Great. Now Drew Carey was gonna get his fat white ass involved. "You stay out of this!" Jason said.

"Apologize to your father," Fred said.

"I'm not gonna say nothin' to him."

"Apologize right now!" Fred said.

Jason looked from one to the other, Fred tall and heavyset with hair plugs,

Chris with pecs so big they looked stupid on him. They'd met in a gay club ten years before, even though Chris said it was a party.

It was sick that he had to live with two fags. It was sick what they did in that bedroom right next to his. Once he got up in the night to get a drink and heard moaning and couldn't get back to sleep.

"Why don't you leave me alone?" he cried, and pushed through them out the door.

"You're not going anywhere," Chris said, grabbing his arm. Jason shook him off and bounded down the stairs of 899 Carroll Street as fast as he could. Those homos weren't gonna chase him. There was nothing they could do.

He dialed Shawn on his cell and told him he was coming over. He walked up Prospect Park West toward the circle, then around, past the big new building, till he hit Vanderbilt. Shawn lived on Bergen between Carlton and Vanderbilt. They'd known each other since they were kids and hung out all the time, even though Shawn went to a different school now. Jason was in eighth grade at M.S. 51.

On his way to Shawn's the week before, he had been walking down Park Place and stopped in the rain to smoke a blunt. He was fumbling in his jacket pocket for a light when some white yuppie lady with a stroller came toward him. When she saw him, she bolted. Prospect Heights was all paranoid white people now; one time he saw a white lady, with one of those expensive Bugaboo strollers, walk right through a dope deal.

Jason hated Prospect Heights and hated Park Slope even more. He'd lived on Carroll Street since he was four. When he was a kid, the neighborhood was cool—kids played in the street—but now everyone in the building had babies. It was always the same story: Some married couple would move in, then within a few years have two babies, then move out and sell to another married couple, and the whole thing would start again. There were all these strollers in the entryway, and sometimes it was impossible to get the door open.

If he could get out of the Slope and live with his mom, he could have a career in the record industry. He loved music, not just rap but old-school R & B, and he liked to walk down the streets listening to his iPod. He made these dope mixes on his laptop, like the Isley Brothers with Jay-Z, Roy Ayers with New Order. He was better than Danger Mouse, even. One night when Fred and Chris were out, he was doing a mix and there was a knock at the door. It was the lady from Apartment Three, complaining that the music was *keeping her daughter awake. He had to turn it down, and by the time he got back to it, he'd totally lost what he was doing.*

He wanted to live someplace where he could mix music as loud as he liked, without headphones, and nobody would ever complain. In New York everyone was on top of each other all of the time, but it wasn't like that in Florida, in the Glades. In the Glades nobody could hear you for miles, and you never saw babies because nobody walked.

Egg-white Quality

COME, YOU moron. *Come, already!* It was ten o'clock at night. Darby was asleep in the next room, and Karen was waiting for Matty to ejaculate. What on earth was wrong with him? They had been having sex for what felt like at least twenty minutes, by which time he usually came, but for some reason he was taking forever.

There were a number of reasons Karen found this troubling. She had already checked her cervical mucus and found that it was EQ, or egg-white quality, a term she had learned from Toni Weschler's book and the many TTC (trying to conceive) message boards she visited on a regular basis. She was pretty certain this was her last day of EQ, which meant it was her best chance of getting pregnant that cycle. They were doing it in precisely the best position, missionary, and if he didn't ejaculate this time, it would be a month before she would be this fertile again.

In the interest of speeding him along, she had fellated him before sex. As much as she hated giving blow jobs, she liked the way they shortened sex. It was like drinking hard liquor before you went barhopping: You spent less money.

She was wiggling her hips the way she always did to help him along, and she had already stuck one finger up his ass, which never failed to make him come a minute or two later. But he seemed no closer than before, and she was starting to get nervous. He was sweating and panting and rolling his eyes to the back of his head, but if anything, his erection seemed to be going away. She wanted to slam him on the back and make him cough up the semen, the way she did with Darby when he gagged on a piece of strawberry. She tried stroking his hair, even leaning up and whispering, "I want your come," into his ear, but at this he withdrew, said, "I need a minute," spat on his hand, and began to stroke himself.

Men were so vulgar. Matty had told her once of a game he played as a teenager called Dead Hand, where he would lie on his hand until the feeling went out of it. Then he'd masturbate with it so it felt like it wasn't his own. Only a male would use his brain cells to think of such a thing.

She had a feeling his distraction had to do with the apartment bidding. At six thirty, Tina Savant had called to say that the bidding was at $749,000 and they were going to do one more round, ending Thursday at noon. Karen had called Matty to consult with him because he'd been so angry that she'd gone to $735,000 without his permission, and after a difficult, drawn-out conversation, she'd finally convinced him they should go up to $761,000.

Karen called Tina with the new bid but even though Matty had signed off on it, he'd been irritable when he came home from work later that night. He kept saying they had overbid, that the real estate market had softened and their bid didn't reflect it. He was afraid there would be another real estate crash in the city, a big one like in the late 1980s, and they might have to sell at a loss.

He was jerking, fast and furious, head cocked, biting his lower lip, eyes closed in concentration. She knew he wasn't thinking of her and tried not to worry about who he was thinking about. Right now the important thing was that he give up the goods. She imagined the millions of sperm in there, seconds away from shooting out of him. They were like millions of hungry apartment hunters all bidding against each other for a mint 3BR with DFPs, SS appliances, and a WD on a pk blk. She knew that if Matty could put aside his financial anxiety, one of those millions of apartment hunters could break out of the throng into the warm, waiting floor-through and find a way to make himself at home.

It wasn't like Karen was in the mood for sex herself. It was hard to feel amorous when you had to think about uterine angle and cervical mucus and then, immediately after, spin around on your butt like a break-dancer to put your feet against the wall so the semen would flow down to the cervix. Sometimes she envied her friends who'd gone through IVF, like Cathleen Meth, who had done four rounds, finally been implanted with twins, lost one of the embryos, and given birth to Jones. With IVF, the man didn't even have to be in the room. Though less romantic, it was also less messy.

Did Matty expect her to do a dance for him or something? Was he angry at her for not getting on top when he knew full well that missionary was the best position for conception? Whatever was standing in his way, she didn't have much sympathy for him. When Matty had first started courting her, it had taken some work on her part to see him as sexy. His bushy eyebrows and poor posture were not what she had imagined, as a little girl, when she thought about her future husband. But over time she had come to love him. When they made love she tried not to think about the parts of him that were unattractive and instead think about all they had gone through together.

Matty stopped his frenzied stroking, collapsed next to her on the bed, and said, "I don't think I can do it."

"What do you mean you can't do it?"

"Every time we have sex now, it's all about getting you pregnant. I have to wake up every morning to the sound of those three beeps on your digital thermometer."

"Waking basal temperature is the most important fertility indicator besides EQ!"

"Maybe we should quit while we're ahead."

"What?" She sat up against the headboard and pulled the sheets to her armpit, before realizing that she was still wearing her top, a red-and-white-striped crewneck from Forever 21.

"We have one great kid. Maybe we should just stop trying."

She felt like she was in a horror movie. Matty Shapiro, whom she thought she knew better than anyone in the world, had become a stranger. "But you've always said you wanted Darby to have a sibling."

"I feel like there's all this pressure at work, and then I come home and there's this pressure here. Everyone wants something from me. Sometimes I wish you'd go back to work. Then maybe I could catch a break."

It was obvious to Karen that he was feeling this way only because of the apartment. He'd been bottling in his feelings, which was why he was bottling in his semen. She had to calm him down. She concentrated hard on breathing deeply and trying to keep her voice well modulated. In *And Baby Makes Three: The Six-Step Plan for Preserving Marital Intimacy and Rekindling Romance After Baby Arrives,* by John and Julie Gottman, she had read that when one partner's heartbeat rose above a certain rate, he became flooded and could no longer listen. In those situations it was useless to talk about anything. "Is this about Carroll Street?"

"Of course it's about Carroll Street!" he said. "It's about everything! You don't know when to back off."

"Look," she said, bluffing, "I'm happy to call Tina tomorrow and retract the bid. But I don't think it would be appropriate to call her at this hour, do you?" He shook his head. "Whatever you're feeling about the apartment, it's important that you don't let those feelings impact the baby thing. We agreed we wanted another child."

"I'm tired of all this responsibility."

"I don't have responsibility?" she said. She was aware that her voice wasn't well modulated, but she couldn't help it. "You don't think it's responsibility raising a young boy to be egalitarian and yet at the same time not a wuss, shopping for a healthy, well-balanced dinner every night, getting it on the table, dealing with every single one of Darby's doctor's appointments, calling Ralph when the dishwasher goes out, getting the forms signed for school trips, organizing playdates, paying the bills, getting your shirts to the cleaners, and straightening up twenty-five times a day? What is all that—a walk in the park?"

"Sometimes I think you want another child because if you don't have one, you're going to have to go back to work someday."

She'd had the same thought herself but had no idea Matty was onto her. She felt like a burglar who'd been discovered by the police in the middle of the act. "That is not true!"

"Then why *do* you want one?"

"I've told you: Darby needs someone to play with, I don't want him to grow old alone, I want him to have help taking care of us, and I feel that children with siblings are better adjusted than children without."

"I think it's because everyone else has two." She could feel her cheeks getting warm, but she focused hard on not screaming at him that he was a goddamn fucking idiot. "Why can't you be happy with what you've got? You've got a great husband and a great child."

She certainly didn't think Matty was amazing at this moment. Pressure was what made him tick, and now he was acting like he needed a break? Who did he think he was? Everything she thought she'd understood about her marriage was being thrown into question. Matty was *Jewish*! All Jews wanted more than one child. It was in the Torah. This was so namby-pamby. It was something an artist might say, not a lawyer, a Jewish lawyer. If he was serious about not wanting this second kid, how could she continue to love him?

As angry as she was, she couldn't help but blame herself. They wouldn't be having this argument if she'd conceived when they first started trying a year and a half ago. If she'd gotten pregnant when Darby was two and a half, then Matty never would have had this opportunity to back down. Because of her own fertility problems, she had given Matty too much time to think, and it was dangerous to give a man too much time to think.

Matty was standing up, throwing on his clothes. "Where're you going?" she asked.

"For a walk."

She wanted to weep but knew it would get her nowhere. What was the point of trying to explain it all to him? Clearly he was flooded. When his blood pressure returned to normal, he would calm down, rethink everything, and go back to his old self. John Gottman said you had to take a break of at least twenty minutes in order to become unflooded.

She put on her robe and decided to check on Darby. She had not broken this habit of checking on him before she went to sleep, even though he was far too old for SIDS. Sometimes from the doorway, she would watch his back rise and fall, and if she couldn't see it clearly, she would tiptoe closer and put her hand on it to make sure he was alive.

Darby was sound asleep, his SpongeBob comforter pulled up to his chin, his face tilted and angelic. She watched his chest and then went into the kitchen.

She was pouring herself a glass of Vintage seltzer when her cell phone rang. She ran to it quickly so it wouldn't wake Darby. Annika. "So nice to hear from you," Karen said. "I wanted to thank you again for having us over."

"Did you go into Melora's bedroom?"

Karen's heart pounded, but almost instantly, the moment of panic was followed by pragmatic calm. She was dealing with someone foreign and naive.

"Why would you think that?" she asked, injecting an offended tone into her voice.

"Something's missing, and I want to know if you took it."

"What is it?"

"That's not important. Did you take something? Because I could lose my job over this."

"I didn't go in Melora's room. What kind of person do you think I am?"

"I just met you yesterday. I don't really know. There are a lot of crazy people out there. Melora likes to meet all of Orion's friends before I have them over, but I trusted you, so I made an exception."

"I'd be happy to meet her. Anytime you want." Annika was silent. Karen could picture her Nordic features brooding.

Karen had been a fool to stay in the bedroom so long. Of course the Swede was on to her. "Listen," Karen said, "I completely understand your concern. You have a very important job, and the last thing you want to do is jeopardize it. But I promise you, I did not set foot in the bedroom. Whatever's missing, I didn't take it. Maybe it was the house-keeper."

There was a pause and then Annika said, "That's what I told Melora. They're Burmese. One of them I really don't like. She has these black eyes."

"You see?" Karen said. "I'm sure it was the Burmese." She paused and said, "You know, I was thinking about your boyfriend."

"Martin?" Annika said. "What about him?"

"Have you thought about calling him?"

"I promised myself I wouldn't call him again."

"Why not? I bet he thinks about you all the time."

"You think so?"

"It's obvious from what you told me that he loves you. He's waiting for you to make the first move." Karen went on like this for a while, with Annika getting increasingly excited and speculating about the pros and cons of calling.

"So do you want to get the boys together again tomorrow?" Karen asked.

"Maybe," said Annika.

"Darby had so much fun at the house. He loved Orion's—"

"I think it's better if we meet in the park."

So she was putting up a blockade. That was all right. Karen would find a way behind it. "Of course, of course," she said. "Why don't I pick you up at the house and we'll walk together?"

"I . . . I guess that's all right." Karen already had a plan. She spotted Darby's Lightning McQueen car on the carpet and shoved it deep into her bag, next to the wallet, which she carried around with her each day.

Atlantic Terminal

THE YOUNG barhoppers and restaurant-goers on northern Fifth Avenue would not have recognized Melora Leigh had they seen the crazed woman limping past them, or, at least, that was what she hoped. She had found a pair of sunglasses in her Majorelle, wraparound Dolce & Gabbana, and with her hair short on one side and long on the other, she resembled an alcoholic punk lesbian who'd just had a lovers' quarrel.

Melora was starting to feel desperate about her lunch with Adam, aware that she looked like a train wreck and unsure how she could fix herself up by one o'clock the next day. Her head was spinning. If she could only stop the thrumming in her ear, she would be able to come up with a plan. Lynn could help her get a wig to cover up the burn, and if she got to Gemma first, she could always sit at a booth and then Adam wouldn't see the limp.

But first she had to figure out how to get home. She knew she could stop any of these barhoppers and ask for directions to Prospect Park West, but she was afraid one of them would recognize her and post something nasty on Gawker.

She took out her phone and dialed Family car service. But it was busy. She tried three times in a row, with no luck. These damn Brooklyn car services were so unreliable.

She would have to hail a cab. But as she turned to face the traffic, all the cabs coming her way were taken, by young, dressed-up twentysomethings going home after a night on the town. After a few minutes she thought she saw a light in the distance, but when he approached, it turned out to be off-duty. If she hadn't canned Ringo, she could have had him wait outside Southpaw and she wouldn't have to battle for yellow with drunken hipsters.

It was a weeknight. It was supposed to be easy to hail cabs in Brooklyn. But these days property values were so high that Brooklynites had disposable incomes they could afford to squander on taxi fares. Melora knew she was part of the reason property values had gone so high, but it still bothered her. The same people who paved the way weren't supposed to have to compete for services.

Her cell phone rang. Stuart. She didn't pick up. She was furious with him for humiliating her in front of David Keller. If she asked him for directions home, he would see her as pathetic. She was tired of being treated like a child. He called twice more, but she ignored him.

Finally, a lit cab approached. She waved furiously and he slowed. As the driver pulled over she saw him take her in—the lopsided hair, dark sunglasses, and uneven posture—and then veer sharply back into traffic.

A few minutes later, near the intersection of Fifth and Bergen, as she was giving up hope, she spotted another lit cab. She arranged her hair in front of her face and tried to stand upright. The car pulled over. *Thank God.* She started to get in.

"Where you going?" he said. He was a Sikh.

"Prospect Park West."

"I go to Manhattan," he spat. "Manhattan only." She wished she still lived in SoHo, if only so she could go home.

"It's only a few blocks away. I think."

"I go to Manhattan," he said angrily, gesturing toward the door.

"But that's against the law. I'm going to call 311."

He took a crowbar from the passenger seat and slapped it hard against the dash. It was so un-Sikh to take out a crowbar. Naveen Andrews in *The English Patient* never would have threatened someone like this. She sighed and got out, and he sped off before she had a chance to get the medallion number.

She passed a children's clothing store, Area Kids; a Spanish diner, El Viejo Yayo; and Triangle Sports. Up Fifth Avenue, she could see the lights of the Atlantic Terminal mall.

What an atrocity. How this Ratner idiot had gotten permission to build it, she had no idea. When Heath was alive, he and Michelle had gotten her and Stuart to sign on to the Develop—Don't Destroy advisory board. Even though Frank Gehry was supposedly going to design the arena, if Bruce Ratner was behind it, it was bound to be ugly.

Why was she thinking about the feasibility of the Nets arena at a time like this? The Ativan made her loopy and unfocused. *Bed. Home.* But how to get home? She felt so tired and out of it. A sign across the street said FLATBUSH AVENUE. That had to lead to Prospect Park West. If she could only figure out which way her house was, she could walk.

Her phone was ringing in her bag. She jerked it out of her Majorelle, expecting Stuart again, but it was an unknown number. "Hello?"

"Melora, it's Michael." His voice was soft and conciliatory, and he was calling himself by his first name, like a friend. She felt reassured already.

"Oh, Michael, thank God."

"Are you all right?"

"No. I'm not. Something terrible has happened. I stole something and I think the police are going to find out and I went off the Zoloft but I'm back on it." She sensed someone behind her, a figure, but when she turned, the street was empty.

"Why'd you go off?"

"Can I see you? Can I make an appointment with you right now? If I can get a cab, I can be at your office in—"

"Why don't you tell me what's wrong?"

She told him everything, starting with the wallet and leading up to the burning hair. "I'm so sorry about all of this," he said, which seemed a little mild given the stakes.

"Do you know how to get to Prospect Park West from Flatbush Avenue?"

"I'm sorry, I don't."

"I'm going to go to jail," she said, and began to sob.

"Everything's going to be okay."

"How do you know?"

"Things are going to work out."

"Oh, Michael, I really hope so!" Her voice sounded high and school-girlish in her head. "I really hope you're right. So can you see me? I know I'll feel so much better when I see you in person."

"Unfortunately—"

"What about tomorrow, our regular time?"

"I thought you had a commitment."

"I do, but it's at one. I could have kept my appointment with you, but I didn't want to. I thought I didn't need you. I was wrong. I'm sorry I lied to you."

"Melora, I'm out of town."

"Where?"

"My mother's ill. I won't be back till Sunday at the earliest and probably not till Monday."

"Where are you?"

He paused, as though uncomfortable with the line of questioning. "The Berkshires."

"That's nothing! I can fly you down from Albany."

"That's not possible."

Melora began to sob. "I can't wait till Monday to see you. I'm supposed to go to this meeting tomorrow, and I look like something out of *Grindhouse*."

"You're going to do fine."

"This isn't a zit, Michael. I lost half my hair!"

She could hear him talking to someone in the background. "I have to go now, but I'm going to see if there's a way I can call you tomorrow."

"Can't I talk to you one more second? I feel like I'm falling apart!" She was aware that she sounded like Ratso Rizzo in *Midnight Cowboy*, pronouncing "apart" with a New York accent, but she could not stop herself. "I'm so scared, Michael!"

"I'll try to call you tomorrow," he said, and cut off the call.

She cried out in frustration. What kind of a shrink had to call you back the next day when you were in the middle of a crisis?

The mall loomed across the street, empty but lit. In every direction there were signs of impending construction, high blue walls where the arena groundbreaking had already begun. Again she sensed someone behind her, and when she turned, she thought she saw a figure duck behind a construction wall. Trying to guess which way to walk, she decided to follow the stream of cars heading to her left on Flatbush, reasoning that they were probably going toward the park.

She crossed Atlantic and walked a long time down Flatbush on wide, empty streets. She passed an Applebee's. Inside, black people ate eggs and pancakes. This definitely wasn't the way to Prospect Park West.

Her scalp was itching crazily, her foot was dragging uselessly behind her. The humidity caught up with her, and the sight of those black people loading up on trans fats made her sick. If Obama got elected he would put in an organic garden, but who knew if he would wind up winning anyway? She leaned over to retch on the street. She vomited enthusiastically, half a dozen good hurls, the last one the most productive, expunging a thick beige current onto the sidewalk.

As she fingered her hair away from her mouth for what she hoped was the final expulsion, she was blinded by the flash of a camera. "Thanks, Melora!" he shouted. Even in her haze, she recognized him: Phil Parnell, the paparazzo who shot all the Brooklyn celebs for *Us Weekly*. Before she could say a word, the asshole had dashed down the street and into the night.

Ground Rules

"CAN I come over?" Rebecca said on the phone. It was ten-fifteen and Lizzie had been about to go to bed.

"Sure," Lizzie said, trying not to sound excited. "With the baby?"

"Theo's sitting. I was out at this thing at Southpaw, and I don't want to go home yet."

Lizzie gave her the address, and fifteen minutes later, Rebecca was at her door. She looked radiant in a slinky red top and form-fitting skirt.

"You look fantastic," Lizzie said. "What were you doing at Southpaw?"

"There was this *Paris Review* thing. It was okay. A little pretentious. A Q and A with Cassie Trainor. It was like unintentional comedy."

"You want a drink?" Lizzie asked. She led Rebecca into the kitchen, feeling embarrassed about how cramped and messy it was. The apartment was a railroad flat, while Rebecca's was a floor-through.

In the kitchen Rebecca noticed the bottle of Terre di Tufi. Lizzie flinched, worried she was going to say Lizzie had gone *Single White Female,* but Rebecca said, "Isn't it good?"

"So yummy. And reasonable!" Lizzie wanted to kick herself: "and reasonable." She sounded like an old lady. She wanted to impress Rebecca, but every time she tried, she stuck her foot in her mouth.

"I tried some of that Argiolas you bought me. It was good."

"Oh, don't worry about it," Lizzie said, embarrassed, fearing the gesture had been too much.

She poured Rebecca a glass of the Terre di Tufi and a smaller glass for herself. They went into the minuscule dining room adjacent to the kitchen and sat at the thrift-store wooden table.

Lizzie was embarrassed by her shabby apartment. Rebecca had to think Lizzie and Jay were real slummers, if not by the railroad apartment then by the Salvation Army furniture.

Rebecca took a sip of wine, her face brooding, and then said, "I decided I'm going to meet the swingers with you."

So Rebecca had had a change of heart. Lizzie wanted to believe it had something to do with her, but she wasn't sure. Rebecca seemed to have an agenda in everything she did.

"Really?" Lizzie asked.

"Yeah," Rebecca said. "I don't think they're for real. I think it's a bluff and that when we get there, there won't be anyone. But I want to see how far they'll go. How far he'll go. We give fake descriptions so we can check them out. If they show. Write that so-called Andy guy and say Victoria has a friend named, um, Tess, who wants to get a drink, too. Another single mother."

Elated, Lizzie said, "We can IM him right now." She fetched her computer from the living room, put it in front of Rebecca, and opened the instant-messenger program. Andy was online.

"Wait a minute, you've already been IM-ing this guy? Did you have Internet sex with him?"

"No! We just exchanged IM addresses. His handle is PSDiddy."

"That right there is reason enough not to swing with him."

But Rebecca finished her wine, and from Lizzie's account she wrote, "I'm really looking forward to meeting you at the Gate tomorrow. I can't stop thinking about it. I was wondering if I could bring a friend."

While they waited for a response, Lizzie went in the kitchen and brought out a few of Jay's beers. The beers were from England and had low alcohol content—session beers, they were called. She wished he had something stronger in the fridge. She thought about running out to the liquor store on Vanderbilt but thought it might look desperate or predatory.

"What is this?" Rebecca said after she had a sip of the beer.

"It's gourmet beer. English. Jay's very into microbrews." Rebecca made a face. "What's the matter?" Lizzie said. "Black people can't drink microbrews?"

Rebecca laughed. Lizzie felt a little funny because it had a different feeling when she said it than when Jay did. This racial stuff was so complicated, and it didn't get any easier with time. Lizzie wondered if this was one of the reasons she was so lonely. There were things you couldn't say to your own partner. You were a stranger and a confidante at the same time.

Lizzie wished she could talk to someone about her marriage, but when she met white women with black kids at Underhill playground, they acted hostile—as though too uncomfortable with their own choices to reach out to someone similar. She figured some had fallen out with their parents and taken it out on the rest of the world; her own mother had taken a long time to accept Jay but finally did, reasoning, perhaps, that even a black man was better than a white woman. Maybe when Lizzie got to know Rebecca better, she could confide in her about some of this.

Andy's reply came in only a few minutes. Past children's bedtime in Park Slope, you could count on the fact that most parents were on their laptops. Surfing was the new married sex.

I thought you didn't like Park Slope mothers, the reply said.

"You told him that?" Rebecca said.

"I figured I should be honest," Lizzie answered, feeling emboldened. She took a big swig of her beer, grabbed the computer from Rebecca, and typed, *My friend doesn't look like a Park Slope mother. She's very cute. Cuter than me, even. No Connecticut Muffin top.*

Rebecca fell over laughing. "Where did you come up with that?"

"Some woman in my new-moms group. I can't believe you haven't heard it before."

Well that's scary, Andy wrote, *because the way I've been picturing you, you're pretty cute yourself.*

"Oh my God!" Rebecca said. "He's hot to trot!"

Her name is Tess and she has the body of Courteney Cox, Lizzie wrote. *I'll feel a lot more comfortable if I have her there.*

"You're amazing at this," said Rebecca from over Lizzie's shoulder.

Rebecca was right. It was as though, under the veil of Victoria and the beer, which Lizzie was drinking quickly so as to maximize the alcoholic effect, Lizzie could be as smart and clever as her friend. Other mothers made her more boring, but Rebecca made her more interesting.

Are there any ground rules before we come? Lizzie wrote.

Pun intended?

No.

Glad you asked. This is just a meeting, but if you do wind up coming to our place another night, the rules are: No meanness. No hurting. No real names. And if there's any bondage play, the safe word is "locavore."

"That is so Park Slope," Lizzie said.

So is Andy your real name? Lizzie wrote.

Please. Like you're Victoria. You're probably not even a single mom. You're probably not even a mom.

I guess you'll have to meet me to find out, Lizzie wrote.

Eight o'clock at the Gate?

How will we know what you look like?

I have brown curly hair and my wife, Alexandra, is blond. We'll be sitting at the front, at the bar.

I'm blond, five-ten, and Tess is a petite redhead.

You sound too good to be true.

Oh, we're true.

After they signed off, Lizzie asked, "So who's going to watch Abbie when you go out?"

"Theo. I'll tell him I'm having drinks with you. He'll be happy. He likes me out of the house."

"Why's that?"

"I'm not very nice to him." Rebecca frowned and regarded the beer label.

"Do you try to be?"

"I don't think so. After you've been angry a long time, it's hard not to be angry. Angry becomes the new normal." Rebecca looked tormented, her face so wracked with insult that she seemed almost deformed.

Lizzie reached for Rebecca's hand and said, "I'm sorry he doesn't appreciate you."

"What am I gonna do?" Rebecca said with a shrug.

"You could leave him."

"I'm Jewish," Rebecca said. "Jewish women don't leave. They die."

Rebecca laid her cheek against Lizzie's hand. Lizzie could feel that Rebecca wanted her. The kiss hadn't been a one-time thing; Rebecca had come over to seduce her.

Lizzie took Rebecca's face between her hands and Rebecca let her kiss her, seeming to soften in her arms. Lizzie felt like she was spinning down into a black-and-white-striped vortex from a 1950s movie. For an instant she could feel the truth, feel Rebecca's desire for her. She wanted to bottle the feeling and wear it around her neck.

As they kept kissing, she put her hand on Rebecca's breast, over her shirt, and moaned from the thrill of getting to touch the places she had imagined. Then her hand was under Rebecca's shirt, trying to get to her flesh. Lizzie swiftly unclasped Rebecca's bra, and the cups dropped open, the breasts flying forth. She caressed them, eyes closed, burying her head in Rebecca's chest.

Rebecca pulled away and lowered her shirt. "I should get going."

"You sure?"

"Yeah."

Lizzie wanted to scream at Rebecca for being so hot and cold, but if she did that, she was afraid Rebecca wouldn't come with her to meet the swingers. She was praying the couple was for real and that if she could get Rebecca drunk enough, she could persuade her to go home with them and make out with her, too.

It was all so confounding. Lizzie had always imagined that the practical aspects of having an affair were easy. You picked up on a mutual attraction and then went about arranging the where and when. But starting an affair was just as hard as dating, which Lizzie had never done much of, since she was only nineteen when she met Sarah. In dating, people played games and tricks to keep their paramours hungry.

It struck Lizzie as ridiculous to have to play tricks on Rebecca when both of them were married mothers anyway. They were already taken, so why couldn't they cut to the chase?

But this was a game, and if it was a game, then she was losing. Maybe in the morning she'd call Rebecca to say she regretted the make-out, and then they could decide where and when to meet.

She went into the bedroom and stood in front of the crib for a long time, staring at Mance's face. She lifted him out of the crib and into her bed, lying down facing her. He stirred and she slipped her nipple into his mouth. As he sucked, she got warm. She wriggled her hand down her pants and touched herself, thinking of what it had felt like to hold Rebecca for those brief moments.

She would have felt weirder if Mance seemed to have any idea, but he was suckling selfishly, as narcissistic as his own father. Her orgasm was angry and fast. After she came, Mance fell asleep, just like a man.

The North Fork

WHEN REBECCA got home that night, she found Theo working on his laptop alone, wearing his reading glasses. "Abbie's in her own bed," he said proudly.

"That's great," she said.

"You're always saying you can't sleep with her in our bed, so I moved her."

"Thanks for doing that." He shook his head, hurt, as though unable to understand why she didn't have more of a reaction. How could she begin to explain it? They had gotten so entrenched it was impossible to begin to know how to dig themselves out.

She went into the bathroom to freshen up. Staring at her reflection in the mirror, she thought back to that dinner party in Carroll Gardens all those years before. Maybe the reason Theo had stopped making love to her was because she was meant to fuck Stuart Ashby. This was why Theo had told her about the businessman in St. Louis. He'd had a kind of marital ESP, known that one day she would have an opportunity to have sex with someone who would make her happy. And because he loved her, he didn't want to stand in her way.

She thought about Lizzie fucking Jay four times a week and wondered whether it was her will or his. It was hard to imagine Lizzie being into a man. It was obvious she was still a lesbian.

Rebecca felt awful about what had happened at Lizzie's apartment that night. She shouldn't have led her on when she didn't really want anything to happen. But Stuart had been so cruel to her at Southpaw, lecturing her about what kind of mother she should be, and she was lonely.

She was worried she'd given Lizzie the wrong idea. And now they were supposed to go meet these so-called swingers. She'd have to find a way to get out of it.

In bed, she put on a sleep mask and turned her back to Theo. "How was it?" he asked.

"What?"

"The performance."

"Cassie's totally psycho."

"Are you just saying that because you're jealous she goes out with him?"

"No."

"Are you jealous she goes out with him?" He hadn't touched her in over a year. What did he care?

"We broke up six years ago. I'm not jealous."

She felt a hand on her back. The sensation was so unusual that she took off the mask and turned over to face Theo to be sure it was actually his hand. "I was thinking maybe we'd try to get away in August," he said. Over the holidays they had gone to San Francisco to visit his mother and stepfather, but it hadn't been much of a vacation. With a baby in tow, vacations meant no sitting, cramped sleeping quarters, and hellish plane rides.

She flopped on her back. "Okay," she said warily.

"I know things haven't been easy the past year, and I think part of it is because I'm so stressed out with work. Tom said he'd give me a week, but he wants me to take it before the end of the summer because we start on the Jane Street condos in the fall. Where would you like to go?"

"It's really up to you."

"I thought you'd be happy that I came up with this," he said, taking his hand away and regarding her with his usual injured pout, a pout that no longer packed any emotional impact.

"I *am* happy. I'm very happy. Should we visit my parents?" Her parents had a house in Beach Haven, on the Jersey Shore, that they'd bought in the 1970s; Rebecca and Theo had taken Abbie for July Fourth weekend but hadn't considered a longer trip because of Theo's work.

"I wanted us to be alone," Theo said. "Just the three of us. I was thinking we could go to the North Fork."

"The North Fork sounds great." She leaned forward and kissed him in the hope that it would end the discussion so she could sleep. She wanted to replay her conversation with Stuart, the first part, before he got distant and cold.

"Did you have a lot to drink?" Theo asked.

"No, just a little wine." She decided not to tell him that she'd gone to Lizzie's, because she didn't want to answer a bunch of banal questions about Lizzie's son and husband. Theo squinted at her but didn't push it any further.

Rebecca had spent all these months blaming Theo for rejecting her, but after that second time, she hadn't really tried to make love to him again, either. Maybe he still wanted sex and was waiting for her to initiate. He'd been making an effort with her tonight, with the vacation, and she had been snappy and unresponsive. Why was it so hard for her to be nice to him when that was what she wanted in return?

There had been nights when he indicated that he might have been interested—one night they'd been watching *A Fistful of Dollars* on TV together, and he had massaged her feet during the movie and looked at her affectionately, but she was so furious at him for going no further that she took her foot out of his lap.

In the spring he'd been stressed at work and told her about it over dinner, and he'd put his head in his hands and said, "My job feels like such a burden sometimes." She could have come up behind him and embraced him, but instead she'd said, "Are you saying I don't chip in? Because I'm busting my ass to pull in my little share with only three days a week to write." And there was that night a few days before, when Abbie had been in the bed and he had touched Rebecca, but she had been too angry to respond.

Nothing was simple in marriage. She had read somewhere that it took two people to form a pattern but only one to change it. Why hadn't she wanted to change? It was as though his sexual rejection gave her permission to blame him for everything that was wrong in the marriage.

It allowed her to make him into the bad guy because the other option—figuring out what it was about her that made him not want to sleep with her—was too painful to consider.

She kissed him, arms around him. His mouth was warm, and his eyes were kind, if not completely inviting. She got on top of him and ground herself against him. To her surprise, he got hard.

Was this the way it worked—nothing for sixteen months, and then one night it all changed? She pulled off his boxers and put her mouth on him. He murmured.

She thought of Stuart Ashby as she sucked her husband, wondering what Stuart tasted like and if she would ever do this to him. Theo turned her onto her stomach and pulled her panties down. So he was angry with her, too; he didn't want to see her face. This excited her. It meant he could find a way to turn his anger into desire. That was a beginning.

He grabbed a condom from his bedside table drawer, rolled it on, and guided himself in. She tilted her head back in pain but also excitement. All a man had to do was sniff another man's interest and it brought him home. Why hadn't she thought of that before? He had gotten only halfway inside her when, from the bedroom, Abbie wailed.

"Fuck!" Rebecca cried.

"Shh," Theo said, still inside her. "She might go back to sleep."

But within a few minutes Abbie was in a full-out cry. "I'm sorry," he said, kissing Rebecca and pulling out.

"Me, too."

"Maybe she'll go back to sleep," he said. He went into Abbie's bedroom. The crying stopped. A few minutes later, Rebecca could hear clinking in the kitchen as he fixed her a bottle.

Page Six

MELORA'S USUAL morning routine was to arise around ten-thirty, sit in the breakfast nook, and read the *New York Post* while sipping coffee and eating a tartine. She would immediately open to Page Six to see if a) she could decode any of the blind items and b) she was in any.

On this particular Thursday, though, she had too little energy to stumble downstairs, so she cried out, "Stuart!" A few minutes later, he came in, already dressed. By his face, she knew it was bad. "Bring me the *Post*."

"I threw it out."

"Well, then go downstairs and get it out of the trash."

He hesitated a minute, then seemed to reason that there was no point in arguing with her. When he came back, his face was grim.

She hadn't even told Stuart the whole story the night before. After she'd puked, she finally found a cab willing to take her, and she got home at eleven, exhausted. Stuart was in bed reading *Bangkok Nights,* and when he saw her singed hair and the now exposed gash above her eyebrow, he gasped. He said he had called her three times but gotten no answer and then wandered Fifth Avenue looking for her before giving up and heading home. He said he was on the verge of calling the police. He begged her to tell him what happened, but she said no, sneaking another two milligrams of Ativan sublingually before drifting off into oblivion.

The photo was on the cover, black and white and grainy, and in it

Melora was caught mid-puke, the pale vomit contrasting with the murky Flatbush Avenue background. She decided she resembled a mix of homeless war veteran, drunken Britney, and that Cambodian guy in the famous picture.

In boldface was the headline MEL NOT WELL and then, in smaller letters, "See page eleven." On page eleven, opposite the regular Page Six items, was another bad picture of Melora from the night before, taken a few seconds after the cover shot, scowling at the photographer.

> **Melora Leigh** has been acting awfully funny lately. Guests at the *Paris Review* fund-raiser **Cassie Trainor** Q and A at Brooklyn's Southpaw, which Leigh attended with hubby **Stuart Ashby,** noted her "odd demeanor" and pronounced limp. "She looked like she was stumbling," said one, "and she was really slurring her words." When the Oscar-winning vixen tried to light her cigarette outside, her hair caught on fire. Later our photog spotted her retching her brains out in front of Applebee's. Perhaps she had just devoured a burger, like fellow Oscar winner **Hilary Swank,** and it went down the wrong way? Ashby was nowhere in sight. Friends of the couple say they have been estranged lately. Let's hope all of this is preparation for a movie role, as we'd hate to see Melora go Winona.

Melora flipped the paper over and cast it aside listlessly, realizing she had three hours until her Adam Epstein. "What's going on?" said Stuart, sitting next to her on the bed.

"Nothing."

"Don't treat me like an idiot. I was so afraid when you came in that I stayed up all night shaking you to make sure you didn't go under. What are you taking?"

"I'm not taking anything. Just the usual stuff."

"Then what happened?"

She flipped over the paper and jabbed her visage with her index finger. "That's what happened."

"I mean what made you sick? What is that cut on your head?" He leaned forward to touch it, and she cowered in pain. He took her hands in his. "Come on, Lor, you gotta talk to me."

She wanted to tell him that when she'd grabbed Neal Harris's wallet, it hadn't even felt like her own hand, more like a marionette's pulled by some unseen human hand up above. The desire had taken hold of her when Bugaboo Dad was peering down into the stroller with his hairy white ass in her face.

That was what was wrong with Park Slope: People's asses were always in your face. She had been inoculated from other people's hairy asses when she lived in SoHo, but in the Slope, there was no escaping them. In the Tea Lounge, the women nursed with their tits hanging out in the open. The singles wore shirts too short, bellies out, bra straps protruding from tank tops deliberately. Mothers changed their babies' diapers on the benches at Connecticut Muffin, the same benches where you sat to drink your coffee. Male joggers wore netted tops that revealed their chest hair and nipples.

Who wanted to see all this? Melora had read the George Clooney profile in the *New Yorker,* in which he said that when you were famous, you had to make your house a nice prison, and she had understood. Her loft on Spring Street had been a nice prison, with the soundproofing on the windows, the wine room, gym, custom-made high-end stereo system, and of course, Lisanne there to fetch whatever she'd needed. It had been protected and remote, and inside, she'd felt safe. Why had they upended their lives for this miserable borough? So they could be gawked at by people with a lower median income? In the two years since they'd moved to Brooklyn, she had lost sight of what was important to her—privacy, insulation, safety—because Stuart had convinced her that those concerns were snobbish.

But slumming it was a pose, like living large was. And in a way, it was worse because it was so dishonest. She was angry with herself for not telling Stuart what she needed. Just because you didn't like most people didn't make you a snob. Her needs were more complex than his, which was understandable, given the fact that she'd been famous since before she had a period.

"I don't know," she said quietly. "I guess I was nervous about the meeting, and I took too many Ativans."

"I've told you those pills are dangerous. Look what happened to Heath."

"I'm not Heath. He was on six different meds!"

"I want to understand what's going on with you. I don't get why you would act out like this when something good is finally about to happen to your career."

"Finally?"

"Let's not pretend you haven't been faltering."

"That's a choice! I'm slowing down to spend time with Orion!"

"But you're never with him. You let Annika take him all the time. You're never alone with him, not even inside the house."

"I took him out for ice cream the other day."

"Honey. You've got to tell me what's going on with you."

"I can't. It's too terrible."

"What is?"

She looked deep into his eyes, wanting him to make things better. "I . . . did . . . something."

"What did you do, sweetheart? What did you do?"

Her phone rang. "Honey," said Vanessa. "I'm on with Lynn."

"Hiiii," said Lynn.

"This must be so hard on you," said Vanessa. How would she know what was hard? How could she know what it was like to be worried you were going to jail? She was heiress to a Greek shipping fortune. She didn't even have to work; she did it as a lark.

"Put them on speaker," Stuart said.

Melora relented. "Stu's on with me, too."

"Hi, Stu," the women said in unison.

This was what it felt like to go from star to has-been, from Oscar winner to *Conan* one-liner. It began with a bad paparazzo photo and ended with a stint on *Dancing with the Stars*.

"Honey," said Lynn. "We love you. Why the yorking?"

"Food poisoning," said Melora. Stuart shook his head.

"Come on, honey," said Lynn. "It's us. Are you knocked up?"

"What? No!"

"You can tell us."

"I have an IUD!"

The women were quiet, and then Lynn said, "*Can* you be?"

"What are you talking about?" Melora asked.

"We have to spin this to your advantage. I'm thinking you're very early, eight weeks along, hence the puke, and then in a couple weeks we let it float that you miscarried."

"I don't like it," Melora said. A faked miscarriage seemed too dirty even for her. It was something the old Melora would have agreed to, and she didn't want to be the old Melora anymore.

"We're just trying to help you," said Vanessa, then let out a long sigh, a sigh Melora knew she could have chosen to mute with the cough buttons they had on the CAA phones, the ones they pressed so they could scream "What an asshole!" about a client without the client knowing.

"Okay, so we go to Plan B," said Lynn. "We say your mother has dementia. An Alzheimer's parent always trumps any bad PR."

"But I don't speak to my mother." Melora had had a falling-out with Marcy shortly after *Poses* took off, when Marcy circulated a book proposal about their relationship, though she never wrote the book. Still, Melora had been so furious with her for wanting to expose her daughter for cash that she'd never reinitiated contact.

"It doesn't matter," Lynn said. "You don't have to take pictures. This is just what we're going to say."

"I'm not going to spread lies about myself to help my career. Can you postpone the Adam meeting till it blows over?"

"Under other circumstances," said Lynn, "that's what I would recommend. That and maybe fucking Samantha Ronson a couple of times."

"But here's the thing," said Vanessa. "First, Adam's only in town for the day. He's editing the Jennifer Garner in L.A., and he took the red-eye in last night just to meet with you." Melora wasn't sure if that was true, but it sounded flattering. "Second, we have it on a very good source that Kate Hudson's agent put a call in to Scott Rudin this morning. And apparently, Scott said, 'Adam's open to all possibilities now.'"

Even Stuart blanched. Melora and Kate were not friends, but they had known each other eleven years, since they'd done a failed CBS pilot together—a David Alan Grier vehicle called *Black at Ya*. On the Chicago set of *The Dueling Donnellys,* they had been cordial if not chummy, and in the furthest stretches of her imagination, Melora had never imagined that Kate Hudson would sell her out like this. But that was Hollywood justice: The moment you slipped out of line there was someone ready to step in.

"Come on," Melora said. "Kate Hudson? She's comedic."

"Nobody took you seriously as an actress till *Poses,*" said Vanessa.

"She's way too young! Rosie's supposed to be in her early forties."

"CGI," Vanessa said.

"I think Melora should postpone," Stuart said. "She's in no state to meet with a director."

"I want this role for you too badly to see it disappear," Vanessa said. "You know he's on a tight schedule with this. You need to convince Adam that you're fine. That the photo was meaningless, a distortion, and that the write-up was libelous. Can you do that? Show him you're a consummate professional?"

"I'll try," Melora said hoarsely.

"I already had his assistant switch the lunch to Sant Ambroeus. Gemma's too busy."

"Now let's talk about tonight," Lynn said. "You two are going to have to go to the *Dueling Donnellys* premiere. It's the only way to counter the bad press and convince the public you aren't on the rocks. We're going to limit the questions, but we want you looking very cozy and happy for the paparazzi."

Melora had forgotten about the premiere. She had half a head of hair, an oozing sore above her eye, and a gimpy ankle. There was no way she was working a red carpet. "I don't want to," she said.

"You've got to," Lynn said. "We're going to dress you up, and you're only talking to *Access Hollywood*. Afterward you and Stuart go to the Gramercy so they get some nice photos of you together; you stay an hour and go home."

"I'm not sure."

"Honey, if you don't show up," Lynn added, "it's only going to feed the rumors that you're a heroin addict."

"*Heroin?*"

Lynn cleared her throat and said, "Just don't go on Jezebel today."

After Melora hung up, feeling ill about both decisions, Stuart said, "What did you do? You were about to tell me what you did."

It had been a mistake to think she could confide in him. He was too selfish to be able to help her. "What do you care?" she asked. "You're never here. You book your movies back to back so you never have to be with me."

"I book my movies back to back because I can't afford to turn things down. I haven't been at this as long as you have."

"But even when you're here, you're so remote. You act like I'm a burden to you."

"Come on. I've been preoccupied with the screenplay."

"If you cast me, you'll get more financing."

"Not in the state you're in now," he said. He was staring at her with pity. It was humiliating to have your husband look at you this way. "Only you can control this, Melora. You can jump off the deep end or you can take charge. There are other modalities besides drugs. Why don't you try meditation?"

"Meditation can't fucking touch what I'm dealing with!" she barked. "It's like a drop of water in an ocean!"

"Did you call Dr. Levine?"

"Of course I did! He's out of town!"

He recoiled. She was approaching this all wrong. They were married. He would have her committed, and that goddamn Dr. Levine would probably get on board with it as soon as he got back from burying his mother.

She had to convince Stuart she was all right. "I'm sorry," she said. "Everything's kind of catching up with me, you know? The movie and Brooklyn. I feel so isolated here."

"I'm sorry," he said, but he didn't ask if she wanted to move. "Look at your hair," he said sadly. "Your beautiful hair."

"It'll grow back."

"At least let me clean the cut."

"You saw?"

"Come on. I'm not an idiot. How did it happen?"

"I bumped it in the bathroom."

"Doing what?"

"Reaching for wine."

Stuart shook his head mournfully and went into the bathroom. He emerged with some alcohol, cotton balls, and a clean butterfly. "I think you're going to need stitches," he said. "Are you sure you want to go to the meeting? You can tell Vanessa and Lynn to go fuck themselves."

"I'll get through it."

"Maybe I should come with you."

"That'll do a lot to restore Adam's confidence."

"Then I'll call Ringo and have him wait for you outside. If you're going to do this, I want to be sure you get home safely."

Melora nodded; if she'd had a car the night before, she wouldn't be working a Natalie Portman in *V for Vendetta*.

The door burst open, and Orion came in with a fencing sword in his hand, Annika following a few steps behind. "What happened to your hair, Mommy?"

"I'm sorry," Annika said, trying to pull him out.

"He can stay," Stuart said, though the last person Melora wanted to see at this moment was her son. "Mommy had a little accident." Annika looked uncomfortable. She'd obviously seen the *Post*.

"It looks yucky," Orion said, and then began shadow-fencing at the foot of the bed.

"Where did he get that?" Melora said, pointing to the foil.

"We signed him up for fencing at Powerplay," Stuart said.

How come she didn't know about this? Nobody ever told her anything, and then they acted surprised when she was out of the loop.

"Watch what I can do," said Orion. He demonstrated some moves with the foil as Stuart looked on, impressed. "I almost hit Darby in the eye the other day."

"Who's Darby?" Melora asked. It wasn't a name Annika had mentioned before.

"A friend of his from the playground," Annika said quickly.

"You were fencing him in the playground?"

"In the playroom," Orion said. Annika's face was red. Melora had known it all along. The Burmese were too honorable to steal.

"You had a playdate here?" she asked Orion.

"Yeah. We met him in the playground, and Annika said he and his mom could come over."

Melora glared at the Swede. "You said he didn't have anyone over."

"It was just one time."

"Were there other kids here?"

"No."

Melora prayed it had been the kid who had taken the wallet, because he wouldn't know what it meant, but she was afraid it was the mother. She'd never liked the neurotic neighborhood mothers, the fatties obsessed with their kids.

She glared at Annika. She was going to kill that Scandinavian bitch. Orion was still fencing, waving the épée wildly. "Too close to my dresser!" Melora shouted.

"Don't take this out on him," Stuart said.

"Don't tell me how to talk to my son."

"*Our* son. Don't raise your voice at him."

"Come on, Orion," Annika said, trying to pull him out the door.

Orion did a few parries, left hand on his hip. Melora couldn't stand his bungled moves, even if he was only four. She snatched the sword away from him. Orion's eyes widened in fright as though she was going to hit him.

"That's not how you do it!" she shouted, then did an expert thrust and parry as Orion watched in awe, having never seen his mother so active.

"How'd you learn that, Mom?"

"*Twelfth Night* at the Delacorte." Revved up, she attempted a lunge, and her ankle buckled beneath her. "Awwwghhh!"

"Are you okay, Mommy?"

"Get away from me!" she cried, collapsing onto the rug and cradling her foot. Why wouldn't the little fucker leave her alone? Why was he always coming into her room when she'd told him a hundred times he had to knock?

Orion's face crumpled and he raced out of the room, Annika following. Stuart shook his head at Melora reproachfully and walked out, too.

"Oh God," Melora wailed, massaging her ankle. With enormous might, she heaved herself up and hobbled into the bathroom to wash her face. She looked in the mirror. And to think she was once voted *Esquire's* Sexiest Woman Alive. She leaned in close and saw a cold sore, just emerging, at the corner of her mouth.

The Stepford Wife

STUART CALLED Rebecca at ten o'clock Thursday morning to ask if he could come over with his script. Rebecca was so excited that she dropped the phone and then frantically picked it up, afraid she'd lost him. Sonam was out with Abbie. Rebecca called and told her to have lunch out, explaining that she was on deadline for an article and needed more peace and quiet.

Rebecca attacked the apartment, trying to whip it into some semblance of order. Rakhman was on the scaffold singing, but because she was so excited to see Stuart, it didn't really bother her. She cleaned the kitchen and swooped up all the toys from the carpet, depositing them in a large basket in the corner of Abbie's room. She picked up the old magazines on the coffee table and stray onesies, footies, and wineglasses, returning each to its rightful place until the living room looked spare enough to be calming.

In the shower, she shaved her bikini line, armpits, and legs, brushed her teeth, touched up her brows, put a quarter-size amount of L'Oreal Absolut Repair in her hair, and dabbed Stella McCartney on both sides of her neck. She put on low-cut black La Perla boyshorts, a loose James Perse white collared button-down, a silver necklace with a circle pendant, and two diamond stud earrings, which she had to shove hard into her holes because they had closed up from lack of use. She made a mental note to take them out before Theo came home so he wouldn't suspect anything. Then she decided it was a sad statement that earrings would be a tip-off to infidelity, so rarely did she wear them.

She examined her reflection in the bedroom mirror. *Not bad for a thirty-five-year-old mom.* She opened Theo's bedside table drawer and took another of the lambskin condoms. She put it in her own drawer for easy access but decided not to change the sheets, for fear of being overconfident and jinxing herself.

Stuart arrived around eleven, smelling of sweat, which Rebecca didn't mind. She loved the smell of male sweat and had been disappointed when, back in the days when she and Theo used to have sex, he would insist on showering first. Theo had been a good lover, skilled and attentive, but always controlled. He never seemed to let go completely during sex, and over time she had accepted that this was how he was; she had learned to be grateful that he cared about her pleasure. In many spheres—cooking, decorating, driving, aesthetics, vacations—he liked things just so. It was probably something that had come from growing up around chaos: You learned to control the things you could. Because Rebecca tended to get easily flummoxed, was the kind of person who sobbed hysterically when lost on a road trip, she liked how good Theo had been at all of that. He was good at things.

The rolled-up screenplay was in Stuart's hand, but he made no move to give it to her. "Nice place," he said. It was nothing compared to the mansion, but at least he was polite.

"Thanks," she said. "If you don't mind Rakhman over there." She closed the shutters, top and bottom, so he couldn't see in.

"Where's the ankle biter?" Stuart said.

"With her sitter. They'll be back around one." She saw him glance at his watch and wondered if he was trying to calculate whether he would have time to fuck her. "Can I get you something to drink?" Rebecca asked. "Water? White wine? I'm going to have some wine. It's so hot I decided I'm allowed." This was the test: If his motives were pure, he wouldn't take the drink.

He gazed at her levelly and said, "Sure."

She filled two glasses and sat down next to him on the couch. He passed her the screenplay. "You don't want me to read it now, do you?" she asked.

"No, I just didn't want to forget to give it to you."

"But it's the only thing you brought."

He blinked at her. Should she hop onto his lap? In the movies these things got off the ground so easily; in real life it was so complex.

"Do you want me to turn up the air-conditioning?"

"It's fine."

"I never know if it's too cold for other people. I'm so hot. Every afternoon I've been watching movies in my underwear." He had no reaction to the word "underwear." Maybe he wasn't interested at all.

"What are you watching today?" he asked.

"I was going to watch *The Stepford Wives*. Have you seen it?"

"The remake? I was at the premiere. Terrible. I was embarrassed for Nicole. Couldn't say hello."

"No, the original. With Katharine Ross."

"Oh, yeah, I think I saw it many years ago, but I don't remember it too well."

"Do you want to watch it with me? I'll make some popcorn. I know it's weird, hot popcorn in this weather, but I can't watch a movie without it."

"I can't have any," he said, looking uncomfortable. "I'm on an Ayurvedic diet."

"What's that?" Rebecca asked, trying not to mock him. You couldn't mock a guy if you wanted him to fuck you, at least not too much.

"It's too complicated to explain, but it's about getting the right types of different foods."

"But wine's allowed?"

"Wine increases the pitta dosha. Ayurveda is all about moderation."

She giggled. The whole thing sounded ridiculous and vain. "So no popcorn?"

"You're tempting me now. I'll have a little."

He told her more about the diet while she made the popcorn, and as she stood in the kitchen archway talking to him, she didn't feel nervous. She felt clear and very smart. Stuart hadn't come to her apartment for coverage.

She served him the popcorn in a bowl. His wineglass was mostly empty, and she filled it. She inserted the disk into the player, sat next to him, about six inches away, and aimed the remote at the TV.

Katharine Ross, wearing a yellow bandanna on her head like the one Rebecca had been wearing in the food handling room, sat alone in the empty Manhattan apartment, staring out the window. A little dog ran across the screen so fast it looked like a cat. Ominous right away. Ross sat in the station wagon with her kids, obviously ambivalent about leaving the city, somehow knowing her husband was planning to turn her into a robot. Something caught her eye on the street—a red-haired man who looked a little like Stuart, crossing with a naked female mannequin under his arm. "Doesn't that give you the shudders?" Rebecca asked.

"Foreshadowing," Stuart said. He took out his phone and typed something in.

Rebecca found that pretentious but opted not to say anything. There were things about him she didn't like, but that was okay. That was the whole point. She wasn't going to marry this guy; he was allowed to be a little annoying.

As the family settled in Stepford and the weird neighbor wife brought over a casserole, Stuart leaned forward with interest. As he did, his knee flopped a little so that it was barely touching Rebecca's. She didn't say anything, but she held her leg very still so that they would remain touching. A current raced between them, and when she raised her glass to her mouth, she saw that her hand was shaking.

When he leaned back against the couch again, he scooted almost imperceptibly closer to her, without seeming to move his butt. This had to be something he'd learned on movie sets—how to make sure he was in the hot spot without seeming to move at all.

"How Park Slope is Stepford?" he said.

"Frightening."

"We think we invented supermoms, but they go way back. Like to the fifties. Except in those days the supermoms were on Valium."

"Would you rather have a wife on Valium," she said, "who gave you a martini when you walked in the door each night, or a happy working wife who didn't do anything nice at all?"

"Definitely a wife on Valium," he said. "Then I could have her at will."

He wanted her. This was happening. "When I watched *The Tenant* the other day," she said, "I wasn't just watching."

"Oh yeah?" His voice was quiet and very close. "You have a thing for Shelley Winters?"

"That scene, in the movie theater . . . it's sexy. The way he gropes her. And she likes it. I mean, I wasn't turned on that they were in a theater filled with perverts, but I was turned on that he felt he could do what he wanted to her."

"Do you always do that when you watch movies?"

"If there's something in them that I like. I went to Barnard, but I'm very turned on by the subjugation of women."

"I knew we had a lot in common."

Stuart put his hand on her thigh. And then, as though it were the most natural thing in the world, he pulled her toward him and kissed her. His breath was sweet but a little cinnamony. Had he chewed gum on his way over? If he had it meant he cared what she thought of his breath. He gripped the back of her neck. He was confident and very masculine. He was a man who knew what he wanted, and the thing he wanted was Rebecca.

Her clothes came off quickly. She pulled off his shirt so she could kiss the same chest she'd admired on the playground. He liked her panties and said so.

When they were both naked and she had sucked him for a while, she got the condom from the bedroom, came back, and started to unroll it onto him. There was a rap on the window from behind the shutters. "Jesus Christ," Rebecca said.

Another rap, more insistent. She threw a blanket around herself and went to the window, opening the shutters only a crack.

"You have key to basement?" Rakhman asked through the window.

"Downstairs mantel," she called quickly.

"I already checked. Wasn't there."

"Ring Apartment One." For a second he seemed to notice Stuart on the couch, but she couldn't be sure. She closed the shutters and went back to Stuart.

He hadn't lost his erection. It flattered her. A man could want her. She wasn't broken. "Do you have the condom?" she asked softly.

"You had it," he said. She looked under the cushion, but it wasn't there, and it wasn't under the couch, either.

His hands were on her shoulders. If they didn't do it soon, the moment would pass and they would never do it. What did the condom matter, anyway? It was a safe time of the month, not too long after her period. And she wanted to feel him inside her.

She rode him, staring into his famous blue eyes, wanting to prolong this first perfect moment. She came quickly, then rocked until she came a second time. He seemed close, and then his body shook and he lifted her off quickly as he came. She knelt and put her mouth around him to catch it so he wouldn't soil the couch.

She lay on top of him, feeling his warm skin. If she had known Stuart Ashby would be her businessman in St. Louis, she never would have gotten so upset when Theo said it.

Stuart kissed her neck and mouth and cheek and forehead and mouth again and pronounced, "You were . . . even better than I imagined."

"Is that a compliment?"

"Oh yes," he said. "You have no idea what I imagined."

She giggled then, a loud, open giggle that surprised her. He had turned her goofy. "I thought about you a lot, too. I thought about you when I first saw you in that Matt Damon movie. I mean, I went home and . . . thought about you."

"You're in good company. Millions of American women did the same thing."

She slapped him on the arm playfully. It was so surreal. She was play-slapping a major motion picture star after he had come over to her apartment to make love to her.

"You right?" he asked.

"Yeah, I'm fine."

"I didn't know you did that."

"What?"

"Smiled."

"Of course I smile."

"Not very often. But I had a feeling I could get you to."

They dressed next to each other, stopping every few seconds to kiss. She wanted to ask him a million questions about what he was like as a child, what he really felt about Melora, if he wanted to have children of his own, and if he would come to her apartment every Tuesday and Thursday for, say, the next seven years. But she knew the quickest way to ruin everything was to go talking about it.

Still, though she had no intention of pinning Stuart down, she was afraid that he would stand, yawn, and say, "I gotta get going." The guy went to bed with Melora Leigh every night. What would he want with a Park Slope mother—whose own husband wanted nothing to do with her?

And because she was certain he was going to leave, she was shocked when he stretched and said, "Why don't we go for a walk?"

The Osborne Garden

LIZZIE WAS having trouble moving. She had taken Mance to the Brooklyn Botanic Garden so he could get some shade, but after an hour of pushing him around and taking him to see the ducks in the Japanese garden, she was exhausted. She stopped on a bench to rest. As she sat there underneath the pergolas draped in wisteria, a couple approached, heading for the fountain.

There was something familiar about the way the woman moved. It was Rebecca. Lizzie's initial response was confusion—she wasn't pushing a stroller—and then she noticed that Rebecca was walking with a man. At first she thought it was Rebecca's husband, but as they approached, she recognized him from the movies. Stuart Ashby.

Lizzie looked up, about to say hi, but Rebecca was so caught up with him that she didn't even see Lizzie, and they passed, laughing loudly together.

How could Rebecca not have noticed her? All she had to do was look over a little. Lizzie made eye contact with nearly every mother she passed, to see the way they dealt with their children and also to see if she knew the kids. But Rebecca didn't even pause at the sight of a mother with a Maclaren.

Even with their backs turned, Lizzie could see Rebecca was smitten: She seemed hyper-focused, her whole posture different. Lizzie had listened to a lot of Ani DiFranco when she was gay and remembered a lyric in a song about a woman who falls for a bad guy: "She bends her breath when she talks to him." That was how Rebecca looked, like she was bending her breath.

What was Rebecca doing hanging out with Stuart Ashby? Had they really just met, or had they known each other a long time? Maybe they were having an affair, and the only way Rebecca knew to talk about it was to say that she had trained him at the Coop. Lizzie was furious with her friend for being so brash as to be seen in public with a married celebrity who was in the tabloids for having a troubled marriage. Just that morning the *New York Post* had run a horrible photo of Melora along with an article saying she and Stuart were having problems. Didn't Rebecca know?

They stopped at the fountain and sat on a stone bench, close. If they weren't having an affair, why were they together in the middle of the day? Somebody like Stuart Ashby didn't need any new friends. He was like Madonna; he'd already met everybody.

How could Rebecca do this to her? Why had Rebecca let it go so far the night before at Lizzie's apartment if she didn't feel something, too? Lizzie had bought Rebecca a pair of earrings at the Clay Pot, before she came to the garden. She planned to give them to her that night at the Gate. They were small sterling disks, elegant and understated, and she had imagined them framing Rebecca's face. They had cost sixty-two dollars and Lizzie had bought them with cash, like she was doing something naughty. How was she supposed to give Rebecca the earrings now, when it was obvious she was in love with somebody else?

She dialed Rebecca's cell, not knowing what she was going to say. She wasn't going to tell her she was in the garden, that was too weird, but she wanted Rebecca to hear her voice. She saw Rebecca fumble in her bag for the phone, look down at the number, then put it back in the purse. She went back to talking to Stuart.

When the voice mail picked up, Lizzie said, rushed, "Hi. I was just calling about tonight. We should get together before we go to the Gate. So call me. Okay?" After she hung up, she felt even more miserable than before. Rebecca had seen her number and let the call go. People didn't do that with real friends.

Lizzie wanted to race to the lovebirds and scream, "The only reason she's sleeping with you is because her husband won't fuck her!" Stuart didn't know that Rebecca was a much bigger loser than Lizzie was. So she wore more expensive clothes, but she was the pathetic one.

Lizzie stood up and began to head toward Eastern Parkway. She looked back one final time as she left, waiting for them to notice her, but their backs were turned, and they had gone on their way toward the Cherry Esplanade.

Lizzie hated feeling like she was saddled with a kid and they were free and alone. Rebecca was lucky she could afford help, but she complained about Abbie as though she didn't have a babysitter at all.

It occurred to Lizzie that she could spend some time without Mance if she let Mona take him; Michelle Obama's mother stayed with the Obama girls all the time while Michelle and Barack campaigned. But that was different. They were older, and besides, it was Michelle's own mother, not her mother-in-law, so she must have felt comfortable leaving them in her care. Lizzie wondered if it would have been different if it had been Barack's mother, the white one, who lived nearby. Would Michelle have saddled her MIL with her kids, or would she have refused to campaign altogether?

Lizzie had called Mona in the morning to ask her to sit that night. If the babysitting went well tonight, then she might let Mona take him during the day, but only for an hour at first. They'd have to take it little by little.

As Lizzie hurried toward the exit, she stewed. Whatever was going on between Rebecca and Stuart, it was obvious Rebecca was besotted. Rebecca was even worse than a breeder: a breeder starfucker.

On Eastern Parkway her phone rang and she jumped, thinking it was Rebecca. But it was Jay. "I'm just checking in," he said.

He liked to call on his own time, but sometimes when she called him, he didn't get back to her for hours. She knew he listened to her messages to see if it was urgent, and if it wasn't, he put her at the bottom of the list. "We're okay," she said. "It's hot." He'd played a gig the night before, but Lizzie couldn't remember the city. "How'd it go last night?"

"Incredible. Two encores."

"Where were you again?"

"Hanover," he said, and sighed as though she was supposed to have his tour schedule memorized.

"That's wonderful! I'm so glad it went well!" But she wasn't really happy for him. His success didn't include her. He seemed to enjoy the escape from domesticity. Who wouldn't? Domesticity was a prison. But she never got an escape, because Jay always acted like his time was more valuable than hers.

"Your mother's coming to babysit tonight," she said.

"That's great. I'm glad you asked her."

"I'm going out to dinner with a friend." She waited for him to ask for more details, but he didn't. He didn't even ask who the friend was. For all he knew, she could be having an affair, but it didn't seem to threaten him in the slightest.

"I miss you," he said.

"We do, too."

"Does he want to say hi?"

"He's been such a pill. It's probably better if he doesn't. What time do you get in tomorrow?"

"Around dinnertime. I'll call when we're outside the city." Lizzie tried to remember the last time she had been excited for him to come home, the last time her heart raced when she heard his steps on the stairs. It was impossible to look forward to seeing him when he made her so angry. She didn't know if he made her angry because he was so irresponsible or because he was her husband. "It's really hard to hear you," Jay said. "Where are you?"

"We went to the zoo and then the Botanic Garden."

She was having a hard time holding the cell phone while pushing the stroller. She hit a crack and Mance tumbled out. He wasn't scratched, but he was startled, and he burst into accusatory tears.

"What happened?" Jay said.

"Nothing, the stroller hit a little bump."

"Was he strapped in?"

"Of course he was strapped in," she lied. "Look, I gotta go." She shoved Mance in the stroller and buckled the harness. He cried all the way home.

Sant Ambroeus

MELORA ARRIVED at Sant Ambroeus looking as fantastic as someone in her situation could hope to look. Lynn had sent over an A-list
crew to help her: Melora's plastic surgeon, Steven Resnick, who had
stitched the cut with invisible stitches; a German transsexual makeup
artist named Toni, who used a three-hundred-dollar Japanese concealer
on the cut and the cold sore; a well-regarded SoHo orthopedist who put
an ACE bandage on her ankle but insisted she come in for X-rays as
soon as possible; and a gay Italian stylist named Alessandro who put
extensions into her remaining hair to cover the patch. To hide the ACE
bandage, Melora selected a long, dark pair of Adriano Goldschmied
jeans, despite the sweltering weather, a black-and-white limited-edition
Marc Jacobs T-shirt that read WHERE IS THE OUTRAGE?, and a pair of black
Satin d'Orsay low-heeled Manolos.

For her nerves she took a hundred fifty milligrams of Zoloft and two
milligrams of Ativan before she left. The orthopedist, Dr. Ash, had given
her some Vicodin for the pain, so she popped a tablet of that, too.

When Melora stepped outside into the midday sun, half a dozen
paparazzi were gathered outside her door—vultures who thrived on
death and distress. She'd felt so horrible after Heath's overdose, when
they stayed outside the house in Boerum Hill. A man had died, and still
they showed no decency!

She recognized the usual cadre of assholes, knowing most of their
first names. Usually, she saw them only at openings or premieres, and it

was unsettling to see them in front of the house. Phil Parnell was at the front of the pack, of course, with a five o'clock shadow and a perpetually red nose. She wanted to sock him in the face.

The cameras clicked like rapid fire, and she felt faint but focused hard on walking steadily, glad she had chosen low heels. Ringo, a burly man of indeterminate Eastern European ancestry, was waiting for her with the limo. Melora had never been more relieved to see him. He ran up to the stairs to escort her down as she kept her head low and ignored the paparazzi's questions: "Is it true you're addicted to heroin?" "Are you putting all your work on hold for now?" "Melora, are you pregnant?"

She pasted a slick smile on her face. As soon as she was inside the safety of the limo, which was soft and did not smell of car freshener, Melora sighed with relief. If only she had kept Ringo. Then there wouldn't be any paparazzi outside her door, because she would have gotten home safely from Southpaw.

When Melora walked into Sant Ambroeus, an upscale Italian restaurant in the West Village, she saw a skinny Ethiopian model at the bar reading a *New York Post*. The girl looked up, noted Melora, and then did a double take. Humiliated, Melora turned her back as she greeted the hostess, a twig with a seemingly fabricated European accent who pretended not to recognize her.

Adam hadn't arrived yet, so Melora took a table in the back and ordered herself a pot of tea whose name sounded like an Indian intestinal disorder. Stuart would have loved it.

Adam Epstein was thirty-five minutes late. By the time he showed up, the Ativan was kicking in and everything felt easy and simple. She had almost forgotten about the throng outside the mansion. All she had to do was stay mellow, and she would knock the meeting out of the park.

"I'm so sorry I'm late," Adam said without providing an excuse. Melora stood and kissed him on both cheeks, then stumbled a bit as she sat back down. She had met him in person only once before, at a Los Angeles Drama Critics Circle party, but their conversation had been brief and perfunctory.

Now, up close, she found herself attracted to him. He wasn't her type—she didn't like Jews in general, and he had an adolescent-Jew thing going on, with long lashes and floppy prep-school-style hair—but something about him was sexy, maybe the intellectual confidence. He grasped her hands in both of his and regarded her with a look that seemed an attempt to disguise pity as high regard. "Hi," he said, like it was a first date. He repeated it several times. She wasn't sure whether to say it back.

The waitress came to get their order, and Adam ordered the Insalata Centocolori, explaining that he had recently become a vegetarian. Melora, who had skipped breakfast, was craving red meat but, not wanting to offend his respect for animals, asked for the insalata, too. "Anything to drink?" the waitress asked.

"Glass of Sangiovese," Adam said, then looked at Melora and added, "What the hell. I had a long flight last night."

"You?" the waitress asked Melora.

Melora was unsure what to do. Given her bad press, she knew it was inappropriate to order anything alcoholic, but because Adam had, she felt he was giving her permission, so she said, "I'll have the same." He seemed to eye her judgmentally, and she wished she could retract the order.

"I want you to know," he said when the waitress left, "that whatever's going on with you, I'm not interested. I've always worked outside the system, and I don't think the personal lives of celebrities are relevant to their work. When we were shooting *Eva and Andie* up in Bovina, the press was crazy for photos of Sandy, because she'd just gotten married to Jesse James and he was up there, too. So we locked down the set and did the movie like a grad thesis."

"Oh, you went to grad school for film?"

"No." He seemed to have a chip on his shoulder about it, and she regretted the question. "I'm totally self-taught. I think film graduate school is a racket, and I've said so in several interviews." She was bombing. There wasn't any point staying for the rest of the lunch. She started to apologize, but he went on. "I just meant we were bare bones on *Eva and Andie*. If you show up at my set on time and do good work, that's all I care about. What you do between wrap and call is your business. I hate the press. If we were living in a different world, it wouldn't be like this. Do you think Truffaut had to deal with this bullshit?"

"No. I don't," she said, wishing she had boned up on her Truffaut so she could reference a few of his films.

The waitress brought their wine. Adam fingered his glass stem but didn't drink, so she didn't, either. She felt like she was in a desert and someone was waving a bottle of Poland Spring in front of her face. "I wrote Rosie for you," he said.

"Really?" She could taste the Sangiovese in her mouth, but he seemed to have forgotten that his was there and took a sip of his water instead, so she drank tea.

"Yeah, I was struggling a lot in those early drafts, and I finally cracked it when it occurred to me that Rosie was the older version of the character you played in *Jeannie Doesn't Live Here Anymore.*"

Melora's jaw fell open. *Jeannie* was an ABC Afterschool Special she'd starred in at fourteen about a girl who becomes bulimic, which was considered groundbreaking with the attention it called to the illness. Melora hadn't actually been bulimic when she shot it; she'd been a cutter, and two years later, when she starred in an ABC Afterschool Special about cutting, she'd been bulimic.

"You saw that?"

"I fell in love with you. To me, Rosie is Jeannie, grown up. She's searching on the inside, very alone, but she lives in a culture where she has to put on a false front. What I'm interested in is the space between the truth and the front. All my female characters have that struggle."

Something about this moved Melora. He'd seen her childhood work and noticed a through line between it and the work she did now. In interviews she always tried to dismiss her childhood acting, but in many ways, she felt it was her best, because she had been so unself-conscious, so pure.

"You know," she said, "I had this dream about Rosie in a bouffant and—"

"You see her in a bouffant?"

She nodded. He reached into his messenger bag and removed a black-and-white photo of a glamorous 1950s wife in a bouffant, looking miserable. "This is my model for the character. Swear to God. I just had a meeting with the costume director and showed her this picture."

They stared at each other as if they were about to have sex. This was going to happen. No one would find out about the wallet. She wanted to crawl across the table and suck Adam's face.

His brown Jew eyes bored into her, and it occurred to her that she had an opportunity to speak honestly. It was so hard to talk to anyone nowadays, so hard to be real. That was why she'd stolen that wallet. Even if it had created a mess, she didn't regret the feeling she'd had when she took it, the feeling for one sliver of a moment that she was alive.

Maybe Adam Epstein knew the pain of feeling like you were different from everybody. That was what *The Undescended* had been about, a young outcast coming of age. Maybe deep down, beneath that cocky New York swagger, much publicized friendship with Woody Allen, and Writers Guild of America Best Original Screenplay Award, Adam Epstein was suffering. Maybe he understood the pain that came from nobody really talking to you like you were there. Maybe when he woke up in the morning he didn't look over at Jessica Chafee and feel lucky to be married to such a beautiful woman. Maybe he felt like Jessica Chafee didn't know him.

Unable to wait any longer, Melora took a deep pull of her wine, opening her mouth wide as she raised the glass to her lips. Adam seemed to remember that his was there and took a faggy sip.

"Can I ask you something?" she asked. He nodded seriously, his eyes still emanating warmth, almost like a movie star's. They were so dark and round. She could feel her IQ rising as she stared into them. "Do you ever find it hard to get out of bed?" Instead of answering, he made a beckoning motion.

"Well, sometimes I feel so tired," she said. He nodded slowly. She was certain he thought she was crazy—now, if not when he'd seen the *Post* photo. But she needed to talk to someone, and because she couldn't tell her bad shrink or her husband how burdensome it felt to be Melora Leigh, she decided to tell Adam Epstein. Adam would understand. "I find it difficult to get out of bed in the morning. Just getting to the bathroom to brush my teeth and getting dressed takes this enormous amount of energy. I can't get my act together to do very simple things. It's like I have these huge weights attached to my limbs, like men on a chain gang. I don't know. Maybe it's a phase. Hormonal. A lot of problems are caused by hormones. Maybe it's because I'm about to turn forty."

He shook his head quickly, like a dog ridding itself of lake water. "Vanessa said you were thirty-seven."

"No, IMDb has it right. I turn forty in October." His Eastern European skin looked several shades paler. "Is that a problem?"

"Not at all. I just—you know when you think one thing and then you learn something else? It's just—weird, you know?" He sipped his wine, regarded the base of the glass with fascination, and then looked up at her. "Go on. Weights on your feet."

She was certain she'd blown it. He thought she was too old for the role even though it said clearly in the script that Rosie was forty-one. There was no point going on. But she was starting to tell him the truth, and when you started, it was very hard to stop. Melora wanted to trust him. He had such a sympathetic brow. This was why women liked to work with him. They felt they could mother him and smother him at the same time. "Well, for years I've been feeling like the problem was me," she continued, "like there was something wrong with me for not being able to get it together. But a couple of days ago I started thinking that maybe I'm not slow. Maybe the problem is that everyone else is rushing too much. And the people who are trying to make me feel crazy are doing it because they have something invested in believing that, whether it's my psychiatrist, or my husband, or my son, or my agent. Did you ever see *Gaslight*?"

"On my top ten!" he shouted excitedly. Finally, she'd broken through. She waited for him to say more, but he didn't.

"Well, I feel like I'm Ingrid Bergman," she said hesitantly. "And it's like I know that everyone's conspiring to drive me crazy, but the problem is I can't find anyone who'll believe me. I can see what a sham it all is, but instead of liberating me, the feeling is . . . depressing. I mean, who can I count on in this world? Who can I count on when I see a picture like that in the *New York Post*? Who can I count on?"

Adam looked beleaguered, but then his eyebrows slanted down on the sides, so he always looked sort of beleaguered. How was he taking this? Was he going to cast someone else, or did she stand a chance of changing his mind by leveling with him? She remembered a story in *Audition* about Barbra Streisand coming in to a play audition looking like a charity case, with vintage clothes, chewing gum. Barbra pulled the gum out of her mouth and stuck it on the bottom of a stool and proceeded to blow them all away with her singing voice. Then at the end, after she left, the casting director went up to the stool, but there wasn't any gum. It had all been a setup, to lower their expectations so she could impress them all the more.

Melora felt like Barbra Streisand without the lungs. "Look," she said. "I know that you read the *Post,* and I know that you're thinking I'm a pretty scary sight."

"You've never been more stunning." Was he humoring her? Was he some sort of bullshitter? It was offensive to be lied to, to your face.

"Adam! This hair is fake!" She lifted a few extensions to show him. "I bummed a light from somebody last night, and my hair caught fire. You know why? Martinis and Ativan don't go together! Ask Lily Allen! Do you know what time I start drinking most days?" She took a big sip of her wine for emphasis, and Adam took a sip of his own as though to brace himself for whatever she was going to say next. "Sometimes eleven. In the morning. I used to make myself wait till six at night. Then I moved it to five, and now I call it wine o'clock so I can start whenever I want. Am I proud of this? No. Do I want it to be like this forever? Fuck no! But I can't go back in the rooms, Adam! I'm too old! The people, the people! I just can't stand the people!"

He was blinking at her silently, his face deadpan. She wondered what it was like to live with him, whether he ever yelled at his wife. "So I drink. And sometimes I take these pills. They go right to the anxious loop in your brain and stop it. They stop the obsessive rumination. Apparently, obsessive rumination comes from early potty training, but I don't speak to my mother, so I never found out when I trained. Have you heard of benzodiazepines?"

He nodded slowly. She went on, "I figured. Your people are by nature very neurotic. You're probably on SSRIs yourself, given your parents' divorce, and if any of the frottage scenes in *The Undescended* were autobiographical, you've probably been on anti-compulsives, too."

She had come here to talk about a movie role and had now segued into public masturbation. She was accusing him of being a depressive. And this was someone she wanted to cast her. She hadn't expected things to go downhill so fast.

"By the way," she said quickly, "I love those NRDC commercials you did. Very new wave."

"*Adweek* called them pretentious," he said.

"No!" she said. "That close-up on the dying man's hand gets the message across. I get so upset when I think about global warming. I mean, I try to do my part. I just joined the Prospect Park Food Coop." He gave no reaction. But maybe he wasn't being mean. Maybe he was a man of few words. It was impossible to build any rapport with someone you couldn't read.

"Anyway," she said, "this isn't what I wanted to talk to you about." She had to get back to the movie. If she could convince him she understood his script, he would have to cast her. "I wanted to talk about this beautiful film you've written, this film about the bleakness at the heart of marriage."

"Is that what you think the film's about?"

"Well, yeah."

"Huh."

"Isn't that what you think it's about?"

"I'm more interested in what you think."

"Come on, Adam! Enough of the bullshit! What do you think your movie's about?"

He paused and took a deep sip of his water. "The enduring power of love."

He was out of his mind. It was like saying *Scenes from a Marriage* was the most romantic movie ever made. If he didn't understand his own work, she would have to explain it. "It's not about love, Adam! None of your movies are about love! Maybe you used that in some pitch with a hedge-fund guy to get financing. But don't try that shit with me."

She had worked hard not to swear since she adopted Orion, but now she was doing it left and right. "I'm sorry I tried that shit with you," he said. She had expected Adam to be inscrutable, but not like this. She had no idea whether she was hitting it out of the ballpark or bombing so badly he would bad-mouth her to the entire industry, turn her into a punch line at a Friars Club roast.

"I know there are other actresses who might come with better PR, but what you'll get from me—and let's be honest here, if at some point this meeting was a formality, the past twenty-four hours have transformed it into something else—is someone who is right for the role, who understands Rosie. Vanessa told me Kate Hudson wants in, and I don't mean to be catty, but if Stu and I go to *Yellow Rosie* at the Pavilion and I see her in a yellow bouffant, I'm going to gouge my fucking eyes out."

"And why is that?"

"First of all, she's a decade too young. Kate Hudson as Viggo Mortensen's wife? He's fifty! Second, I'm sorry to say it, but the girl's got no instrument! She wants to have one—that was why she worked so hard on *Almost Famous*—but drama is not her forte. I'm telling you, all that single-process goes to a woman's brain, Adam!" His eyes fluttered up to Melora's mane. "You think *I* dye? Oh, Adam, I'm a real blonde." She stood up and started to unzip her jeans, but he held up his palm.

She sat back down. "Just so you know," she said, "I'm willing to do frontal. In fact, I think the one thing this picture is missing is some good period 1950s bush. And because I'm Method, I'm already growing, Adam. I'm already growing. Think of me as the Robert De Niro of the pussy." The waitress brought the food and then dashed away as though afraid she was going to catch something from Melora.

The Robert De Niro of the pussy? What had she said? "I'm sorry," Melora said quietly. "I've been under a lot of stress lately."

"I understand," he said.

"Actually . . . my mother has dementia."

"I thought you didn't speak to her."

"That's why it's so painful."

His eyes seemed sad and sympathetic. Maybe she should have gone with dementia in the first place.

"Adam," she said, folding her hands on the table and scooting in her chair, "if you cast me in this picture, I can promise you one thing: You will get the truth. I had this acting teacher, this Russian teacher at Stella in the early eighties. Misha Slovinsky. In Misha Slovinsky's class, we would do our scenes, and at the end of each one, no matter how good it was or who had performed it, he would say, 'I dun belif it.' And then he would explain what hadn't been believable and why. His comments were always completely on the mark, and you'd come away going, 'How is this man so savvy?'

"Well, one day I did this scene out of *Hooters* where Ronda the homely one talks about how she's not beautiful. Misha was very into casting against type, so he cast Ricki Lake as Cheryl, the hot one, and me as Ronda. So I did the scene, and it was that magical thing where everything sort of clicks, even there in the dingy classroom with the sparse sets and no makeup. And at the end of the scene, Ricki and I sat there in the two chairs—you had to face the class while he critiqued you—and he leaned back in his seat, folded his hands, and said, 'I belif it.' Adam, if you cast me in your movie, you will belif it."

Adam's eyebrows seemed to droop all the way down the sides of his head. Had she depressed him, or was he just thinking deeply? "I believe you," he said. His tone was so even and measured that she couldn't tell how he meant it. Was he expressing faith in her or terror?

If he cast her after all this, it would be some sort of miracle. But a part of her no longer cared. Of course she wanted the role, but she felt as though it was out of her hands. She had gotten an opportunity you rarely got in this type of meeting—to show him who she was. If he couldn't see that she was right for Rosie, it was his loss. It meant he didn't get it. With a temerity she had been unable to summon when Robert Downey, Jr., cheated on her with Nancy Travis or when she found out that Sarah Jessica Parker had beaten her out for the role of SanDeE* in *L.A. Story*, Melora believed that if the project was meant to be, then Adam would cast her.

Ravenous, she stabbed her lettuce with the fork and shoveled it into her mouth. She took a big slug of wine to wash it down, and it splashed all over her WHERE IS THE OUTRAGE? tee.

Accepted

WAS IT possible that the Tina Savant conversation had really happened? On her walk to Melora's mansion, Karen kept replaying it in her head, convinced she had imagined it. But every time she checked her cell, the number was right there, under Incoming Calls.

It had happened at twelve-thirty, as she was on her way out the door with Darby to pick up Annika and Orion at the mansion. Tina Savant had called to say their offer of $761,000 had been accepted.

Karen had nearly dropped the phone when she heard the word "accepted." It had been such a long period of near misses that she had expected 899 Carroll Street to be another one. But it was really happening. They had played their cards right, and it had paid off. By the fall they would be in the North Slope, in an apartment with enough bedrooms to allow her to conceive.

When she called Matty at the office to give him the good news, he was silent at first, as though frightened they had overbid, but at last said it was good that she'd been aggressive, because the truth was he loved the apartment, too. Then he said he was sorry about their fight the night before and that they would have to celebrate the accepted offer with a bottle of champagne when he came home from work.

It excited her that he wanted to celebrate, because that morning, after her post-coffee bowel movement, she had noticed some egg-white cervical mucus—which meant that today and not yesterday was actually her Peak Day, and she stood a chance of conceiving if she and Matty had sex that night. She hoped he could get hard. His erection quality seemed to exist in reverse proportion to positive real estate news.

At the corner of Ninth Street and Seventh Avenue, she passed a newsstand and paused, as she always did, to glance at the tabloid magazine covers. On the magazines there was the usual smattering of bump watches. On the rack below, a *New York Post* photo jumped out at her. It was a woman vomiting, and the headline was MEL NOT WELL. Karen opened to page eleven, where she read the whole story, clapping her hand over her mouth as though to stop a wave of sympathetic vomit.

As she read the article, she felt a wellspring of sympathy for Melora. Russell Crowe and Sean Penn could get drunk or fight all they wanted, and it only made them more popular, but when it was a Lindsay or a Britney or a Melora, the story was totally different. This was what Hollywood did to women. If they weren't invisible, they were mocked as shrews or surgery addicts or, the worst of all insults, bad mothers.

She wondered if the photo had anything to do with the wallet she had taken from Melora's drawer. She had a feeling it did. Melora was in trouble, but Karen could save her. Karen knew what it was like to have the walls of your life come tumbling down before you. Only someone who understood could help.

Karen closed the paper and pushed Darby north, toward Garfield. Around Seventh Avenue and Seventh Street, she noticed a black man, tall and lean, come out of a passing van. He had a guitar strapped to his back and carried a small duffel bag. He seemed to be walking next to her for a while, looking at her. She feared he was a pervert or a pickpocket, but then he turned toward her and said, "Karen, right?" pointing at her with a big smile.

"What?" she asked, though she knew right away.

"I thought it was you. You don't remember me? Brooklyn Tech? Class of '94?"

It was Jean Pierre-Louis, the Brooklyn Tech trumpeter and taker of her virginity. He had lost at least forty pounds since he was seventeen and blossomed into a strikingly handsome man. His skin was dark like Seal's, and he had the kind of head shape that worked well with the shaved look. She couldn't believe how attractive he was.

"Right, right," she said, hoping her voice sounded calm and well modulated. "Of course I remember you, Jean."

"I go by Jay now. J.P. is my stage name. All my friends call me Jay."

"Jay," she repeated. He had even changed his name. It was hard for her to imagine that this was the same awkward tubby boy who had fumbled with her bra. "What do you mean stage name?" she asked.

"I'm in a band. I played trumpet when you knew me, but I switched to guitar at Oberlin." He gestured to a case on his back. "I just got back from New Hampshire. That was the touring van. My wife thinks I'm coming back tomorrow. I decided to surprise her."

"Oh," she said. He had a wife. "So you're married."

"Yeah. Her name's Lizzie. Two and a half years. We live on Park Place. It's only like two blocks from where I grew up, but it's so different now." She hadn't even known he was from Prospect Heights. They'd never discussed it. They were talking as though they'd known each other well in high school when, after those few phone calls, they had gone back to being strangers. "What about you? Do you live in the Slope?"

"Yeah, we're a couple blocks down that way," she said, waving toward the south. She added, "We just got an offer accepted on a place on Carroll Street, actually. We'll be moving in the fall."

"That's great."

She noticed Darby staring up at Jay and said, "This is Darby. Darbs, this is Mommy's friend Jay."

"Hi, Darby," Jay said, tousling his hair. "I got a little one at home myself. Mance. He's one and a half."

Karen's heart thudded. She knew she should be happy for him, but the news distressed her. She wanted him to be scarred from their sex, the way she was, and the fact that he had a healthy baby proved he wasn't. Everything was simpler for men. "Congratulations! Is he your first?"

"Yep. I love being a dad. I mean, it's hard work, but I love it."

He was taking out a photo now. The baby was light-skinned. So the mother was white. It didn't surprise her. He'd probably never dated a black woman. She wondered what the mother looked like, whether she was fat or skinny, pretty or short.

As Karen stared at the photo, she thought about what their own baby would have looked like. She had imagined it from time to time, and in the months after the abortion, she had dreamed of the baby, dreamed that it was a boy and she was smothering him in her sleep without realizing it. She imagined that this Mance's half brother was up in heaven looking down on Mance and wishing he could play with him.

Their son would be sixteen now, she realized. She would be the mother of a sixteen-year-old.

"That's an interesting name—Mance," she said. "Where does it come from?"

"Old blues singer. Mance Lipscomb. How crazy is this?" Jay said as they kept walking side by side. "I haven't seen you in all this time, and then I run into you on Seventh Avenue. I guess eventually, everyone who has a kid moves to the Slope, huh?"

"I thought you lived in Prospect Heights."

"Same thing," he said with a half smile, like she was silly for casting a distinction. But it wasn't silly. Prospect Heights was nothing like Park Slope. It wasn't even off the park.

"You know," she said, "as much as people make fun of this neighborhood, I love it. I've made so many friends."

"You should meet Lizzie. She could use a few more friends." The last thing Karen wanted to do was spend time with the mother of Jean Pierre-Louis's child, but instead of saying this, she smiled vaguely, so he would know she wasn't in the market for new friends.

"So are you working, or . . ." he asked.

"Oh, no, I'm with him. He's in nursery school, but he's off for the summer."

"Lizzie's at home with Mance, too," he said. "It's so hard on her. I keep telling her to get some help, but she doesn't want to. She used to be in publishing. What did you do before you had him?"

"I was actually a school social worker for a while, in the South Bronx." Since he was the big shot with the music career, she felt the need to impress him, if not with a hot career then with her political commitment to helping poor children. She wanted him to imagine her with all those difficult black children and see her as tougher and nobler than the average upper-middle-class white woman. "But after I had Darby, we thought it was better for someone to be at home with him. My husband's a lawyer, and he works long hours. I read this evil book, *The Feminine Mistake,* that said all women should work, but I think it's a crock. It's so individual. You can't make a blanket statement about what all women should do."

They chatted amicably for a few more blocks, and at Garfield, when she turned right, he said he'd walk with her. He told her about his band and how surprising the success was. He told her Mance's birth story, which involved a tub at the Brooklyn Birthing Center, and he said his mother was still living in Prospect Heights.

She wondered what it would have been like if she had given him a chance back then, after the terrible thing that happened. After that night at the dance, he had called and asked her to get pizza, but she declined. They were too different. They had nothing to say to each other, and besides, she was embarrassed by his weight. She herself had been slim then and felt that if she dated him, it would mean not only that she couldn't get a white guy but also that she couldn't get a skinny black guy.

Now she thought about the photo she had seen of Barack Obama as a boy in the Honolulu airport on the one day he met his father. He had been so pudgy in the picture, but today he was skinny and handsome, a compulsive exerciser.

The adult Jean reminded her of the adult Obama, slender and confident, bearing no sign of the fat kid he once was. Maybe his band was doing well and soon he would be as famous as Lenny Kravitz or John Legend.

Karen's parents would have hated the idea of her dating a black guy—around the house her father sometimes used expressions like "sooty" to refer to blacks, to Karen's great chagrin. But maybe he and her mother would have changed their minds once they got to know Jean. Karen still wouldn't have kept the baby, of course, but maybe she would have told Jean about it, and he would have come with her to the appointment, and the loss would have bonded them, like in that movie

Juno, except Juno had the baby. Maybe it would have made them so close that they would have dated long-distance during college and afterward gotten married and had a child, a child who was possible because they'd been smart about the first.

But it was silly to play that out. Beyond their obvious differences—Prospect Heights/Park Slope, Haitian/Irish, black/white—she never would have married a musician. When you built a family, you had to have stability. Jean's wife was brave to have chosen to have a baby with him, given the financial insecurity, not to mention all the temptation he probably had on the road. He probably had groupies in every city, good-looking guy like that.

They had arrived at Prospect Park West and Garfield Place. Karen saw paparazzi clustered across the street outside the house and wondered if it was because of the photo. "What's going on?" Jay asked.

"My friend lives here. She's an actress. Melora Leigh."

"What did she do?"

"Oh, you know, they just like action shots. I'm going to have to go past them to ring the bell." She felt excited that he was going to see her entering a throng of paparazzi. Though he knew they weren't there for her, she felt they gave her status by proxy.

She was about to cross the street when he said, "You know, there's something I always wanted to tell you, but I never got the chance."

She knew what he was going to say and wanted to stop him. "You were my first," he went on. "I told you you weren't, but that was a lie. You probably knew."

"Well . . ." This was too painful. She lowered her face, wanting to end the discussion, but he took it as a judgment on his stamina.

He laughed. "I wasn't very good back then. It's so embarrassing. I'm much better now. I mean, not that—I—you know." And then he grinned, able to laugh at himself because of the disparity between who he'd been then and who he'd become.

Karen found his false humility insulting. Stamina was a male concern, frivolous, while women had to worry about pregnancy and abortion—not to mention all the STDs that were easier for women to contract than men.

Jean's mild embarrassment only drove home his total ignorance of what had happened to her that night. He had no idea how much he had made her suffer, not only at sixteen but all these years later. She had run that night through her head a thousand times, wishing she had stopped him.

Working in the Coop child care room once, when Darby was only one, she had gotten in a conversation with a skinny father on her shift. She was fretting about how long it was taking Darby to learn to walk, and the man made some joke about how she needed to have a second kid so she wouldn't be so neurotic. Noting his four-year-old daughter playing with the train set, Karen shot back, "*You* only have one child."

"That wasn't the number we were going for," he said.

She didn't want to have to go around telling people that one wasn't the number she was going for, and because of Jean Pierre-Louis, she was afraid she would have to. Because she couldn't tell Jean any of this, she hated him more. Because of this near-stranger, she recorded each basal temperature as soon as she woke, without even even getting out of bed to pee, and then wrote the result on a chart tucked into her bedside table drawer. Because of Jean Pierre-Louis, she ate high-fat Ben & Jerry's ice cream each night because she had read that ice cream increased chances of conception, eradicating any marginal effect on her cellulite from the Masai Basic Technology shoes.

She hated this man who had reinvented himself physically and in name, even in instrument. Their sex had left no meaningful imprint. He had no idea what he had done to her.

"I should go in," she said, patting him on the shoulder.

"It was so great to run into you," he said.

"You, too," she said. She lingered a moment as he crossed and headed north, his guitar swaying as he walked. He even seemed taller than he used to be. She looked across the street at the paparazzi waiting for Melora. She reached inside her bowling bag and stroked the wallet. Maybe Melora had found out it was missing, and that was why she was going crazy. Even if Karen never had another baby, she mattered to Melora Leigh, although Melora didn't know it yet. She mattered to all those photographers.

Karen crossed the street and fought her way through the throng, who took halfhearted photos of her as though doubting she was anyone important. She rang the bell. Annika came to the door and yanked Karen in.

"What's going on?" Karen asked.

"There was a photo in the *Post*. It's a disaster. I tried to call you to tell you to meet us in the park, but you didn't pick up." Karen looked at her phone. She'd been so busy talking to Jean that she hadn't heard it ring. "Just one second and I'll get Orion," Annika said.

"I think Darby left one of his toys here the last time," Karen said. "It's a little Lightning McQueen car, from *Cars*."

"I left my Lightning McQueen here?" Darby said, crestfallen.

"I'll look for it later," Annika said briskly. "Orion! Let's go!"

"I want it now!" Darby screamed, and for once Karen was grateful that he was spoiled.

Annika looked uncomfortable but finally nodded. "Maybe you can look for it," she said to him. "Wait right here," she said to Karen, and headed up the stairs with Darby.

"Of course," Karen said. As Annika climbed, Karen turned quickly and swiped a key set off the rack. She waited a few more minutes and then pulled the car out of her purse. "Here it is!" she shouted up the stairs. "I just found it on the living room rug!" Then she shoved the key set deep into her purse.

Mona Pierre-Louis had paid for her groceries and was turning to the exit worker to show her receipt. Sixty-four years old, she'd been going to the Coop since 1978. She'd belonged so long that while newer members had five-digit membership numbers, Mona's was 122. In recent years she liked shopping there less and less. The place was always so crowded, and the white people were all so pushy, slamming right into you with their carts and strollers without even saying "excuse me." In the old days, when François was still alive, the members were more relaxed, maybe because most of them were stoned.

She didn't have anything against white people, per se. Her daughter-in-law, Lizzie, was white, and although it was sometimes difficult for Mona to accept that Jean hadn't married a Haitian, she now tried to see white people through the prism of having a half-white grandson. One of the reasons she had come to the Coop was to get some organic cookies for the boy, Mance, for whom she was sitting that night.

Mona had been surprised when her daughter-in-law called to invite her but had agreed. Mona's son, Jean, a musician—he'd changed his name to Jay, but she refused to use it—was often traveling with his band. Mona tried to reach out to Lizzie but felt the girl was rude to her. The day before, she had given her a sun hat for Mance, but Lizzie hadn't seemed to like it. It was like she was the only one who knew how to dress him.

The exit worker was a pinched-looking white woman with gray hair tied in a bun at the nape of her neck. The woman made small talk with a friend before taking his receipts to check them.

This was another problem with the Coop. The members were so selfish nowadays. Checkout workers chatted with friends or flirted, with no regard for the rest of the people standing on line. Over time the members had lost sight of what a coop was about.

Mona stepped forward and handed the worker the receipt that indicated how many shopping bags she had. After the woman counted Mona's bags and checked them against the receipt, she said, "Can I look inside your purse, please?"

"No, you may not," Mona said.

"It's a new policy. We're supposed to search bags." The woman pointed to a sign that read, THE COOP HAS THE RIGHT TO RANDOMLY SEARCH MEMBERS AT EXIT.

So what if there was a sign? "But you didn't search that man in front of me! You didn't search your friend!" A few people turned to stare.

"It's random," the woman said, pointing again to the sign. "There have been a few pickpocketing incidents, so we're supposed to do random searches."

Pickpocketing? The nerve of the woman. A black man was the Democratic nominee for president of the United States, and Mona had to put up with this? "I'm not a pickpocket!"

"I'm sure you're not, but if you'll hand me your purse, I can look inside and then you can go." There was a line of shoppers building up behind Mona, and she could feel them glaring at her, thinking she was making a mountain out of a molehill. But this was no molehill. "Ma'am, you're welcome to talk to the team leader if you—"

"You want to search me because I'm black!"

Behind her, on the line, she saw a white woman roll her eyes at a white man. Mona's cheeks burned.

"This has nothing to do with that!" the exit worker shouted, standing up as though Mona had wronged her and not the other way around. "I told you, it's random."

"There's nothing random about it. You're assuming that because I'm black, I'm a thief."

The team leader, a slim bearded man, came up behind the exit worker. "Ma'am," he said to Mona, "if you'll come with me, we can straighten this whole thing out."

"I am not coming with you!"

Mona set down her grocery bags and ran out onto the street. She walked as fast as she could to Union Street, sat down on a chair in front of Tasti D-Lite, covered her face, and cried. The Met Food on Vanderbilt was getting better these days anyway, the produce much higher quality than it used to be, and there was a gourmet grocery on Flatbush for anything the Met didn't sell. It wasn't worth the Coop's 40 percent savings for her to be humiliated like this when all she was trying to do was feed herself.

She was about to head home when it struck her that if she gave up, she would be part of the problem. It was easy to run away, to bury these things, but she had an opportunity to do something about it. The Coop was supposed to be sensitive to these kinds of issues, and if she could get it reported to the right people, they might be able to do something. She went back inside, past the entrance desk, and climbed the stairs to the office. That was how she found out about the Minority Issues Task Force.

Notting Hill

THAT AFTERNOON, while Abbie was napping and Sonam was cleaning the kitchen, Rebecca dialed Lizzie. Rebecca had a bad feeling about the swingers thing but figured she would humor Lizzie by showing up. She might even get some good material for a new novel set in Park Slope. And she was afraid that if she didn't show up, Lizzie was going to go nuts on her, go Glenn gay Close.

"Hi," Rebecca said. "I got your message."

"Are you having an affair?" Lizzie asked.

Rebecca moved her mouth away from the phone so she wouldn't sound like she was breathing hard. Then she said, "Why would you say that?"

Lizzie told her she had seen them in the garden. Rebecca's mouth got dry, and she had the sudden fear that Lizzie would tell Theo. She had to play it cool. It wasn't like she and Stuart had been holding hands or anything.

"Why didn't you say hi?" Rebecca asked.

"You guys looked like you didn't want any company. I think you're having an affair with him. And I think it's lame."

This was exactly why you couldn't open up to other mothers. They were guaranteed to have more problems than you did. Rebecca never should have told her she'd met Stuart. Lizzie was jealous of her for having a life, for finally getting laid for the first time in a year and a half, the longest drought she'd had since before she'd lost her virginity. Why hadn't Rebecca picked a normal mom friend who would have been happy for her for getting to fuck a movie star, who would have asked how he was in bed?

"Come on," Rebecca said. "What would a guy like that be interested in me for? That's so *Notting Hill*."

"Well, it seemed like—you guys seemed intimate or something," Lizzie said.

Rebecca was elated that they had come across this way because it meant there was something mutual, and the one thing you couldn't do when you were in a relationship was see it from the outside. "No. He's like that with everyone."

Remembering the disappearing condom, she lifted the couch cushions to see if she could find it, but all she found were a few pennies and a pistachio shell. Where was the goddamn thing? Had Stuart taken it on purpose because he wanted to bareback? Did that turn him on or something? She got down on her hands and knees and looked under the couch. She found one of Abbie's long-lost toys, a purple Hello Kitty ball.

"Why were you with him?"

"We ran into each other on Seventh Avenue, and he said something about wanting to see the Cherry Esplanade. I offered to take him. He said he'd never been there before."

"But they moved here two years ago!"

"You know celebrities. They never plant roots. So what time should we meet tonight?" Rebecca pulled the couch away from the wall and the unused lambskin condom dropped, wilted like a dried flower, onto the floor. It had gotten wedged between the couch and the wall. Sonam had come out of the kitchen and was sweeping. Rebecca wrapped the condom in a paper towel and deposited it in the garbage under a dirty diaper.

"You still want to come with me?" Lizzie asked, sounding surprised.

"Of course I do. It'll be a kick. It's not like we're going to do anything . . . right?"

"Right."

"So where do I meet you?"

"Come to Loki at seven-thirty and we can grab a drink before we go to the Gate."

There was a noise in the background on Lizzie's end and then an excited shout. Lizzie said, "Jay came home early. I have to go." And just like that, she hung up.

Lizzie had sounded happy to have her husband home, and Rebecca envied her, but only for a moment. Lots of women were glad to have their husbands walk in the door, but Rebecca had something much more exciting than a husband.

The Walker

WHEN MELORA got in the limousine on the way home from the meeting, she swallowed another Ativan. She settled back onto the seat as Ringo headed into afternoon traffic. Adam was probably on the phone to Kate Hudson, or Julia, even. That would be terrific. Julia Roberts stealing Melora's third Oscar. Her phone rang. Vanessa. "How'd it go?"

"Um . . . all right, I guess." What was Melora supposed to say? If she told her what she had said at the meeting, Vanessa would lose her mind. The key was to play it close to the vest.

"Can you tell me anything else?" Vanessa asked.

"He said he doesn't care about the *New York Post*."

"Scott Rudin cares about the *New York Post,* and he's got to okay anyone Adam likes."

"Did you talk to Scott already?"

"I left word."

Melora could see the next year of her life. Adam would refuse to hire her, saying she made Amy Winehouse look stable; CAA would drop her; the other agencies would blackball her; and she'd sign with some sheisty manager who was so desperate he'd take anyone. CAA would bad-mouth her to the entire industry, and in a few more years she'd be doing infomercials, Lindsay Wagner–style, or worse, starring in documentaries such as *Searching for Debra Winger.*

Her cell phone rang. Stuart. "Sweetheart, how did it go?"

"I wish I knew."

"What do you mean? You're not making any sense."

"He's impossible to read."

"Of course he is. They all are. But did you get any indication of how he responded to you?"

"None."

"Did he say anything at the end, something that might—"

"He just said it was a pleasure to meet me."

"Huh." He sounded worried, but not about her. The only thing he cared about was getting *Atlantic Yards* to Adam Epstein, and if she didn't get the part, the entire Leigh-Ashby clan would be on Epstein's shit list.

"What do you care if I get cast or not? What does it matter, anyway?"

"What do you mean what do I care? This is the best script you've gotten since *Poses*."

"I don't know," she said sullenly. "I think it's overwritten."

"Are you on something?" he asked. "Did you take anything before the meeting?"

"What? No!"

"You're slurring your words. If you showed up blitzed on your pills . . ."

"What? What if I did?"

"You know, I should have taken that poison away from you. You're a danger to yourself."

Lynn rang on the other line, and Melora switched over without saying goodbye. "How was it?" Lynn asked.

"Maybe he likes quirky."

"Quirky is not you, Melora! Quirky is Sylvia Miles!"

"I did the best I could. I really tried."

"That's all you can do, honey." An image flashed before Melora's eyes of unbuttoning her jeans. She thought about telling Lynn but decided against it. Lynn was an old woman, Melora couldn't shock her too much. "Now, I don't know what you were planning, but I feel very strongly that you should do your shift today."

"What?"

"At the Coop. It's in forty-five minutes."

Melora had Outlooked Lynn her shift schedule after joining the Coop, but in all the craziness over the wallet, she'd forgotten about it. "Oh God," she said. "I want to go home and go to bed."

"Sweetheart, if you're going to be a no-show on the first shift, it'll just fuel the rumors. Someone will figure out you missed it, call in an item, and they'll tie it to the vomiting. Adam might find out."

"I'm sure I won't be the first person in the history of the Coop to miss a shift."

"The whole point of joining was to be spotted."

"You don't know what I look like right now."

"I do. Toni sent me a cell picture. You'd never know you were missing half your hair." Melora gritted her teeth and popped another Zoloft.

The traffic was so bad going into Brooklyn that Melora didn't get to the Coop till a few minutes after the shift was supposed to begin. On her way in, an angry middle-aged black woman pushed past her out the door. This was another reason she regretted her decision to join: The members were so high-maintenance.

As soon as she got on the shopping floor, her throat closed and she began to have trouble breathing. Oh God. She had to get out. Had to get some air. What if they'd already gone through the videotape and she'd been spotted? What if undercover cops were waiting for her to return to the scene of the crime so they could apprehend her right here? She looked around. Everyone looked like spies, with their shifty expressions and extraneous headgear.

Maybe there was something new in the Coop newspaper about the pickpocketing. If they had reported on it the week before, there might be an update now. She dashed to the rack by the cashiers, but it was the same issue, with the story on people who'd fallen in love at the Coop.

She thought about that trick, Schrödinger's Cat, where the cat wasn't dead until you actually opened the box. She was suspended in a pre-opened box time in which she had done nothing wrong because so far nobody knew. This buoyed her for about a minute, until she replayed the lunch in her head and realized that even if she didn't get caught, it didn't matter, because Adam Epstein would never cast a lunatic.

As she turned to go back to the entrance desk, she saw a big yellow sign above the doors. PICKPOCKET ALERT—WATCH YOUR VALUABLES! She shuddered and looked down. Everyone was watching her. They were going to get her sooner or later, she knew it.

At the desk she signed in and introduced herself to her team leader, Craig, a short man with a neat beard. "I want to do checkout?" she said, wheezing a little. She would have to touch up her makeup before she sat down.

"All the checkout stations are taken. You're going to have to be a walker."

She resisted the instinct to make a streetwalking joke, something about how at least hookers got paid, and instead asked, "What does a walker do?"

"You walk people to their cars or apartments with their shopping carts and then bring the carts back to the Coop."

She had seen the walkers in the neighborhood, as ubiquitous in Park Slope as lesbians with dogs. They wore orange vests and chitchatted with the shoppers for blocks and blocks. She didn't want to do it, but at least this way she would be outside. Outside she couldn't do anything stupid.

"Go outside with Julie, and she'll explain what to do." He pointed to a tall, pale woman in her forties with an intense, slightly psychotic look.

Julie handed Melora an orange vest and led her into the sweltering heat of Seventh Avenue. Any day now she would be spending her days in an orange jumpsuit and look back on the orange vest with nostalgia. "So this is a really simple job," Julie said. "You wait out here, and when someone asks for a walker, you go with them. You're supposed to ask where they're going, to be sure it's not out of the boundaries." Julie handed her a yellow ditto with the boundaries demarcated on it—about ten blocks in every direction. "If they ask you to stop anywhere on the way to their car or their house, you have to explain that's not allowed. Also, you're not supposed to carry the groceries up any stairs for them." They sat side by side on a bench. Sweat ran down Melora's neck, dissolving any remaining makeup from the Adam Epstein lunch.

Within a few minutes a Hasidic mother asked Julie to walk her. After they left, Melora sat there weighing the benefits of ditching the vest and bolting home. The paparazzi would be there, waiting for her. Someone was probably calling them right now to tip them off. What if Phil Parnell took a shot of her pushing the cart? Would it be good publicity or bad? At least it wouldn't look like she was running from the scene of the crime, if it turned out the video showed her taking the wallet. She could say it was a lookalike, an imposter. But there were no skinny blondes in the neighborhood. All the women still had baby weight, even the ones whose kids were in grade school.

A dumpy, redheaded woman, in mom jeans and a wrinkled "718" T, came out of the Coop with a humongous gray shopping cart. Then she retreated back inside and came out, pushing a blond boy in a Maclaren. "Can you walk me?" she said, and then did a double take as she recognized Melora.

"Where are you going?" Melora asked.

"Fourth and Fifth. Oh my God. I'm sorry. It's just— Oh my God, it's you." Melora glanced at her map. It could be worse. Fourth Street and Fifth Avenue was only eight blocks away. It could have been ten or twelve. "I'm so sorry," the woman said, shaking her head.

"Why?" asked Melora.

"That picture. In the *Post* this morning. I—felt so horrible. I mean, it didn't even look like you. The first thing I thought when I saw it was that they had doctored it, like that Mischa Barton ass shot." Why had Melora joined this godforsaken place? "So was it? You, I mean?"

Melora didn't say anything. She looked from the cart to the stroller, thinking about the pain in her ankle. She reasoned that whatever the kid weighed, it was probably less than the groceries. She put her hands on the stroller handles and began to push it toward President Street. After a few steps, the boy turned around, spotted Melora, and bawled, "No, Mama, NOOOOOOOOOOOOO!!!!!!!!!"

"It's okay, Jones. It's all right." His Abu Ghraib–style screams indicated otherwise. The woman turned to Melora guiltily. "Why don't I push him and you can push the cart?"

Melora relented. She walked a few feet ahead of the woman to discourage conversation, but the woman caught up with her and said, "Why were you throwing up? The press is so quick to say it's drugs or whatever, but there are a lot of reasons someone could throw up that have nothing to do with drugs." Melora considered the possibility of stranding her with the shopping cart, but this was exactly the type of woman who would write in to Gawker and call her a Coop deadbeat. She tried to guess the wordplay Gawker would use in the item headline: IT'S NOT EASY BEING GREEN.

"I had food poisoning," Melora answered wearily.

"What did you eat?"

"Clams."

The woman nodded like she wasn't convinced but wasn't going to push it further. "Was it hard for you to do that scene in *Poses*?" Melora stared straight ahead. They were on President between Seventh and Sixth. "You know, where you die from the sleeping pills? I mean, wasn't it scary pretending to be dead?"

How was she supposed to answer this? Like she was talking to James Lipton? Was the woman going to pull out a card with the next question? At first Melora opted to say nothing, but this was one of those people who took silence as encouragement. "It was a challenge," Melora said, "but I felt it was worth it."

"I guess that's what they pay you the big bucks for, huh?" As she pushed, Melora's hands trembled from the Ativan, the Vicodin, and the crushing heat.

"I saw Stuart and your son on the playground yesterday. He was very cute. Orion, I mean. Well, Stuart also. They're both very cute. He was talking to this woman I know, Rebecca Rose?"

Of course he was. He loved chatting with women and always ate it up when he got recognized. Melora imagined that the mother was Asian. There were a million Asian mothers in Park Slope, all married to short ugly Jewish guys.

"Rebecca said he was her camp counselor in Vermont," the woman said. Stuart had never been a camp counselor in Vermont. Was this woman messing with her head? "He said it was a miracle he was allowed back in the country afterward."

What was Stuart doing going around making up lies to stay-at-home mothers? She would have to ask him about it when she saw him.

They were heading down Sixth Avenue. Melora stopped to take a few deep breaths. "Are you all right?" the woman asked.

Melora nodded. She couldn't puke again, not in public, even if it meant she had to swallow it. But it was so hot, and the shopping cart so heavy. If only that stupid team leader hadn't been such a Nazi. This bordered on unfair workplace practices, to make someone walk for hours in the sweltering heat. SAG would never allow this.

Melora could feel beads of sweat popping on her lower lip. She wiped her lip with the back of her shirt. "Stuart was such a doll to Orion on the playground. Really attentive and kind. You're so lucky to have met a guy like him. I don't believe any of those rumors about, you know, the two of you being on the rocks. I think people just say that because he's not on the deed."

They were at Carroll and Sixth, waiting to cross. What happened next felt like a slow-motion action scene in a movie. Melora watched it from above, hovering like a ghost. Her hands loosened on the cart handle, and the cart rolled elegantly into the avenue, a speeding white van slammed into it, and the groceries scattered violently everywhere. A bag of Sesame Blues popped and exploded on a windshield, covering it with round dark chips. The van driver cursed, slammed on the brakes, and got out to inspect the damage. Melora hobbled on her good foot toward home, certain she wouldn't get a work slot credit now.

Swingtown

JAY HAD come home that afternoon unexpectedly, and though Lizzie had been excited to see him, she was also resentful that he felt he could barge in on her with no warning. Her hostility seemed to excite him, and they wound up making love on the living room floor while Mance played in his crib.

He said that since Lizzie was going out that night anyway, he was going to see some friends play at the Living Room. If only he knew where she was going, what she hoped was going to happen.

When Mona arrived at a quarter to seven, Lizzie asked if she wanted anything to eat, and she shook her head, taciturn, and said she'd already eaten. Lizzie was carrying Mance on her hip while trying to finish getting dressed, and Mona said, "Here, let me take him."

"It's okay," Lizzie said, more harshly than she meant to. Mona frowned and watched Lizzie struggle to get both heels on while holding him. Lizzie felt so bad that she set him down on his grandmother's lap.

She expected him to fuss, but he didn't, instead reaching for Mona's big costume earrings. Mona looked ten years younger holding him, as though she missed having a baby. "Well, hello," she said, nuzzling his nose. He laughed. Sometimes he seemed happier around other people than he was around Lizzie. It made her wonder whether she was doing the right thing by staying home with him.

"I've already given him dinner," she said. "And there's milk in a bottle in the fridge. You should bathe him around seven-thirty and then feed him the bottle right after. You heat it up in some water—don't use the microwave."

"I know not to use the microwave," Mona said, surly.

"And you might have to sit with him for a few minutes. You can bring the rocker in from the living room and sit by the crib. If he gets really fussy, you can put him to sleep in our bed. I don't mind."

"I won't need to do that," Mona said, as though there were something wrong with it.

"You have my number if you need me," Lizzie said, hoping that Mona didn't call with an emergency right in the middle of the swing—if it got to that point. "I'll probably be back by eleven at the latest, and I'll get you a car home. I hope that's okay."

"Go, go. Enjoy yourself. Where you going?"

"For a drink with a friend. Another mother."

"That's good—two mothers getting out alone."

"She's really cool, actually. Her name's Rebecca."

"Well, you and Rebecca have fun."

"You, too." She kissed Mance, waiting for him to cry, but he didn't. When she slipped out the door, she could hear them both laughing and had the eerie feeling that Mona had made a joke about her to her son.

Lizzie found Rebecca sitting at the bar of Loki in a colorful canvas skirt and a green scoopneck blouse. She was already sipping a glass of wine, which meant she was trying to get in the mood. Lizzie was elated.

"You look great," Lizzie said, pecking her on the cheek.

"Thanks, so do you."

Lizzie was pleased with her outfit—a clingy black sleeveless vintage dress that hit her curves in all the right places. She had done her short nails in bright red. She took out the box of earrings and set it before Rebecca with a big smile.

"What's this?"

"Just a little something."

Rebecca opened the box. "You got me earrings," she said, frowning.

She was so ungrateful. Lizzie pretended not to notice. This was going to be a perfect night. "Put them on."

Rebecca put them on and turned to Lizzie. "Thank you," she said. She looked so radiant in the light, so sparkling.

Lizzie had it all figured out in her head. Even if the couple didn't show she was going to try to get Rebecca drunk enough to make out with her. Maybe she could even get Rebecca to come back to her apartment. She could say goodbye to Mona and make love to Rebecca in her own bed; Jay wouldn't be home till late anyway.

And if the couple did show, it would be even easier. They would be unattractive, of course, but she decided that she could use this to her advantage; they could flirt with them enough to get a rise out of them, then leave. Whatever happened, it was going to be good. Even if Rebecca didn't know it, she wanted Lizzie, too. Otherwise she never would have agreed to come. And once they were together for real, she'd forget all about Stuart Ashby.

It was only a block from Loki to the Gate, and as they walked, Lizzie joked about the height and hair-loss level of Andy, wondering whether she'd ever met Alexandra on one of the playgrounds. Rebecca seemed muted, and Lizzie realized she would have to get more liquor in her system.

As they were about to cross Third Street to the Gate, Rebecca hesitated. "What is it?" Lizzie asked.

"Are you sure you want to do this?"

"Of course I'm sure, *Tess.*"

"Maybe you should do this alone." Rebecca was a user, plain and simple. How could she abandon Lizzie now, after all this?

"You don't even know what's going to happen. They probably won't even show."

"But they might. And—I don't know, it makes me uncomfortable."

"Why? They won't be looking for us. They're looking for a blonde and a redhead. If we keep arguing, they're going to see us."

Rebecca nodded and they crossed. As they went in the door, they spotted an attractive couple sitting at the bar, matching the description Andy had given, but Lizzie didn't look too closely for fear they would be onto them. The Gate was a dark, old-school-style tavern that had televisions above the bars and specialized in draft beers from all over the world. The women took a booth against the wall behind the couple so they could gawk. "Oh my God," Lizzie whispered, as she got a closer look.

"It's the Hotties," Rebecca said. The only attractive couple in the neighborhood had shown up looking to swing.

Andy had tan, Judaic skin and curly wild hair, and the torso of a surfer or kite boarder, strong but not overbuff. Alexandra was a slender woman with long hair in two Heidi braids.

Lizzie glanced quickly at Rebecca, whose mouth was hanging open in a half smile. This was good. The hornier Rebecca was, the better Lizzie's chances.

Andy looked over his shoulder at the girls, and they kept their heads down. "I think they're onto us," Rebecca said.

"We should order a drink, maybe, so we seem normal."

Lizzie went up to the bar and ordered two vodka tonics. "Now they'll definitely be onto us," Rebecca said when she plunked the drinks down on the table.

Lizzie took a big drink of her vodka tonic and watched Rebecca do the same. "What the fuck are we supposed to do?" Rebecca said. "He keeps looking at us."

"I don't know. Talk to them, I guess."

"I thought this was a bluff."

"It was, but . . ."

Andy was getting up and coming over. He said, "You're supposed to give accurate descriptions when you say you're going to meet someone."

"What are you talking about?" Rebecca said, at the same time as Lizzie said, "We had to check you out first." Rebecca glared at Lizzie for giving them away.

"You're both very beautiful," he said. Rebecca took a big swallow of her drink. "Which one of you is Tess?"

"This is," Lizzie told him, pointing at Rebecca. He sized them up.

His wife was getting up from the bar. She walked with her legs turned out, as if she had been a dancer once, and she was wearing a high-necked 1970s-style cream sweater and a pleated skirt. It was the kind of nerdy look that only someone this attractive could get away with, as though she had played a bit part on *Swingtown* and decided to keep the clothes.

"I'm Alexandra," the woman said, and the two of them sat down opposite Lizzie and Rebecca, who introduced themselves by their fake names. "I love your earrings," Alexandra told Rebecca. Lizzie crowed.

"Why don't we get another round?" Andy said.

The Dueling Donnellys

FOR THE *Dueling Donnellys* premiere, Melora went with beige Marni twisted gabardine pants, 2005 silver Manolo mules, and a clingy black Chloé top that made up in glamour for what the trousers lacked. Toni had come over at six to redo Melora's face, and when Melora regarded herself in the mirror, she was pleasantly surprised, coming off as together and sleek, the opposite of her internal state. Stuart looked stunning in an off-white Tumi shirt and Rogan jeans.

The paparazzi were still outside their house, but on Stuart's arm, she didn't mind as much. Ringo was waiting with the door open, and Stuart hurried her in, slamming it on the photographers. "Animals," he said. "First poor Michelle Williams, now us. Don't they know this is a residential neighborhood?"

When they got out in front of Loews Nineteenth Street, Lynn was waiting for them. "Sweetheart," she said, kissing Melora. "You look gorgeous."

Melora saw flashes coming at her from every direction. The reporters' questions came immediately: "Is it true you two are splitting up?" "Melora, are you going into rehab?" "Are you putting your career on hold indefinitely?" and "Is it true your mother's been suffering from dementia?" Melora smiled sweetly, but it was all she could do not to scream at them to get a life, they were ruining the world. They were horrible. Where was the outrage?

"Not taking questions," Lynn said, leading Melora and Stuart to the *Access Hollywood* reporter, a pretty black girl with straight hair.

"Melora," the *Access Hollywood* reporter said, sticking a mike in her face. "How does it feel to be here in New York celebrating a film that was shot in New York?"

Melora began to calm down. Softballs. Lynn had prepped her. "It's so wonderful, really, and I'm just glad that all this production is coming back to the city." Stuart squeezed her hand encouragingly.

Over his shoulder she saw them coming. Two cops, white and burly. They had staged it this way for maximum publicity. They were going to handcuff her right here on the red carpet in front of all the hangers-on and paparazzi. She turned to face them.

But they merely adjusted the barricades that had been put up to keep the crowd back from the carpet. Heavenly God! They were just crowd police! She wanted to race over and embrace them both.

Down the line Melora could see Kate Hudson and Vince Vaughn answering questions from other reporters. There must have been fifty of them, some European, standing two and three deep.

"This film is about a contentious brother-sister relationship. Can you relate to that?" the reporter asked.

Melora was almost home free. "Well, I'm an only child, so not really. But I can certainly understand how a sister would be protective of her brother."

"And did you enjoy working with Vince? A lot of people have said you make a very natural brother-sister team."

"You know, he's a doll to work with. Just a really free, very open actor."

"Patricia Field designed the costumes for the movie. How did you enjoy working with her?"

"Pat is a genius. A living genius. The way she expresses character through wardrobe, it's just—I can't say enough good things about Pat Field."

"That's great. So do you and Stuart have any special plans for the summer?"

"We're going to try to get away, but for now we're just relaxing at home." Melora thought about saying "in Brooklyn," but decided against it, figuring it would only draw to the mansion the two remaining Manhattan paparazzi unaware of her PR woes.

"Stuart, what are you working on these days?"

"I have a part in the new Kevin Smith, which comes out in September, I think. I play an Australian sex-machine salesman. Case of typecasting, I guess." The reporter gave a big, appreciative smile, and Lynn ushered them away—wise, Melora thought, to let Stuart get in the last word. He was better with the one-liners.

Inside the theater, Lynn and a handler led Melora to a greenroom off the stage, where she, Kate, and Vince were to sit until Arnon Milchan introduced them all to the crowd. In the old days premieres weren't such events. You could do the press line and then dart out. Now they had to introduce you to the audience, turn it into theater.

Stuart had said he'd wait for her in the limo, and then after she made the appearance, they could grab dinner at Bar Blanc before the party at the Gramercy. Melora never watched her own movies and wasn't about to start now.

In the greenroom she found Vince and Kate chatting amicably as their press reps typed away on BlackBerries. Melora greeted them.

"You look awesome, baby," Vince said. "Really. Awesome."

Kate kissed her on both cheeks and said, "How come you didn't do any press?"

"I did. *Access Hollywood.*"

"I understand," Kate said. "I wouldn't want to talk to anybody, either, after that horrible picture. I mean, I've hated Murdoch for years but that was . . . cruel."

"That Stars Without Makeup bit *Star* had of you last week was pretty cruel, too."

Kate turned away. Melora sat on a couch on the opposite side of the room with Lynn. "You should have let it go," said Lynn reproachfully.

"She provoked me," said Melora.

"I know, but you can't stoop to her level. She's got a lot of romantic problems."

"What about Lance Armstrong? I thought they were hot and heavy."

"Oh, come on, now. A thousand dollars says they don't make it to Christmas."

As Melora watched Kate's mouth move, she was convinced Kate was bad-mouthing her to Vince, saying that Adam Epstein had already called to cast her in his film. This was torture, being stuck in a room with her nemesis. Melora was beginning to doubt Lynn's judgment. First she'd suggested the Coop, now this. Melora had had a chance to sign with Stuart's rep, Ina Treciokas, two years before, but had stayed with Lynn out of loyalty.

She had to get a pill under her tongue. She reached in the Majorelle, pried a couple Ativans out of the vial, and coughed to slip them in. She thought she saw Kate notice.

The stage door opened, and the handler beckoned them out to the stage. Vince and Kate readied for their entrance, taking last-minute looks in the greenroom mirror. Kate did a scary hair flip, turning her back to Melora. Vince adjusted his shirt collar and went next, clearly trying to keep them apart. Melora followed as quickly as she could, but the heavy metal door shut in front of her. She fumbled to open it again, while the handler was turning the knob from the other side. Vince and Kate were already waving to the cheering crowd by the time Melora took her place next to them, looking dazed and wobbling slightly on her feet.

Come to Bed

WHAT'S TAKING so long? Karen was lying in bed waiting for Matty to come in. After their celebratory dinner of chicken couscous and a bottle of Chandon Brut, he had given Darby a bath and put him to bed, then said he had work to do and went out into the living room. She figured he was anxious about sex. She had suggested it, but only obliquely, during dinner, saying just that they could "spend some time together" after Darby went to bed. She hadn't even mentioned her EQ mucus.

Now, as she looked at the clock, she realized he'd been in there an hour and a half. The time had flown by—she had to send a few e-mails for the Audacity of Park Slope voter registration drive in the Grand Army Plaza greenmarket that she was helping to plan, and then she got caught up in a Jennifer Weiner novel, and now it was nine-thirty. She couldn't keep her eyes open much longer.

She put on her robe and went into the living room. The back of the couch faced the hallway, and as she approached, she noticed vigorous movement. There was something foreign and private about it, and her first thought was that he was sobbing.

She came into the living room silently and saw it all at once—his hand moving up and down against a large close-up on his laptop of something going in and out of a shaved vagina. Then the penis pulled out and a hand was stroking it and the vagina turned upside down and above it—on the same body—was *another* hard penis, attached to a buxom Asian woman with what were clearly fake breasts. The vagina wasn't a vagina after all. It was an . . . asshole. The woman was a man.

The woman, or whatever it was, was murmuring, "Oh, give it to me." And then the man—the original penis—turned toward the camera, and the woman with breasts put her penis into his . . . what could only be his . . .

It was Karen's gasp that turned Matty around. He slammed his laptop shut and leaped up, zipping his fly. "Jesus, you scared me!" he said angrily, as though she—and not he—was the guilty one.

Karen felt sick. It wasn't that she assumed he didn't do it; all guys did, especially men with high-pressure jobs. But this was not the old in-and-out. What had she seen? She couldn't even begin to decode it. She had imagined pornography before, but this was something entirely different. A woman, with a woman's breasts, and a penis—not a fake one, a real one with hair and veins? There was nothing about this in *The Surrendered Wife*.

Did it mean he liked men, or whatever that—thing—had been? That minotaur? How could he have the nerve to look at that when Darby could wake up and walk in at any minute to ask for a glass of water?

"I was waiting for you to come to bed," she said.

"I thought you were asleep," he said, like a moron.

"I can't believe you," she said.

"I got on that site by accident. I don't even know how—"

"Stop it."

He came around the couch and tried to touch her, but she scrambled out of his arms. "I'm sorry," he said. "I don't even know how I found that."

Her mind kept flashing back to the terrifying image on the computer screen, the image she couldn't make sense of. Who was she married to? How could Matty be attracted to what he saw on that screen and also to Karen Bryan Shapiro? If this was what turned him on, it had to mean he hated her.

"I don't have secrets from you," she said, thinking of the wallet and realizing instantly that this was not true.

"I love you so much," he said helplessly.

"You ruined everything," she said. "We got such good news today. This was supposed to be a special night. And now every time I remember it, I'm going to think of . . ."

She went into the bedroom and slammed the door, trying to figure out what to make of this. Her husband was a mystery to her. He had hidden himself from her, and he had done it because she wasn't enough for him.

Who knew what he did in his spare time? She'd seen the ads in the back of free newspapers. For all she knew, he was spending his money to have sex with those . . . things.

She wanted to be enough for him. That was the whole reason you got married: because you found someone who needed you. Matty didn't need her to get off, and he didn't even want to make another child with her. He didn't need her to help him be a father because he didn't want to be a father again.

But there was someone else who needed her. Someone whose life she could impact. She grabbed her bowling bag from the foot of the bed. She would make Matty sleep on the couch, and after she was certain he was asleep—Matty could sleep through any strife—she would take a car service to someplace pristine and beautiful. The Gold Coast.

Badly Drawn Boy

"CAN I buy you another round?" Alexandra asked the women. They had all moved to the back room of the Gate, dark, with tables around the perimeter, and quieter than the blaring front room adjacent to it.

"I'll have a dirty martini, two olives," said Lizzie. She had gone through a martini phase with Sarah during the lesbian jitterbug craze of the mid-nineties, when the Gap commercials came out. The more she drank, the more Rebecca would drink.

"I'm still working on this," Rebecca said, pointing to her vodka tonic. Lizzie was afraid this meant she wasn't sold on the couple. How could she not be? In Park Slope it didn't get any better than this.

While Alexandra went to the bar to get Lizzie's drink, Andy sat opposite the women, looking from one to the other like he was the fox in the Jemima Puddle-Duck stories that Lizzie read to Mance.

"So how do you two know each other?" he asked.

"We're sisters," Lizzie said suddenly. Rebecca glared at Lizzie.

"You're sisters?" Andy asked, perking up.

"Yep."

"Who's older?"

Lizzie pointed at Rebecca. "I wasn't sure that would be okay with you guys, so I didn't mention anything about it," Lizzie said. "I hope it's cool."

"Just so you know," Rebecca said quickly, "we like to do things together, but we don't like to do things *together*."

"Oh," said Andy.

"Except when we drink," said Lizzie.

"Well, *she* likes to do things together," Rebecca said, looking at Lizzie meaningfully. "But I don't. So she lives with it. That's sort of what being a sister is about. So how old are your kids?" Rebecca was a human prophylactic. It was like she was trying to make this as unsexy as possible. Why had she come?

"Two and four," said Andy. "Boys."

"Are they home?"

"Oh yeah. With their sitter. She's not expecting us till late." He raised his eyebrows, looking like Groucho Marx. "What about you? How old are yours?"

"My Cyrus is one and a half," Lizzie said, "and Tess's daughter . . . Sunshine . . . is the same age. We like to do everything at the same time."

Rebecca slitted her eyes at Lizzie, clearly not liking the name Sunshine.

"Your daughter's named Sunshine?" Andy said. "That's such a cute name."

"Yeah, well. She's filled with it. Sunshine, that is." Rebecca took a deep swallow of her drink.

Alexandra came over with Lizzie's martini and two shots. She sat next to Andy, across from Lizzie. She and Andy clinked and did the shots.

"They're sisters," Andy said. His wife frowned as though disbelieving.

"So how long have you guys been doing this?" Rebecca asked.

"Doing what?" Andy said.

"Um . . . meeting people."

"Not long," said Alexandra. She seemed unhappy and uncomfortable, and it made her less attractive. "We started with these very good friends of ours, on vacation in Aruba, and then decided it was something we wanted to pursue."

"So are we the first ones you . . . met besides your friends?" Lizzie asked.

"No, we've met a few couples on craigslist, but they weren't like us,"

Andy said. "Not our type of people, if you get what I mean. That's why we posted on Park Slope Parents."

"How many responses did you get?" asked Rebecca.

"Including the death threats?" asked Alexandra.

"I know!" Lizzie cried. "They went crazy on you!"

"Alex didn't expect it," said Andy, "but I did. Nobody in Park Slope has a sense of humor."

"We got one response from a couple who seemed legit," Alexandra said, "but they said a few things in their e-mail that made us nervous, so we never met them."

Lizzie's curiosity was piqued. "Like what?"

"The guy said he and his wife were interested in deviance, too. I didn't like the word 'deviance.' "

"You did the right thing," Lizzie said.

"I don't get it," Rebecca said. Her voice slurred, and she looked even angrier than usual.

"Get what?" Alexandra asked warily.

"Why do you do this? Was it a joke? You can tell us. We won't be offended."

"It's not a joke to us," Andy said carefully.

"But why swing? I mean, you guys are hot. You probably have a smoking sex life. So why'd you want to add to it?"

"We believe that an open relationship strengthens the bond," Andy said.

"Come on, seriously," Rebecca said. "Did one of you cheat or something, and this is what you decided to do as a compromise?"

"What are you, a shrink?" Alexandra said shortly. Rebecca was in danger of ruining the whole thing, Lizzie thought. Whatever the couple's motives were, they didn't want to share them. Rebecca had opened Door Number Three, the door of a couple's dark places.

"She's trying to say she finds you both very cute," Lizzie said quickly.

"Well, the feeling is mutual," Andy said, and then laughed, a nervous, effeminate laugh that contrasted with his muscular appearance. Maybe he was one of those attractive but insecure men who had no idea how much he had to offer. Lizzie imagined that Alexandra was a psycho ex-dancer who had cheated on him and had him by the balls.

"You know, you two don't look anything alike," said Andy.

"Everyone says that," Lizzie said quickly. She couldn't tell if Andy believed they were sisters or was going along with it to see how far they took it.

"Why don't you sit on my lap?" he asked Lizzie.

She swallowed hard. What was he expecting her to do with him? What if someone she knew walked in, a mother from the neighborhood, and told Jay? He would kill her. Lizzie didn't want to be in this loud bar with this weird couple, no matter how attractive they were. She wanted to be alone with Rebecca in her bed, stroking her hair, kissing her like before . . .

A song came on by Badly Drawn Boy, a British pop group. Lizzie had heard it many years before and loved it. "The Shining." It was slow and beautiful and made you fall in love with whoever you were with. "I love this song," Lizzie said.

"I'm glad," Andy said. "Do you want to dance?"

She nodded. This was nerve-wracking. Before she met Sarah, she'd slept with only two guys, one in high school and one in college. She wondered what Jay would think if he knew she was here with a couple who wanted to swing. Would he be angry or laugh it off because they were parents? How come he never worried that she would cheat on him with another man?

Lizzie and Andy slow-danced on the floor. A couple hipsters at other tables stared at them as if they were weird. Alexandra watched from the table, her face flushed, either with anger or alcohol.

"You two should dance," Lizzie said as she and Andy swayed past the women.

"I think I'm good," Rebecca said. But Alexandra stood up and took Rebecca's hand. Rebecca hesitated and then got up. The women held each other like it was an eighth-grade dance, Rebecca's arms on Alexandra's shoulders, Alexandra's arms on Rebecca's waist. Lizzie could see instantly that Alexandra wasn't interested in women at all and was doing this only for Andy's benefit. She felt sad for both of them.

"So is your older son at P.S. 321?" Lizzie heard Rebecca ask Alexandra.

"We're in 39."

"Which one is that again?"

"Eighth and Sixth."

"Oh, right, right," Rebecca said. "I hear it's getting harder to get those variances." It was like she was trying to make the evening as unromantic as it could be.

Andy had moved his hands down to Lizzie's butt and was nuzzling her neck. She felt awful and afraid. But this had been her own idea. Alexandra started to kiss Rebecca and Rebecca took a step back. Some of the hipsters were whispering to each other.

Still standing, Andy started to grope Lizzie, kissing her neck and face. His hands were messy and all over the place. Lizzie didn't like it. He was sloppy and sexist, and it made him less attractive. She wanted to run away with Rebecca so they could laugh about him together, laugh so hard they fell on top of each other.

"Maybe we should take a break," Lizzie said, darting for the table again. The others followed. Andy sat opposite her and leered. "Do you guys have any weed?" Lizzie asked.

Andy nodded. "We should probably go outside, though," he said.

They all stood on Third Street, a few doors down from a house where Lizzie had had a playdate a couple months before. Andy took out the joint. "You think we're okay out here?" Lizzie said.

"As long as we do it quickly."

Andy lit the joint for Lizzie, who inhaled and coughed. "You sure you want some?" Rebecca said. Then, to Andy, "She's still breastfeeding."

"Only a little," Lizzie said. She shot daggers at Rebecca and passed her the joint. You weren't supposed to bring up nursing in the middle of a swing. Not that Lizzie knew what you *were* supposed to talk about.

"I thought you said your son was one and a half," Andy said.

"He is," Rebecca said loudly. Rebecca was trying to humiliate her, mocking her for wanting this to happen. Lizzie wanted to slap her.

Back inside, Andy sat next to Lizzie and said, "You're so beautiful." Then he was kissing her, everywhere, a full makeout. Lizzie looked across the table at Rebecca, who seemed to be smirking. Taking Andy's cue, Alexandra kissed Rebecca, pushing the hair from her face. "That's okay," Rebecca said. "I'm good."

This was Lizzie's last chance. Maybe the pot would kick in and Rebecca would finally make out with her. She broke off from Andy and turned to kiss Rebecca. As she got her mouth on Rebecca's, Rebecca pulled away and reached into the pocket of her purse. She examined her phone and laughed aloud. Then she stood and said, "I gotta go."

After Rebecca left, Lizzie wasn't quite sure what to do. She was too stoned for her rage to sink in. The pot made her lonely. She had been so excited about this night, about her makeup, wardrobe, and scent. It wasn't even nine o'clock, and she was alone at the Gate with two Park Slope parents, two Park Slope parents who, when it came right down to it, though attractive, weren't all that interesting or smart.

"That wasn't your sister, was it?" Andy said.

"No." Twenty minutes later, Lizzie was on their king bed between them, not sure what she was doing there but lacking the will or perhaps the energy to leave.

The Afterparty

NARS WAS the sponsor of the *Dueling Donnellys* afterparty at the Private Roof Garden of the Gramercy Park Hotel. Melora posed for a few photos with François Nars himself, and when the cameras stopped flashing and the two of them moved away, he eyed her cut and said he had a much better concealer than whatever she was using.

At her table Melora ordered white wine from the waitress, certain that Stuart would reprimand her. Instead, he ordered a whiskey. Maybe all the drama was getting to him.

Their dinner at Bar Blanc had been stilted and hostile. Both had drunk heavily as she described the lunch with Adam, and Stuart seemed to grow more forlorn. She wanted him to tell her he was rooting for her, but she felt as though he was ashamed of her.

Kate and Vince were several tables away, laughing merrily with their entourages, which included Mischa Barton, Luke Wilson, Adrien Brody, and Lucy Liu. Melora was sitting with Stuart and Lynn and no one else.

Someone had separated Melora and Kate on purpose, and though Melora was relieved not to have to make small talk with Kate, she was envious that the other table seemed so lively while she was stuck with her husband and her publicist. Even Stuart kept looking over as though he would rather be at Vince and Kate's table than his wife's.

In the old days she and Stuart would have had a dozen friends with them. But tonight she hadn't even thought to invite Cassie and David.

When the waitress brought the drinks and she'd had a few sips of wine, she started replaying the lunch in her head. Maybe Vanessa had heard something and hadn't gotten a chance to call her. It was only six-thirty there. She dialed CAA and asked for Vanessa's office. She saw Stuart stiffen as though nervous for her, which only made her more uncomfortable. The assistant, Ryan, picked up. They were always men with names like Ryan, Tim, or Dan. Very heartland, very chipper. They were straight but acted gay and lasted six months each. "Hey, Ryan," she said quietly, trying to sound light and in control, as if she'd been out of the country a year and had never even heard of the *Post*. "It's Melora."

"Hey, Melora," he said cheerily, his voice not betraying the events of the past day. "Let me see if I can get her."

She counted off the Mississippis on her fingers. By the time she got to seven, she knew what was coming. "She stepped away," he said. "Can I take a message?"

"Just tell her to call me."

"Was she in?" Stuart asked. It was obvious she wasn't in. Was he trying to rub her humiliation in her face? "I'm sure the lunch went better than you thought," he said, but his words sounded empty and discouraging.

Had she really tried to show Adam Epstein her pubic hair, or had it all been a dream? Had she gone to the Coop to do a shift? Had she really let that shopping cart roll down the street? She flashed back on that scary mother who had been asking her all those questions. "Were you ever a summer camp counselor?" she asked Stuart.

"Crikey, what are you talking about?"

Melora noticed Kate get up with Lucy Liu. At first she thought they were heading for the bathroom, but they came right up to Melora's table and smiled. "I'm so sorry to impose, Stuart," Kate said, "but Lucy's been wanting to meet you forever, and I told her I'd do the honors."

Lucy, in a slinky off-white dress that left nothing to the imagination, extended her hand. "I loved you in *End of the Day*," she said to him, ignoring Melora.

Melora watched Stuart's face perk up. "It was a brutal shoot, but I'm proud of the result."

"I'd love to work with you someday. I hear you're writing some-thing . . ."

"Oh, it's early yet."

"I hear it's set in New York. I love working in New York. I grew up here, you know."

"Of course I know."

"Well, if you have any roles for me, please send it along." Lucy shook his hand again.

Melora couldn't help what she said next. She turned to Kate and said, "Did you call Scott Rudin this morning about *Yellow Rosie*?" Melora saw Lynn cover her face with her hand.

"What are you talking about?" Kate asked. Lucy Liu looked as though she was noticing Melora for the first time.

"Because I want you to know that I would never do that to you. I don't profit off of other people's downfalls. I've been in the business thirty years, and I had a lot of opportunities to muscle in on other women, but that is not how I operate."

"Me, neither."

"You're lying! You're such a lying bitch," Melora said. Lucy Liu gasped.

"Hey," Stuart said.

"Honey," Lynn said, putting her arm around Melora protectively.

"Get offa me!" Melora shouted. And then she lunged at Kate, trying to scratch her eyes out. But she was a second too slow; Stuart grabbed Melora from behind and yanked her back as Kate gaped in horror and Lucy whisked her out of the room.

"You're a very fucked-up woman!" Lucy cried.

"You crazy bitch!" Kate called.

"We're getting out of here," Stuart said. Lynn rushed them to the stairs and they bounded all the way down to the street and the limo. Stuart and Melora hopped in, the paparazzi snapping photos of their stricken faces.

"What were you thinking?" he screamed at her after they had pulled away. She could feel the flashes getting pictures of them arguing. The cameras went through tinted windows now. They saw through dresses.

That was how the Kerry daughter had gotten in all that trouble at Cannes. Technology had no morality.

"You were on the call this morning!" Melora screamed. "She's trying to get my part!"

"She could charge you with attempted assault!"

"She provoked me!"

"You're a liability to everyone around you. It's one thing to ruin your own life but another to ruin mine."

"I knew it!" she said. "All you care about is your own career! You didn't want to get married till after *Poses* took off. And now you're afraid I'm going to get in the way of you getting your movie made."

"That's not true," he said calmly. "You were the one who wanted to get married. You said you wanted the world to know how much you loved me."

She had no memory of this. He was always accusing her of saying things she'd never said, and he did it with this same certain, patronizing expression, just like Charles Boyer. "I never said that!" she said.

"You did!"

There hadn't been a prenup, and she was beginning to regret it. She'd suggested one at her business manager's bidding, but Stuart had been opposed to it, saying, "Only in America do you plan the downfall of the marriage before it's begun." Shamed, she had dropped it. Now, if they split, he could take half of everything she'd made since they married, and half the proceeds from a sale of the house, even though she had bought it with her trust.

"You're a liar!" Melora cried, feeling the wine and Ativans sloshing around in her brain. She felt like her head was going to explode. "You only want me to get this part so you can suck up to Adam Epstein, and you know that if he casts Kate, you've lost the chance to show him your script."

"That's ridiculous. I have friends in common with Adam. I could have gotten it to him months ago."

"He's the first director I've had a chance to work with since Paul who actually has some producing chops. You just want to use me to get to him. You didn't care how I was doing until that *Post* photo came out."

"You sound crazy now. You don't even know what you're talking about."

"I'm not crazy!"

His face softened. "Look," he said. "I want to help you, Lor. But you have got to tell me what's going on. This morning you said you did something. What was it? You have to tell me or I can't make it better."

"I can't. It's too terrible," she said, and then everything caught up with her and she began to sob.

"What is? Did you kill someone?"

"Warm."

"What do you mean—warm? Is this a joke?"

"Think the Ten Commandments."

"Adultery?"

She shook her head. And then she told him. Everything. About feeling compelled to take the wallet, and the article in the Coop newspaper, and how they were probably going to take her to jail. The only part she left out was how the wallet had gone missing from her bedside table. She was too afraid he would call her an idiot.

When she'd finished, he took her into his arms and she sobbed into his shoulder. It was such a relief to tell him, to have him know her. They were a team. She'd been silly to think he was using her. Like he said, all he wanted was to help her.

"I don't get it," he said. "We don't need money. You don't have to steal."

She had hoped he would understand, but he didn't. He didn't get that the moment had been like an orgasm for her. She had done it and then she had felt calm. If only she could feel that way again. "Of course it's not about money," she said, pulling away.

She had made the mistake of marrying someone better adjusted than she was, someone so low-key, so humble, and so grateful for his success that he didn't see how anyone could be successful and unhappy. She shouldn't have opened her big mouth.

He tapped on the divider and it went down. "Make sure you wait until she gets into the house, okay?" he told Ringo. "Let me out here."

"What's going on?"

"This is a lot for me. I need a break from you."

He was leaving her? With no warning? "What? What are you talking about?"

"I'll be back later. I just need a little space." It was the worst thing a man could say to a woman.

They were on First and Eleventh. "Where are you going? Please don't leave me."

Ringo stopped the limo, and Stuart got out. She watched him through the glass like she was never going to see him again.

Crosby Street

REBECCA ROUNDED Fifth Avenue heading north. She dialed him as she was running, then ducked into a storefront, eyes peeled for Lizzie. She was relieved to get away from that ridiculous scene at the Gate. The couple was cute but way too insane for Rebecca.

"I can't stop thinking about you," Stuart said. "Can you meet me?" He had become forthcoming. She lapped it up. This was what she had missed as much as the sex: the flattery. In the early throes of love, you complimented each other. Then you got married and spent the rest of your years hurling insults and complaints. Marriage was disappointment verbalized.

"Yeah, I think so," she said. "But I shouldn't be too late." Theo wouldn't care where she was. He was probably fast asleep, curled next to Abbie in their bed, as he was most nights.

"Me, neither." She didn't ask him to elaborate. She didn't want to know about Melora or Orion. She wanted him to exist solely for her. "A friend of mine has a place in SoHo. Can you meet me there?"

"Who's the friend?"

"I'm not telling."

"Is he male?"

"Maybe."

"Is it someone famous?"

"Everyone I know is famous."

"Uh-oh," she said. "Is it Russell's place? Guy Pearce's?" He gave her the address and hung up.

She caught a cab at Carroll and Fifth and leaned back against the seat as they cruised across the Brooklyn Bridge into the city. She pulled the Lizzie earrings out of her ears and stuck them in her purse. They weren't her style, way too hippie-dippie for her taste. She felt embarrassed at the awkward sentimentality Lizzie had displayed. She pitied her and felt sick for her at the same time.

As the cab moved, Rebecca peered up the Bowery at the towering luxury hotels, thinking about the SROs that had been torn down to make room. She looked out the window at all the rich Euros and trust fund kids who had taken over SoHo and the Lower East Side, and she didn't feel as furious as she usually did about how money had ruined the city. She felt romantic. New York was big enough for all of them. The skyline would survive.

When she got to Crosby Street, she saw Stuart waiting, and then he came to the cab window and paid the fare. Rebecca saw this as romantic and not sexist. He wasn't treating her like a whore. He was treating her like a princess, though there was a fine line. Without a word, he led her through a gate, down a quiet courtyard, and into a sleek modern building where they waited in a bare-bones foyer for an elevator. They said nothing to each other, but inside the elevator she threw herself against him. She felt him stiffen against her. He moaned in her ear, "I want to be with you again."

"Me, too," she said. "I want to be with you all the time."

The elevator opened into a spacious, pristine loft, decorated with modernist furniture. It was generic-feeling, like a hotel room, with no personal photos or touches. Who lived here? George Clooney? Brad Pitt? She thought she had read something in the *Observer* about a Lenny Kravitz apartment on Crosby Street. It was probably his, except Lenny Kravitz had a lot more style than this apartment showed. Was this where all Stuart's girls came? Did hookers come here? Had Stuart had other affairs in this very same loft?

"This is so *The Apartment*," she said, going to the window and looking down onto the street, where she saw a couple stumbling out of a bar, leaning against each other. "I feel like Jack Lemmon's gonna walk in any second."

"You do have a certain Shirley MacLaine thing going about you," he said, standing behind her, his arms wrapped around her front.

"You mean I'm suicidal?"

"A suicidal girl is very sexy. What are you drinking?"

"Jameson on the rocks." She hadn't drunk whiskey since she was single but felt that when you were having an affair, you were supposed to drink liquor. And it was an affair, because this was the second time they had gotten together.

She regarded the Vitsoe shelving system and tried to guess whose loft it was from the books, but they were all generic—design, indie movie books, and James Frey. All the celebrities read James Frey. She surreptitiously opened a drawer, but the only thing inside was a blank French notebook.

He gave her the drink and got himself a beer from the sleek stainless-steel Sub-Zero. "That's terrific," she said. "You need beer goggles for your assignation?"

"Of course not. You have a great assignation."

He patted her on the butt and led her down a hallway to a flight of stairs going up. A few minutes later, they were on the roof, SoHo at their feet. There was a garden, professionally landscaped and brilliant. She breathed in the sweet smell of the city. The air was cool, and she was happy even though her heart was racing. They sat on two chaises, and then she lay back and looked up at the glowing night sky. Instead of feeling lucky or incredulous that she was on a roof in SoHo with a major motion picture star, she felt like it all made sense. It took a special woman to lure a man away from a movie star, and she was special.

The same smug pride all those SHAMs felt rearing their children, she felt now with Stuart. It had taken her a third of her life to figure out what she was good at, but now she'd landed on it: fucking Stuart Ashby.

Everything she'd gone through with Theo since Abbie had been born was worth it because it had led right here to this rooftop on Crosby Street. Everything would work out. Whether this lasted or didn't, whether she stayed with Theo or left, it would all work out.

But she wanted to be with Stuart and had already been imagining a life with him since the day she met him in the food-handling room of the Coop. She would divorce Theo, Stuart would leave Melora, and then she and Abbie would move into a fabulous condo with him, maybe even on Crosby Street. They would make love all the time, three or four times a day, and he'd be great with Abbie since he had already blended into another family, and when he went off on a movie shoot, they would come with him. Through her association with him, she could get a hotshot literary agent and a publisher for her novel, and then she and Stuart could adapt it together, going on to garner so many Oscars they would put Melora's paltry two to shame.

Stuart got on top of her and lifted her skirt. "I love your body," she said, embracing him.

"I love yours. I wanted this when you trained me. I could see you, in my mind, splayed. This splayed. Displayed." He kissed her torso through her shirt and then unbuttoned her blouse and buried his head between her breasts, pushing her back on the chaise. Everything that had felt wrong with Lizzie felt right with Stuart.

"I brought a condom," he said. "You didn't seem very good at keeping them around." He reached in his pocket and took one out. She was flattered that he had thought of this. Then he got it on, quickly and effortlessly, and he was inside her, kissing her neck and cheek. As he rode her, she gave in to the feeling of this beautiful man inside her. For a moment she didn't have a husband or a baby. She was just a beautiful pussy. She was sex and they were sex and they both knew it. He seemed to know exactly how to move, how to curve himself to please her, and within a few minutes she was coming and then he was.

"I wish we could be together like this every day," she said.

"You mean twice?"

"Yeah, twice. I need to see you twice a day. You're like medicine. Without you I feel sick."

He pulled out and turned, and a moment later, the condom disappeared—where had it gone?—and he was dressed, lying beside her and taking another sip of his beer. He was the kind of guy who could dissolve a used condom into thin air.

As she put her clothes back on, she told him she had read his screenplay. She had read it in one sitting that afternoon at the dining room table while Sonam vacuumed around her. She'd been impressed. The dialogue was better than she would have expected for an actor, and the story was well paced and smart.

"Yeah?" he asked. His expression was urgent and a little anxious; this flattered her because it meant her opinion mattered. "So what'd you think?"

"I liked it. Very gripping and gritty but authentic. I had a couple ideas for how to flesh out Lucy."

"What are they? I know she needs some work, and it's very important to me to write a strong woman."

"I think you should make her have had a kid with her ex-husband. A son. She has a very removed relationship with her son until the end, when she foils the terrorist plot in the Atlantic Mall, but after the muffin-shop guy kills her ex-husband. After that, instead of ending on that crane shot of his funeral, where she's in uniform, you should have her take custody of the son. And they build this newfound close relationship, and you go out on the two of them putting flowers on Jimmy's grave, her hand on the child's shoulder."

"That's not bad! That's really bloody brilliant, actually! Exactly what this pass needs. There's someone I want to show it to, and he writes really strong roles for women. He's going to love that."

"Who is it?"

"It's a producer, but he also writes. That note about her having a son is perfect. I'd never thought to make her a mother."

"It just kind of came to me," she said, "on its own."

Rebecca enjoyed his intellectual interest nearly as much as his sexual interest. It made her feel important. She was more than a freelance writer taking care of a baby. She was an adviser to an independent movie, one that might actually get made. She had a vision of herself attending the premiere on Stuart's arm. Even if they weren't together by the time the movie came out, maybe he'd get nominated for an Oscar and thank her in his acceptance speech as the one who'd made the script click into place. Maybe he'd even give her points, the way Spielberg had given Harrison Ford on *Raiders*.

"We should sit down together one day and you should give me all your notes," he said. "Naked." He kissed her and she put her hand on him.

"Oh, I had another idea," she said excitedly. "You know that chase scene on the Prospect Park Carousel?"

"Yeah?"

"You've got to move it. Carousels are too cliché. Any chase scene involving clowns, carousels, or umbrellas is a bad idea."

"But I'm trying to get in some signature locations."

"I think you should set it in the Grand Army Plaza arch."

"There's an inside?"

"Yeah, Abbie and I saw a marionette show there. It's dark, with these narrow winding staircases. It has a very distressed feeling. Very Fosse does Weimar."

"I gotta call the Mayor's Office of Film and ask them about it," he said, and typed a note into his phone.

"Overall, the script is really gripping," she said, "but I have to say, it's a fantasy that all that intrigue happens in our neighborhood. Nothing ever happens in Park Slope."

"I know. I tell people that it's a movie about Park Slope if Park Slope were interesting."

"The neighborhood was a little grittier in the seventies, when it was more Irish and black. Did you know Laurence Fishburne is from the Slope?"

"Yeah, we got in a conversation about it at the opening night of *Thurgood*."

Of course he knew Laurence Fishburne. She had to tell him something he didn't know. "Did you know that a United Airlines plane crashed on Sterling Place in 1960? It collided with another plane over Staten Island and then fell on a church. Killed a hundred thirty-four people. There's a condo there now, where it happened. I don't think the people in there know. There's no sign or anything."

"Maybe I could find a way to work in the plane crash," he said, typing on his phone again.

"Nothing like that happens in Park Slope anymore," she said. "It's so slow. I don't think I can take it much longer."

"Take what?"

"The mothers. The fathers. It's so phony. Everyone's selfish, but they pretend not to be. This guy was mugged near my apartment, and he posted about it on a message board. People said he was bringing down their property values. Park Slope has the worst qualities of the Upper East Side combined with the worst of Berkeley, California. I mean, at least there they're genuine hippies. In the Slope it's yuppies pretending to be hippies."

"Oh, come on," he said. "It's a great neighborhood. Where else would you go?"

"Philly, maybe. My parents live there and could help us. There are all these lofts going up downtown. And Theo could commute."

"You don't want to move. In the words of Kyra Sedgwick in *Singles,* I think that a) you have an act, and b) hating Park Slope is your act."

"It's not an act. I really hate it. There's nothing keeping me here. Abbie's too young to have made any friends. I wanted to like it because it's pretty and the public school is good and there's the Coop, but I don't. I'd stay if I had a really good reason to stay."

"And?" he said, and took her hand.

She tried to be silent but couldn't help herself; she was giddy with love and needed to tell him. "You're the only thing that makes me want to. I always thought that if something exciting happened to me, I would have to go out and find it, you know, someplace else. In Manhattan or something. I didn't expect it to come to me. You're like that plane landing on Sterling Place."

On the cab ride back to Brooklyn, they made out the whole while. She got out at the corner of Carroll and Eighth and couldn't stop kissing him goodbye. "I'll call you," Stuart said, and she wrenched herself out of the cab.

As she walked from the corner to her building, she saw a figure on the stoop. At first she thought it was Jason, the boy upstairs with the gay dads, but as she got closer, she saw that it was Lizzie.

She was sitting halfway down, chin in hand, glaring. "That was him in the car, wasn't it?" she said.

"Who?"

"Come on! You left me stranded with those psychos for an actor! How could you do that? I got my mother-in-law to sit. I cut my nails. I bought you earrings!" Lizzie saw that Rebecca wasn't wearing them. "You took them out! You don't even like them."

"I do. I just— They're not my style."

"I've never met anyone so selfish. Why did you come?"

"You said it was a joke."

"It was a joke."

"So what's the big deal?"

"You're a really fucked-up person, you know that? At first I thought you were sad. I mean, this attractive woman, and her husband won't have sex with her. But now I can sort of see why. You're mean." That was what Theo said to her all the time. Was it true? Had he been punishing her for becoming cold? Now it didn't matter. Now she had Stuart and nothing mattered anymore. "You wanted a baby, so you married him," Lizzie went on, "and then when you got the baby, you stopped being nice. Then he figured out that you never really loved him, and he's punishing you for it. I don't blame him."

Maybe Lizzie was right and she had never loved him. Maybe it wasn't enough to love someone for what he made you feel about yourself.

"You don't know anything about him. You've never met him," Rebecca said.

"Abbie's going to need so much therapy when she grows up because of you."

"What about Mance? Mance is growing up with a closeted lesbian for a mother. You don't think he's going to have issues?"

"I'm not a lesbian. I'm bisexual."

"Give it up," Rebecca said, unable to help herself. "You're a dyke. That Andy guy was hot and you barely looked at him. You're into chicks. You only got married because you were too afraid to be a lesbian mom. That was too out-there for you, too transgressive. So you had to transgress another way, by marrying Jay. But it didn't work. You're still gay."

"If you hate black people so much, you shouldn't let your daughter play with a black child."

"They don't really play. They don't even parallel-play," Rebecca said.

Lizzie was staring at her, her expression hard. And then she covered her face with her hands and started weeping like a small child. "Everything was going so well," she said through her hands. "Everything was going so well till I met you."

"That's not true," Rebecca said, patting her gingerly on the back. "I'm sure things were pretty bad already."

The Bizarre Injustice
of the Playdate

WHEN KAREN first tried to figure out Melora's alarm code using the keypad on her phone, she had been confused, thinking the numbers would spell ORION. But after a few tries mimicking the pattern she had seen Annika's hand make, she realized the code was OSCAR. Of course. For a security code, you had to pick something that everyone in the house would remember, but not something obvious like a birthday. So they had gone with Oscar, what Melora had two of and what Stuart coveted.

Karen felt a rush of nerves as she typed, not having a plan for what to do if she got it wrong and one of the burglar reps came on the intercom or if it turned out that the house was under armored guard. But then she heard two quick beeps and shut the front door behind her.

The mansion was quiet as she climbed the stairs. She hoped everyone was a light sleeper and then wondered in fear how many people lived here—Annika, but the cook, too? Were there assistants? Groundskeepers? There could be dozens of people sleeping here, entire maids' quarters that Annika hadn't shown her.

On the third floor she made her way past the playroom to the master. She pushed the door open and found Melora asleep alone, a copy of *Eat, Pray, Love* on her chest. She appeared deep in sleep, her skin pallid. Where was Stuart? It was as though she'd been waiting for Karen, as though she wanted her to visit. There was a gash above Melora's right eye. Karen hoped she hadn't done something drastic, like try to hurt herself. Maybe they'd had a lovers' quarrel and that was why he was gone.

Karen moved to the edge of the bed. Melora's fingers were slender and long, like a pianist's, but also bony; on sites like Jezebel.com, bitchy posters frequently commented that Melora showed her age in her hands.

Karen found a potato-chip chair by the dresser and lifted it silently next to the bed. She felt like a hospice nurse tending to a dying patient. That could be another career for her if she ever went back to work: helping people die. She could say and do the right things to make them go in peace. Maybe if she did something like that, something good for other people, then God would reward her with a second child.

Melora was so lovely sleeping, like in the dream sequence in the Jane Austen movie where she was awakened in a pristine English garden by her real-life suitor kissing her on the eyelashes. Karen took her hand and stroked it slowly. Melora stirred, and then her eyes fluttered open. She was disoriented for a moment, but then she saw Karen, realized she was a stranger, and sat up in bed. "Who are you?"

"It's okay," Karen said. "Don't be afraid. I'm Karen. I've wanted to meet you for a really long time, actually, but you're never around."

Melora looked confused and a little afraid, like she wasn't sure whether she knew Karen from somewhere. "I'm . . . busy," Melora said, her words slurred. She was on something—who knew what? So the *Post* item had been true. Karen wondered what she was on—downers, or maybe something worse, like heroin. All the celebs did it nowadays, and there had been rumors about Heath even though the autopsy had shown it was sleeping pills. It was a good thing Karen had come in; maybe if she hadn't woken Melora, the poor thing would have died in her sleep, another celebrity casualty of brownstone Brooklyn.

"I know you are," Karen said. "We're all busy. It's very hard to be a mother. Everyone expects so much of us, and we get so little time to ourselves. Are you thirsty? You look thirsty." Melora nodded. "Let me get you some water."

Karen went into the adjoining bathroom and filled a glass she found on the marble double sink vanity. The toilet was enclosed in its own room. Melora could do her business while Stuart bathed in the clawfoot tub without hearing any sound effects. With all these luxuries, it was a wonder Hollywood's divorce rate was so high.

The glass was a fancy tinted thing, the kind of thing she'd never keep in her bathroom because Darby would break it. But Karen figured Orion never came in this bathroom. Melora paid people to make sure of it.

Karen came out and handed Melora the water. As she drank, some of it splashed on her chin. Karen dabbed at the mess with the corner of her shirt. She felt protective of Melora. Where was Stuart? Why wasn't he in bed next to her, taking care of her in a time of need? Hadn't he read the *Post*? "Where's your husband?" she asked.

"I don't know."

"Is everything all right?" Melora didn't answer. So they were on the rocks. It was true. "What did you think of that book?" Karen asked, pointing to the paperback. Melora said nothing. "We read it in book group. Very controversial. Some of the women felt it was disingenuous of Gilbert to get a book contract before she set out to experience those things. I say, 'Go you.'"

"*My* issues were completely different. They had to do with the premise. She got divorced because she didn't want children and her husband did. I don't understand that. I knew I wanted children from when I was a very young girl. I can't imagine not being a mother. Motherhood is such a creative act. I mean, it's not like what *you* do for a living, but it's still a miracle. I want another child, but we're having trouble."

Melora stared straight ahead. Karen went on, "I thought about adoption, but I'm too afraid of the emotional unknowns. You're asking for trouble when you take castoffs. I guess you weren't afraid. I mean, it's so brave of you. And so giving. People like you are really making a difference. I wish I could be like that. I don't know why we're having so much trouble getting pregnant. I think it's because Matty masturbates too much."

"Please get out of my house," Melora said. Her tone was not threatening so much as desperate, and Karen pitied her. But she wasn't afraid. She felt strong. It had been such a terrible day. Jean Pierre-Louis, with his cluelessness, and Matty, with his betrayal, had sapped her of her strength. Now Melora was giving it back to her, resuscitating her.

She was in the movie star's bedroom, and for some blessed reason, Stuart wasn't here. That was a sign that she was meant to talk to Melora one-on-one. She had been waiting for her opportunity, but fate had kept them apart until two days before, when she'd met Annika on the playground. She had met Annika so she could meet Melora.

"Don't be afraid of me," Karen said. "I'm here to help you." Melora winced, and Karen put her hand on top of hers. It was warm and pulsing. "I've wanted to meet you for such a long time," Karen said, "but every time I come over, you're out."

"So you're the one."

"What do you mean?"

"Who took it."

"Our sons love each other," Karen said, not liking Melora's ugly term "took it." She hadn't taken it like a thief, the way Melora had taken it from Neal Harris. She had saved Melora by removing it, so no one dangerous could find it. "You should have seen the way they connected that day at Harmony. Darby has a lot of friends, but I've never seen him take to another child like that. I'm always a little apprehensive when he makes new friends, because for some strange reason, when Darby makes a new friend he really likes, I don't care for the mother. Either she works and she's patronizing to me, or she's gossipy or keeps a messy house. The bizarre injustice of the playdate! But when I saw Darby and Orion taking to each other, I was so happy, because I *like* you. Even without having met you, I knew that I liked you. I felt that when I saw *The Main Line*. I rented it when I was in college. I don't even know why. It was a Saturday night, and all my friends were at a party, but I was tired and stayed in. I was going to get *The Usual Suspects,* but it was out, and I found *The Main Line* under Drama. You were so good in that. So real. I felt like we could be friends even though you were only a kid in it. I mean, as far as I'm concerned, that work and Robert MacNaughton's in *I Am the Cheese* are the greatest young-adult performances in the past half-century. Forget about Anna Paquin. Paquin Schmaquin.

"And then all those years later, you wound up in the Slope. Of all the neighborhoods in all of brownstone Brooklyn, you chose to settle down in mine. Just sixteen blocks from me. So I was happy that our sons got along. And excited to get to know you. I thought you'd be here when Annika invited me over, but you weren't. Then I realized why. You're hiding from your family because you're suffering. Why did you do it?"

Melora was leaning back on her pillow so hard she seemed to want to disappear into it. "I mean," Karen went on, "it couldn't have been for the money. Did you want to be caught the way Winona did? Was it a cry for help?"

Melora looked listlessly out the window. A streetlamp was glowing through the gauzy curtains. "I wanted to do something," Melora said after a moment. "I never do anything anymore."

"Sure you do. You're taking care of this child, and you're working— I couldn't get tickets for the Neil LaBute, but I heard it was wonderful— and I'm sure you're reading scripts."

"Not really," Melora said.

"You poor thing," Karen said, feeling sorry for Melora. "You don't know how wonderful you are. You're better than Gwyneth or Hilary or Kate or Cate. You put them to shame. I care about you so much. I don't want you to throw everything away. So I'm going to hold on to the wallet for you. Which is really much better. You couldn't run the risk that Stuart might find it. It's lucky for you I took it out of his reach."

The more Karen talked, the more excited she felt. "But if I have something of yours," she went on, "it's only fair that you have something of mine. And the something of mine I want you to have is, well, me. Normal people, when they move to a new neighborhood, they get to know their neighbors. But you didn't. You never chatted with other mothers on the playground or had a housewarming, and according to some of the Berkeley Carroll mothers, you haven't shown up to any fund-raising events or any of the class get-togethers. Only Stuart goes. It shouldn't be this way. People need to become part of a community, Melora, even people like you.

"So I'm going to help with that. Lucky for you, it turns out I'm going to be moving a few blocks away in the fall. On Carroll Street. We got the accepted offer today, as a matter of fact. And I want to feel like I can pop in here whenever I'd like and ask you for a cup of sugar. Or ask your chef for one. So I'm gonna hold on to this key and drop by from time to time. You can tell the people who work here that I'm a friend of yours because I am. I mean, I'd like to be." Karen hadn't considered the logistics of how she would explain the friendship to Annika, but she could come up with something. "And don't try to change the lock, because then I'll have to do something I really don't want to do."

"Just because you have it," Melora said, her voice raspy and weak, "that doesn't prove I took it. If you go to them with the wallet, they'll think you took it. It'll be your word against mine."

Karen pulled a small RadioShack digital tape recorder out of her pocket. "I don't think so." She felt like she was on *Law & Order,* one of her favorite shows.

Melora's lips were so white she almost looked dead. "Oh, sweetie," Karen told her, "I don't want you to think of this as a burden, because it's not. It's going to be so wonderful. We'll sit outside under the Japanese maple and talk. We'll go for dinner together at Stone Park and Applewood, and the minutes will fly by. I want you to talk to me the way you talk to your friends. And please do not for a moment think that I would ever sell your secrets to the tabloids. You can trust me the way Drew Barrymore trusts Nancy Juvonen. In fact, you should give me your cell phone number, so we can reach each other all the time. What is it?"

Melora's mouth hung open and drool trickled out of one of the corners. Karen dabbed it with her shirtsleeve. Melora rattled off the digits. Karen entered it and then dialed it. "This way you'll have my number, too, so you can answer whenever I call." A moment later, the iPhone on the bedside table rang. An old sound, like from the 1940s. "That's such a great ring," Karen said. "Did you program it in?"

"It comes with the phone," Melora said wearily. She didn't have to be such a bitch about it. How was Karen supposed to know? Not everyone could spend three hundred dollars on a cell phone. But maybe someday Karen could, when their apartment value had soared so high she could open a home equity line of credit.

Melora's eyelids were starting to droop. Karen stood and lifted the comforter at the bottom and tucked it around Melora's feet. Melora's eyes were like saucers as she looked up at Karen. She needed help, she was afraid. In her eyes Karen saw the baby she might never have.

"Shhhh," she whispered. "It's all right." She ran her hand across Melora's forehead and went to the door.

Honey

MELORA COULD hear the covers moving. She worried the strange woman was crawling into bed with her, but when she opened her eyes, the woman was gone and Stuart was snuggling up next to her. He rubbed her shoulders.

She didn't know what time it was or whether the woman had really been there. She must have been a dream. All those drugs. They made you hallucinate. "I'm sorry about tonight," he said.

"Where were you?" she asked.

"It doesn't matter. I'm sorry about tonight."

"Do you really think Kate's going to charge me with attempted assault?"

"We can talk about this in the morning. Just go to sleep, honey."

His body was so warm next to hers, and he was calling her "honey." Maybe nothing had happened at all, not the woman by the bed, not Kate Hudson, not the Adam Epstein meeting. Maybe Melora hadn't even stolen the wallet. In the morning she would wake up and realize the past week and a half had been a long, weird nightmare, like in *Our Town*, in which she had played Emily in the Lincoln Center revival.

It had all been a nightmare that gave her a sense of what life would be like if she didn't change her act. And now that she knew, she and Stuart would fall back in love the way they were in the beginning. They would go back to appreciating each other. "Do any human beings ever realize life while they live it," Emily had said, "every, every minute?"

If Stuart was calling her "honey," then he loved her. He was hers. She felt guilty for snapping at him all the time. When he was near her, she was always yelling, crying, or sleeping. She was like a little girl. He wanted a woman.

"Let me suck you," she said.

She pushed him down and pulled his pants from around his waist and put her mouth around him. She felt like the old Melora, if only in this way. The old Melora wasn't afraid of sex; she loved it, reveled in it. She was good at it. He seemed to resist at first, but then he let her take him, and a few minutes later, he rewarded her.

She fell asleep with him in her mouth. With the drugs in her system, it was easy.

THE COOP COURIER

Cooperative Cooperators Help Nab Pickpocket

By Alison Wein

By reviewing videotape with police officers of the shopping floor, as well as engaging in some handy gumshoe work, the Coop has an alleged perpetrator of the two pickpocketings that took place on the evening of July 5.

Tape showed a man picking the pocket of Laird Goldwasser, 39, a City College professor. All staff was shown the tape so they could be on the lookout for the perpetrator should he—or she—enter the Coop again. When the man—not a member—returned on July 16, entering through the exit door, an off-duty staffer recognized him and alerted the team leader, who alerted the police. The man was arrested in front of the Coop and did not resist. He was found to have a long history of drug and theft violations.

Goldwasser's wallet was later recovered on his property. The alleged thief, a 42-year-old resident of the South Brooklyn Homeless Men's Facility, was charged with the pickpocketing. However, it was not clear from the videotape who was responsible for the second pickpocketing alleged to have occurred that day.

That alleged pickpocketing was not captured on video because the camera stationed where the pickpocketing is believed to have taken place did not contain any videotape. The member of the Audio-Visual Team responsible for changing the tape had not been performing his duties for many months, leading to a gap in the tape.

According to Coop General Administrator Vivian Shaplansky, "The member had been showing up for his shift and signing in but leaving early, unbeknownst to his team leader, so the tape in that location was not changed."

The AV Team member who neglected to perform his duties will face disciplinary action. His shopping privileges have already been suspended.

Said Shaplansky, "This incident proves why it's so important for everyone to do their share," adding that in the future, "videotape changing will be performed by Coop staff members."

Told that the videotape issue prevented his thief from being caught, pickpocketing victim and member Neal Harris said, "I wish I had my wallet back. My thief is still out there, so beware."

Shaplansky urged members to guard their personal possessions zealously and report any suspicious activity to a team leader. The Coop has already implemented a random bag search at the exit and posted a sign alerting all members to the policy.

"We wish it hadn't come to this," said Shaplansky, "but we want our members to feel safe. We hope the search itself is a deterrent to all sorts of theft and that in the future we can get rid of the policy. But in the meantime, we must be vigilant."

Dipshit

THE PROTESTERS on Seventh Avenue were loud and agitated. There was a group of about twenty of them, holding placards that read FIGHT RACIAL PROFILING, BOYCOTT THE PPFC, and IT IS NOT COOPERATIVE TO BE RACIST! It was nine-thirty A.M. on a Wednesday in early August, peak time for Coop shoppers who had dropped their kids off at day camp or were doing a little shopping before work.

Rebecca didn't usually read the Coop newspaper, even when the lines were long, as she was bored by the politically correct controversies. But the week before, while standing on an endlessly snaking Express line, she had picked up a paper and learned that members of the Coop's Minority Issues Task Force were planning to boycott the Coop because of perceived bias in bag searches. The bag searchers were supposed to search randomly, but apparently, they were searching more black people than white people, and the black people didn't like it.

The protesters were mostly black, but there was a sprinkling of Boomer whites who looked disappointed that it was no longer 1969, and seemed elated to have a new cause. The races stood in separate groups, segregating themselves even though the point of the protest seemed to be racial harmony.

Rebecca did her best to ignore the protesters—during college, there was a protest every day on the steps of Lehman Hall by some group of Transgendered Students or Israel Divesters. But as she turned to go in the door, a young, butch-looking white woman shouted, "The people united will never be defeated!" right in her ear.

Rebecca was hit by a wave of nausea. She'd been feeling vaguely nauseated the past few days but had attributed it to stress about the end of the affair. After that night on the roof three weeks before, Stuart had never called again. She had debated calling or texting to find out if he was injured or away on a film shoot, but she knew the death knell of any relationship was when you started telling yourself that the guy had been struck by a car.

Was it all because she'd said she wanted to see him every day? He had said he wanted to see her, too. And after that night on the roof, she hadn't even tried to contact him.

Could a man fall back in love with his wife on a dime? Whatever problems he and Melora had, it was hard for Rebecca to convince herself they could be solved instantaneously. The only conclusion that seemed even remotely plausible was that she'd been too critical of his screenplay and injured his pride.

She put her hand out to the building to stop herself from vomiting, and it occurred to her that maybe the nausea had nothing to do with stress. *Oh God*. Her breasts had been tender the past week, but they were always tender before her period, so she didn't think much about it. *No no no*. That one time. When Rakhman interrupted them.

But one time? And Stuart had pulled out. She didn't think a woman could get pregnant when the man pulled out—even though in eighth-grade health education, the teacher made extra sure to explain that she could.

On Crosby Street she and Stuart had used protection. Was it possible his sperm were so superpowered that even a tiny drop of Cowper's fluid had been enough to knock her up? Why had she gotten involved with an alpha man? Why hadn't she chosen someone diminutive and beta, with low count and low motility?

Inside the Coop she swiped her card and took a detour to Aisle Two, where she grabbed a three-pack EPT off the shelf, next to the organic cotton tampons, and rushed to the bathroom by the produce aisle. It was hard for her to pee on the stick while also making sure that Abbie didn't unlock the door to the bathroom. She had to press her arm against Abbie, who was reaching up for the door handle, while she used her other hand to hold the stick in position. Abbie saw what she was doing and tried to grab for the dipstick, and Rebecca had to block it with her thighs.

She hadn't taken one of these tests in so long, two and a half years, when she and Theo were trying for Abbie. In all her years of singlehood, even with the broken condoms, the condoms put on after a few minutes of barebacking, and the dangerously close withdrawals, she'd never once had a scare.

She counted to five as she peed, wondering what happened if you peed longer or shorter. Then she closed her eyes and held the stick away from her body, flat, because it said on the insert that you had to or the results would be invalid. As she counted, she tapped her Havaianas flip-flops together and said, "There's no way I'm pregnant, there's no way I'm pregnant," very softly, like a prayer or a mantra.

"No preg ant," Abbie repeated.

There was a rap at the door. "Just a minute!" Rebecca shouted. Nobody could wait a goddamn second at the Coop. It was why she hated the place.

She opened her eyes and looked down at the stick. The indicator displayed a dark purple +. She thought about that word, "dipstick," which sounded so much like "dipshit." Only a dipshit got herself knocked up by a man who wasn't her husband. She shut her eyes, and when she opened them, the + was still there, an unyielding mark of color next to the lonely-looking horizontal control line.

Warren Tofsky liked to bike in Prospect Park in the mornings, even though he lived in Brooklyn Heights. He worked as an accountant for the city, and after he tooled around the park, he would take the Brooklyn Bridge to his office on John Street. The park calmed him, soothed him, and though it was hot, he was going every morning in the summer to try to drop the weight he'd put on when he, his wife, Judy, and his two-year-old twins, Leila and Maya, vacationed for two weeks in the Hudson Valley. They had cooked a lot and he and Judy drank a bottle of wine every night, feeling celebratory and relaxed, and he had come back to the city a few pounds heavier.

Warren had met Judy late in life, each after a failed childless marriage, and now he was a fifty-one-year-old father of toddlers, which always struck him as strange. He was only a father and was old enough to be a grandfather.

Judy herself had also been old when they'd met—and she wanted children desperately. They'd gone through years of fertility treatments, and finally, with the help of an egg donor, she got pregnant with Leila and Maya.

The twins were the love of his life. When he parked his bike in front of their building on State Street every night, the girls would race down the stairs on their pulkes to greet him, then throw their arms around him, shouting, "Daddy! Daddy!" This moment was the highlight of each day.

On this Thursday morning, Warren was looking forward to his bike ride, hoping that the humidity would make the park less crowded. He preferred as little company as possible on the roads and never biked on weekends because *he hated the weekend warriors with their Italian bike shorts and loud patter. His own bike was a vintage Raleigh Sturmey-Archer that he'd bought off craigslist a few years before, and he took pride in owning a clunker.*

At Fifth Avenue he turned right toward Carroll and then hung a left. He preferred taking Carroll to the park because Union had more traffic. As he approached the intersection of Carroll Street and Eighth Avenue, pedaling hard up the steep hill, the light was just changing to red. He glanced at his watch. Leila had spilled her cereal that morning and he'd stayed to wipe it up, and as a result was late getting out the door. It was already eight-twenty, and he was supposed to be at his desk by nine. He decided he could clear the avenue, and at the intersection he pedaled harder, glancing quickly over his shoulder as he did so. He saw the SUV for a split second, high up and dark, and then he heard a screech and a crack. The last thing he thought before he lost consciousness was that this was why God had given him and Judy twins: because they would always have each other.

Bonding

THE WAVERLY Inn was crowded for August—a dead month in the upper echelons of New York society—and Melora was glad to be there. Adam and his wife, Jessica Chafee, had invited her and Stuart to dinner, and she was looking forward to getting to know her director without the duress of the Sant Ambroeus lunch.

The lighting was dim and warm, and Adam was going on about how happy he was with the costume design that Ann Roth had come up with for Rosie and how perfect Melora looked in the A-line bubblegum-pink silk taffeta dress she would wear for the opening shot of Rosie looking forlornly out the kitchen window while doing the dishes.

He had called Melora two days after their lunch to say he was casting her not because she was the best actress for the role but because she was the best actress over five-ten for the role. He didn't mention anything about her behavior at Sant Ambroeus or the photos that had run the next morning in both the *Post* and the *News,* and the following week in *Us Weekly, Star,* and *Life & Style,* of her lunging at Kate Hudson at the Gramercy Hotel. He said only that he had always envisioned Rosie as towering over the Viggo Mortensen character and that if she didn't, the whole movie wouldn't work.

The pre-insurance questionnaire Melora had filled out in July asked her to list all medications she was currently taking and the reasons for taking them, as well as any medical professionals who were caring for her. For her other roles, she had always written none, but certain that the Fireman's Fund would request a urine sample, this time Melora had answered honestly: that she was on Ativan as needed to treat anxiety, under the direction of Dr. Michael Levine. It turned out there was no sample. The fund had bonded her without requesting fluids or even demanding a set minder.

She was set to leave for Sofia on August twenty-first and was arranging to enroll Orion in a well-regarded international school there. After firing Annika, she had hired a midwestern NYU grad named Suzette, who was proving to be as unflappable as Annika had been high-maintenance. Stuart had promised to join Melora in Sofia after he was done campaigning for Obama in Florida with George Clooney. He had never offered to spend this much time on one of her film shoots, and she was certain this meant they were turning a corner in their relationship.

Since Adam had booked her, she and Stuart had made love almost every night. When it was over, she was so happy and calm that she needed only one milligram of Ativan to sleep. That was practically nothing. Mainly placebo. Any night now she was going to try to sleep without any at all, but she wanted to get in a good rhythm first, after everything she'd gone through in July.

She had also stopped Zoloft, instead focusing on sunlight, exercise, and omega-3 supplements from Back to the Land. (The entire family had been expelled from the Coop by the Disciplinary Committee and charged for the damaged groceries and shopping cart after the woman Melora walked with had reported what happened.)

While they were waiting for their appetizers, Melora sipped a glass of prosecco. "I'm so fucking jealous of you for booking this role," said Jessica. She wore her black hair in a bob, kept her head low, and spoke in a deep mid-Atlantic croak—even though she was from Sunnyvale, California. "I wanted Adam to cast me," Jessica went on, "but after *Eva and Andie,* he felt we needed a break. Now I regret not fighting for it. Mark my words, Melora. I think you're gonna get another O."

"Oh, come on!" Melora said, not wanting to jinx herself with further discussion of awards.

"Just don't fuck my fucking husband," Jessica said.

Stuart laughed. "I'll drink to that," he said, raising his glass. Melora looked around the table at all these people who respected her and felt she was worthy of being there, at this elite restaurant by the Edward Sorel mural. For the first time since P. T. Anderson had called to cast her in *Poses,* she felt that her life was coming together. She raised her glass. The trio turned to her expectantly. This was the perfect moment. She had planned her speech while getting dressed for the dinner, figuring out exactly how she was going to segue in.

"You know," she said, "I've always seen the artistic process as a series of gifts passed from individual to individual." She was cribbing from something Misha Slovinsky had said but didn't think she was in danger of being found out. "It begins with the writer as he pens his script. Then he gives the gift to the director, who gives it to the actors, who finally give it to the audience. So I'd like to toast the gift you've given me, Adam, and the gift I hope to give our audience someday."

Adam didn't seem as impressed by her eloquence as she had hoped when she was preparing the speech at home, but Jessica nodded enthusiastically. After they had all set down their glasses, Melora looked at Adam and said, "Stuart's a screenwriter, too, you know."

"Honey," Stuart said, putting his hand on her hand.

She hadn't told Stuart, but she had invited him along to the dinner so she could bring up the screenplay. It was crazy not to share this new-found success with Stuart. She had been talking to Dr. Levine about the Middle Way, nonextremism, which was what you practiced when you were neither self-indulgent nor self-mortifying. It had been self-indulgent of her not to want Stuart to share in her success, to keep it separate from him because she was scared he would surpass her. Even if he surpassed her, he wouldn't leave her. He loved her. He had stayed with her through the worst crisis of her life, and it had only bonded them more. It was as though they had been through an airplane crash together. Now that she had some power, she wanted to give some to the man she loved.

"He's very modest about it," she said, "but it's really good. It takes place in Brooklyn."

"In the Slope," Stuart said, "but also downtown. It's called *Atlantic Yards.*"

"Good title," Adam said. "What's it about?"

"Well, the genre is—I guess you'd call it a dark action-adventure. It deals with terrorism and fear of Arabs, and there's also a female cop character who's struggling with her feelings about motherhood and ultimately learns how to be a mother."

"Sounds interesting," said Adam. "Nobody makes honest movies about race these days. I hated *Crash*. In what world would any of those people be friends?"

"I know!" Stuart shouted.

"To me that was the *Life Is Beautiful* of race movies," Adam went on as Jessica watched his mouth move. "I was so upset when it got all that acclaim that I tried to get a friend of mine at *Film Comment* to write an essay on it, but he was afraid to cross Paul Haggis. Said he had a screenplay he wanted to get to him someday."

Stuart chuckled, paused to sip his Bordeaux, and said, "My movie's sort of about 9/11 more than it's about race. No one's ever made a movie about how that event changed New Yorkers, changed the way they look at each other. In a way, *Do the Right Thing* was the best 9/11 film ever made, and that came out before it happened."

Adam nodded enthusiastically and repeated, "Before it happened." Then he said, "So what phase are you in? Still writing it, or—"

"Capitalization. It needs twenty million to be done right, since it's imperative to the narrative that it be shot on location. I'm about halfway there."

"He's going to direct it, too," Melora said.

"Are you going to play the cop?" Adam asked Melora.

"Yes," Stuart said, facing her lovingly. "I can't imagine anyone else in the role." He put his hand on Melora's knee.

This was news to her. They hadn't talked about *Atlantic Yards* since the night of their fight in the limousine. But Melora wasn't surprised that he wanted her, given everything they had gone through together. You could get what you wanted in work, as in life. You just had to go about it in the right way.

"I'd be happy to take a look if you want a new set of eyes," Adam told Stuart.

"Really?" Melora squeezed Stuart's hand under the table.

"Yeah. I mean, it sounds like it's beyond my purview, but I'm always interested in films set in New York City. And you're the husband of my star. I need you on my good side, man."

"I am on your good side, mate. Huge bloody fan."

Adam scribbled down something on a napkin. "This is our home address."

This was better than Melora could have imagined. All these years she had wanted Stuart to need her the way he had at the beginning. Now, finally, he did. The fact that he was accepting help from her was a sign of how much had changed. You could take help only from someone you trusted.

After the appetizers arrived, her cell phone rang softly in her bag. The Waverly had a strict rule against cell phones, but Melora had kept hers on deliberately. She silenced it and lifted the phone surreptitiously, in her Majorelle, to see who the caller was.

When she saw the number, her body went cold. "Excuse me," she said, clutching the phone in the bag before darting outside to answer.

Everything in Melora's life was coming together with this one exception. She had read the article in the *Coop Courier* about how the thief was still at large, and she guessed Karen had read it, too. Karen still had the wallet—and the tape recorder, with Melora confessing.

Over the past few weeks Melora had waited for Karen to call her, but she hadn't, and Melora had convinced herself she wasn't going to follow through. She couldn't even remember exactly what Karen looked like, and when she passed heavyset mothers she would look the other way, afraid that one would grab her by the arm and ask why she hadn't called. Every time her cell phone rang, she jumped and glanced at the number. And it was never Karen. It was as though she'd been granted a pass. Until now.

"Hello?"

"I've been meaning to call you," Karen said. "How are you?"

"Fine," Melora said.

"Can you meet me at Stone Park?"

"Tonight?"

"Yeah, Matty's with Darby and I finally had a moment to get away . . . How's ten?"

That was in an hour and a half. By the time Melora had to leave, they would be finishing their main courses, and she'd have to hop in a cab. She'd have to leave Stuart alone with Adam Epstein and Jessica, to have all that fun without her. To talk about Lucy and the incredible things Melora was going to do with the role, without her being there to hear them compliment her.

"All right, I guess."

"Can you call and ask for a table in your name? I tried to reserve one, but they say they're crazy busy."

Melora said she would and, with a sigh, dialed the restaurant and got the table. If this sicko only wanted Melora to help her with restaurant reservations, score her Knicks tickets or Broadway premieres, she would have been fine with it. But she wanted company, and that scared Melora more. She dropped her phone into her bag and trudged back into the restaurant, trying to come up with a plausible excuse to duck out early.

Someone to Remind You

KAREN HAD wanted to call Melora sooner, but the past few weeks had been insane. With the presidential election only three months away, she had been doing a ton of work, organizing house parties and phone banking for Obama. On top of all that, there were so many things to do with the new apartment. Their real estate lawyer, a friend of Matty's, had looked over the contract and made a few minor amendments regarding the air conditioner and blinds, but other than that, it was in good order. Karen had arranged for an inspector to come, and after he told them some concerns he had about a leak in the bedroom ceiling, they were able to bring the price down two thousand dollars, to $759,000, which felt like a deal. Karen and Matty had signed and returned the contract. They were planning to put down 15 percent, and 10 percent was already in escrow till the closing, which wouldn't be scheduled until Karen and Matty passed board approval.

When Melora came in the restaurant looking resplendent, dressed casually in a high-necked off-white cotton top and skinny jeans, Karen waved wildly at her from the bar, where she had been waiting. Melora gave a half smile and came over.

Karen threw her arms around her, and Melora coughed a little as Karen accidentally bumped her epiglottis. "You look gorgeous," Karen said. "Where are you coming from?"

"A dinner," Melora said with a slight tone of irritation.

"Where?"

"Ah, the Waverly."

"Oh my God! I've been wanting to go there since it opened, but I know it's impossible to get in. I wish you'd told me. I could have met you there. Joined you. Did you see anyone famous?"

"No." Melora looked down sullenly. Karen didn't believe her. Didn't Melora know that if she acted pleasant, she herself would have more fun? Karen didn't want their get-together to feel like pulling teeth. "Was Graydon Carter there?"

"No."

"Come on, there had to be somebody famous. Besides you, I mean."

"Gwyneth Paltrow was near us."

"What's she like? Is it true she was a bitch to the fat girls at Spence?"

"I don't really know her," Melora said, looking off into the distance.

Karen got it. Melora didn't want to gossip about other celebrities. Maybe she was friends with Gwyneth. And that wasn't really the point of knowing Melora anyway. Karen just wanted to be with her, to listen.

"God, I'd love to go there," Karen said. "Do you think you could get me in someday?"

"I could look into it."

"I'd really like you to," Karen said.

The host asked them if they were ready and led them to a table by a window. The waitress came and handed them the menus, and Melora regarded hers sadly, closed it, and said she wasn't very hungry. Karen didn't like her somber face. It made Karen feel bad, like she was torturing Melora by inviting her to dinner. But this friendship thing was new to Melora, and Karen had to try to be understanding. Melora wasn't used to opening herself up and letting herself be vulnerable.

Karen glanced at the door. It was Thursday night, a peak restaurant night. She wanted a neighborhood mother to see her dining, but then she wondered what she would say if the woman asked how they knew each other. It would be hard to come up with an excuse for how she and Melora Leigh had come to dine together late at night at Stone Park. Maybe if no one she knew came in, she could let it drop, casually, on the playground that she'd befriended Melora.

But that was wrong. In real friendships, you didn't feel the need to talk about the person when she wasn't around. In real friendships, you were protective and tight-lipped. At Rosh Hashanah services at Garfield Temple one year, the rabbi had talked about *lashon hara,* the evil tongue, and said that according to rabbinic law, it was wrong to talk about someone who wasn't there, even if you were saying good things.

"So who were you at dinner with?" Karen asked.

"Adam Epstein?"

"Adam Epstein? Are you working with him? I enjoyed *The Undescended,* although it was a little graphic for my taste." Melora told Karen she was acting in his next film, *Yellow Rosie,* and going off to shoot it in Bulgaria in a few weeks. She said it was the lead role and that Viggo Mortensen was going to play her husband.

"So was anyone else at the dinner?"

"Stu. And Adam's wife, Jessica Chafee."

"She's amazing! Everyone thought she was going to pop after *Eva and Andie*—but it never happened. I think she couldn't recover from the hooker role she did after. Remember? In that movie with Ed Harris? I forget what it was called."

"*Leg Man.*"

"Right!" Melora had probably been up for a role in it herself, but Karen didn't ask in case Jessica had booked it over her. "The hooker thing hurts women. Look where Elisabeth Shue wound up after *Leaving Las Vegas.* She never works."

"She had children," Melora said.

"Mira Sorvino played a hooker, and she doesn't work anymore, either."

"She had children, too."

Karen could tell Melora didn't like this line of conversation. It was probably too close to home. The movie sounded like a good role for her. Who knew? If she did well in it, it could get her career back on track.

The waitress came to take their orders, and Karen got Tempura Fried Oysters and Spring Lamb, plus a glass of Riesling. Melora ordered a seltzer with lime.

After the waitress left, Karen waited for Melora to ask her a little about herself, but she didn't. So Karen took the lead. "Darby and I went to Old Navy today," Karen said. "I had to get him some back-to-school stuff. The lines were crazy. I didn't think it would be so bad on a weekday in August, but black people really like to shop! Getting to the Atlantic Mall is always so stressful, but Darby likes the bus ride. He's very into trucks and buses right now. I thought that phase would be fleeting, but it's not. Does Orion like buses?"

"Yep," Melora said, looking out toward the sidewalk with interest. Karen turned to see what she was looking at, but the street was empty.

"So, Old Navy. Right. We got him some cargo pants and long-sleeved shirts because— You know, it's funny. At GapKids he's usually a 4T, but at Old Navy he's only a 3T. These urban children are so obese that everything runs big. Not that I blame the parents. If you read Michael Pollan, you know that since the Nixon administration, the government has had a vested interest in making soy and corn commodities cheap, and those two foods happen to be the backbone of fast food. The people in these communities don't have access to fresh produce, although I did notice that the Grand Army Plaza greenmarket takes EBT cards now, food stamps, which is a step in the right direction. Where was I?"

"You were saying why you wanted new clothes."

"Right. I wanted Darby to get some cute clothes because we're not sure if the coop board is going to ask him to come to the interview, and we figured we should be prepared. I don't know what the protocol is regarding children, do you?"

"You don't have to bring them."

"Phew. Because he can be very unpredictable around adults. The meeting's still a while away. September twenty-fifth, tentatively. I was hoping it would be sooner, but these things take forever. I'm kind of nervous about one of the women in the coop. I don't know if she's on the board or not." Karen told Melora the story of the woman in Apartment Three and how she'd yelled at her. "Do you think I should call her and make nice?"

"No. Just hope she forgets she met you."

"I don't think that's going to happen. She had such a stick up her ass. I think she has it in for me. Any woman named Rebecca's going to be a bitch. Remember that *Sex and the City* episode where Charlotte and

Trey were in sex therapy and Charlotte named her vagina Rebecca? Matty said he found that anti-Semitic, but I think he's too sensitive."

Melora smiled faintly. "They're asking us for all this stuff for the meeting," Karen continued. "A financial package. It's really specific. You even have to send them the blank pages from the mutual fund reports—and they want three personal reference letters."

Melora hadn't seemed very interested in anything Karen was saying up until now, but she seemed to perk up, her eyes growing warm and alive. "I could write you one," she said.

Karen couldn't believe it. All this time she had wanted a real connection with Melora, and now she had one. On their first girl date. Melora was being generous of her own accord. She was using her position to help someone else, which was the whole point of having a position in the first place. It had to mean she cared about Karen.

"Really?" Karen said. "Are you sure you're comfortable doing that?"

"I did one for Jerry and Jessica Seinfeld when they were applying at the Beresford."

It was almost too good to be true. "But—how would you say you knew me?"

"They don't care about that. I can say our sons are friends. It's true, isn't it?"

"It sure is. That would be incredible."

Melora seemed upbeat for the first time that night.

"Oh God, I hope this works out!" Karen cried. "I think we'll be so much happier in a bigger space. I want to have a room for a second baby, and I have this idea that if we have three bedrooms, I'll be able to get pregnant. The more they study fertility, the more of a connection they're seeing to stress. Matty and I are going to try again this cycle, a week from tomorrow."

"That's great." Melora looked lost in thought, like she wasn't fully listening.

"I don't have a lot of time left. I read this book *Creating a Life,* and it said a woman's fertility plummets at twenty-seven. I'm thirty-two!"

"Well, if it doesn't happen, you know, there's nothing wrong with having one kid. It's easier, for one."

"How would you know? *You* have round-the-clock help. *You* could have six kids and find a way to manage it." Annika had called Karen the day after Karen's tête-à-tête with Melora and told her she'd been fired. Then she started swearing at Karen in Swedish. After that Karen hadn't heard from her again, but she assumed Melora had hired someone new.

"That's true," Melora said slowly, "but I don't want six kids. I want one. Only children are very independent. I'm an only child. There are a lot of great things about being an only. FDR was an only child, you know."

"So was Roy Cohn."

"You shouldn't worry so much," Melora said. "If it's meant to be, you'll have another baby."

Karen thought about what a wonderful person Melora was, how different from other celebrities, how giving, and how lucky she was to know her. She felt bad for poor Neal Harris with his lost wallet. But in a way, the pickpocketing had been a good thing. If it weren't for Neal Harris's stolen wallet, she and Melora wouldn't be sitting together at Stone Park. "You're so great," Karen said. "You're a really special person. I mean, you care about me. I love that about you." Karen leaned over and squeezed Melora's hand.

"Things will work out," Melora said. "I know they will." Melora knew exactly the right thing to say to make a person feel better. She was a woman of few words, but those words were choice. Melora was smiling like Mona Lisa, as though she had some beautiful secret. Karen knew what it was: She was pleased with herself for offering to help Karen. Karen was happy that Melora was happy.

"I know they will, too," said Karen, "but sometimes you need someone to remind you."

Ghost Bike

THE MEMORIAL was already up, and the man had been dead only a day. Rebecca had heard the accident the morning before—a crash and then a parade of police sirens and ambulances that got closer and closer and stopped. She could see all the emergency vehicles out the window. Later, when she had come out with Abbie, she'd seen the overturned bike and a huge SUV standing catty-corner to it, on the northeast corner of Carroll and Eighth. Yellow crime tape sealed Eighth Avenue for an entire block, and cops had directed passersby toward Prospect Park West instead. Rebecca had known as soon as she saw the bike that he was dead.

Today there were flowers and newspaper articles and a handwritten note reading, "Imagine a world with no cars." There was a photograph of the man—round-faced, happy. In the articles it said he had twin daughters. Just like that, it was over. His wife probably worried about other things when she said goodbye to him in the mornings—terrorist attacks—but not bike accidents. Abbie reached to touch the flowers, and Rebecca steered her away as though something terrible might happen to her if she touched something close to death.

Down the block from the memorial, someone had locked a spray-painted white bike to a street sign—ghost bikes, they were called, put up by a cyclist advocacy group. Rebecca knew they were only trying to call attention to a safety issue, but she hated the fact that every time she left her apartment, she would have to see that morbid symbol. She had done nothing, yet a ghost bike would be parked on her block forever.

Rebecca headed east on Carroll toward the public library in search of Stuart. She had already called him a few times and gotten voice mail, so she didn't see the point of phone-stalking him again. She had decided to try to find him in person.

In the two days since she had taken the test, she had tried half a dozen others to be sure it wasn't a false positive. She was no more certain of what to do than she had been inside the Coop bathroom, but she felt it was important that she talk to him. She was in pain about something, something connected to another person, and the logical thing seemed to be to go to that person.

Over the past two days, she had prayed for a miscarriage, which she knew was awful and wrong, but it was early, and the baby wasn't a baby yet. If she miscarried, then she wouldn't have to make a decision about whether to keep it. She had even tried hitting herself in the stomach but couldn't bring herself to do it hard enough to do any damage.

There were so many problems with keeping it. She would have to decide whether to tell Theo the truth, or—the only option more horrifying than telling him—find a way to trick him into believing it was his. And to trick him, they would have to . . .

If she told him about Stuart, who knew what he might do? She couldn't bear the thought of him leaving her. He might even try to take Abbie from her.

The logical thing was to get rid of it. But she wanted to tell Stuart first. She would tell him her plan, and he would agree, and then she would know she was doing the right thing.

The newly constructed library plaza was crowded with sunbathers sitting at the metal tables arrayed in front, and children playing in the fountains that lined the steps. If Rebecca hadn't been so stressed, she would have stopped to let Abbie wander in. Instead, she took the handicapped ramp, veered left for the elevators, and got off at the second floor.

In the Society, Sciences & Technology room, she breezed past the new titles about how to avoid home foreclosure and how to redo your kitchen. She scanned the room for Stuart. But it was mostly black college students taking notes from big textbooks.

She swiveled Abbie's stroller around, and as she was heading out, Stuart strode right toward her. He had his laptop under his arm and was frowning at his phone. "I thought I'd find you here," she said.

He flinched nervously and instinctively, as though she were a fan, before recognizing her and flinching in a different way. "How did you know I'd be here?"

"You told me this is where you work."

"Oh, right, right," he said distantly, as though they'd had the conversation months and not a few weeks before. He hadn't remembered telling her. She had all their conversations memorized, but he hadn't remembered this simple detail.

"Can we talk?" she asked. He hesitated. "Can we go somewhere? It's important. There's a restaurant on the top floor that's usually pretty quiet. Please?"

"Let me get my stuff," he said after a moment. He went to one of the cubicles and grabbed his laptop bag.

The path to the restaurant was long, up the elevator and then down empty, ominous winding hallways with black-and-white photographs of Brooklyn history on the walls. As they walked, they were silent. Not long ago this would have been sexy to her, walking down a long, winding hallway with Stuart, but now it felt grim.

The restaurant was hopping with nannies and their charges. No one took any notice of Stuart or Rebecca. She had the thought that it would be a perfect place to see a lover and wished that she had come here with Stuart back in July, when things were different.

They found a table by the window overlooking Prospect Park. The sky was blue and brilliant, the sun beating through the window.

"So what did you want to talk about?" he asked.

"What happened?" she blurted.

"What do you mean?"

"You just disappeared on me," she said. She hadn't meant to sound accusatory, but her voice sounded strained and high to her. "You fell off the face of the earth. And you didn't come to your Coop shift yesterday."

"That's a long story. I wanted to call you. I've thought about you a lot."

She could feel her heart pulsing in her throat. Maybe this was all a big misunderstanding. Something had happened that prevented him from calling her—his mother had died, Orion was gravely ill—and now that he was dealing with whatever it was, they could be together again and have the baby. "You have?"

"You're the best thing about this neighborhood." He smiled wryly. "It's just—I have a lot going on right now. Professionally. And it's been hard. It's not a good time. To be in touch. But I've wanted to call you." He put his hand on her hand. "That night on the roof was incredible."

She wasn't sure what he was talking about with the "a lot going on right now" stuff, but he was saying he *had* been thinking about her. She mattered to him. There was something between them, bigger than sex if smaller than love. He would go through this with her, come with her to the appointment. And then maybe in the waiting room, he would change his mind and . . .

"When I met you at the Coop," he said, "it was like I finally understood why I moved to Brooklyn. So I could meet you. But then things took off, maybe faster than I thought they would, with my movie, and—"

"You mean you showed it to that producer?"

"I'm going to. So I'm rewriting. And the thing is, this producer, I only know him because of . . . because of *her*. So I have to be careful. I mean, I can't run the risk that she . . . or it might blow my chances with this guy. It's her connection. I have to stick around. But it's not that I don't care about you. Because I do."

So Melora was helping him, and he was too scared to step out on her. It was so cowardly and base. Rebecca pitied the actress. Stuart had treated Rebecca horribly, but he was treating his wife even worse.

"Anyway, I'm sorry I haven't called. So what's going on? What did you want to talk to me about?" he said.

"I'm pregnant," she said. Her throat was dry, and her voice came out like a croak.

Three distinct reactions passed across his face: confusion as to how it had happened; concern for himself; and the last and most galling, conviction that he wasn't responsible. "What?" he said blankly. "Are you sure?"

"I took four tests."

"They could be wrong."

"I visited PeeOnAStick.com. The blogger says false positives on EPTs are much more rare than false negatives."

"How do you know it's mine?"

"Believe me," she said quietly. "It is."

"How am I supposed to know that?"

"Oh, come on! What do you think—there are a million guys looking to have affairs in this neighborhood? If there were, I wouldn't have been so hard up when I met you."

"What about your husband? I don't know what you do with him."

"We haven't had sex in over a year." She thought about saying a year and a half, but that was too embarrassing. She couldn't believe she was amending her state of sexlessness to make herself less pathetic, but just because you were in a crisis didn't mean you had to humiliate yourself.

"How am I supposed to know that's true?" he said.

"You want him to sign an affidavit?"

He put both hands on the table, looked out the window at the park, and then looked back at her. "Do you want to be pregnant?" he asked quietly.

She wasn't sure, but now that she knew he was using Melora to get to this producer, she was ashamed that she'd harbored hopes for him. He was too selfish and caught up in his world. "Of course I don't," she said.

"Okay, then. You're a smart woman."

"This isn't as funny as the movie *Knocked Up*," she said.

"That movie would have been better if it were eighteen minutes shorter." He reached across the table and squeezed her hand. "This is awful. I'm sorry."

"I should have been more careful," she said. "I shouldn't have let you . . . I don't know what I was thinking. But a girl's not so on the ball about her cycle when she hasn't had sex in a while."

"But didn't I . . . ?"

"Yeah, you pulled out when we were in my apartment. I didn't think it could happen, either. I mean, I never had any accidents before. Maybe I'm super-fertile since Abbie. Sometimes that happens after a woman has a kid. Her body gets primed for pregnancy or something." They stared at each other silently as two young black female library workers made small talk at a table nearby.

"I don't know what I'm going to do." She wanted to cry, but the anxiety was so big that when she tried to sob, nothing came out. She hadn't known that a lack of tears could be worse than tears.

"I thought you said what you were going to do," he said.

"I did. I just thought you should know. I thought before I did it that you should know."

He put his hand into his pocket. "You want a little . . ."

She shook her head. Didn't he get it? It wasn't about money. She wanted him to come with her, or to offer to come, but he said nothing. If she was the best thing about the neighborhood, why wasn't he offering to help her? Wasn't he her friend? Even if the baby wasn't meant to be, nobody deserved to go through this alone. And then—to have to hide it from Theo? She didn't even know how it would be possible, with the bleeding and whatever else might come after.

"Thanks," he said. And then he took her hands in his, leaned in so their faces were almost touching, and said, "Maybe some other time . . . when you've worked everything out, and I'm in a different place . . . You matter to me, Rebecca. I know you know that." He leaned over and kissed her on the cheek. "You're stronger than you think you are." It sounded like a bad line from a movie. She wondered if this was what she had been to him—research on how "real" people lived. She wondered if during those moments she had felt close to him, he had been playing a role. "You'll be all right," he said, and left.

After he left, she thought back to that moment when Rakhman had interrupted them. Why hadn't she looked harder for the condom? Had she done this subconsciously, on purpose, so she could get out of the marriage?

She had been so scared of divorce. Maybe this was her way of allowing herself to get out of her marriage: by creating circumstances so unforgivable that Theo would have to walk out on her and she could blame him, and not herself, for the divorce.

But she didn't want to raise a child alone. She had a hard enough time being a married mother of one. How could she be a single mother of two?

Even in that terrible moment in the Coop bathroom, she had fantasized about raising it with Stuart. What an idiot she was to have hoped. She was a Barnard girl and yet had made the two oldest mistakes a woman could make: getting married to have more sex, and getting pregnant to keep a man.

She took out her phone and dialed her mother at the house in Beach Haven. "Hi, sweetheart!" her mother exclaimed happily. Though they had visited her parents a month before, Rebecca didn't call very often. It was as though, in her depression, she had shut herself off from her mother, afraid that if she opened up about small things, she might open up about the big thing and then be unable to take it back.

She felt bad for not reaching out to her mother more often, for not checking in and telling her the small details of life. She felt bad for visiting them in Philly so rarely when they were only ninety miles away. Someday her mother would be dead and she wouldn't get a second chance.

"How are you?" her mother asked.

"I'm okay," Rebecca said, swallowing hard. "Abbie wanted to say hi to you." She put the phone to Abbie's face, but the baby said nothing and tried to grab it. "She was saying 'Gammom' before, but she's shy now."

"That's all right. So is it hot there? I hear it's been a terrible summer."

"Sweltering. I wish we were there with you."

"I told you, you can come whenever you'd like. It's lonely here with just the two of us. Dad's out on his bike."

Everything had been so simple for her parents. They met, fell in love, had two children. Had they ever had a sex drought? Had her mother ever cheated? It was hard to imagine that anyone had sex droughts in those days. Even in the seventies, the gender roles were more traditional. Men were expected to want it and women to give it up on command. And there was no Viagra or Cialis then to help them. It seemed that in those days, even though life was harder with the economy and the gas crisis, everyone was happier. Rebecca wondered if there was such a thing as too many choices.

She wanted to tell her mother everything that had happened but didn't know how to begin. Her mother would think she was crazy for getting pregnant. She would tell her to get rid of it, probably. Her mother was pragmatic to a fault.

Abbie was reaching for the phone. Rebecca tried again to put it to her mouth, but again Abbie clammed up. "I wish I was a kid again, jumping the waves," Rebecca said.

"Is everything all right?"

"Yeah," she said. "Give Dad a kiss for me when he gets back."

Rebecca turned her head toward the window and looked down. She saw two new mothers entering the park—she could tell they were new mothers by their car-seat carriages, ambling pace, and exaggerated poses of interest. She had always seen new mothers as odious and stupid, but from this high up, they just looked nervous. She watched them walk together until they were swallowed up by the trees.

The Boycott

IT WASN'T the same taking care of Mance without Rebecca around. It was draining. Lizzie went to all their haunts—the Third Street playground, the Teat Lounge—but Rebecca was absent, as though she had never lived in the neighborhood at all.

It was a humid Friday afternoon around four, and Lizzie was on her way to pick up some dry cleaning on Seventh Avenue. First she stopped on Sixth Avenue to buy nipple ointment at Boing Boing. Mance was going through a biting phase in which he would chomp down hard on her nipple and then look up at her with devilish eyes. She had tried all of the tricks—distracting him, lecturing him, taking away the breast— but nothing stopped the biting the next time, so she had decided to treat the symptoms instead of the cause and hope that the phase passed.

After she and Rebecca had stopped spending time together, Mance nursed more often. Lizzie felt it was as though he had sensed her shame, and now that there was no one around to make her ashamed, he had relaxed, too.

It had been three weeks since the fight on Rebecca's stoop, and they hadn't spoken since. Lizzie had spent the first few days being furious with Rebecca for ditching her at the Gate, and the next few feeling ridiculous for having been deluded enough to think something would happen between them.

It was obvious that the two tiny makeouts had happened only because of alcohol. Rebecca had practically admitted as much when she told Lizzie about her problems with her husband.

Lizzie was relieved not to be pining for Rebecca, not to think about her all the time the way she had for those few brief weeks. Sometimes, purely as an exercise, Lizzie tried to summon the level of interest in Rebecca that she'd had at the beginning, but when she thought about her, she no longer felt her heart flutter.

But she missed Rebecca's sarcasm and her intelligence. None of the stay-at-home moms at Underhill made fun of their babies like Rebecca. She wished the two of them could go back to being friends, but Rebecca clearly didn't want it, and there was no way Lizzie could force her.

As for the Hotties, every time Lizzie had flashed back on that awful night, she'd been ashamed of her cheap ménage. How could she have gone home with them—with a couple she could see any day at any playground, with their children? So far she hadn't passed them on the street, but there was a reason: Their apartment was on Sixth Avenue and Eighth Street, and now she steered clear of the South Slope. You weren't supposed to shit where you ate. That was probably why she and Rebecca were the only ones who had answered the ad.

As she had suspected, Jay had no idea what had happened. She got home before he did, put Mona into a cab, and had time to shower before he got back from his friend's gig. She felt guilty for about a day before she realized there was no way he would find out and that it was silly to feel bad.

These past few weeks he had been more distracted than ever. It turned out there was a new late-night talk show starting up on Comedy Central and shooting in New York, with a young Jon Stewart–like comedian as host. His name was David Keller, and he was looking for a house band. Apparently, he'd seen a few of One Thin Dime's gigs, and he was interested. Tonight Jay was playing a gig in L.A. and David Keller and a bunch of network people were expected to attend. Lizzie was hopeful, because if he got the job he would have to stop touring, but there had been near misses before, and she knew not to get too excited.

She bought the nipple ointment and then hung a left on Union toward Seventh. She turned right on Seventh and saw a large crowd in front of the Coop. There must have been fifty of them, about two-thirds black; they were holding angry placards and standing in a row, stretching almost all the way down the block. While they stood there, some Coop shoppers walked through the line and into the Coop, while others stopped, observed, and went away. A stout middle-aged white woman with a WNYC tote bag was observing, her face skeptical.

"What's going on?" Lizzie asked.

"They're boycotting," the woman said. "Because of racial profiling." Then she saw Mance and got an uncomfortable look.

"What do you mean, racial profiling?"

"They're saying the random bag searches aren't random."

Lizzie wondered how Mance would feel if someday someone searched his bag just because he was black. Now that a black man stood a chance of becoming the president, she thought a lot about what Mance would be like when he grew up. She wanted him to reach as high as Barack Obama, but she knew that no matter what his station in life, at some point he would be the victim of racism and misunderstanding. Nothing changed fast in America.

Maybe the Coop really was racist and these protesters had a good case. They looked like ordinary people, not overpoliticized, just angry. Lizzie started to pass in front of them, heading south, when she spotted Jay's mother, Mona, in the crowd. Even though the babysitting had gone fine that night of the swingers, Lizzie hadn't invited her again.

Lizzie stopped the stroller and greeted her. "I didn't know about this," she said. "What's going on?"

"Oh, it's awful," Mona said. "I never told you, but they searched me without permission." Mona told her what had happened and how she had joined the Minority Issues Task Force, which had organized the protest.

Lizzie was aghast that they had treated her so badly. "Why didn't you tell me?"

"I was still in shock. I told Jean. I'm surprised he didn't mention it." Mona bent down to look at Mance, rubbing his head affectionately and murmuring something in French that Lizzie couldn't understand, despite all the French she'd had in high school and the three classes she'd taken at Hampshire. This was another reason Lizzie never felt comfortable around Mona; she and Jay were always speaking French to each other.

"Where's his hat?" Mona said.

"What?"

"The hat I bought for him. The sun's so strong. How come he's not wearing the hat?"

As Lizzie was deciding what to say, she saw some motion down the street, near President. Cops, a dozen of them in riot gear, with helmet shields pulled down over their faces. They moved swiftly and with purpose, reminding Lizzie of Nazis. "What's going on?" she asked Mona. Mona turned to look.

After that, everything happened so quickly that there was no time for Lizzie to register what was going on: Within seconds the cops had surrounded the group in a big semicircle, standing shoulder to shoulder. Then they were cuffing everyone. Someone shouted, "There was no order to disperse!" Onlookers yelled protests as the cops arrested everyone in a line. Other passersby saw the cops and then beelined across Seventh Avenue to stay out of trouble.

A short, Italian-looking cop with dark eyebrows flipped Lizzie around, away from the stroller, and frisked her. She couldn't believe it—his hands running down her body, patting her down, breasts, crotch, thighs. "You don't understand," she said. "I was just walking down the street." She pointed to a white mother pushing her white baby past, but the cop took no notice.

"She's not a part of this," Mona said.

"You can tell it to the judge," he said, and then he was cuffing Lizzie with sharp plastic cuffs that stung. Another cop cuffed Mona, who cried out, "You're hurting me!"

"Be gentle with her!" Lizzie shouted.

She always thought from the Law & Order episodes that you got your Miranda rights read to you when you were arrested, but he didn't say a word. The plastic cuffs were tight, and she didn't like having her back turned to Mance. "You don't understand!" she shouted. "I don't even belong to the Coop. I do FreshDirect." She bent down next to the stroller on her knees. "I can't leave my baby!"

"Is there someone here who can take him?" he asked as though noticing Mance for the first time. She tried again to explain to him that there wasn't, but his face was cold and unforgiving. This was all business to him. Lizzie began to cry, certain that they were going to take Mance someplace awful, like Child Protective Services. She had read about the Danish woman who'd left her carriage on the street while she dined on St. Marks Place and then had her baby taken from her.

"What do I do?" Lizzie said to Mona.

"Call someone!" Mona shouted as another cop led her to a police van.

Lizzie scanned the faces in the crowd. Every time she walked down Seventh Avenue, she ran into someone she knew, another mother or a friend from Hampshire or a Prospect Heights neighbor who belonged to the Coop, but today she recognized no one.

"I can take him," the WNYC woman said. Lizzie thought about how smug the woman seemed when she'd said "racial profiling." She didn't like her, but she seemed trustworthy, and her face looked softer now than before. She was old-school Park Slope and seemed like she might have grown children herself. And anyone who supported public radio couldn't be all bad.

"I have a friend," Lizzie told her. "She lives a few blocks away. She can take him. Keep calling her until you get her." And then Lizzie rattled off the number she had known by heart since the day that Rebecca had first given it to her.

The cop stood nearby, annoyed, as though all of this was an inconvenience, as though Lizzie didn't have a right to get someone to care for her child even now that he was arresting her. Lizzie repeated the number three times to be sure the woman had gotten them right, and then she leaned down and whispered to Mance, "Mommy'll see you soon," even though she wasn't sure that was true. The officer whisked Lizzie away, leading her into the van. The white woman steered Mance out of view.

Changing the Game

"SO THEY arrested her without cause?" Theo was asking. "I find that hard to believe." It was almost seven at night, though the sky was still light, and he and Rebecca were standing at the Lincoln-Berkeley swings, pushing Abbie and Mance.

After the woman at the Coop had called around four-thirty, Rebecca had rushed over from Third Street, where she had taken Abbie. Her first big decision was what to do with Mance's stroller. Though it wasn't a monumental choice, she took enormous pride in her ability to make it. She hung it on a hook inside the Coop, then carried him while pushing Abbie, with the other hand, to her apartment. She fed both of them leftover pizza (she had no idea the last time he'd eaten) and let them play in the air-conditioned apartment awhile before packing Mance in the Ergo carrier and heading out with both of them to Lincoln-Berkeley.

Around six, Lizzie had called from the Seventy-eighth Precinct to check on Mance. She sounded scared but mainly concerned about her son. Rebecca said he was doing great and promised to put both children to sleep in Abbie's crib that night if Lizzie didn't get out in time. Rebecca volunteered to send over a lawyer—a girlfriend from Barnard—but Lizzie said one of the protesters had already gotten in touch with Sarah Kunstler.

"I'm so glad you have him," Lizzie said. "I'm glad that woman reached you."

"Oh, come on," Rebecca said. "I'm sure you would have done the same for me."

"I guess I would have. But it still means a lot."

Later on Jay had called. He was in Los Angeles and would try to get on a red-eye that night. He said he would come straight from the airport.

At six-thirty, when he got off the train, Theo had called to say he wanted to meet Rebecca at the playground. He rarely got home before eight-thirty but had pretended to be sick so he could spend some time with Abbie outside before it got dark.

Over the past few weeks, since her night on the roof with Stuart, Theo had been unusually affectionate with Rebecca. But she had been so distraught about the affair that she'd been cold.

When Theo arrived at the playground, he'd been shocked to find Rebecca pushing not one but two toddlers on the swings. She had explained the sequence of events several times according to what the Coop lady had told her, but he still didn't seem to grasp how frightening it must have been for Lizzie.

"It was a racial protest, wasn't it?" he said.

"So?"

Theo angled his chin toward Mance significantly. "So Lizzie *was* part of it."

"No, she wasn't! She doesn't even belong. She was just walking down the street and went to say hi to her mother-in-law. They arrested her. This is all Bloomberg's fault. Ever since the Republican National Convention, the cops have been out of control. They never would have arrested her if her kid had been white."

"Don't you think that's a little paranoid? We've got a black guy running for president."

"So? Doesn't mean there's no more discrimination." He could be such a dolt. She knew he was for Obama—they had talked about it— but sometimes she felt like he said things to bait her, to test whatever residual political correctness she had left over from Barnard.

Theo was playing the whistling game with Abbie, in which he pretended to look away for a second, whistled innocently, and then scared her by making a monster noise. Rebecca hated when he played this game—she was bothered by his manic investment in Abbie's joy—but Abbie was already shouting, "Again!"

"You should try this with her," he said. "She loves it."

"Oh, we have our own games."

"Really? Like what?"

Rebecca didn't have any games with Abbie. She didn't like speaking in funny voices or making weird faces or even playing Open Shut Them, but she didn't want to sound like a bad mother. "They're secret games. Right, Ab? Don't we have secret games?" Abbie nodded. Theo went back to his whistling and Abbie clapped in delight.

When it was the three of them, Rebecca would watch him play these silly games with Abbie and wonder why he couldn't chill. Push her on the swing while talking to Rebecca. Or push from behind, for God's sake.

But tonight it didn't bother her because she had Mance to focus on. She felt proud of how well she had managed to handle two babies at once. This was an easier crisis than the one she'd been turning over in her mind obsessively for the past two days.

She pushed Mance high and then, feeling unusually energetic, ran under the swing to the other side. Mance howled in delight. "Another Underdog?" she asked, and she did it a few more times. Theo looked at her curiously, not used to seeing such demonstrativeness from her. "You want to go higher?" she cooed to Mance. Talking to children about swinging was like talking about sex. "More?" she said. "You want *more*? You want to go *really* high now?" She imagined what it would be like to be able to play like this with a child of her own. If there were two, then they each got one.

She missed Stuart suddenly—his interest in everything that came out of her mouth, the way he cocked his eyebrow at her one-liners or watched her face when she talked, even if that was just a trick he'd learned in acting school for when a scene partner had a long monologue. She missed being wanted.

If she had a baby, she might be wanted again.

Babies were selfish—they needed to be to thrive—but she had never gotten a chance to enjoy Abbie's neediness because Theo had always responded to her needs before Rebecca had a chance to. He had taken two weeks of paternity leave when Abbie was born, but they'd felt like two months. He would race to Abbie at the slightest wail, scoop her out of the crib when she woke, and change her at the poopy cries before Rebecca, in pain from her cesarean incision, could even stand.

Rebecca had never anticipated that there could be such a thing as too much help. But, feeling like a failure for not having been able to push Abbie out, she wanted other ways to prove to herself that she could mother.

When Abbie's umbilical-cord stump had fallen off, Rebecca had decided to give her her first tub bath. She readied the baby washcloth, tub seat, and one of the six yellow duck towels they'd gotten as baby gifts, and just as she started to bathe her, Theo looking over her shoulder from behind, she got a phone call from *Allure* asking if she could interview Jessica Simpson in Los Angeles in two days because another writer had fallen through. She left the room and had a long conversation with the editorial assistant about flight plans, and when she got off the phone Theo was sitting on the couch, cradling Abbie in the duck towel. He had robbed Rebecca of a milestone, even if, as he argued later, it had to be done. She had felt hijacked and realized the hijacking had begun the day Abbie was born.

Before Rebecca's labor began, in all those months of midwife visits to St. Luke's, she'd thought she was the patient, but as soon as they arrived at the hospital, it became clear that the baby was a patient, too. Before her eyes, everyone's allegiance shifted. She labored for hours in the hot tub and on the rocking chair, and every ten minutes, it seemed, the midwife would put a Doppler against her to check on the baby. Rebecca told herself things were going to turn around, that the excruciating pain would end in natural birth, but after two hours of fruitless pushing, the midwife frowned and said, "We need to get you on Pitocin. The contractions are weakening."

Weakening. Already Rebecca was beginning to feel like a failure. Could she make her contractions stronger? Could she rest? Couldn't they give her vitamin shots, like in a Jacqueline Susann novel, or steroids, like the athletes took? Wasn't there some way to turn it around?

In labor and delivery, after they put her on the Pitocin drip and the midwife watched the fetal heart monitor and Rebecca saw the look of concern on her face, she understood. The baby's survival took precedence over the mother's. Which was how it needed to be, of course, and how it had been since the beginning of time. Childbirth was the very beginning of a long, brutal process of learning that you were no longer the most important person in the world.

But if she had been able to forgive the midwife for her shift in allegiance, she was unable to forgive Theo. Yes, he had massaged her diligently during her thirty hours of labor. He had brought the iPod, although she'd screamed at him to turn it off. He had fed her ice chips and water and told her things were going to be fine. And when the attending came in and suggested the cesarean, he had put his face up against the doctor's and said, "If anything happens to her, I am fucking going to kill you."

But after the baby came out and she heard a cry and someone brought Abbie to her face—she couldn't hug her because her arms were pinned down—Theo was saying he would go with the baby. He wanted to be sure she didn't get switched. Suddenly she was all alone.

The doctor sewed Rebecca up, and afterward she lay on a bed in recovery, enormous boots on her legs to prevent a blood clot, as a hostile West Indian nurse sat next to her, eyeing a monitor. Rebecca was there for three hours, apart from her newborn, apart from her husband, who was too afraid to leave his child to come visit Rebecca. His loyalty had shifted, along with the midwife's. His daughter mattered most now.

She kept waiting for Theo, but her first visitor was the midwife, who finally escorted her to maternity, where Theo wheeled the baby in to meet her mother.

Rebecca wanted a do-over, this time with a child who would not be a tug-of-war rope. If by some chance she could find a way to raise the new child with Theo, as his own—a possibility that provided numerous logistical challenges—then she would get her do-over. She would know forever that the baby was hers and not his. He could never take it away, and he wouldn't try to. He already had his. If she couldn't change the player, maybe she could add another one and, in so doing, change the game.

But if she was going to convince Theo that he was the father, it required them to do something that had proved impossible for the past seventeen months. And they would have to do it soon. She was crazy even to consider what she was considering, but she had to try.

"We should get them home," she told Theo, patting him on the back. Even this small gesture of affection felt phony. She waited for him to turn to her suspiciously, but he was focused on Abbie, who was pointing at a sneaker in a tree.

Rebecca lifted Mance out of the swing and into the Ergo. He was lighter than Abbie and easy to carry. They walked out side by side, with Mance twisting his face around to see his friend.

Palazzo Chupi

THOUGH THE tabloids would later report that it was Julian Schnabel who told Melora about the condo at Palazzo Chupi, it was actually Liv Tyler. Liv and Melora had the conversation at an Obama fund-raising barbecue that David and Cassie had thrown in their backyard. Everyone Melora knew in the industry was raising money for Obama these days. She got at least a few invitations a week, and as much as she wanted the guy to win, the Obamamania was getting annoying.

Liv and Melora were lying on chaises, sipping white wine and chatting about child rearing, and eventually, the talk turned to real estate, with Liv complaining that it was no fun taking Milo to the Bleecker Street playground anymore because the *Sex and the City* tour groups always came in after getting cupcakes at Magnolia. "The tour people are afraid of pigeons," Liv said distastefully. "The West Village used to be so homey, but it's turned into a tourist trap. And now that Milo and I don't need so much space, I'm thinking of moving to the Meatpacking District."

There were rumors that Liv and Royston's split had driven Steven Tyler into rehab, but Melora felt it was inappropriate to inquire. "The Meatpacking?" Melora asked. "That's even worse. All those Bridge-and-Tunnels going to the clubs?"

"I don't mean like West Fourteenth," Liv said. "I'm thinking a little south of there, like West Eleventh. They're calling it WeWeVill, West of the West Village. Yesterday I checked out a condo in Palazzo Chupi."

"What's that?"

"You don't know about it?" Liv asked, leaning in and setting her wine on a patio table. "It's in Julian Schnabel's building, on top of their pad. The whole place is like Venice. All these terraces overlooking the water. And it's bright red. Richard Gere bought one last fall, and he's looking to flip it. I did a walk-through, even though it's out of my range."

Melora found that hard to believe; she figured Givenchy was paying Liv millions for the spokesperson gig. "What's the asking?"

"Fourteen. Are you thinking of moving? I thought you guys loved Brooklyn."

"I'm not so sure anymore. I mean, Stu does, but I find it really claustrophobic. And it takes forever to get into the city. I want to live someplace that feels like a neighborhood but lets you have Manhattan at your fingertips."

"You should check it out. Terra-cotta terraces, this incredible pool in the basement—shared, but still. French doors everywhere, a colonnade running across the north side. And Hudson River views."

"How many bedrooms?"

"Four. And four baths. But after the mansion, it might be too small for you guys. It's just one floor."

Melora tried to imagine it. She liked the idea of looking at the water. It was the one thing she missed from her time in Los Angeles. Your brain was clearer when you lived near water. It was a natural antidepressant. Since the move to Brooklyn, she, Stuart, and Orion had taken a few day trips to Fairway in Red Hook, but a supermarket view of the Statue of Liberty wasn't the same as living on the Hudson.

The cost was high, and she wasn't sure her business manager would approve, especially in a weak housing market. Despite all the critical acclaim, *Poses* had made most of its money on DVD, and those residuals were smaller than theatrical. And all the indie movies and the Neil LaBute play had forced her to dip into savings. Stuart would have to kick in at least $1 million toward the down payment, which he hadn't for the mansion, and she would have to sell her house in Silver Lake. That, combined with the mansion money, which she was hoping would be at least $6 million, would make it barely doable.

Orion would have to leave Berkeley Carroll, but he was an adaptable kid. She could get him into Little Red or City & Country.

But she was afraid Stuart would resist. He was still so devoted to the neighborhood, even after everything Melora had gone through at the Coop. The few times they'd talked about her "rough patch in July," as they always referred to it, he'd said that what had happened was because of her internal state. Brooklyn represented something to him that it didn't represent to her—stability, hominess, and normality.

For her it had always been foreign. She liked the idea of going back home to the West Village, raising Orion nearby to Charles Street, where she'd grown up, even if everything was different, even if all the mom-and-pops and bodegas were gone.

But there was another reason she was eager to get out of Brooklyn, and that was a five-feet-four-inch woman with a four-year-old kid. Melora had thought about calling the cops with an anonymous tip to say that she knew who had the stolen wallet. But Karen had that goddamned recorder. She had proof.

Karen had already called her for another girl date, this time to al di là, and though Melora had put her off till Monday night, she was dreading it. She had to get the wallet and tape recorder back. That was why she had offered to write the reference letter, which she had penned through her teeth, describing the fat shrew as "morally outstanding" and "an asset to any cooperative." Melora had a feeling that when Karen trusted her, she might be able to convince her to hand it over, but that hadn't happened yet. It was such an ugly predicament: to get Karen to trust her, she had to keep spending time with her. Thank goodness she was going to Sofia soon.

Melora told Liv she had to make a call and darted to a corner of the garden. She dialed Michael Levine. When Dr. Levine had come back from the Berkshires, Melora had booked a two-hour session with him and explained that if he wanted to continue being her shrink, he would have to be available on demand. She said she would pay him $1,500 for every call and that her goal was not to abuse the privilege but simply to know that it was available to her. Under this arrangement, he would keep his phone on at all times, and if it rang during one of his sessions, he would have to excuse himself to take it, ending the session if need be.

When she first proposed it, he seemed offended by the notion and said he needed to think about it. But he had called her back a few days later to say he would do it for $2,000. He said it was the only way to justify his time away from other patients. She was shocked that a Buddhist would try to bargain her up, but he was an Upper East Side Buddhist, after all.

It took only a few minutes for him to call her back. "Melora," he said. This was the first time she had used the lifeline, and she could tell he was nervous.

"I'm thinking of leaving Brooklyn," she said.

"I don't understand. You mean leaving Stu?"

"I heard about a condo in WeWeVill, and I'm going to try to see it before I go to Bulgaria."

"Where's WeWeVill?"

"West of the West Village. What do you think?"

He was quiet. "I know you haven't been happy in Brooklyn for some time."

"I think this could be the key to feeling better, Michael. I could get away from these people, this oppressive neighborhood, the Coop, and . . . her." Michael had told her she should turn Karen in because extortion was a federal crime, but Melora was too nervous about the tape recorder. "I can't stand it here. I have to get out. I think Brooklyn has been the cause of all my problems."

"Places don't cause problems."

"Sure they do! I was fine in SoHo. I mean, relatively fine. Everything's going so well for me now. I just feel like I could use a fresh start." Her voice was rising in volume, and she saw Liv glance over curiously from across the garden. "Anyway, I think I'm going to take a look. This could be the key to getting back, you know, to who I was before. Someone who's not afraid. I think I need a change of space."

"It sounds like you're thinking very clearly about this."

"I am," she said. "Thank you, Michael." She hung up. Maybe the call hadn't been worth $2,000, but it had left her certain that she would do the apartment walk-through before she left for Bulgaria.

She mouthed the words "Palazzo Chupi" as she made her way back to Liv Tyler. Even the name sounded whimsical and bright. What was that expression—"real estate is destiny"? How could you live in a place called Palazzo Chupi and not be destined for beautiful things?

Holding

LIZZIE WAS brought to the Seventy-eighth Precinct in a van with a dozen other protesters. She had started to think of herself as a protester, even though she wasn't, because she was so aggrieved that she had been arrested without cause. The van had no seats, and they were all on the floor. Lizzie was sitting next to Mona.

"We weren't blocking the entrance," Mona kept saying, weeping.

Lizzie had always kept her mother-in-law at a distance, but she felt sorry for her, having to put up with this at her age. She wasn't sure which was worse—that the cops had been rough with a sixty-year-old woman or that they had separated a mother from her child.

When they got to the station house, Lizzie wanted to run home. She was only a few blocks from her apartment, and yet she couldn't leave. Inside the station house everyone was searched, given vouchers for their possessions, fingerprinted, and photographed. Then they were separated by gender and put in different holding cells.

The women's cell was about eight by eight, a cage like out of *Barney Miller*. There was one bench. The women sat grimly, the older ones on the bench, Lizzie and some of the younger ones on the floor.

"They're all together in this," said a pretty young black woman with short dreads. "Bloomberg, the Coop, the cops."

Lizzie wished that Mona didn't have to suffer through this, that she could go through it for both of them. She was sorry that she hadn't let her take Mance after that one night.

Maybe if Mona had been spending the day with Mance today, she never would have been at the protest in the first place. Mance wasn't only Lizzie's, even though she had birthed him. He was his father's and his grandmother's, too. Mona didn't look like Lizzie, but she was just as much Mance's blood as Barack Obama's white grandmother was his. It wouldn't hurt to let Mona come over one or two nights a week. Then Lizzie could finally get out on her own, drink wine in a bar, see her friends from Hampshire, even go to the gym.

"I didn't mean to be so bossy that night you came to sit," Lizzie said. "I just wanted to be sure you knew what to do." Mona nodded, too distracted to want to have this conversation right now, in a jail cell.

A nice light-skinned Hispanic cop said Lizzie could use the pay phone. She took Mona with her.

After Lizzie dialed Rebecca she tried Jay. He didn't answer the phone until the third try. When she told him she'd been arrested, he was silent, and when she said Mona was with her, he didn't believe her, so she had to put her on. Mona started crying again while she talked to him in French.

Back on with Jay, Lizzie explained that Mance was with her friend Rebecca and gave him Rebecca's cell number. "How did this happen?" he said.

"It wasn't my fault. It happened really quickly and . . . I wasn't even in the group. There was no order to disperse."

"This is New York City," he said. "You should know better."

"The only reason I stopped was because I saw Mona."

"If I had known she was doing this, I would have told her not to."

"Everything's going to be okay," she said. "I'm taking care of her. And Mance is fine. Really. He's in good hands. What time is your gig?"

After another hour in the cell, the nice cop brought them a pizza. At nine o'clock they were transported, cuffed, to Brooklyn Central Booking on Schermerhorn.

BCB made the Seventy-eighth look like a palace. The women's cell had peanut-butter-and-jelly sandwiches scattered all over the floor and reeked of urine. A sign said DO NOT EXPECT TO BE RELEASED TILL THE MORNING. That was when Lizzie knew she would spend the night there. A white crack whore slept on a pillow of sandwiches. A black girl no older than sixteen was on a pay phone, having a loud argument about how she hadn't even been driving the car.

Lizzie helped Mona get comfortable on a gym mat and then lay under a bench and prayed to God that Mance would never have to see a place like this. She was thirsty, but there was no water. Women squatted over the toilet all night long. She tried to drift off to sleep, and as she tossed and turned, her back aching, it struck her that this was the first night she'd been away from Mance since he was born.

Annika had been crashing at her friend Eva's place until she landed a job with a new family. Eva, a Swedish nanny she'd met through the Swedish nanny mafia, worked for a family in Williamsburg who owned a bar, and she had her own two-bedroom flat on the top floor of the house. She was traveling with them in Europe for August and had said Annika could stay there till she got back.

Since Annika had been fired by Melora, she hadn't been sleeping well. She never should have let that stupid Karen in the house. She'd had a bad feeling about her but had ignored it. She knew Karen had taken something from Melora's room, and that was why Melora had fired her. Money, probably. It was so obvious from the look on Karen's face when Annika found her at the top of the stairs. But she had never guessed Melora would pick up on missing cash. She was always out of it, on her Valium or whatever those pills were. She could barely keep track of anything. Annika didn't understand how someone could be on all those pills. In Sweden you were expected to handle your problems without drugs. Annika didn't understand why these Americans, who were supposed to be self-sufficient, had so many crutches. It seemed the richer someone was, the weaker she got.

Annika was lonely. She missed Martin. Though she'd been pining for months, she still hadn't gotten up the courage to get in touch with him. It seemed wrong. His wife was expecting a baby, and you weren't supposed to mess with a man whose wife was pregnant.

But tonight she was afraid she wouldn't sleep. She wanted to talk to him.

She was worried that she wouldn't be able to get another nanny job, even though Stuart had called to say he'd write whatever reference she wanted.

Annika downed some vodka she found in Eva's freezer. She dialed Martin's cell phone. It was loud when he answered, and she knew where he was—at the Dominican dance club in Washington Heights where he had taken her once. At first his tone was distant, but then she said she wanted to kiss him, and before she knew it, he said he would meet her.

She missed his body on top of hers, missed his huge dark cock. Every time they made love, she felt like she was in a porno film, so different was Martin from the boring Svens she'd dated in Täby.

While she waited for Martin to come, she put on Vipe Out. She loved indie rock, but when she had lived in the mansion, she could listen only through headphones because Melora was so sensitive to loud noise. There were good things about being unemployed. Maybe she could get a job at a gym as a personal trainer. It was too hard being a nanny, even though the room and board was an incredible perk.

She blasted the music and shadow-boxed, wondering how long it would take Martin to get there. Washington Heights was a long way away, and he would ride the train, because he didn't have the money for taxicabs. She showered and changed into tight dark jeans and a white tee. She had small breasts and the body of a twelve-year-old boy, but Martin never seemed to mind.

He liked to take her in a naughty place. When she told him anal sex was all the rage in Sweden, he had gotten so excited; the girls didn't want to lose their virginity, so they had anal sex before vaginal. He said Sweden sounded like a country built for him.

When Martin arrived, she could smell the liquor on his breath. Johnnie Walker Black Label was his favorite drink. He looked better than she'd remembered—he was short, only five-two, but muscular. She loved watching him fight. He was so fast and spry, and in the ring his face was totally different—hard and tough.

She ran her hands down his arms. "I missed you," she said.

He grinned and asked if there was anything to drink. She gave him some vodka. She poured his straight, hers on the rocks, and they drank together as they sat on the couch. They talked a bit about the gym and his new clients, and she told him she was working with a new trainer at Kingsway. She told him what had happened with Melora, and he said he was sorry, she'd find a new job. Their relationship had never been about talking. Sometimes it was good to have a language barrier.

He smiled his shiny white smile and put his arm around her, and then he flipped her onto her stomach on the couch and got on top. She asked him to come inside her. They'd occasionally had regular sex before they broke up, and she wanted it now but figured he felt too guilty about his wife to do it that way.

They would get there again. There was time.

Afterward they channel-surfed and ordered takeout Mexican. It was so good not to talk, to be with someone in this easy way. When she said goodbye to him, she knew they were together again, and it made her happy.

Lysistrata

WITH MANCE sleeping soundly in Abbie's crib and Abbie next to Theo in the queen, Rebecca went into the bathroom to take a shower. She spent a few minutes with the razor and gave herself a whore bath. She didn't want to spend too long in the bathroom, though, or Theo would suspect something and get self-conscious.

She toweled off, went in the bedroom, and put on a white transparent V-neck with a pair of two-hundred-dollar gray and black silk panties she'd gotten years ago at La Petite Coquette. She wanted to look available but not too available, and Theo had always liked boyshorts, high, full-coverage underwear that reminded him of old Sears catalogs.

She got in bed next to him and took out a book on elder-parent care that she was reading as research for an *Elle* article on the sandwich generation. The words swam before her. Theo was typing on his computer, his reading glasses on. In his Buddy Holly glasses, he looked so handsome. If she hadn't been so angry with him the past year and a half, she would have felt lucky to be married to such an attractive guy.

She put her hand on her belly under the covers. It was starting to swell already, the baby making its presence known early, as though to ensure its own survival. Soon she would be showing. She had heard about that before—how you showed earlier with the second baby because your muscles were stretched out from the first. There wasn't much time to do this. She dated the conception at three weeks and one day before. It was already pushing it to think she could pull one over on him. If she waited any longer, it would be too late; she'd look too far along too early, and he would know. She would have to figure out what to say to the doctor.

She turned to watch Abbie sleeping. She was beautiful—her hands were folded under her chin, her chin tilted up like she was praying. Children looked so vulnerable when they slept, while adults looked ugly and unkempt.

"Isn't she incredible?" Theo said. He stroked Abbie's head.

"I can't believe she'll be two soon. Our daughter is going to be two!"

"I wish she would stay like this forever," he said. "Someday she's going to be embarrassed to be seen with me."

"We'll drive ourselves crazy if we think about that now." Rebecca snuggled up to Abbie, nose to nose.

"You did a great job making her," Theo said.

"You helped."

"Yeah, but you grew her in you. You did everything right."

He was rarely this tender to her. He was being this way because he'd seen her looking at Abbie with love.

She tried to remember the last time she had been kind to her husband. She had always figured it was a few months after Abbie was born, before he began to reject her. But she remembered how jealous and angry she had felt with him after he gave Abbie her first bath, and the baby couldn't have been more than a week and a half then. Maybe Rebecca had become cruel to him before he stopped touching her, cruel because she knew she was being replaced. It was so hard to go back to before the rut.

Rebecca saw what she'd been doing wrong all this time: She had been trying to go through the front door when he wanted to be approached from the side. He needed to be approached through the door marked Father because the one marked Husband was locked.

"Oh God," she said. "I was so neurotic when I was pregnant. I didn't even take Tylenol or eat sushi or—what was the thing about cheese? If you eat soft cheese, you might get Lysistrata?"

"Listeria," he said, laughing, although she knew it was listeria and had said "Lysistrata" to get a chuckle out of him.

"I'm sorry I've been a bitch," she said. "Sometimes I'm so over-whelmed, taking care of her, that I take it out on you. You work so hard. I'm sorry I get upset when you don't want to go out on date night with me."

His face softened. "I love to go out on date night, but sometimes I'm tired. I don't want going out to feel like another obligation, you know? Sometimes it seems easier—"

"—to stay here."

Abbie stirred in her sleep, and Theo ran his hand down her features, shushing her. He always knew how to quiet her. Rebecca didn't. She inched closer to her child and put her hand over Abbie's body on Theo's arm, trying to make it seem more like a going-to-sleep pat than a come-on. He put his arm on hers, crisscrossed. She shifted upward in bed so that his arm was on her butt.

"I like these," he said, running his hand down the smooth panties. If it worked out, she would have to write the boutique owner a letter, like an infomercial: "My husband didn't have sex with me for seventeen months, but after I put on a pair of your boyshorts . . ."

"I found them at the bottom of my drawer," she said. "This is what happens when you never get a minute to clean out your clothes."

They had started to make love the night she'd gone to Southpaw and Abbie interrupted them. He had wanted her then. But was it only because he could sense Stuart's interest? Was it because he suspected she might stray? Men were more intuitive than women gave them credit for. Now that there was no Stuart, could he be interested? *Oh God. Oh God. Please please please make this work.*

She closed her eyes, and he took his hand off her butt. She heard stirring, shifting. He was turning his back to her, going to sleep.

She massaged his shoulder. "That feels good," he said. He was in a white undershirt, and she tried to get at his flesh through the neck hole. It was hard to get a good angle with Abbie between them, so she climbed over her daughter, rolled him onto his stomach, and got on his back.

"What did I do to deserve this?" he said.

She put all her energy into the massage—as though her life de-pended on it, which it did—and was able to muster a level of attention that he always complained she never had. Theo was moaning with plea-sure, but it wasn't until she'd been at it a good fifteen minutes that she allowed herself to lie on top of him and brush her breasts against his back. He turned over and looked up at her, put his hands on her shoulders. He was hard, but only semi.

Shit shit shit. He knew something was amiss. She would have to level with him. If she couldn't explain why she was interested, he wouldn't trust her interest. In so many ways, their relationship since Abbie's birth had been gender-reversed; he wanted her to touch him more, while she wanted him to have sex with her. It had never occurred to her that there might be a through line between touching him and sleeping with him. She had been so angry with him for withholding sex that she never felt affectionate enough to touch him lovingly.

"Abbie needs a sibling," she said, and kissed him.

His body stiffened with intensity, but she suspected there was ex-citement beneath. She was sitting on him, her panties still on; Theo was in his Calvin Klein boxer-briefs.

"I don't think I could ever love anyone as much as her," he said.

"Everyone thinks that about the first child."

"But I mean it," he said.

"Even if you do," she said, "don't you want her to have someone to be there for her forever, after we go?"

He looked suspicious of her change of heart; in the past, when they had discussed this, she had made dark comments about how you needed to have sex to make a baby, or she'd said that she could barely manage one. "I thought you only wanted one," he said.

"She needs a playmate." *Please please please love your daughter the way I think you do.* "And when we're old, I don't want her to be alone. It's not fair to her."

"Two children are harder than one. And Abbie's so amazing. What if the second one turns out to be a terror? A boy?"

"He'll have her to whip him into shape." Her heart was pounding so loudly, she was afraid he would hear it and be onto her, know the stakes were high. "Can't you imagine how nurturing she's going to be? She loves her dolls."

"A doll isn't a baby," he said with a laugh.

He loved Abbie too much to make room for another. This wasn't going to work. She would have to terminate the pregnancy or terminate the marriage.

"I know, but you should see her on the playground. She's so sweet with younger babies." Rebecca was moving her hips against his. "She likes to push them on the swings. And when she sees a baby, she likes to stroke its head. It's so adorable. Don't you want her to have a companion?"

She bent down to kiss him again. With other men, this kind of talk would be a deal breaker; with Theo, it was an aphrodisiac. For him the line between penis and heart was direct, but she had felt too scorned to see it.

"I love you," she said. "I love you for being a good father. For caring so much about Abbie and taking care of us so well." She pulled down his pants and sucked him for a few minutes. Words were one thing, but a little insurance never hurt. And then she was pulling off the undies he liked and getting on top of him, Abbie blissfully unaware. Rebecca prayed she wouldn't open her eyes and interrupt them again. If she'd had a little more foresight, she would have slipped Abbie some Benadryl. She realized with horror that Mance, in Abbie's room, might wake up at any moment. With two children, you had double the chance of someone ruining things for you.

But Abbie's room was silent. Theo flipped Rebecca over and took her missionary-style. She murmured, "I love you," into his ear. He had always liked it when she told him this during sex. She did love him— for not knowing what she had done, for wanting to give her a baby, for being brave enough to make love to her after all this time.

And though it took longer than she remembered it taking before everything had gotten off track, after a while (twenty minutes? twenty-five?) he shuddered and collapsed on top of her with a huge harumph. "I had a lot in there," he said.

"I know you did," she whispered. He was thinking about his sperm count. Thinking how good a shot he'd gotten off.

He climbed off, and they lay there panting on their backs. "What are you thinking about?" he said, putting his hand on her wrist.

"The night Abbie was born."

"What part?"

"You never visited me. I was down there for so long, and it was so cold, and you never came to say hi and see how I was doing."

"They wouldn't let me," he said.

"What are you talking about? I thought you were staying with her to be sure she wasn't switched."

"I was for a little, but then I asked if I could see you, and they said you couldn't have visitors yet. Hospital regulations. I told you this."

"No, you didn't." Had he told her and she'd opted to forget it? He'd never abandoned her. He'd been there all along, but there were these new rules, and she didn't even know all of them herself.

She turned her legs to face the wall over the headboard, like she did when they were trying to make Abbie. As she lay there, hands crossed over her stomach, for a second she could almost feel herself getting pregnant.

Toleration

"YOU'RE AN ice queen, Rosie," Viggo was telling Melora, in character. They'd been in production a month, but Adam had saved till the final week the scene where Rex, Viggo's character, leaves Rosie after twenty years of marriage.

Melora and Viggo were standing under the hot lights on a sound-stage outside of Sofia. She was wearing a crisp cotton sundress with an elaborate girdle underneath, scrubbing the kitchen counter as he told her he was leaving. This was the sixth take, and Melora wanted it to work. After the first five, Adam had given her direction, and each time she thought she had taken it well, but when he called "Cut," he would frown, lick his lips, and step onto the set.

Melora was supposed to be scrubbing the chrome faucet while Viggo ended the marriage, and Adam wanted tears. She had been able to cry, but after the last take, Adam had said it was too expressive, too soap-opera, and that he wanted something more internal. That was what she was focusing on now: being internal. Whatever that meant.

"Is it Annie?" she asked Viggo, a reference to his secretary.

Viggo went into a long speech denying that he was having an affair. This was the moment Melora was supposed to start crying. She did some sense-memory exercises about a bad fight she'd had with Fisher Stevens at Odeon once. She tried to remember the smell of the restaurant, in hopes that this would trigger some emotion, but the smell eluded her, and though tears flowed, she knew Adam would say it was too much of a performance.

"Cut," Adam said, taking off his headset. She looked up. Viggo sighed and walked off the set to light a cigarette.

Adam put his arm around Melora and guided her into the glaring heat outside. "Was it the wiping-the-tear thing?" she said desperately. "Because I don't have to do it."

"It wasn't the wiping-the-tear thing. Keep that."

He guided her out of the building down an alleyway as the second AD, Kelly, a gay man who resembled the comedian Carrot Top, murmured something into his headset. Kelly seemed frustrated. Melora didn't know why she gave a shit about the second AD's frustration, but she did. She was holding everyone up. She hated feeling this way. Since she was ten, she had gotten self-esteem from being good at taking direction, from working well and fast.

She wanted Adam to give her a line reading so she could do it right. There were only eight more days of shooting, and aside from this scene, the shots were all easy: pickups and a few missed country-club close-ups.

He led her down the side of the soundstages, where they sat on a ledge under the beating sun. He looked at her. "Remember Sant Ambroeus?" he said.

"Yeah." She didn't like him bringing up the meeting. She didn't like thinking about that time; it seemed so distant from who she had become.

"That's who I want you to be here. That woman. In this take I saw what was missing. You need to be the high-status person in the scene, even through the tears. You're coming off as a victim. I can't stand that. It's too Hollywood. I know what I'm asking you to do is tough. There was a similar scene with Patty Clarkson in *The Undescended*, when she gets the phone call from the nursing home that her mother is dead. Your tears should be tears of liberation. He's walking out on you, but it's finally giving you the chance to build a life for yourself away from him. I want to see you feeling two things: You're realizing that you can be free at the same time you're experiencing the sting of his rejecting you first. Does that make sense?"

"Sort of." Directors were so impossible—the more New York, the more difficult to decode. The upside was that if you worked with a genius like Adam Epstein, he could carry you on his shoulders to the Oscars. The downside was that it was like pulling teeth to get him to be coherent.

"I didn't cast you because you're tall, Melora," he said. "I cast you because of your strength. You think you're weak, but you're stronger than anyone else on this set. You were when you were a kid, and you still are. You're the girl I saw in *Jeannie Doesn't Live Here Anymore.* I need to see her on film. I didn't want to say it earlier in the shoot because I thought it might make you too nervous, you know, jinx you and make you totally screw up the rest of the movie." That was reassuring. "But we need this scene. You have got to empower yourself. I want you to be as strong as you were with me that day at Sant Ambroeus."

What a way to put pressure on a girl. She would have preferred that he let her go on thinking he'd chosen her because she was tall.

If only she had brought an acting coach. After Adam cast her, she had called Harold Guskin to try to get him to come to Sofia with her, but he was off in Dublin for six months, helping Rachel McAdams on the new Sam Mendes.

She could see Viggo up the street, smoking and chatting with Kelly, the second AD. She could feel her costar's impatience. Melora hated being the Difficult Actor on-set; she wasn't used to it. She wanted to get it right. She had to get it right. This was the most pivotal scene in the film—the Oscar moment—and if she didn't nail it, it would ruin the picture.

Until this moment everything had been falling into place so perfectly: Stuart and Orion were staying with her at the hotel, and Orion was doing great at the international school; they'd brought along the new nanny, Suzette, who was wonderful with Orion; and two weeks before, Richard Gere had accepted her bid of $12 million on Palazzo Chupi. Now all they had to do was sell the mansion. Stuart said he would prefer to stay in Brooklyn but if she really wanted to live in Manhattan, he understood. He loved the apartment in Palazzo Chupi, declaring that a water view was exactly what he needed in order to write well, and when she asked about him kicking in money toward the purchase, he agreed to give $1 million, as long as his name was on the deed. Now all they had to do was sell the mansion.

Though Kate Hudson had given a *People* interview in which she called Melora a "whack job," she had not pressed attempted-assault charges. That turned out to be a good thing, because Melora had signed a contract to play Lucy in *Atlantic Yards* and didn't want anything to jeopardize it.

Adam had loved Stuart's script (which Stuart had rewritten in a crazed week at the Brooklyn Public Library), signed on as co–executive producer, and gotten Scott Rudin on board, too. They had booked Kal Penn of the *Harold & Kumar* movies as the terrorist muffin-shop worker, and as a result Stuart had gotten another $5 million in financing from a Gujarati tech guy. Production was set to begin in March.

Two thousand nine was going to be a great year. She could feel it. *Yellow Rosie* would garner her a third Oscar, and if it didn't, *Atlantic Yards* surely would. After the Oscar win, she would do a couple more years of quality features and then find a dark cable comedy vehicle, maybe for Showtime or AMC. If Glenn and Julianna and Kyra could do it, why couldn't she? She could insist on producing, which was where the real money was anyway, and maybe come up with a clothing line and another perfume. But in order for all of that to happen, she had to nail the Rosie scene.

"Do you get what I'm saying?" Adam asked, taking her hands in his and staring at her so closely it seemed almost like he was going to kiss her. "Because you need to tell me if you don't."

"I totally get it," she told Adam. "Strength. Could you give me a few minutes in my trailer?"

"We're already behind schedule," he said.

"Ten minutes. I promise you. Just give me ten." He nodded. She raced down the street, past Viggo and Kelly, and into her trailer.

It was nearly five minutes before Dr. Levine called back. She was furious. "What took so long?" she said.

"Alec Baldwin," he said. Baldwin had come out of Levine's office one day when Melora was waiting, and she and Levine had had a long talk about what the sighting had brought up for her. Levine didn't be-lieve in being overly protective of his other patients' privacy; it was some Buddhist thing in which they were also supposed to be a big community.

"Oh, Michael," she said on the phone. "It's not working!" She broke into tears, telling him how unclear Adam was being. "I think he's going to fire me."

"Well, that's not going to happen."

"How do you know?"

"I just know." He could be smug sometimes, more like a seer than a shrink. If these phone calls didn't start paying off, she would have to hire a life coach. They cost the same amount and didn't talk like fortune cookies.

"I'm not sure about that, Michael! This is a pivotal moment in the movie, and he seems really concerned that he's not getting it. I think he's going to fire me and cast Kate Hudson. Or Maggie Gyllenhaal. I don't think I can do it. I don't think I can give him what he wants. I'm not good enough."

Dr. Levine was quiet for a long time, and then he said, "You can tolerate the frustration."

"What?"

Again, Yoda-like in its inscrutability: "You can tolerate the frustration."

"I don't get it."

"Yes, you do."

Levine was worse than Adam Epstein. They could start a club of inscrutable Jews. "I'm sorry, Michael, I just don't understand."

"The frustration won't swallow you. It's not bigger than you. It's okay to be frustrated."

"I know it's okay. I *am* frustrated! What I don't know is how to play the scene!"

"If you can tolerate the frustration, you can play the scene." The guy could write for Kevin Costner. "Think about that for a little."

There was a knock on the door. "Just a minute!" Melora hung up and sat on the edge of the bed. She looked at the wall, at the framed black-and-white photographs Stuart had taken of Orion on Slaveykov Square, and tried to make sense of Levine's words.

Tolerate. She remembered a Jerry Seinfeld routine about people with lactose intolerance: "I just won't stand for it." What did it mean to tolerate something? It wasn't the same as mounting it or conquering it. To tolerate something meant you put up with it, you got through it. Levine had been trying to tell her that nothing she had to deal with was bigger than her: the difficult scene, Adam's inability to communicate clearly, the challenge of acting.

Frustration. She had told Michael she was afraid she would fail, and instead of telling her she could tolerate the fear, or the stress, he had said the frustration, which seemed to put Adam at fault and not her. Levine was right. It was frustrating that Adam couldn't articulate what he wanted, that he wasn't happy with what she'd done, and that he kept making her do more takes. It was even frustrating that he had taken her aside in front of everyone and that Viggo was blaming her for the long day and that she was famished but couldn't break for lunch till someone else said she could.

Melora Leigh wasn't frustrating Adam Epstein; Adam Epstein was frustrating her. On the next take, she would think about Adam and his total inability to communicate.

You can tolerate the frustration. She walked out of the trailer into the summer sun. Viggo looked up. "Everything okay?" *You can tolerate the frustration.*

She nodded. He'd gotten so smug since *The Lord of the Rings* and she was irritated by his whole Renaissance-man thing, with his publishing company, painting career, and poetry. It was annoying. Why couldn't he be content with acting? He had the easy job in the movie because his character was the foil for hers. But that was all right. She didn't have to love him. She just had to play the scene with him. *You can tolerate the frustration.* There were a lot of other actors she could think of whom she would have preferred to have playing her philandering husband, but Viggo would do. He was good enough.

On the soundstage, Adam was talking urgently with Scott Rudin, who seemed to have just arrived; Melora hadn't noticed him earlier in the day. Scott greeted her with a kiss on both cheeks, but his eyes were worried. She could tell they'd been talking about her. How awful that today of all days, Rudin was on-set.

She checked herself, hearing Dr. Levine's voice inside her head. *You can tolerate the frustration.*

"How you doing?" Adam said. His voice was tender but patronizing.

"I'm ready," she said.

The makeup woman stepped in to dry the sweat from her brow. After the seventh take, there was no eighth.

Prostaglandins

"DO YOU have any questions for us?" Theo asked the couple as Rebecca wondered when the meeting would end. It was the last week of September. The board meeting was in Theo and Rebecca's living room, and Karen and Matty had just told everyone how excited they were to take out the garbage twice a month as part of cooperator duties. It was the usual bullshit interview where the couple dressed up and tried to make themselves likable and the board asked stumpers like "Do you have any questions for us?"

The secretary, Peter Boland, a diminutive father of two who designed tongue depressors, scribbled notes for the minutes. The treasurer, Chris James from Apartment Four, grabbed another chocolate graham cracker from the bowl Rebecca had put on the coffee table. Chris didn't care much about the future of the coop because he was already in contract on his place—he'd gotten $725,000 from a young married couple with a trust fund—and he, Jason, and Fred were moving to Kensington. Tina and Steve, who were allowed to sit in on the meeting, according to the house rules, were smiling anxiously and periodically looking at the other board members' faces to see how they were taking to Karen and Matty.

Rebecca didn't like this Karen any more than she had the day she had rung Rebecca's buzzer—there was something pushy and weird about her. But she was too tired to put them through the ringer.

These days she was too tired to get revved up about anything, especially not a coop board meeting. Between the exhaustion and the morning sickness that had shown no signs of abating over the past seven weeks, she was having trouble taking care of Abbie—even with the help from Sonam—and each night she felt like she'd been run over by a truck.

Theo had been shocked that Rebecca's pregnancy had taken so quickly, but also delighted and proud that it had been easy. One week before, Theo had accompanied Rebecca to her first visit with her new OB, a Frenchwoman in Soho, and she'd seen the heartbeat on the ultrasound. It had been a terrifying feeling to lie there and realize that this thing growing in her was real, as Theo stroked her protectively.

When the doctor asked her the date of her last period, she had been prepared and fudged a little, saying, "July twenty-fourth," with the same straight face she'd used when she went into convenience stores to buy wine coolers as a teenager. She was worried that later on, when the baby was bigger, the measurements might not match up to the date, but she figured a big baby would raise fewer alarms than a small one. And there was probably some message board somewhere for women who had done the same thing and had advice about it she could use.

Theo had been so excited when she told him she was pregnant that he'd suggested they tell his mother and stepfather, but that made Rebecca too uncomfortable. She said she wanted to wait till three months had gone by. "I just don't want to get them worked up," she said, "in case, you know, if something . . ."

"It's so beautiful to see you excited about this baby," he had said. And then he'd said maybe they should have three.

"I can't think of any questions," Matty said in the board meeting. He asked Karen, "Do you have any questions?" and put his arm around her protectively.

"Nope, I think I'm good." Then she giggled and said, "I read in a real estate book that when a board asks if you have any questions, you should say no." She laughed again. Her husband looked nervous.

"So I think that's it," said Theo. "We talked about being self-managed and the job wheel. I don't know if you got a chance to look at the minutes, but we just had the facade redone, and the building's financials are very healthy. Definitely healthier than Lehman's." The stock market had been crazy lately, with Lehman filing for bankruptcy and the government bailing out AIG. Two weeks before, the market had fallen almost eight hundred points in one day, after the House had rejected the bailout bill. Theo had tried to explain it all to Rebecca, but she still didn't get it all. She watched *The Rachel Maddow Show* each night through the haze of nausea and exhaustion.

"Oh, I had one more thing," Peter Boland piped up. He had the Abe Lincoln–style beard that was increasingly popular among Park Slope fathers. "I see that one of your reference letters was from Melora Leigh. How do you know her?"

Rebecca's mouth got dry. When she'd gotten the reference letter in the application package, she, too, had wondered how Melora Leigh had come to be friendly with an overweight plebeian. She hated the idea that someone only two degrees removed from Stuart was about to move downstairs from her. She'd even had a nightmarish vision of Melora telling Karen that she knew all about Stuart's affair.

Rebecca thought about Stuart all the time and how he'd said in the library that he might be in a different place someday. Maybe he had gotten his movie deal and didn't need Melora anymore. He would call Rebecca up, and she could leave Theo and be with him and Abbie and the new baby forever.

Once her phone had rung late at night, and she had rushed into the living room to look, but it was a wrong number, a Spanish-accented woman asking if Luis was there. Rebecca hung up, devastated.

Over the past month and a half, she had harbored hopes that she would run into Stuart in the neighborhood. But the shades of the mansion were drawn and the windows dusty, and it didn't look like anyone was there. The front garden, with the lilies, remained well maintained, but that didn't mean anything; they hired people to do that. She had even typed his name into IMDb and found that he'd been cast in a Christopher Nolan movie, but all it said about the shooting schedule was "preproduction."

She never saw Orion or Melora, either, or even the nanny. Maybe Melora and Stuart had split up. She wondered if this Karen woman knew what had happened.

"We met on the playground," Karen said. "Our sons are friends."
Rebecca didn't buy it but said nothing.

"What's she like?" Peter asked.

"Oh, she's as normal as can be. Just like you and me."

"I loved her as Princess Xaviera," Peter said.

"I'll be sure to tell her," Karen said.

Everyone shook hands and made polite awkward pleasantries. Rebecca led the couple to the door. Matty was making a loud joke with Theo, and Rebecca found herself next to Karen. Karen lowered her voice and said, "I didn't want to say anything in front of everyone else, but are you expecting?"

How did she know this? It was spooky. Rebecca was barely showing and wearing such a loose blouse that surely no normal person could see. What kind of weirdo would ask this of a stranger? What if she'd been wrong? "Um, it's really early," Rebecca said. "So . . ."

"I thought so," Karen said.

"How did you—"

"I'm good about these things. Congratulations. Darby loves babies. It's great that there will be so many little ones in the building. So is your daughter in nursery school yet?"

"Uh, yeah. Beansprouts."

"Oh, I hear wonderful things about it."

After Karen and Matty had left, Tina and Steve Savant sat back on the couch and smiled anxiously. The poor couple had already had a deal fall through in June; obviously, they didn't want that to happen again, especially not now that the housing bubble had officially begun to burst. They were probably ecstatic that they'd had the good sense to list in the summer and not the fall, after the markets had plunged. "So what did everyone think?" Theo asked.

"I don't like her," Rebecca said. "I mean, I know we're not supposed to say that, but . . ." She told the story of how Karen had shown up before the open house, trying to get a look at her apartment. "I'm not sure someone that pushy is a good fit for the building." Tina Savant shot daggers at her.

Theo put his hand on Rebecca's knee and said, "So she was aggressive. Who cares? They're paying seven fifty-nine. Do you have any idea what that does for the building's property value?"

Chris said he was fine with them, and Peter said he'd had all his questions answered. Rebecca didn't care if this woman moved in. She would never talk to her anyway. She had more important things to worry about than whom she approved at a coop board meeting.

"All in favor?" Theo asked. There was a chorus of ayes. Tina looked like she was going to explode with delight.

After everyone left, Rebecca cleared the graham crackers and tossed them in the garbage. All the things she used to enjoy, like sweets, now made her sick. In late August she and Theo had gone to Greenport for a week, and she'd been miserable, nauseated all the time. She'd spent the whole time lying on the bay beach in front of their cottage, unable to read or concentrate.

When she was finished clearing the dishes, she thought about working on a story about sex in the workplace for *Mademoiselle,* but by the time she got her computer on, she was too tired to write. She would have to ask her editor for an extension, and she was nervous, afraid the editor might hesitate to hire her again, perceiving her as a difficult writer. Though it was too soon to know, she was afraid there would be a recession and the media industry, already weak, would suffer. If that happened, she had to keep up good relationships.

Everything about the pregnancy was difficult, and she worried that it meant she would have a difficult child. It wasn't too late to change her mind, but that would only entail more lies, and she was anxious enough about the big one.

In the bedroom she took off her clothes and climbed under the covers. She slept naked most of the time now that she and Theo weren't fighting. Theo came in a few minutes later, after watching some baseball on TV. "I should stay up and work a little," he said, "but I wanted to say good night first." He got in bed and snuggled against her. "We're up for this project I'm really excited about."

"What's that?"

"A condo in Julian Schnabel's building. The owners want us to put in a gym facing the Hudson."

"I hope you get it," Rebecca said absently. He was working late hours all the time, and she was worried that when the baby came, he wouldn't be as available as he'd been to help her with Abbie. She had taken his paternity leave for granted then, even resented it, but couldn't imagine the thought of not having his help the second time.

"I love you so much," he said, kissing her neck. "I was looking at you in the meeting and thinking about how beautiful you are."

This was what she had wanted from him for so long, this level of adoration. And yet he felt it only because she was pregnant. It was all a big lie. She wanted him to want *her* the way Stuart had.

If only she could run into Stuart in the neighborhood! He would look at her belly and see the tiny bump, realize she was keeping the baby, and want to be with her. If he saw how resplendent she was, he would want to raise the child with her. He didn't love Melora. He was only using her for her connections; he had practically admitted it that day in the library. A part of him had wanted this child—that was why he had been so cavalier about the condom that time in her apartment. A man who truly wanted no connections wouldn't have been blasé about birth control, would he?

And even if he was going to stay with Melora, maybe Rebecca could talk to him, tell him about the baby. Maybe he could be in the baby's life somehow and they could find a way to be friends.

Theo was hard, pressing himself against her. She played dumb, made exaggerated noises of exhaustion. Why didn't the sex make things better between them? Before, when they weren't having it, she was convinced it would solve all their problems. She would no longer resent him and he would no longer see her as a stranger. But now that they were having sex, it was fraught.

She couldn't stop worrying about the pregnancy and the birth, fearing she'd made the wrong choice by keeping the child. One night, tossing and turning, she'd had a brief thought that the baby might be redheaded before remembering that red hair was a recessive trait and both parents needed to have the gene for that to happen.

"I think you should go for a vaginal birth," Theo said into her ear. "I know you could do it. You're so strong. And you went through so much before. I don't want you to have another C-section."

"We have time to figure it out." She didn't allow herself to think about the birth. Even after seeing the heartbeat in the doctor's office, the whole thing still felt surreal to her.

He was trying to push it in. "I thought you said you had work," she said.

"It can wait a little while."

"I'm so sleepy."

"That's all right. You can pretend you're sleeping." Where had this cocksure man been all those months, the one whose desire was so strong he didn't care if she was into it? Who was this new person in her bed? Maybe he'd had an affair, too, and was demonstrative because he had something else on the side and had stopped resenting her.

"I don't know if . . ." But his hand was already down there, guiding it in. Theo was turned on by pregnancy. He was the Brad Pitt of Park Slope fathers.

"You know what I love about this?" he said into her ear. "We don't have to use protection."

"But it's so early," she said, appealing to his concern for the baby, if not for her. "We might hurt it."

"Oh, come on," he said. "That never bothered you with Abbie. All those prostaglandins will be good for the baby." He flipped her onto her stomach, and she turned her face to the side so she could breathe.

Union Street Bridge

KAREN AND Matty were walking home down Prospect Park West when Matty got the call from Steve Savant. Karen could tell it was good news from the way Matty nodded excitedly and said "Thanks."

After he told her, she jumped up and down, ecstatic, and they hugged for a long time. They were going to have the second child. She knew it. Since that miserable fight in front of the computer screen, he hadn't said a word about wanting only one child, and they had done it unprotected twice during her fertile times. There was no conception, but she was hopeful; she wouldn't be fully able to relax until they were settled on Carroll Street anyway.

Karen felt it was perfect that they had heard about the board approval when they were on Prospect Park West, the Gold Coast. She had been so certain the Rebecca woman would vote against her, despite the reference letter from Melora, that she hadn't allowed herself to get her hopes up.

When she first told Matty about the letter, he said he didn't believe Melora was her friend, but she said she had been at the playground a few times and that they'd gotten chatty. Matty thought the letter was overkill and might even backfire, but Karen convinced him that in coop board meetings, there was no such thing as overkill.

The women had gotten together twice more, at Little D and al di là, before Melora had left for Bulgaria, and Karen was excited for the friendship to bloom even more once she returned. Melora treated both times and didn't seem to have a problem with that, but she tended to say little. Things would get better once they were real neighbors. They would stop by each other's houses, and in the winter they'd make Christmas cookies together, and maybe one night Melora would invite her over for a party with fabulous Hollywood people.

Inside Karen and Matty's apartment, they told her mother, Eileen, who had been babysitting, that they'd been approved. She hugged them both. Karen hadn't told Eileen that she felt the apartment could help her conceive, because she knew her mother would think it was ridiculous, but Karen could already see herself calling later with the good news. Then there would be photos of Darby and his sibling on the refrigerator right next to the ones of Patrick, Logan, and Kieran. Maybe Karen would even have a third.

"Karen was great," Matty said. "I was nervous, but she acted very comfortable."

"I knew you would get it," Eileen said. "I told you not to worry. Who wouldn't want to sell their apartment to such a perfect family?" Karen didn't feel that any family of three was perfect, but soon they wouldn't be a family of three.

After Eileen's car service arrived, Karen took a shower. When she came into the bedroom, she found Matty sitting in bed working on his computer—he often worked in bed now instead of the living room, as though to reassure her that he was on the up-and-up.

Everything had come together because of Melora's letter. How many ordinary couples came equipped with a personal reference from an Oscar-winning actress? Melora was a friend now.

Karen dressed by the side of the bed. "Where you going?" Matty asked.

"I have to get milk at Union Market," she said. "I'll be right back."

"Be careful," he said. "It's late."

She went to her desk drawer and took out the digital tape recorder. The wallet was still in the bowling bag purse, where she carried it every day, brushing against it when she took out ChapStick or Darby's sunscreen.

Outside, she walked to a car service on Seventh Avenue. "The Union Street Bridge," she told the driver. "And it'll be round-trip."

The bridge was deserted but oddly beautiful. She got out of the cab and went to the railing overlooking the Gowanus Canal. There was a child's rocking horse teetering on top of a houseboat. She wondered who had put it there.

She opened her bowling bag and threw the tape recorder into the canal. Then she took out Neal Harris's wallet, removed the three hundred dollars in cash and the MetroCard (expiration still six months away), put them in her pocket, and threw the wallet as far out as she could. It didn't make a sound as it went in.

The Swing

IT WAS a crisp September Sunday on the Third Street playground, and the place was hopping with dads on duty who chased their children absently while reading the Sunday paper. Lizzie had trekked down with Mance to get a break from Underhill, which lately had been feeling claustrophobic and repetitive.

She, Jay, and Mance had spent the day lolling around the apartment, going to Brooklyn Flea to browse, and walking home all the way down Vanderbilt Avenue. After the arrest, Jay had been furious with her, but his anger had soon turned to indignation as he concluded that it wouldn't have happened to Lizzie if Mance hadn't been black. He said it was probably good that she had been there with Mona because otherwise he didn't know how Mona would have gotten through it.

Jay's gig in L.A. the night of the arrest had gone well, and the band had auditioned for *The David Keller Show,* going through three rounds of callbacks and finally getting hired as the house band. He would be making $200,000 a year to work twenty hours a week, and he was getting on the AFTRA health plan, since it was a TV show, which meant Lizzie and Mance would be insured, too. Jay was around the apartment more at night, and when he did go out to friends' gigs, sometimes he brought Lizzie with him. They hired a sitter and went for drinks afterward or dinner before.

Lizzie couldn't believe that their life was changing so fast. She wouldn't have to go back to work right away, unless she wanted to, and lately she was thinking of opening a vintage store on Vanderbilt Avenue, although she knew it would take a lot of work and money.

Since the night of the arrest, Mona had taken Mance every Wednesday from ten to five, and she seemed to love it, exuberant when she brought him back at the end of the day and filled with stories about the friends he'd made. Though Lizzie and Mona weren't close, they had reached a workable détente. Lizzie got the break she needed to allow her to miss Mance, and Mona got the time with her grandson that, Lizzie realized, she had been longing for since he was born.

Lizzie was thinking she'd hire a sitter one day a week, when Jay's gig started, on top of the help Mona was giving them. It was the strangest thing—she hadn't gotten arrested on purpose, of course, but since the arrest, everything had gotten better. Jay was finally giving her what she needed without her having to say anything.

Lizzie lifted Mance out of the stroller and carried him to a bucket swing. He was buoyant and playful, smiling at Lizzie as she pushed. He had become so much more expressive since the summer. He had a dozen words—all one syllable—but it was still exciting to her when he pointed up at the sky and said, "*Plane!*"

She had just done an Underdog with him and was returning to the other side to push him when she saw Rebecca and her husband coming toward the playground. Theo was pushing Abbie in the Maclaren—Lizzie could see she had gotten tall—and Rebecca was holding Theo's arm.

Lizzie hadn't spoken to Rebecca since the morning she'd gotten out of jail and had called to thank her. (Jay had picked up Mance and met Lizzie and Mona at the courthouse in the morning, after all the protesters were released on an ACD—adjournment contemplating dismissal.) Rebecca had sounded so generous and sweet about having taken Mance that Lizzie thought they would make plans again.

But when Lizzie called, she always got voice mail. And she didn't have Rebecca's home number; they had never exchanged them. Clearly, Rebecca wanted nothing to do with her. But that was all right. It wasn't worth it to pursue someone who wanted nothing to do with you—not a man, a woman, a lover, or a friend. Lizzie had been lost for a long time, and Rebecca was just the worst of it. She felt clearer now, or at least more calm, about her life, and she wanted the feeling to last. She hoped it would. She hoped Jay wouldn't lose the David Keller job at the last minute, but she had a feeling that even if he did, they would be all right.

Theo was more handsome than Lizzie had imagined him—one of the few good-looking dads around, with floppy hair and a tall, slim build. Rebecca looked stylish in dark tight jeans and an Indian-style white tunic.

She wasn't sure Rebecca had seen her but then they came into the swing area and Rebecca plopped Abbie in the swing next to Mance. Rebecca recognized Mance before Lizzie—oh, the public liability of having a black baby in a white neighborhood!—and then turned to Lizzie and kissed her on both cheeks, an affectation she had never used before. She said, "How are you?" and shook the swing to get Abbie's attention. "Look, Abbie, it's Mance!"

"How are you guys?" Lizzie asked.

"We're really good," Rebecca said. "This is Lizzie," she told Theo.

He reached forward and shook Lizzie's hand. "Theo," he said. "I'm glad they dismissed the charges."

"Oh God, me, too," she said. "People are telling me to sue the NYPD, but I don't want to go through all that. I don't know what I would have done if they'd taken Mance, and . . . held him at the precinct or someplace worse. Thank you so much for taking him."

"Don't worry about it," he said. "He's an easy baby. And a great sleeper. You're very lucky."

Theo was pushing Abbie's swing. Rebecca smiled and waved at Mance while Theo did some sort of whistling game with his daughter.

A short woman came into the swing area with an older toddler and put him in the swing on the other side of Mance. Lizzie noticed that he was wearing kneepads and wondered if he was retarded or a danger to himself. But his face seemed normal, and he was verbal, even if he seemed old for the bucket swings. The woman kept looking over at Rebecca and Theo and finally waved at them excitedly and said, "I thought it was you! How are you?"

"Pretty good," Theo said. "Congratulations on the sale."

"Oh, we're so excited about it. We can't wait."

The woman talked a little more with Theo and Rebecca about closing dates and move-in deposits, and then she said, "I was telling Rebecca how excited Darby's going to be to have a baby in the building."

Theo turned to Rebecca, frowning, and said, "You told her? We haven't even told my parents."

"She figured it out," Rebecca said, reddening and glancing quickly at Lizzie. Lizzie didn't understand what they were talking about, and then Rebecca said, "We're expecting. In April." She said it as if someone had died. Then she seemed to realize her tone was serious, pasted on a fake smile, and slipped her arm around Theo's waist.

"I'm sorry," the stout woman said. "I didn't mean to let it slip like that. I'm such an idiot."

Lizzie glanced at Rebecca's stomach and could see a slight bulge. Of course she was pregnant; she was wearing loose clothing.

Lizzie felt repelled by the news. Everything about it was wrong. If it was the actor's child, then either Theo didn't know, or he did know and had agreed to raise it as his own, which was sickening. Or maybe Theo was the father and he and Rebecca had worked things out at exactly the same time she'd started up with the actor. It was possible Rebecca herself didn't know whose it was. Lizzie couldn't imagine carrying a baby without knowing whose it was. Every scenario around this pregnancy made Lizzie uncomfortable. She knew more than she wanted to.

"Congratulations," Lizzie said. "That's wonderful. I'm so happy for you both." She said "both" deliberately because it was formal, and because she wanted Rebecca to know that she had moved on. Theo kissed Rebecca on the cheek and then patted her belly in a proprietary way.

The other mother went back to pushing her son, and Theo, Lizzie, and Rebecca made small talk for a while. Rebecca stood nervously, as though Lizzie were going to come out and tell him about Stuart Ashby. Did she really think Lizzie cared that much about her stupid affair, cared enough to blab to her husband? It was so self-centered to think that the world was going to tell your secrets. Rebecca thought she was the center of the universe. This was why she would never make real friends. You couldn't make friends if all you ever thought about was yourself.

Abbie started to fuss, and Theo took her out of the swing. "You want to run around a little?" he asked.

Rebecca turned to Lizzie and said, "So great to run into you," which clearly could not have been further from the truth, and followed Theo as he carried Abbie to the bouncy bridge.

"I'm Karen, by the way," the short woman said.

"Lizzie."

Karen was gazing at Mance and shaking her head. "What a beautiful boy," she said. Lizzie was used to these compliments from white parents and had long ago learned to decode them. They were commenting on the fact that he was biracial, but they didn't know how to say this, so they said he was beautiful. "What's his name?"

"Mance."

"Mance," Karen repeated, her face going pale. "What an interesting name. Where's it from?"

"He's named after a blues musician," Lizzie said. "Mance Lipscomb. It's short for 'emancipation.' "

Karen got a tense look, as though she hated the name or had had a boyfriend named Mance who had broken her heart. It was the strangest reaction Lizzie had ever seen. "Great name."

"What's your son's name?" Lizzie asked.

"Darby." Lizzie hated it—it was one of those names the child would never be able to grow into.

"So how do you know Rebecca?" Karen asked.

"We met right here, actually, on Third Street. Our kids play together, although I guess at this age, it's mainly parallel-playing."

"Wait till they get older. It's so exciting when they make real friends and you can finally get a break."

Karen didn't seem like the kind of woman who looked forward to getting a break from her son, but Lizzie nodded and said, "I know. There're a lot of things I'm looking forward to. Like getting rid of the stroller. I can't wait till he gets old enough for us to walk places."

"You'll miss all of it," Karen said. "The diapers, the night waking, the nursing. It goes by so fast. I still can't believe Darby's in pre-K this year. He goes to the Garfield School. So do you live around here?"

"Not far. Prospect Heights. What about you?"

"Well, our closing's in two weeks, but right now we live not far from Ninth Street."

"Do you guys go to Harmony? I love that playground. This summer I took Mance there a lot. We walk the loop past the ball fields to watch the kids playing."

"Did you read about that rape?" Karen asked.

"That was a while ago." Lizzie felt very cold.

"You know, they caught him," Karen said.

Even though Lizzie had convinced herself that the man on her street wasn't the same one, she was relieved to hear this. "Really?"

"It was in the *Brooklyn Paper*. West Indian guy. Wanted for three other rapes."

"And they're sure it's the same guy?"

"He confessed. It was definitely the same one." They pushed the boys silently for a while, and then Karen said, "So what do you do? Or . . ."

"Actually, I'm at home with him now." Lizzie had tried out different ways of answering this question and had landed on "I'm at home with him now" because she preferred the adverb form, "I'm at home," to the noun form, "I'm a stay-at-home mom," and the "now" because it implied that it wouldn't be forever.

"Me, too," Karen said. "We thought about a nanny, but it didn't make sense. I was a social worker, and after taxes I would have cleared about five thousand dollars."

"I know what you mean!" Lizzie said. "I was in publishing. And I liked my work, but not enough to want to hire someone else to take care of him all day."

"You know, whatever your choice is, you should try to be happy with it. In this neighborhood a lot of women will try to vilify you for choosing not to work, and I think it's unfair. Women should do what's right for them. And everyone should leave them alone. I'm reading this wonderful book right now, *Maternal Desire,* by Daphne DeMarneffe, and she basically says that a) women have an innate desire to become mothers, and b) there's nothing wrong with that."

"I couldn't agree more," Lizzie said. Lizzie decided Karen was more intelligent than she had given her credit for. Yes, she had named her son Darby, which was worse than Jackson, even, but Lizzie liked her. Though she couldn't really see them hanging out one-on-one, she was excited to have met someone she might run into if she came to Third Street again. It could be so slow with no one to talk to, so endless.

Karen helped Darby out of the swing, and he went running off. She gave Lizzie a big, generous smile and put out her hand, which was small but firm when Lizzie shook it. "So great to meet you. Now, you take care of that beautiful baby."

"I will," Lizzie answered with a smile. Karen ran after Darby. Lizzie wanted to keep talking to her, because Karen listened and Lizzie felt like she could be herself around her. With Rebecca, she'd always felt that she had to be bigger or bolder, but with Karen, she felt that she was enough. Karen looked older and wasn't a fashion plate, but Lizzie wasn't sure that was so important. Motherhood wasn't a fashion show. You just needed friends you could rely on.

Still, she decided not to go with them, because she didn't want to seem overeager. Instead, she pushed Mance with extra vigor and watched Karen from a distance as she scooped Darby away from a wild, heavy tire swing.

Something Else

AS SHE came, Melora planted her hands on the upholstered wall behind the headboard of the bed in their hotel in Sofia, as though willing herself through it. Her orgasm was so intense and wonderful that she was afraid Stuart would know she had been faking for the past two years. How could he think that her mild five-second eruptions had been real compared to this ecstatic and unbridled, seemingly endless little death?

He was looking up at her with such dazed appreciation that she expected him to accuse her of deception. But he said only, "You're a tigress!" and after a few minutes of nuzzling, he finally lifted her off.

Lately, she'd been feeling in love with Stuart. She felt elated and schoolgirlish when she returned to the hotel to find him toiling away on *Atlantic Yards*. She was ashamed she had been cold to him before, so snappish and unforgiving. She was lucky to have him as a husband, to have that delicious combination of intelligence, strength, and humor so hard to find in Hollywood men.

"You were amazing," she said. These days she could feel everything more strongly—smell, touch. He seemed bigger in her. She never would have said this because it would have implied that he was small before, but she felt it. The antidepressant had desensitized her not only to her own pleasure but to the pleasure of having her husband inside her. She had even mentioned this to Dr. Levine in one of her phone calls, and he said that a lot of things changed when you went off anti-depressants.

"God, I wish I had a cigarette," Melora said, collapsing onto the pillows next to Stuart. She was trying to quit and had stopped carrying them around, though she had bummed a few on-set from Viggo.

Stuart was pulling at a beer, and he handed it to her. It was all right, but no cigarette. He put his arm around her and chugged contemplatively. "You're incredible these days," he said.

"I feel like I am," she said. "I just feel so . . . into it."

"You weren't before?"

"Of course, but not like this. I feel this urgency, like I have to have you. You know, I miss you when I'm on-set. I think about you all the time." That morning she had taken one of his T-shirts to her trailer so she could smell it between takes.

"I miss you too, sweetheart," he said, but she could feel him thinking about what he was going to do next. He was so active all the time. The busier he got, the less available he was.

"Let's order room service," she said. They had eaten at the restaurant only an hour before, but Melora was ravenous. She reached for the menu by the side of the bed. "I want fried chicken. Do you think they have fried chicken?"

"What are you—pregnant?"

"Don't even joke. Do you want something?"

"I'm not hungry, sweetheart. But order whatever you'd like."

"I wanted to eat with you," she said.

"I'll watch you," he said.

While she was on the phone ordering, his cell phone rang. She could hear him saying things like "finishing funds," and then he was pacing the floor and talking so loudly she had trouble getting in her order of a bottle of prosecco and a roasted chicken.

"Hold on a sec, Adam." He pressed the mute button on his phone and turned to her. "We just got another ten million from an oil baron in Dubai. I can't fucking believe it." Then he pressed the button again, and before she knew it, he was sitting at his desk in front of the laptop, taking script notes.

The jealousy rose in her chest. He now had a closer relationship with her director than she did. Sometimes at night Stuart went to Adam's rental house to work on rewrites with him. Stuart had even gotten Adam into Ayurveda, once he found out that he was vegetarian, and at craft services now, Adam was always going on about his doshas.

Melora felt all the old fears: that Stuart would leave her, move on from her, even if they both won Oscars . . . She had to cut off the thoughts before they took over. *You can tolerate the frustration.*

Melora's phone rang. Stuart looked up at the noise, annoyed, as though it was all right for him to take a call but not her.

It was Karen. The thorn in her side. Melora had already conjured nightmarish images of playdates with her on the Bleecker Street playground, where Liv and the other celebrity moms could see her. They would all want to know what she was doing with such a hog, and Melora didn't know what she was going to say. She picked up, glancing nervously at Stuart.

"I have good news," Karen said.

"What's that?" Melora asked listlessly. She would have to tell her they were moving sooner or later, but she was nervous.

"We had the board meeting yesterday. They approved us."

"That's wonderful."

"Did I catch you in the middle of something?"

"Not really." Melora was always in the middle of something, but that never stopped Karen from wanting to chat for half an hour.

"Well, I just wanted to tell you," Karen said. "We're going to be neighbors! And it's all because of you."

"What do you mean?"

"The letter." Melora had already forgotten about it. "The husband in Apartment One seemed really impressed that I knew you. He said he loved you as Princess Xaviera."

"All men do. It was the cone bra."

"Even so, I think it helped. So I was calling to thank you."

"Anytime."

"And I also wanted to tell you something."

"What's that?" Karen was going to say she'd decided to decorate her living room just like Melora's or that she wanted Melora's help getting Darby into Berkeley Carroll.

"I wanted you to know that I don't have the wallet anymore. It's in the Gowanus Canal. And so is that tape recorder."

Melora's throat felt open and wide. This was what happened when you learned to tolerate frustration. Everything else fell into place. It was like clapping your hands if you believed in fairies: You could make things happen if you wanted them badly enough. "Thank you," Melora said. "Thank you for doing that."

"I realized I didn't need them anymore. Because . . . we're friends now."

"Yes."

"So when are you coming back? We'll have to have a special dinner to welcome you back!"

"I actually wanted to mention something to you. Stuart and I are moving to Manhattan."

"What?" Karen sounded like this was a personal affront. "What are you talking about? Where're you moving?"

"Downtown."

"Where?"

Melora didn't answer. She didn't have to tell Karen anything now. She didn't have to be nice.

"Did you sell the mansion yet?"

"Not yet."

"What are you asking?"

"Excuse me?"

"Forget it. I'll look it up. I don't Google you so much anymore now that I . . . know you."

Another call was coming in. Melora glanced at the display. Carol Gornick. The Sotheby Homes broker. Melora told Karen she had to go, and Karen said goodbye in a cracked voice. Melora would change her cell number as soon as she got a chance.

"I'm so sorry to bother you so late," Carol said.

"What is it?"

"You've got a serious offer on the mansion."

"What is it?"

"Six two. And apparently, you know the buyers."

"I do?"

"Maggie Gyllenhaal and Peter Sarsgaard."

"Oh my God," said Melora. The highest offer they'd gotten until now was $5.2 million from some French media bigwig. But this was a real offer, and she knew they'd be crazy to wait for something better, especially with the housing market sinking.

With the $6.2 million from the mansion, the $2 million she'd gotten for her house in Silver Lake, plus Stuart's contribution of $1 million, they would have to finance only $3 million on Palazzo Chupi. That was a stretch, but Soften, the perfume, was bringing in good money, and the DVD sales for *Usurpia* were outrageous. If it got tight, she could take a bad action movie or have the promotions guy at CAA look into a spokesperson deal, like Gwyneth's Tod thing.

It was hard to imagine the Gyllenhaal girl in that beautiful house, sleeping in the master, Ramona in Orion's bedroom. Every time Melora walked past, she would . . . What was she thinking? She was never going to walk past. She was never going back to Brooklyn again, not even if John Turturro asked her to be a BAM trustee. Who cared who lived in the mansion? If Maggie and Peter wanted to stick it out a few more years before drawing the same conclusion Melora had—that Brooklyn was no place for the famous—it was their mistake to make.

"They adore your house," Carol went on. "She's been admiring it from afar, she said. They think they could really build a family there."

"That's wonderful. But I have to talk to Stuart."

"Of course, of course."

He wasn't even glancing over to see what her conversation was about. He was telling Adam, "But I feel like she hasn't really *earned* it."

Melora got off, staring at Stuart meaningfully. She wanted him to get the hell off the phone so she could tell him about the offer. This was important. It was about them. But he was acting so self-important, he almost reminded her of herself.

She breathed out through her mouth. *You can tolerate the frustration.* She would tell him soon enough. He would be off in a few more minutes, and even if he wasn't, soon her room service would be here and she could drink her prosecco and eat her roast chicken, maybe finish

Eat, Pray, Love. With all those things to focus on, it wouldn't really matter even if Stuart stayed on for an hour.

Naked, she got out of bed, went to him, and rubbed his shoulders. He swatted her hand away, engaged in conversation. *You can tolerate the frustration.* She decided to take a shower while she waited for the room service to come. There was always something else you could do.

Lee Nielsen's favorite thing to do on fall evenings was rake the leaves in his front yard in Ithaca. Marcello would romp around next to him as he gathered them into big bags made just for this purpose and supplied by the sanitation department. Sometimes his neighbor, a Daily News writer named Hank who had moved from Cobble Hill, would wave from his porch across the street.

Lee had never imagined that he and Kath would leave the city so quickly, but after the mugging, everything had happened at lightning speed. Kath was devastated when he told her, and when the police came to get the report, she kept breaking down in tears. Soon after that she started to have trouble sleeping, and it got so bad that she had to ask their family physician for medication. Lee hated her being on it, worrying about the long-term effects, but she said she needed it every night to sleep.

Over the summer they had gone to visit friends in Ithaca, and on a whim they wound up going into a Realtor's office, looking at the house, and making an offer that day. Their offer—$599,000—was probably more than they could have paid if they had bought two months later, after the insanity in the stock market, when housing prices had begun to dip, but they had far more space for the money than they ever could have gotten in brownstone Brooklyn. Now Marcello was thriving at the local nursery school, which cost only $9,000 a year, and Kath was making lots of new friends. She didn't take the sleeping pills anymore.

Ithaca turned out to be a community that Lee hadn't thought existed anymore, with cool, smart artistic people who weren't boring or at all suburban.

And he had never imagined getting so much pride out of owning a house. He could stand in his own yard and know that behind him stood a two-story home. He had grown up on the Upper West Side in a doorman building, so the concept of stairs was exotic to him.

At night in Ithaca you could hear the crickets. His favorite thing to do these past few weeks, when it was just beginning to get nippy, was sit on the front porch after dinner, drinking a beer and staring up at the sky. Marcello might have a less exciting life than Lee had had, growing up in Manhattan, but he would go to a great public school and do well there, and Kath felt that mattered more.

The following summer they would join the Cass Park pool. With all the money they saved not living in the Slope, they were planning to go away for two weeks to a rental in Chatham, on Cape Cod. Another Ithaca family had recommended Chatham, and Marcello was ecstatic to spend time with his friend.

"Look, Daddy!" he cried now, throwing a bunch of leaves in the air. "It's raining!" Lee put down the rake, scooped his son into his arms, and threw him onto the leaf pile as he shrieked with delight.

Much Better These Days

THANKFULLY, THE protesters were no longer standing in front of the Coop doors when Karen got there to shop on a cool September Monday, a few days after they'd been approved by the board. In August, after a bunch of protesters were arrested for blocking access, the Coop stopped the random bag searches. Now there were no more demonstrations, but the black people in the Coop eyed the white people with hostility. If Karen checked out her groceries with a black woman worker, the woman would act short and hostile, as though Karen had had anything to do with the pickpocketing or the bag searches.

When Karen finished her shopping, she got on the checkout line with Darby. The Coop was so crowded on this particular morning that the line snaked all the way to the bread section, three aisles long. It was creeping forward slowly; Darby was on his second bag of Pirate's Booty when Karen saw Arielle Harris approaching with her baby son in a shopping cart. Realizing that she had outbid the Harrises on Carroll Street and never gotten a chance to gloat about it, Karen touched Arielle's shoulder.

"Hi, Karen," said Arielle. "How are you?"

"I've just been insane lately," Karen said. "Did you know we got the apartment on Carroll Street?"

"No, I didn't."

"We close October fifteenth."

Arielle's face got long, and Karen was convinced it was jealousy, but instead of congratulating Karen, Arielle said, "Oh, you poor thing."

Karen got a terrible feeling, cold and spooky, as though Arielle were a doctor about to tell her she had a terminal disease. "What do you mean, 'poor thing'?"

"You didn't read the City section today?"

"No." Karen had been trying for four years to read the newspaper, but Darby was so demanding in the mornings—and had not gotten any less so over the years—that she had given up. Now they didn't even subscribe.

"Huge article about redistricting. It turns out everything east of Eighth Avenue and north of First Street is in District Thirteen now, not Fifteen."

"I don't understand."

"P.S. 282 is your zoned school now. Not 321."

Karen gasped. P.S. 282 was even worse than P.S. 107. It was two-thirds black and one-third Hispanic, Karen had learned from a mother on Third Street who had told her the entire spiel after looking into it for her own daughter. And it wasn't considered failing, so it was almost impossible to get a variance. It was the worst kind of school there was: too bad to be good but too good to be bad.

"Apparently, it was because of the overcrowding at 321," said Arielle. "The community education council railroaded it through. Did you already put down a deposit on the apartment?"

"Yes," Karen said, her throat parched.

"Can you get it back?"

"I—I don't know."

"When I read the article, I was so relieved we didn't get the apartment. I mean, if we'd gone higher, we would be in your position. And with the craziness in the financial markets these days, I'm actually glad we're renting. Neal thinks there's going to be a huge housing crash in New York—even worse than the one in the late eighties. He says in a few months we're going to see prices dropping as much as fifty percent, so we're not going to look again till then.

"But you shouldn't worry too much about the school." She clapped

Karen on the arm and said the most ominous words that one mother could say about another mother's school: "I hear it's getting much better these days."

After Arielle left, Karen didn't know what to do. She could breach the contract with cause, but there was no cause. There had been no false claim; the apartment had been in District Fifteen when they looked at it.

She looked at Darby, innocently eating his Pirate's Booty, and she wanted to cry. He would become a Crip in fourth grade, make friends like The Wiper. He would wind up going to Queens College or BMCC. He would never learn the correct pronunciation of the word "ask." She should have stayed where she was and sent him to P.S. 107. Compared to 282, 107 was Saint Ann's.

It wasn't fair. Things weren't supposed to go like this for people like Karen. She was a Good Person. She raised her child well. With the money they'd be spending on their mortgage, there was no way they could afford both the apartment and private school, at least not now.

She hated her neighborhood suddenly. She didn't know what she was doing here when the people were so odious and selfish. The sorry state of the Department of Education alone was enough to make any good parent leave the city. She lifted Darby out of the cart, his Booty spilling out all over the floor, and raced him outside into the day.

That night at the dinner table—takeout Chinese, since she had left her grocery cart in the frozen-food aisle—she told Matty the news. He stopped, his fork still in the air, and rubbed the crease between his eyebrows. "Aren't there other schools in District Thirteen?"

"Sure, but there's no guarantee we would get into any of them: 282 is our zoned school now. And we'll never get him out of it. P.S. 8, in the Heights, is in Thirteen, but it got an F on Joel Klein's report card. I think we should try to get out of the apartment. Can't we call a lawyer and find out our options? Tell him we bought under one assumption and that assumption changed. I'm sure Steve and Tina could find someone else. I know there were other bidders. And even if the Harrises wouldn't want it, there are probably other people who—"

"Stop it," he said. He swallowed his bite of chicken with cashew nuts, then said, "We're not backing out."

"But I can't send him to that school!"

"You wanted to move. That's what we're doing. If we breach, the best-case scenario is that they keep seventy-five grand of our money, and the worst-case scenario is that they sue us. Is that what you want? You were the one who was so set on doing this. And now we have to deal with this, and with everything going on in the economy. I just wish you'd listened to me and stayed where we were."

"You wanted to move, too."

"I was having second thoughts about it as early as last spring when the markets started to tumble. I don't know if I'm going to have a job in another year if things keep going the way they're going."

"But you're about to make partner."

"No one is safe. *No one is safe.* And you think we should just throw away our deposit?"

"No."

She tried to picture the apartment in her head. It had seemed so spacious when they saw it, but now she imagined that it was smaller. She couldn't remember the floor pattern and had a sudden fear that the living room had a herringbone parquet pattern. How could she live with herringbone floors?

"Look," Matty said, "if Obama gets elected, a lot of things could change. We might get more education money for the city, and they could reconsider this whole plan. And even if they don't, we can look into private for middle school. We'll revisit the whole thing in seven years."

"*Seven years?*" Karen cried. It sounded like a prison sentence.

She went into the bedroom and dialed Melora, but the number had been disconnected. And now the wallet and the tape recorder were in the Gowanus Canal, where they were of no use to Karen at all.

She needed someone to talk to about all of this, someone to vent to, even if there was nothing she could do. She just didn't want to feel alone.

She took out the small local phone book from the shelf underneath her bedside table. There it was, listed under his last name on Park Place, just like he had said.

She thought for a second about how she would say she'd gotten the number. Then she realized she had nothing to worry about. She could say Rebecca had given it to her, since the two of them were friends.

"Lizzie?" she said. "It's Karen Shapiro. We met on the playground the other day. How are you?"

Beautiful Leeches

IT WAS a little chilly for a walk in the park, but Rebecca was desperate to get out of the apartment. As soon as Abbie woke up from her nap, Rebecca bundled her up in a jean jacket and took her outside in the Maclaren. She tried to walk the loop every day, to keep her weight in check and also to help her mood. She had been all over the place emotionally and found that it uplifted her to be near the trees.

She entered at Garfield Place and headed down past the ball fields, skating rink, Audubon Society, and zoo, and even though it took her an hour and a half, she enjoyed it. She liked the fresh air and the landscape of changing leaves, finding that nature was the only antidote to her blue mood.

Though she didn't feel great, she looked great—everyone said so—and had packed on only nine pounds in twelve weeks. She was doing prenatal yoga a few times a week and was glad to see that her ass hadn't gotten any fatter than before. Her OB, Dr. Maucotel, said that eating carefully was one of the best ways to ensure the baby would be small and thus increase her chances of natural birth.

She buttoned her APC cotton trench coat and tightened the belt around her waist. Her birthday was in the fall—she would be thirty-six in a few weeks—and her anniversary was in the fall. This was the only time of year when she didn't mind living in Park Slope. It made her feel like everything she put up with was worth it, because there were beautiful leaves on the trees and you could smell people's wood fires when you went outside.

As she made her way toward the mouth of the park, she saw a male figure running beside her. There was something familiar about his gait, and she realized it was David. When they had dated, David hated exercise—he smoked Drum cigarettes and consumed frozen food—but now he was running in the park. That was what happened when you got rich and famous: You treated your body like a temple.

She thought about how David knew Stuart and wondered if he might know where Stuart was. "David!" she called.

"Rebecca! How are you?" He came closer and ran in place, which Rebecca found incredibly annoying. She kept walking, David jogging next to her.

"I'm all right," she said. "What are you up to these days?"

"Cassie and I just got engaged." So it was real. It wasn't a fleeting tabloid romance. They were getting married.

"Oh my God, congratulations."

"Thanks. We don't have a date yet. But we're thinking next fall at Brooklyn Society for Ethical Culture. Cassie loves fall weddings. She is gorgeous," he said, indicating Abbie. "Her hair's so long! How old is she now?"

"Almost two."

"Is it terrible yet?"

"Not too bad," she said. "We're actually having another one in the spring." She wasn't sure why she'd said it—maybe because he had said he was engaged and she felt the need to one-up him.

"Oh my goodness, *mazel*! So how far apart are they going to be?"

"Two and a half years."

"That's a perfect distance. Close enough for them to be friends but not so close that it's overwhelming."

He sounded like a Park Slope mother himself, obsessed with repro-duction and child spacing. "What about you?" she said. "Are you tying the knot because you and Cassie are thinking of having one?"

"God, no. We have way too much going on." He waved his hand. "She's going to start recording an album soon, and I just got a talk show ordered by Comedy Central. I'm calling it Dick Cavett meets Jon Stewart."

David had success upon success. That was how it worked when you were a single man. You got the right girlfriend, and it moved you ahead in your career. And if you did have a kid, it didn't change anything because you were a man and didn't have to take care of it. Even if he and Cassie had a baby someday, it would be easy because they were rich. It wouldn't hurt his career, and it definitely wouldn't lead to less sex, because he was too narcissistic to subjugate his needs to those of a child.

Rebecca remembered reading a book for one of her articles that said women's earning power went down after they became mothers, whereas men's earning power went up. The mommy tax, it was called. She wanted to blame Abbie for her floundering, but she'd had Abbie in part because she already was.

She wondered if she envied David because he was a man and would never be beholden to a child, or because he was so successful and she wasn't. Since the pregnancy, she had given up on the idea of resubmitting her novel. She was too tired to work on it, and she could barely make her paying-article deadlines. Once the baby came, it would be impossible.

"Kids are so demanding," David went on. "They're great, but . . . they're leeches." He rubbed Abbie's head. "Gorgeous, beautiful leeches."

Rebecca thought about the baby inside her belly and felt certain David knew where Stuart was. The mansion was empty all the time. Maybe David would tell her that Stuart and Melora were no longer together.

"I never got to thank you for the ticket to Cassie's gig," Rebecca said. "I really enjoyed it. So nice of you to invite me."

"Of course, of course, no problem."

"It was so exciting for me, getting to meet Melora Leigh. And her husband. Movie stars!"

"They're very sweet. Both of them. Genuine, you know?"

"I never see them around the neighborhood anymore. I used to all the time."

"They're in Bulgaria. Melora's shooting the new Adam Epstein, and Stuart and Orion went with her."

Rebecca swallowed, trying to maintain her composure. He had traveled across the world to be with his wife. He had joined her on her shoot. How could Rebecca have been so stupid as to think he would leave Melora? How could she have been stupid enough to think the affair—if two times even constituted an affair—meant anything to him? He hadn't even tried to contact Rebecca to find out what she had decided. She was dead to him, and the baby was, too.

And the line about "when I'm in a different place" had been a lie. He'd known he would never walk out on Melora, and he'd misled Rebecca on purpose, to seem like less of an asshole.

"Oh," she said. "When do they get back?"

"They're not coming back," David said. "They're moving to Manhattan."

So she would never see him again. There were good things about that and bad. She wouldn't have to worry about hiding her pregnancy from him, and she would never run into him by accident, six months pregnant and glowing, and have to explain that she'd decided to keep his baby after all.

But she would never get to spot Stuart again, not even from a distance, and see if he looked happy with his wife. The baby would never meet him. He would never be in his child's life. He was gone, and now she was left with her huge, colossally stupid decision. This was one of the many downsides to getting involved with a celebrity: Eventually, they all traded up.

"I think I'm going to walk this way," Rebecca told David, indicating the pedestrian path next to East Drive. "Across the meadow."

"Promise you'll e-mail me pictures of the baby," David said.

"I'm sure I'll see you before then," Rebecca said.

"You look radiant. Congratulations again." He kissed her on the cheek and ran up toward the memorial arch. She watched him—a single man in a sharp tracksuit, running to keep himself fit for a beautiful millionaire fiancée fifteen years his junior.

Rebecca veered off East Drive onto the grass and toward the pedestrian path. She found a bench and sat, facing the stroller out so Abbie could watch the West Indian soccer players on Long Meadow.

She put her hands on her belly and thought about what David had said—how babies were beautiful leeches. Why, oh why, had she chosen to bring another leech into the world?

The circumstances of its birth would be complicated, and she would have to lie to it forever—not only to Theo, which was awful enough, but to the baby, who would someday be a child. Even if she wanted to forget about Stuart, did everything possible to pretend she'd never met him, which would be difficult enough since he was famous, the baby would always be there to remind her. Stuck to her. A leech. A leech who might turn out to resemble his father.

What if she made it through the pregnancy, lying to the doctor and to Theo, and the baby came out looking like Stuart? In ultrasounds the baby was hidden, a black-and-white mystery, like a cut-paper silhouette. But when the baby came out, its face would tell the story of its creation.

What if, by some weird stroke of genetic fate, the baby *did* come out redheaded after all? Red hair was the giveaway of infidelity. There was a saying about it—"I'm going to beat you like a redheaded stepchild." What if the baby turned out to be a pale, redheaded boy, and as soon as Theo saw him, he knew?

He would leave her. Of course he would. She had gone too far with her businessman in St. Louis. She wasn't supposed to get pregnant with the businessman's illegitimate child. If only she had been smarter about picking a lover. It was one thing to have unprotected sex and another to have unprotected sex with a carrottop. She would have been better off sleeping with Rakhman the facade worker.

One of the soccer players scored a goal, and his teammates cheered and clapped him on the back. Abbie started at the cheer.

It was ridiculous to worry about hair color when it probably wouldn't be an issue. Recessive meant the baby had to have it on both sides, and there was no way Rebecca had it on hers. She was Jewish, of dark Russian stock. She was descended from generations and generations of brunettes.

But what if there was a hidden red-haired gene in her family that she didn't know about, some great-great-great-grandmother with Cossack blood? She would have to pray she found a redhead on Theo's side, too.

What if she couldn't?

What if she had a triumphant vaginal birth and then the doctor handed Theo his son and he saw the bright red hair of Stuart Ashby? He would walk right out of the hospital. And he would take Abbie from her. She knew he would.

Rebecca scanned her brain, trying to remember the precise defini- tion of "recessive trait." Could it skip two generations? Three? She had learned about all this in ninth-grade biology class but couldn't remem- ber the details. Some scientist had figured it out in the late eighteen hundreds. Mendel. He'd studied peas. She could remember Mendel and peas but nothing else.

She took out her phone and typed "red hair recessive," but the page wouldn't load. It was impossible to get a signal in the park.

Acknowledgments

THE AUTHOR would like to thank and acknowledge the following individuals and institutions: Charles Miller, Ernesto Mestre-Reed, Will Blythe, Daniel Greenberg, Marysue Rucci, David Rosenthal, Sophie Epstein, Monika Verma, Ross Miller, Jessica Rose, Greg Siegel, Tara Rullo, Cindy Whiteside, the Brooklyn Writers Space, and the Brooklyn Public Library.

About the Author

AMY SOHN is the bestselling author of the novels *Run Catch Kiss* and *My Old Man*, and the nonfiction *Sex and the City: Kiss and Tell*. She has been a columnist at *New York* magazine, the *New York Post*, and England's *Grazia* magazine and has written for *The Nation, Harper's Bazaar, The New York Times*, and *Playboy*. She has written television pilots for such networks as ABC, Fox, HBO, and Lifetime. Raised in Brooklyn, she still lives there today.